CRUISE SHIP CRIME INVESTIGATORS

CRUISE SHIP SERIAL KILLER
OCEAN PACIFIC

STUART ST PAUL

FIRST EDITION

Copyright © 2019 Stuart St Paul

All rights reserved.

DORIS VISITS BOOKS
Northwood, England.

ISBN: 9781548952839

ACKNOWLEDGMENTS

Laura Aikman for once again collaborating on the creative voice and characters. A great actor can can get into how people think and speak, long after the writer thought they knew how the characters thought and spoke. Laura is an actress who is not only known for films, theatre and television credits but she voices animation. Sometimes she is four or five characters in the same show, the same scene, sitting in a loan studio talking to herself. She has a great creative input. She is as some of you may know, my daughter. Credits on IMDB

My son **Luke Aikman** for the focus to the synopsis. That is a very different talent. A great actor lost to the business world – see Fever Pitch.

Thanks to **Jean Heard**, my wife for the many reads and corrections long before others would be able to understand the ramblings of a dyslexic who has written in code. Without her there would be no Doris….. see the guides on www.youtube.com/c/dorisvisits

Thanks to **David Whithington** who we found as a friend after the first novel. He runs a friendly cruise advise site called 'How To Cruise'. He has become a moderator on most of the Doris Visits chat sites which this team run, and so kindly offered to moderate an early version of this book. As someone who knows cruising well he was very welcome on board as proof reader.

MAP of our fictitious cruise ship.

1200 Guests   700 Staff

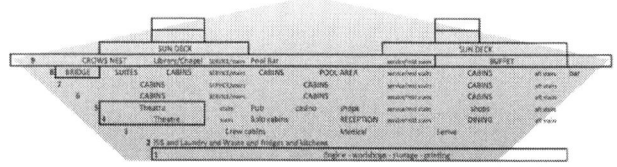

CAST AND CREW LIST AT THE END

…. As you get into the book you can check out your own world map.

This is totally a work of fiction on a fictitious ship. Any references to ships, locations or crew grades are to give the book a true sense of reality and authenticity in this dramatized work. All names, references, characters, ships and incidents are all a product of the author's wild imagination.

1 SECOND NIGHT IN THE PACIFIC

Tapping his wine glass with a spoon, the ship's Captain stands,

"It's time for those who dare to join me in absolute darkness," he shouts, unnecessarily into the microphone. He is English, the consummate entertainer, and the American guests love his accent and hang on his every word.

The masked diners at the vast banquet fall silent. The purpose of a masked ball is to remain anonymous, to be able to dine, mix and dance with strange partners. The dress code is more fancy than formal, though many choose their black opera suits and a simple Venetian masquerade mask. The night starts with supper in the huge, ornate grand dining room that seats about six hundred. Although few will have separated from their partner, to be truly vulnerable, some will be completely unrecognisable and unknown. Excitement is high most nights, but being alone in the middle of the planet's biggest ocean, over seven hundred nautical miles from the Panama Canal transit they left behind two days ago, puts even more electricity in the air.

After dinner, most guests will move to the ballroom and dance, but Captain Neil Reynolds has a daring alternative on offer. He fully understands the magic of the warm nights, alone, mid-ocean on a smallish ship of twelve hundred guests and a relatively small crew. Tonight is his favourite party piece. He wears a simple Highwayman's eye cover and a cape over one shoulder, so the epaulette on the other still boasts his grade.

"Tonight is a new moon, a magical phase where desires are set and intentions made, but more importantly the sky is perfect for stargazing. Unless you have an inside cabin, you will never have seen such darkness!"

A roar of laughter rings out, as mocking the cheaper cabins is an allowable joke on any ship. The Captain knows how to control his audience.

"This is not a night for the faint-hearted. Just because the moon cannot be seen, it doesn't mean its powers are hidden or reduced. Quite the contrary! 'Tis the time it is at its most impish, most playful and most dangerous. Think long and hard before you join me on the sun deck."

"Woo!" is the cry from the pantomime crowd lead by the waiters. The Captain smiles and continues, playing the goblin even more, whisking his cape up he barks,

"The moon's strange powers impact our behaviour, increase awareness you never before recognised. Perhaps few of you will dare, preferring to dance at the Grand Masked Ball. But as I turn off all the ship's external lights, I challenge you to absolute darkness. With everything so dark and silent, the buzz of our increased technology, artificial intelligence, vending and machinery will whir louder and louder, threatening to come to life…"

The Captain begins to walk towards the exit, gripping his radio microphone and circling his cape.

"In Hindu tradition, fasting on this day will

prevent widowhood! Too late for those of you that have eaten! On the night of the new moon, the bodyweight of honey bees peaks – as does the weight of us cruisers."

He gets another laugh; cruisers love to laugh about the wealth of food or gluttony on a ship. He stands on the room's exit steps, next to a rarely used grand piano and looks back, enjoying his large audience, knowing that for most, this is the end of his show. Few will risk the dark.

Stargazing is not normally held on the night of the masked ball because there is too much going on, but the weather is about to change. That means a change in visibility and less stability on deck which would make turning lights out a risk. His show tonight is right on the full moon.

"Schizophrenia increases, madness and aggressive behaviour are made worse, but! For us here, under a dark sky, the ship slowed almost to stationary for silent running, with nothing anywhere on the horizon. Tonight is perfect! No other ship for miles, no city, no traffic, and no industry to offer light pollution. It will be the darkest night of your lifetime."

The diners may be a little concerned now, but the waiters add another lower tone chorus of "wow!" Some of the staff are veterans, maybe thirty years of service on the same ship, working nine-month shifts with just a month or two home to see the families they financially support. The Captain flicks his cape then adds even more drama to his finale,

"Do not underestimate how frightening and disorientating this can be."

The waiters lead a worrying cry, "Oooh!"

"You have ten minutes before lights out. No late

arrivals are permitted on deck, no glass allowed on deck. Members of the crew will be at every doorway to assist. Ten minutes. Do not be late!"

Captain Neil leaves dramatically, his cape billowing behind him. The haunting laughter through the address system is added by someone else; someone they will never see.

2 MASKS ON, LIGHTS OUT

Holding their shoes and lifting gowns, ladies look down through their masks to master the exterior metal steps up to deck ten, the sun deck. Elevators at all three points on the ship are busy to get guests up to deck nine; aft, midships and the front or bow. There are no lifts to deck ten, the sun deck.

Men assisting ladies, and vice versa, engage in an added level of fun which suggests they may not be their usual partners. Those looking up already will see that even with the ship's lights on, the night is dark and the sky clear with stars easily visible.

"Please settle," announces Captain Neil, "you have just minutes to find a chair, lay on the deck, or hold onto a rail. Please come away from the stairs because you will lose all orientation when the lights go out."

The large deck circles a funnel and machinery section and stretches from the middle pool to the front. It is full, and those without sunbeds are on the deck sitting or laying flat on their backs.

"I suggest you lay down flat and look up," the Captain suggests. "Quickly now."

Like a Mexican wave falling to a slow end, every guest in the middle of the deck lays down, looking up.

The deputy captain walks amongst the guests with a keen eye on safety that allows Captain Neil Reynolds the freedom to perform. He is many years younger than Neil, slimmer, and has an olive skin which does not glow white like his superiors.

"Deputy Captain Vasile Nagy to Stair Guards, confirm doors closed and stairs clear."

"By number," is Nagy's short sharp command into his radio.

"Number one, port forward deck doors closed and clear," is the first voice on the radio.

"Number two, Sir, port side forward sun deck stairs and deck nine clear." The replies continue as Neil ensures his microphone cable is safely over the rail and safely away from the guests. He is an engaging man, smiling and appearing to enjoy himself but also looking for potential problems. This light-hearted routine is a well-rehearsed drill and every officer is eyeing the public. Turning all the lights off is a very serious thing to do, and it only happens when they know each and every guest is safe.

"One minute to go!" Captain Neil shouts, making his way in a circle back to the stage where his microphone is waiting. He holds on to a side rail with his left hand, the microphone in his right. He may be well-rehearsed, but he too is subject to risk statements and procedures as well as the attraction of the sky.

"Clear to go, Captain," is Nagy's report, heard on the radio.

"Can you all hear me?" The captain asks the guests over the address system on the sun deck, which is pure showmanship as he knows they can.

"Yes." Is the combined reply.

"This is for your eyes only. A phone-free zone

until I announce you can use them, as even the light from your screen will destroy what you are about to see. Look up in five. Four. Three. Two. One."

The guests count down each and every number with him, until he makes the final command,

"Lights off!"

As the lights on deck vanish, mother nature lights hundreds and hundreds more stars in the sky and boosts the power on the ones that were already there. There are wows and gasps of amazement. The chatter builds to an exciting din as the amazing sight continues to reveal itself. The pitch dark of the night is ignored because the sky is mesmerising. It is a vision none of the guests will ever forget and will share for the rest of the night.

"Few have seen the sky from the middle of the Pacific Ocean. This body of water is over one-hundred-and-sixty square kilometres. It is larger than all the landmasses on earth combined," Captain Neil narrates, still craning his neck to look up. His tone reveals his pride in this spectacle.

"More stars than you can ever have imagined, too many to name. If you look high over the port side, you can see Mars, the big red planet. Got it? To its side coming back is the constellation Libra, next, more directly over us is Virgo, then continue on that line; Leo, Cancer and then Gemini."

As Captain Neil explains the bright stars above, a few guests shuffle around in the darkness straining to see as it is difficult for them to turn their head when lying flat. They are all mesmerised.

"If you feel the need to pollute the night with your cell phones, now is the time. You have a final few minutes," Neil suggests.

Cell phones light the deck with a blue glow. Many who were laying down decide to sit or stand. Others move in the flat blue haze. More and more phones point to the sky, some to take photographs, others are using a 'star app' which names all the stars.

"Lights back on in five, four, three, two, one. Lights on!" Neil shouts.

"Lights on, repeat, lights on," Nagy says into his radio.

The re-appearance of the deck lights make most of the stars vanish. It is now as if someone turned the lights off in the sky. Still enthusing with excitement, guests rush for the stairs keen to continue their evening, others crowd the captain, or officers, while some check their phones to see if the pictures worked out for them.

"Man overboard! Man overboard!" cuts through the din, and echos up from deck nine below. With no ability to look over deck ten down to the sea, officers rush past guests and descend to deck nine which has a drop to the ocean. Captain Neil Reynolds excuses himself and finds a private space to raise his walkie-talkie.

"Note position. Someone give me a status report!"

3 MAN OVERBOARD

An officer in whites leans over the starboard rail of deck nine, next to a guest who is still pointing and shouting, "Man overboard!" on loop.

Further down the deck, a junior officer is in the rigging, powering a searchlight and scanning the sea methodically as he was taught in training. The light first comes in towards the side of the ship, then slowly scans back out to sea, turns and traces back to the ship again on a slightly new line. It passes a floating mask, re-centres and holds on it. There is a gasp from the crowd. An officer raises his walkie-talkie,

"Captain. A mask is floating in the water, starboard side. No sign of a person."

"Bridge, this is the Captain. Maintain position. Plot the coordinates from when the lights went out versus our position now. Launch three port side lifeboats. Man overboard, this is not a drill," he commands privately, "Captain to security, Officer Ruby Jenkins, prepare all your staff for a potential muster station check. Please join me on the promenade deck, aft."

Chatter continues on the communications and codes are repeated as the Captain descends the external steps to the crowded pool deck. Having seen the mask, guests are moving from the starboard side to the port side to watch the lifeboat crew in action on deck six below, where they are hung. The sea is lit up in all directions. The sounds of locking devices, chains and motors all play a new tune commanding attention.

The Captain walks along behind guests and looks out at the face mask. He pulls out his phone and takes a photograph. The crowd begins to swell, guests now joining from the bars and lounges. One engages him,

"Captain, tell them to spread out, all the guests on one side will make us tip over."

"Don't worry, there is no chance of that."

"That's what they said on the Vasa!"

"That was three hundred years ago, Sir, boat building has come a long way." The Captain excuses himself and raises his walkie-talkie.

"Officer Jenkins, let's get security officers on all decks, we'll need crowd control."

Neil moves swiftly towards the port side to lean over and check on the progress of the lifeboats. Seeing they are being launched, he cuts back to starboard, to the officers manning the mid searchlight. He scans the sea for a guest in the water. He opens communications again,

"Bridge, I need two rear searchlight operators, meet me at the port side aft lamp on deck five." He looks up at the spotlight operator above him, midships. "Let the forward searchlight stay on the mask, you scan the sea for signs of life or any other debris."

"Yes, sir."

"As soon as you can, hand this job over to an engineer and meet me down on five."

The Captain ducks inside the ship at the rear staircase, and seeing the queue for the lift and the excitement at the guest stairs, he turns down the corridor and enters the door marked 'Crew Only'. He runs, taking two steps at a time on the white metal stairs, flashing around the tight corners of the undecorated area. He reaches the deck seven, then six and is out on deck five in no time. He looks out again to the dimly lit sea, as he makes his way to the rear of the ship. Engineers and officers are firing up more lights. The decorated female officer in suited black uniform, Ruby Jenkins, turns and stands to face him. Her name badge clearly states 'Head of Security'. She wears flat shoes, ready for action. Her slim frame boasts square formidable shoulders that balance her long hair. Her good looks might fool you to question her position in what is so often a man's post. The male engineer reports first,

"Sir, we have travelled just three nautical miles since lights-out. Radar is showing nothing. The first life craft is nearly back at our number one position and is in communication with the bridge."

"We need a headcount, Sir," Ruby states, in a west coast American accent.

In the distance, the searchlights of the lifeboats back at position one are wiping back and forth in the water. Each crew member, every team knows exactly what they have to do from the many drills they perform each week.

Captain Neil turns back to his officers. "Why do they always do it in the middle of nowhere, days from civilisation or help?"

"Can I prepare for a muster station roll-call of all passengers to discover who is missing, Sir? If anyone. Let's hope it's just a mask and a false alarm." Ruby says.

Captain Neil hesitates, "First let's put out a message to ask if anyone has lost a mask overboard. Half of the passengers will be asleep. If we can solve this without waking them, or interrupting the ball it would be a better outcome. If we go straight to muster stations, anyone who has lost a mask overboard will be too embarrassed, or afraid to admit it."

Ruby nods in agreement.

Deputy Captain Vasile joins the Captain and Ruby, "Sir, I think both of you need to join me back on the sun deck."

"Can't you deal with it, Vasile?" The captain asks.

Vasile leans in so as not to be overheard. "No Sir. A guest has been murdered."

4 THERE'S BEEN A MURDER

A full five decks up again, a very large lady lays still and lifeless at the side of the sun deck, her feet near the rail. She is wearing an elegant long black dress, short stubby heeled black shoes, and a hat with a veil. Beside her is a matching clutch bag and her hand is gripping a walking stick. Standing above her are three medics in green jumpsuits and two officers in whites. Their bags of equipment surround her, but no amount of technology is going to bring her back to life. Behind them stand four deckhands waiting for orders.

"The team were stacking the sunbeds when one came over to wake her. They called the medics." A young officer explains.

Ruby Jenkins moves from behind the Captain to kneel beside the body, she looks up to the medics. "Why do you think it's a –." Ruby starts.

"Excuse me, Ruby." Captain Neil cuts her off to address the deck team that found her. "Gentlemen finish making the sunbeds safe, then please report to Madeline in Human Resources. Not a word to anyone about this until we know what's really happened. Not one word." He says.

They nod and resume working. Ruby stands up next to the Captain as he addresses the small team around the body.

"In order. Ruby, please have this area taped off at the bottom of all access stairs, and have all crew or guest doors with access into the ship locked. This area is closed. Next, please brief Madeline in H.R. to interview the deckhands and ask for their cooperation in not spreading rumours. If need be, have someone from security with her, but I think your team will be stretched tonight. If they need counselling or help, see if Maddie can handle it. Let's get photography up here to detail the mask before it sinks, then match that to guests they photographed earlier this evening. Then the body, pictures from every angle before it is moved."

"Yes, sir," Ruby and the team of officer's reply.

Ruby and the young officer leave. Neil turns to his second in command, "Vasile, go to the bridge and take over. Note in the log that I am on special duties concerning another guest to be detailed later."

Vaslie goes. Neil is left with the medics and the other young officer. He looks down at the body and mumbles to himself, thinking out loud, "I'm thinking that mask is no more than a distraction to allow the murderer to get away." He looks up, directing his attention to the medics. "That's if it is a murder. What makes you think that it is?"

The medic with two stripes eases forward and answers. His badge reads 'Manesh Hunjan, Senior Medic'. Neil knows him. He knows most of his crew despite constant changes.

"Sir, she had no pulse on arrival. When we looked at her chest to attempt CPR we noticed blood, but not a lot. Then we saw multiple small stab wounds."

"Why not more blood, Manny?" The Captain asks, looking down at the body.

"She is so big sir, the blade could only make wounds to her front, her bleeding would have been internal." Manesh offers.

"Maybe the blade pierced her heart and she died instantly." Ruby offers, re-joining the conversation.

Manesh looks down at the body. There are bloodstains on her chest area, but she's wearing a very dark dress, so it's difficult to see them.

"Sir, Miss, with respect to the lady, she is so very big. The length of the blade needed to reach her heart…" Manesh hesitates, embarrassed.

"A sword." Ruby offers, pulling the dress aside to see the wounds again, and getting blood on her hands and sleeve. Manesh offers her some wipes to clean her hands.

"Sorry sir, but I agree, it would take a very long blade and she was laying in a huge group of people, and no one noticed her die?"

"No one noticed a sword, a sabre would be more than enough. But surely any large blade would drip, leaving a trail?" the Captain reflects. "Gentlemen!" He shouts to his deck crew, stopping them stacking beds. "Leave it now. Please report to Human Resources and make statements. Thank you. Use the far stairs." He points at the staircase on the other side of the sun deck. The Captain looks around, then back to the team. "This is a crime scene. We need to find any blood trail; we need fingerprints on the door handles. Ruby, you are in for a very busy night."

She acknowledges that and turns away. She sees a member of her team waiting below on deck 9, offering her a roll of tape. She holds out her hands and it's thrown up. Jason, one of the house photographers is there with his camera ready. She waves indicating he should join them via the rear stairs, then indicates to her teammate that the near stairs should be taped off.

Neil turns to Manesh again, "OK, leave the body here until Ruby gives you clearance, but I'd like it out of sight, in the morgue and this deck cleaned and open well before sun up. Brief doctor Yates to set up an autopsy room,"

Manesh addresses his team in an Asian dialect and they rush away, leaving him with Neil who bends down again and to the lady who has made every effort to look her best for the party. "Can't have been easy for her to get upstairs. She made a real effort to see the stars."

All of her clothes look expensive. Neil takes out his phone and photographs her shoes and her hand gripping the clutch bag. He then separates the bag from her hand and photographs it. Using a tissue, he opens the bag and takes out the one magical thing every cruiser carries; her cruise card.

"Donna McGovern. Were you travelling alone?" He says gently, though Manesh can hear. He looks to the walking stick, then scans her again for clues he may have missed. He pulls out his walkie-talkie.

"It's Captain Reynolds. Please patch me through to Mr Stevens, hotel manager… No, don't worry, I'll ring him," he says concluding his on-air chatter and clipping his walkie-talkie back to his belt. He takes his phone and speed dials, as Jason approaches. He nods, allowing Jason to start taking pictures.

"Roy, it's Neil. We have a dead guest on deck ten. Maybe another overboard, but I'm beginning to think that the second is unlikely. Can you do a passenger check on a Donna McGovern; family, contact details, anything you have. Thanks."

Neil watches Jason and Manesh work, then looks over the edge to the deck below being securely taped off. He turns back to the body being photographed and Ruby working.

"Can you get the detail of all the jewellery she's wearing. It looks expensive. Necklace, bangles and rings," Ruby says into her phone, addressing her team. "Jason will have pictures for you."

A young Officer Cadet, mesmerised by the scene playing out before him stands beside Neil, who shares his thought, "You won't have dealt with anything like this in training?"

"No, Sir."

"There is very little to steal onboard a ship, apart from in the shops, but they're covered in cameras. That makes other guests targets to a thief."

"That is rare, Sir," Ruby interjects. "This was not a robbery. Unless she was wearing another expensive piece."

"I photographed her in the Atrium earlier, I remember her smile. I can check against those photographs," Jason offers.

"Better remove all pictures of her from the photo gallery," Neil adds.

"Of course, sir," Jason replies. He then nods to Manesh, "I'm done here."

"My team can move the body then?" Manesh checks.

The young officer seems uneasy.

"What is it?" Neil asks. He has been around long enough to know that everyone sees things differently, everyone's mind is focussed differently, and the young officer has been watching everything.

"This deck was full of people. The murderer has escaped. He obviously didn't want to be caught." The young officer starts.

"Or she," Neil adds.

"Or she. So, they would have had to have covered her mouth with some force to ensure she didn't scream. Her mouth should have bruises."

"The doctor will find all that in the autopsy," Manesh confirms, looking up at him.

"But her jaw looks very strange. Is it broken, or is her mouth is full?" The officer asks.

"Did you move her mouth?" The Captain asks Manesh.

"No Sir." Manesh replies, "We checked her neck for a pulse, her wrist, then found the blood on her chest, the blood on her dress, and the multiple stab wounds. She was dead. We called security."

Neil nods. His focus falls on her mouth, it is awkwardly closed as if her jaw has been broken in the struggle. The medic pulls her chin down to reveal her mouth is stuffed with red material. Jason photographs as Manesh takes it from her mouth.

The captain takes over and holds the top corners allowing it to unfold, revealing it's a red napkin from the dining room with words written in black ink.

'Scatter, you featureless puppets, scatter.'

5 MIAMI

The scorching hot Miami sun beats down through the large window of a long time disused commercial retail unit. Without functioning air conditioning, it's punishing. Kieron Philips, dressed in a tourist's Miami Beach T-shirt, shorts, short white socks just below his huge calf muscles, and pumps, he looks like someone whose luggage was lost on the plane. He collapses in a chair, wiping his brow and face with the base of his shirt. It is no longer white.

"Nice!" Hunter Witowski mocks in his deep voice. "Can't take the heat? I thought you did multiple tours in Iraq and Syria!"

"Witowski, you know nothing about me apart from the online press rubbish and what that clown of a ghost-writer invented for the book. I don't recognise myself in that heist book."

"No, I have a full jacket on you," Hunter boasts as he walks out of the door to lift one end of a desk left out on the sidewalk. He waits for assistance.

Kieron gets up and joins him, taking the other end. He lifts it, and walks in backwards as Hunter pushes forward.

"You might have been CIA, but they never really know what's going on," Kieron adds, provoking him.

"Remind me how we became partners?"

"I solved a crime on your last ship, I got your wife back from kidnappers, taking a bullet I might add. Then I had to find my own daughter, who you allowed to be kidnapped from right under your security-chief-nose. Then I shared my job offer as an International Cruise Ship Investigator with you. You should read my biography." Kieron answers.

"A bunch of unrecognisable lies, written for you because you can't write!" Hunter adds.

"Just scan the detail of how I went to your rescue. That bit's true!"

"You mean I saved your sorry white-sock-wearing British butt, then got you gainfully employed here in the heart of the cruise world; Miami," Hunter says.

Kieron drops his end of the desk abruptly, just inside the unit so Hunter crashes into his end, still outside. Hunter reacts so it narrowly misses his bare feet in open toed-shoes.

"The heart of the cruise world?!" Kieron laughs, as he walks outside into the empty car park to look at the parade of boarded-up commercial units.

"The realtor said a very desirable neighbourhood."
"Hmmm."
"'A lot attached to a very popular restaurant'." Hunter points towards the brightly painted diner on the corner.

"Near to all local facilities including a bank and a successful progressive college?"

"They wouldn't be on our lot," Hunter shrugs.

They are both tall, physically fit men with frames that suggest they were carved by many years of military service. Hunter looks relaxed and at home here in Miami. Both have scars, or as their domestic passports might suggest, identifying marks. Hunter has two healed bullet wounds to the left shoulder, Kieron has an old scar that starts just below the sleeve of his shirt on his right arm, and pops out over the neckline.

Kieron gestures out at the area, "This is Miami, in the greatest country in the world, and the shops are all closed down?"

"Business has moved to commercial outlets at the new mall, making these great units available! Lots of parking, easy access!" Hunter boasts.

"For the ships to pull up right outside." Kieron torments.

"We'd be mega-flush if your daughter hadn't left our forty million on the last ship," Hunter argues, accusingly.

Kieron nods slowly, "But had that chunk of cash come off the ship as you'd planned, the Portuguese police would have it firmly in their pension plan and we'd be locked up right now with nothing,"

Hunter disagrees, shaking his head.

"Why not put some of what we do have into better offices, somewhere near the cruise companies?"

Kieron suggests.

"We don't show favouritism or allegiance by being near anyone shipping company," Hunter counters.

"Tick that box!" Kieron smiles.

"Wild Mary's Breakfast Bar next door and an office away from prying eyes. Here's where we plan how to get our money off the last ship!"

Kieron walks up and slaps Hunter's cheeks between his hands, "Fine. You plan that. I'll work out how to spend the cash on a new office," he says, walking back into the unit and grabbing a bottle of water.

Hunter walks in and stands silhouetted in the doorway. "Don't ever slap me again."

"It's a British thing."

"Don't care! Don't do it."

"You're not supposed to like it."

"I know, I watched Benny Hill, but don't," Hunter says, deadpan.

"How about we call this bromance off? We're kidding ourselves. We're not going to be offered loads of work on cruise ships; they're not riddled with crime. They got rid of us, sleight of hand. Fwhhip, gone! … First you see us, then we're in a derelict unit on a brownfield site, in a forgotten area of Miami, where inside we have a 'contemporary space'… meaning nothing,"

"I'm going to do that British slap on you in a moment, but with a little American force." Hunter states.

"That's not how it works. It's not meant to be forceful, it's a comedy thing. It only works when the bigger guy slaps the smaller guy."

Offended, Hunter stands bolt upright. "Why are

you here?" He asks.

"Seriously, what do we have to offer the shipping industry?" Kieron counters.

"We are experts in training cruise personnel." Hunter insists.

"Then we need an office in Goa, not Miami. When was the last time any ship employed Americans or British?" Kieron insists.

"Oh, you mean like me or you?" Hunter rebuttals.

"Apart from us?" Kieron asks, "and look where we are now."

"Sitting pretty, about to walk next door and have breakfast in Wild Mary's. We'll figure how to get back on that ship and get 'our money' that's locked in a trunk. Only we have the key!" Hunter exclaims, pointing at the plain white wall which has a nail knocked into it, with the key hanging on.

They both notice a very large wet patch swelling below the dangling key. Water is dripping from the nail and from the key.

"You banged that in there." Kieron accuses.

"I banged it in because you tried with the heel of that pathetic plastic sandal and failed!"

Bang. Water bursts out, the nail flies across the room and the key is gone.

6 WE'VE MET BEFORE

Officer Ruby Jenkins sits behind her desk looking sideways at security monitors. She is holding a picture of the masquerade mask recovered from the sea and trying to match it against footage date and time marked from last evening. There are more than one of its kind, just as other masks are repeated. Captain Neil Reynolds enters, and closes the door behind him.

"You should get some sleep, Ruby. The lifeboats are on the way in. They found a body just after sun-up. They've radioed in to confirm the cruise card in the jacket pocket is of Eric Clifford, the second guest missing at your roll-call last night."

"I can't sleep; we have two dead bodies."

"You're out of hours. You have to take a six-hour break. Let's assume, for now, that Clifford killed Donna McGovern, then jumped ship. I've closed the starboard decks so we can bring his body back onboard undercover," Neil explains. He moves back to the door and tries to insist she take his advice. "I'm going to shower, change, and grab something to eat before I have to take his wife down to identify the body,"

"Then ask her if she understands the note," Ruby says harshly, sliding the evidence bag containing the red table napkin towards him.

He is tired, but re-enters and reads it again, 'Scatter you, featureless puppets, scatter.' He shakes his head.

"Not something we find from a rudimentary autopsy," Ruby says.

"When the boats are locked back in, we'll power on to Tahiti and start to make up last night's lost time. Later, you can figure out the why and wherefore. First, we give his wife some time, then you can have your autopsy. That's after you've rested."

The Captain leaves but Ruby sits firm, something is annoying her as she scans the pictures of the dead woman, Donna.

"Why come on board with your wife, then murder another woman? Beats me… let's take a look at your wife."

Ruby punches up Betty Clifford's picture in passenger records. She looks strong, smart and happy from the picture. She shows off a wide smile that would not be allowed on a government passport.

"Why are you so happy, Betty? Why are you so very bloody happy?"

Ruby trawls the data on Eric and Betty Clifford. Date of cruise booking is just over one year ago. Standard cabin, upgraded to a balcony cabin. Ruby clicks on upgrade history. It states they paid full price for the cabin class they booked so were upgraded when unsold bed space went on sale. The reason being that it was to be their fortieth wedding anniversary during the cruise. Ruby checks the anniversary date against the itinerary. The ship will be visiting the island of Bora Bora on that day.

"Bora Boring." She says, as she picks up her phone and dials.

"Captain. Ruby Jenkins. Just a heads up for when you do the identification later. Eric and Betty Clifford were to celebrate their fortieth wedding anniversary the day we are in Bora Bora."

"Thank you, Ruby, now goodnight."

She smiles at his gratitude and feels the pull of her bed, but she is still uneasy. She checks the list of their previous cruises on this ship, which only frustrates her more. Then details for occupation.

"I don't think I can sleep tonight, Eric. I want to understand your relationship with Betty and your apparent madness. Show me how you're a puppet master… reveal your twisted logic." She muses to herself.

Ruby scrolls down and finds 'unemployed' as the occupation. She jumps screens, searching for Eric

Clifford on social media. His profiles are inadequately filled in, as she would expect from users of his age, who neither have to sell themselves to get a partner in life or a job. She stops and looks up at the cruise stops for the huge world cruise itinerary.

"Southampton to Cadiz, we stopped in Cadiz… There was a puppet museum in Cadiz!"

Ruby produces a wide mischievous smile. She has found something. She pulls another folder from her desk and it drops open at Cadiz. She leafs through and finds that the puppet museum was on the walking tour of the city. Back to the computer, she checks the Clifford's purchase history and discovers that they took the tour to Seville.

"Damn. Seville is miles from Cadiz. They wouldn't walk to the puppet museum from there… Or would they? Would Betty get angry? Angry Betty."

Ruby picks up her phone and dials.

"Hi 'Lucy Excursions'? It's Ruby in security."

"Hello, Ruby security. I hope you are busier than I am." Lucy replies.

"Don't. Though you could come and help me, or at least tell me what time the Seville excursions got back when we were in Cadiz?" Ruby listens and writes down 1552hrs, circles it and looks at the clock, "I've not been to bed yet."

"That is the least romantic offer I have ever had."

"Sorry Lucy, I must try harder."

Ruby goes into her records of 'ship leaving and entering times' for crew and guests and sees that Betty Clifford entered the ship 1615 hours, but Eric did not board until 1725 hours. All aboard time was 1730 hours.

"Where were you going without Betty, Eric? Eric?

Methinks puppets. How far is puppet land?"

Ruby pulls up a map and discovers the puppet museum is just behind the station, next to where they docked. "Eric Clifford, you puppet master, you're playing a game with me."

She types into a search engine 'puppet master Cadiz'. She watches the first result, a 'Cruise Doris Visits' YouTube film entitled 'The Puppet Master of Cadiz'. As she watches the huge collection of puppets, strung and full-sized, she writes the name, 'Francisco Peralta – The Puppet Master of Cadiz'. The film leads her to another, a guide to Cadiz, and she sits back watching, trying to connect the dots. She looks back at the picture of the napkin which and interrupts the film by typing the phrase into the search engine.

'Scatter, you featureless puppets, scatter.'

The first result is, 'Seven Pillars of Wisdom, day 1 of 240'. She hits print-screen.

"What am I doing? I need to sleep. And it's a fucking book!" She exclaims.

The PDF form of the book is actually all online. It is written by T E Lawrence. She opens a second tab and runs a search on T E Lawrence. 'Thomas Edward Lawrence, Lawrence of Arabia, British archaeologist and army officer. Worked as a spy. Lead the Arab Revolt against the Ottomans in World War 1. He diarised his affairs and they became a book, then a classic film.'

"So classic, none's ever seen it," she says sarcastically.

Ruby sits back in her chair, "I'm tired, Eric. This is not a joke anymore."

She looks at the first tab she opened. The book starts with a poem which she reads over and over. It is complicated, or just written when language was used in a different manner.

"Can I make sense of this madness?" Ruby asks herself jumping screens and following links from one cyber wormhole to another.

Lawrence was born out of wedlock in Wales, though neither of his dead parents are from there. He died in 1935 and is buried in Moretown, Dorset. Printscreen. Lawrence used the name T. E. Smith when working at an engineering firm of national importance. She recovers the print of the poem. Then she leafs through all her printed sheets and nowhere can she find the line, 'Scatter, you featureless puppets, scatter.' Ruby reads the poem again focusing on the first line,

"'I loved you, so I drew these tides of men into my hands and wrote my will against the stars.' ... They were all stargazing, but it makes no sense."

Ruby reads the screen. 'Sometimes one man carried various names. This may hide individuality and make the book a scatter of featureless puppets, rather than a group of living people...'

She highlights it and hits print.

"I can make a case for that being the masked ball, I suppose, but this needs hours of research," she says wearily to herself.

Feeling the ship is at full speed again, her head falls to the desk, exhausted. She checks her watch. Time has evaporated and all she has found is possibly irrelevant nonsense. She once again dials the Captain.

"Ruby, I thought I told you to get some sleep!" Neil answers.

"Sir, have you identified the body with Mrs Clifford yet?" She asks.

"No. I am about to."

"Ask her to bring her passport, and her husband's."

"Passports are with the hotel staff. They always are on a world cruise."

"I'll meet you there. I may have something on that phrase, it's from a poem; it might be nothing but I sense it needs looking into." Ruby says, putting the phone down, then pulling the print from the machine. She slaps her own face and dashes out.

7 BANK JOB

Like the opening of a cheesy movie, Kieron and Hunter are a huge unnerving presence, loitering in the reception of a large bank. They have observed that the security guard by the door has taken notice of them, and signalled to his colleague who is patrolling the other side by the manager's office.

"They think we are staking the place out," Hunter whispers to Kieron, turning away.

Kieron watches them as the far guard starts to walk towards them, always able to take cover behind the rounded counter.

"Nice stalking. I hope they don't shoot us, it would strange to have come this far and get whacked in a bank by a pair of trigger happy old-timers." Kieron says.

"Turn away, you're making them nervous," Hunter says.

"I'm making them nervous? You sure they're not jealous I've taken a six thousand, nine hundred and eighty-nine square foot unit all to myself just down the road?" Kieron asks.

"Don't make any sudden moves, don't reach in your pocket, and stop looking at them,"

Kieron turns to Hunter, miffed, "You're serious! I can't put my hand in my pocket or I'll get shot? Like Butch Cassidy?"

"I'm just saying, they think you look suspicious. If you go for a weapon, they might pull one on you."

"I don't have a weapon."

"Look, Kieron, you're in America now, dressed in a stupid beach get-up, so cops are bound to be jumpy. You get pulled over in a car, asked for ID anywhere, don't make a fast move to a pocket," Hunter explains.

"You're telling me when that door, which we are waiting to open, opens, if I reach into my pocket for the passport they've asked me to bring, for ID, they'll shoot me?" Kieron asks, looking at the door they're waiting at.

"What do you think? You've worked the front line."

"I think you're probably right, I just never expected to be on the frontline so soon after trading Iraq for sunny Miami,"

"Digs against my country will also get you shot. By me. Just behave, you're in Southern America, people carry guns."

"I never realised Miami was in Southern America."

"Where did you think it was?"

"North Cuba."

Hunter nearly goes for him, but the door opens.

"Should I put my hands up?" Kieron asks.

"Mr Witowski and Mr Philips?" Both of them walk forward to the bank clerk holding the door open. "I'm Ron Stone, here to help you guys."

As Kieron gets level with him, he stops, "Ron,

would you tell your two guards back there that we're here to open an account, I'm British and I'm not used to being shot in the back as I go for my passport."

The young manager smiles, and waves for the two security men to stand down. The guards relax, hands away from their guns. Kieron pulls his passport out and the door closes with them inside.

"Big mistake, Ron. If I had a gun, you'd now be dead or captured, they would be out of the game as we are behind the bulletproof counter," Kieron explains.

Hunter shakes his head in disbelief. Kieron holds out his hand to shake that of a very nervous Ron Stone.

"Kieron Philips. I and Mr Witowski run a security consultancy a few blocks down on Orange, next to Wild Mary's. You ever need any help, just give us a call. We could probably be here quicker than the police."

"Am I being robbed?" Ron asks nervously.

"No," Hunter replies, as his phone rings. "Excuse me, sir."

"Witowski." He answers flatly, turning away.

Kieron signals for Ron Stone to lead them on.

"We require a safety deposit box, Ron, for these two parcels." Kieron says, putting them on the desk, "and we need to open an account. Here's nine thousand dollars in cash and my passport. When Mr Big Business gets off the phone he'll give you his ID."

Hunter follows, talking into his phone, "We're kinda busy at the moment. How urgent is this? … Well if you don't know, and you're just fishing, d'you mind if I ask you to call me back when this is a contract?"

"So you're by Wild Mary's?" Ron asks, still trying to suss the two men out.

Kieron hands over forms. "Bank deposit box application form all filled out. Bank account application all filled out. Joint names, we will be filing as a company."

"Witowski and Philips." Hunter interrupts.

"Philips and Witowski." Kieron corrects him, then continues. "References from our previous employer, a cruise company whose main account is with your Dodge Island office."

They watch Ron hand their money to a teller who machine-counts it. He puts it in a band, then stamps the deposit paperwork. The teller signs across the stamp, Ron Stone signs below the stamp and hands the receipt to Kieron.

"That's a receipt for your deposit. I'll walk down to you tomorrow with the account details. I'd like to see where you are."

"Fantastic," Kieron enthuses, "we have nearly seven thousand square feet of a modern contemporary nature."

"It needs work, Ron, but we're good for it," Hunter adds, giving Philips a sly look as Ron turns away.

"Now, I'll take you to the safe deposit."

Kieron and Hunter follow Ron around and down some stairs to a basement.

"Who was on the phone?" Kieron asks Witowski.

"Possible first job,"

"Same company?"

"No, biggest cruise company on the seas."

"And you told them we were very busy?"

"I did."

In the cellar, a safety deposit box is placed on the shiny steel desk in the middle of the room adjacent to the vault. They walk up to the floor to ceiling steel bars separating them. Beyond the walls are safety deposit boxes top to bottom Their every move is watched by a third armed security guard.

Hunter throws his parcel in the box, Kieron throws his parcel in, the box is closed. They lock it, slide it through the gate into the vault, and watch a fourth armed guard take it and lock it in place.

"How is there enough trade for a safe depositary out here?" Kieron asks.

"This is Miami. You don't ask questions about money." Hunter pockets the key.

"You could put a nail in the wall for that," Kieron mocks with a grin.

The men follow Ron back up the stairs and into the reception. He stops by the guard at the door to the street. "You guys ever need extra hours?"

"Dialogue's free man," says the guard.

"I could have had a gun," Kieron says to the guard.

"We weren't worried about you. We were worried about the big guy," the guard says.

Kieron looks at his badge. "Isaiah Success? That's your real name?"

"No, I wear someone else's badge, in case I shoot a smart arse."

Kieron follows a very amused Hunter out into the harsh sunshine.

"I liked him," Hunter says with a smirk.

8 FRIED GREEN TOMATOES

Witowski and Philips are walking the blocks back to their unit in the almost vacant lot. Turning at Wild Mary's means they are home; their unit is attached to the back of her diner.

"Shall we go in and introduce ourselves?" Kieron smirks.

"Rude not to," Hunter says, stepping back and opening the door.

Colour is the first thing that hits. The seats are all red and cream, the floor is spotlessly clean, white and black tiles laid in a simple but effective chequered pattern. Standing just inside the entrance, they survey the space. To the left where the diner wraps around the corner, there is more room. A classic jukebox sits switched off and looking very dead, like it hasn't been used for years. In front of it is a small dance area. They notice the sign to the left of them. 'Only dance on tables after they have been cleared'.

"Funny," says Kieron.

"What can I get you, two gentlemen?" A confident, happy African American lady asks, through a wonderful smile.

"That's a welcome that'll have us coming back," Hunter starts.

They move to the right, where another sign reads, 'no dancing on the tables'. This side, there are stools at the counter. A middle section has tables for two bar-side, and doubles the other side where a walkway separates them from the tables for two against the window roadside. The men are led to sit with a view of the empty parking lot.

"You two handsome gentlemen sit down here in the window where Mary can see you," she says, putting menus on the table.

"And the ships come in," Kieron says.

"Sorry?" She asks.

"We can see the ships come in."

"He's British. Strange sense of humour," Hunter says, looking at the menu.

"Nice jukebox," Hunter says.

"Nineteen-fifties, Wurlitzer-twelve-fifty."

"Still play?" he asks, looking around at it.

"You got a quarter?"

"Sorry, I only have Benjamins," Kieron says, looking to Hunter, then her.

"I get your humour now, love your accent,"

Mary reaches behind her to take the coffee pot off the counter, turns the cups on their table up for use and starts to pour.

"No one really calls 'em Benjamins now, not down here. They calls 'em yards. Not that many round here would have one… We don't get many British people in here," she leans back on her stance and looks at him, "Say something else."

"Mary? Do you get much trade here since the local merchants moved to the mall?"

"I like that. Real nice."

"Do you?" He asks.

"Do I what? What was your name?"

"Kieron Philips," he says standing, "and the pleasure is all mine." Kieron takes her hand and kisses it. "My question, is, do you get much trade here since the mall opened? I ask because we are your new neighbours. The first unit that way."

"Well if you are opening a trade that needs people, you could be in the wrong place."

"We are maritime consultants."

"What kind of time is that?" she asks.

"Maritime. Shipping."

"We don't get many ships pass by," she says.

"Two eggs, easy over and some grits, please,

Mary," Hunter cuts in.

"You'll be wanting fried green tomatoes with that," she instructs.

"I will?"

"You will, my mama's recipe, and she used to sit where you're sitting," Mary says, and turns to Kieron. "You eating or just waiting for a ship?"

"I'll have the same please, Mary," Kieron says. "Who sat here?"

"No one sat there. Stan!"

"I heard!" Stan shouts back. He has already cracked eggs next to the sliced tomatoes on the griddle. He's a large man, must be twenty stone.

"I'll be back with food. Mr Philips, maybe you could look in my restroom, where water seems to be coming in from your unit next door. Is you trying to float a ship?" Mary leaves.

"Folks around here have a good sense of humour," Hunter states.

"Me. I'm their fun apparently," Kieron comments.

"You're different," Hunter says, and he gets up and walks to the restroom. Philips follows.

The restroom is clean and functional, and she has floor cloths rolled to dam a canal, so water runs to the floor drain. But the water is not coming from their joining wall, it is from an internal wall. Kieron steps out of the restroom and opens the next door along, which is a storage cupboard. Water is running down the 'party' wall to the floor and out of the sidewall to the restroom, guided by the same ingenuity of cloths.

"Considering the mess, she was very polite," Kieron says, heading back to the table.

"She's probably been ringing the landlord, no idea

she had new neighbours."

"No, it must be a shock to see people around here," Kieron delivers, but it doesn't niggle Hunter who sits down.

Mary is setting two plates ready for them.

"Think this might become a routine for us, Mary."

"You boys are more than welcome. What's your name?"

"Hunter Witowski."

"Hunter, I like that name. What did he say his name was?"

"Kieron."

"Like Chevron, with a K?"

"That's it," Kieron says, to be easy.

"Then I hope that's not an oil spill you got going down my wall," she nods, looking Kieron up and down. Kieron is struck dumb.

"Kevron, your food's getting cold."

"Mary. We hope to be away a lot," Hunter starts.

"I was getting excited about the trade."

"I don't wanna disappoint, so how about I pay for breakfast even when we're not here, if we can run a phone extension through to you, and you can tell folk who visit or call, that we are not in."

Mary puts her hands on her hips and stands, thinking.

"Are all your friends stupid enough not to know that if you ain't here, you ain't here?"

"He doesn't have any friends," Kieron adds quickly.

"Oh, they're your friends, I get it."

9 FORMAL IDENTIFICATION

Ruby enters the medical centre and is pointed towards a closed consulting room door. The lit red sign says 'NO ENTRY. IN USE'. She knocks and goes straight in. It is a basic examination room, a bed on a trolley, a desk, and a chair where Betty Clifford sits below an x-ray film lightbox. She looks both sad and afraid. A worried Malaysian nurse sits with her holding her hand, but stands when Ruby moves closer, allowing her to take the chair. Ruby looks at Betty for a short while before eventually sitting.

"Mrs Clifford, my name is Ruby."

Mrs Clifford nods, confused. They both look up as Captain Neil enters. The Captain has the effect of grabbing attention, it is as if guests know him personally. Mrs Clifford's face relaxes instantly, finally someone who will solve everything.

"Sir, this is Mrs Clifford. Betty, this is Captain Neil Reynolds," Ruby says.

"Mrs Reynolds. I'm so sorry it's been such a horrid night."

"I still don't know what's going on," Betty says, "where is Eric?"

"Unfortunately, we found a body in the sea. Seeing as your husband is missing, we need you to take a look. Hopefully, it's not him and he will still turn up." Neil explains softly.

"No, it can't be. We've been together forty years, never been apart!" Betty cries, "he'll turn up drunk, always does. I wish he'd stop drinking."

Neil takes her hands and she gets to her feet, he puts his arm around her to comfort her, but they all know the inevitable. He was found with cruise card ID in his pocket.

"Mrs Clifford, I brought both your passports down. It's all part of the identification," Ruby starts, "What was your maiden name?"

The Captain looks at Ruby, wondering where this unusual question is leading.

"Harris." She says. "Been a long time since I used that."

"Have you ever used any other name? An alias?"

Betty shakes her head.

"And your husband, has he always used Eric Clifford?" Ruby asks.

Betty nods. The Captain looks concerned for her and indicates that Ruby might wait.

"Shall we go through, Betty?" He suggests.

Betty is resistant, but Neil leads her to a connecting door marked 'Operating Theatre'.

"Ready?" he asks.

Betty, though a strong lady, begins sobbing with fear, but she nods and follows him in. He puts an arm around her as they both stand by the body hidden under a white sheet. Everyone is silent. Neil indicates to the nurse to fold back the sheet.

Betty buckles at her knees and gasps for air.

"No, No," Betty begs.

Neil holds her up.

"Betty, I'm so sorry, but we need to hear you formally identify that it's him."

"It's not, it's not him. That's not Eric." Betty whispers, exhausted by emotions.

"Betty, we need you to look again. This body has been in the water so he might look different, but if it is Eric, we need you to identify him."

"No. It's nothing like him."

"Ok." Puzzled, Neil walks her to a nearby chair. The nurse goes to cover the body, but Ruby lifts the sheet again and checks the face against a picture she has printed from the guest information sheet.

"She's right, it's not him," Ruby agrees.

"Of course I'm right, I know my husband… Where is he?" Betty cries. "Drunken sod."

"Has he done this before? Stayed out all night?' the Captain asks.

"Every cruise," Betty blurts, "enjoys himself far too much."

"We're looking for him, Betty. We'll find him," Neil reassures her, before passing Betty Clifford to the nurse. "Let me get you some water."

"I'll take a large gin!" Betty says, her handshaking.

Neil grabs a plastic cup and pours her a water at the sink. He hands it to her.

"I'll work on the gin."

Neil turns away and leaves Betty with the nurse. Ruby is close behind. They stop in the consulting room, confused.

"Never been apart in forty years," Neil starts.

"But he stays out all night drunk," Ruby snaps, with a little annoyance. "I found this."

She offers him her print-out of text with a passage highlighted. He reads, 'Sometimes one man carried various names. This may hide individuality and make the book a scatter of featureless puppets, rather than a group of living people: but once good is told of a man, and again evil, and some would not thank me for either blame or praise.'

"Where's this from? A book?" Neil asks.

"Lawrence of Arabia," she explains, "I thought that the puppets on the napkin referred to our masked ball. An assumption I should never have made."

"We played Lawrence of Arabia here in the cinema a few days ago, long before we went through the Panama Canal. I watched it. I don't remember those lines," Neil says, punishing himself.

"It's from the introduction of the book. I don't know what they mean in the book, to be honest, I don't know what they mean here."

"No, but we do know we have at least two dead bodies and a third missing person. Could drunken Eric be our murderer and now he's in hiding?"

Doctor Simon Yates enters, interrupting any further train of thought.

"That's not Eric Clifford, Simon. But he must be from this ship to have had Mr Clifford's cruise card in his pocket. You had better label him unknown and do a full autopsy," Neil suggests.

"I can do my best, but we don't have testing equipment on board. There are six stages to an autopsy; the Y-incision and removal of organs you see on TV is just the start. Checking the stomach contents, I can do. I can collect samples, I can also do a head and brain examination, but without the proper tests, there can be no conclusion, no stage six."

"Do what you can, keep meticulous records, pictures and samples, and keep me fully informed, thanks, Simon," Neil says.

Neil walks out of the room and exits the Medical Centre with Ruby following him.

"Ruby, ensure Jason from photography realises he is a key member of this team. Not just to cover everything, which we must do, but to run facial recognition software on our John Doe. Can Jason check his picture against all the passenger pictures on guest files?"

"I'm on it, sir."

"A guest will report John Doe missing unless he's travelling alone, which would narrow it down. And we need to find Mr Clifford."

"He might not be the murderer, sir," Ruby suggests with a shrug.

"No, these are all assumptions. I shall make that very clear when I report everything to head office. But someone seems to be playing with us."

10 FIRST CALL

A yellow cab pulls up outside Kieron and Hunter's unit. They wade out through the flooded water, step into the street and lock the door, which now has a huge sign on it, 'When unattended please enquire next door at Wild Mary's'.

"Should we not leave the door open so the water can flood out? Then the ships might be able to sail right up outside." Kieron mocks.

"The place would get wrecked," Hunter says, turning and walking towards the cab.

Kieron stays looking through the window of the unit for a few seconds more, then joins Hunter in the cab.

"Where we going?" The driver asks.

"Dodge Island," Hunter replies.

"I thought all these here units were lying empty, waiting to be flattened," the driver says, pulling away.

Kieron turns to Hunter, then to look out the window, lips pursed.

"Remember when we had real jobs? You know for

the world's biggest cruise operator?" Kieron asks.

"How do you measure biggest? Money, wealth, power, number of ships? Number of customers? Number of awards? They can all find a reason to be number one…" Hunter pauses for effect. "But they all have one thing in common."

"Give me a clue."

"When they have a problem, who they gonna call?"

Kieron thinks for a moment, "Ghost Busters?"

Hunter shakes his head.

"OK. I give up. Who?" Kieron asks, really pushing Hunter's buttons.

Hunter ignores him.

"Yeah, who?" Interrupts the cab driver, "because my brother is good at sorting stuff out. He's got a boat, and lots of friends, you know what I mean? Which terminal you want?"

"Can you drive the loop and then drop us off by the firehouse?" Hunter asks.

"Sure. What's the big problem? Let me call him. He has friends who work in the firehouse," the driver continues but they ignore him.

As they reach Dodge Island, it becomes obvious that it is cruise central; buildings, terminals, car parks and ships, all with cruise operators and ship's names. It is huge and impressive.

"Why don't we have an office here?" Kieron asks amazed by the sheer size of the industry. There is ship after ship. "This is a whole island of cruising. It's endless."

"It would drive you mad, trust me, Wild Mary's would seem like a Buddhist retreat if we had a place here."

The cab stops by the firehouse and the two men step out. Kieron, still with wet feet, is shaking them in between trying to catch Hunter, who is off at speed,

"Is it far?"

"Three blocks down. We're late."

"Why didn't the cab drop us there?"

"His brother's looking for work and he's a hustler. This is ours and gonna stay ours."

"Wait!" Kieron stops, slips his shoes off, takes off his wet socks and slips his sandshoes back on.

"That's a better look actually," Hunter says, pointing at the rubbish bin on the sidewalk.

"I was going to wash and dry them."

"No. You don't need white socks where we're going."

"They don't wear socks a few blocks down?"

"They don't wear socks in the middle of the Pacific."

"We're catching a ship? What? Which one is ours?" Kieron asks, pulling out his passport from his pocket, checking it's there before reseating it in safety.

"Our ship is in the middle of the Pacific, two days out. Too far for a chopper. The operator's not turning the ship around, so they rang us."

"Because of our new teleporting invention?" Kieron asks.

"My guess they want us to drop in. A little more extreme than Madeira. But no one will be shooting at us."

"Drop in? To the Pacific?"

"It's what we do." Hunter states.

"Is it?" Kieron questions.

"Before nightfall."

"I'm so glad you told them we were busy." Kieron

smiles, "because the answer is no, this is not what we do."

"We both did it for years."

"When we were younger. Not now, we've both had desk jobs. We're old!"

"We got my wife back. Dropped into the sea then."

"That was abseiling height from a stationary chopper!"

"It's what makes us different; 'extreme cruise ship crime investigators'."

"We're detectives now?" Kieron is now further amused. "Like the flying doctor, but flying detectives?"

"I knew you'd get there in the end," Hunter smiles, walking on again and turning on a verge of grass to an office block and looking up.

"And why is there such a rush?" Kieron asks, following him but still off the pace.

"Because the customer is in a panic," Hunter drawls calmly as he holds the door open for Kieron to walk in. "Whenever he looks at you, just say 'no worries'."

"What might our customer's worries be?"

Both men are inside the building, Hunter lets the door swing closed and they are cooled by efficient air conditioning. Kieron stands under a unit.

"Come on, let's go. They're in a panic, man." Hunter encourages.

"'No worries'," Kieron replies, barely moving, "do they have a spare office here?"

"No!"

"No worries."

"Can you just speed up?"

"Us slowly walking says 'no worries'. A lot is told

in body language, you know."

"I hope not."

"Well what kind of body language do I need, what is their problem?" Kieron asks.

"They are not sure but they've either had two or three murders overnight."

"Two or three."

"And that's not as big as their next worry."

"What's that?" Kieron asks, watching Hunter press the elevator button for floor eighteen.

"Our fee," he smiles.

"What is our fee?"

"They never asked, which is why they should worry."

11 OFFICIAL KIT FOR JUMPING

Two waterproof kit bags are pulled from the trunk of a limousine and dropped on runway tarmac. Kieron and Hunter, both in unzipped bright yellow survival suits, pull their parachutes out of the trunk and swing them to their shoulders. The driver checks they have everything and closes it, as a security officer from the company walks around to see them go.

"What we didn't discuss, is that it could be terrorists," the officer levels.

"None of anything you told us equates to terrorists. Does that mean there's something you didn't tell us?" Hunter asks.

Kieron looks sternly at the security officer; he has spent years working for politicians and military bosses where the truth is not always told to those on the mission. He was not expecting to be back in conflict at any level, but certainly not terrorism.

"Absolutely not, you have my word on that. But in your kit bag, there are four handguns. Security will lock them away as soon as you arrive."

Hunter nods, but Kieron's look lingers before the two men walk towards the waiting plane.

"This is bulky and uncomfortable," Kieron moans.

"You moan about how the military's not given proper kit, now you moan when you get it. This has US coast guard approval, NMD, SOLAS-"

"Yeah, Yeah, Yeah."

"- and is the accepted safety equipment of our employer and their insurers," Hunter explains, he's been a company man for some years.

"Approved for dropping us out of a plane into the ocean to meet their cruise ship?" Kieron turns and walks towards the plane. "I've never seen an Airbus like this." He shouts back.

"EADS HC-144 Ocean Sentry, it's a US Coastguard re-design of the military airbus, used for search and rescue, the fuel tanks are enlarged. In fact, it's all fuel tank."

"A flying liquid bomb?"

"It's one of the only options. The ship will be 900 or more miles away," Hunter explains, dialling on his cell phone as he walks. "Is that Cruise Ship Crime Investigators?" he asks into the phone.

"They're out," is the reply he hears loud and clear.

"I know, Mary! Me and Philips are about to get on a plane, out to the Pacific," he shouts above the noise from outside the plane which has the engines running. The crew start waving at them to hurry.

"Then you still out," she says.

"We're still out."

"Then you two owe me for your lunches."

"I thought the deal was for breakfast?"

"No, the deal with Mary was for full board," the phone goes dead.

"They seem in a hurry for us to get on board. Who was that?" Kieron asks.

"Our office manager."

The two men climb in and drop their kit bags. The Captain of the six-man crew turns around and gives a thumbs up. Hunter returns it and the door is closed and locked in an instant.

The plane taxis away fast. Both men pull on headphones and listen to the crew exchange.

"What's the hurry?" Hunter shouts into the comms.

"Weathers changing fast and you guys want to jump, right?" They hear back, as the engine's power and the tail lets them know they are turning. Kieron gestures with his face and hands, 'are you sure?' But that is all too late. He is in a survival suit, with a chute on, in a plane that has started take-off procedure.

"We are clear, hold tight," the Captain relays down the comms.

"Nice," Kieron grumps, not down comms, "I haven't even done this for Queen and country since I was…" he fumbles, unable to think of a time.

"What was that?" Hunter shouts.

"I said, all this effort could make our fee look pretty small," Kieron shouts to Hunter, their heads now close together.

"I don't think that's an issue. I like that when people call us, price is never something they ask about," Hunter smiles.

"What was the file-sharing you were talking

about?"

"I asked them to set up a data centre in Miami. They were impressed with the idea, so it should happen."

Hunter checks his watch; it is three in the afternoon as he feels the plane lift. He presses his headset to communicate.

"What are the chances of getting us there before dark?"

"I gotta be honest guys, you're about an hour late to guarantee that. But that ship will be lit up like Coney Island," the pilot communicates.

"Sounds like you're a long way from home," Hunter says.

"Where's home?" the pilot jokes.

"I hear you," Hunter agrees, then something hits him.

"What?" Kieron shouts.

"I forgot to ring Elaine."

"You rang Mary, but you didn't ring your wife? What time does Elaine normally expect you home?"

"About seven," Hunter shouts. He looks to see if his mobile has service, but even if it did, she would never hear him and his inner glove will not allow a text.

"You should be on time to call her from the ship. That's if you survive the drop and they can find us in the water." Kieron shouts. "You might try the whistle as we pass over."

Hunter puts his left hand to his chest and feels the whistle attached to his suit.

"I have a torch too," he shouts back.

"I'm sure you do; it is an 'approved' suit."

-

"There she is!" Is the shout from the pilot, which wakes both Philips and Witowski. It's far from quiet in a twin-turboprop plane but both these men have learned to grab sleep when they can, even in a war zone. They look down through the window.

"Coney Island!" Hunter shouts into his communication.

"I'll circle back, drop down to fourteen thousand feet and slow down as much as I dare in this wind," the Captain says, and the plane is banking before either of the two soldiers have given a thumbs-up back. They grab the small kit bags and clip them on, they house the guns and ammunition.

"One more thing," the pilot adds, looking back. "Don't get it wrong. Because I'll be away as fast as I can, by the time I near Miami I'll be flying on fumes and I don't want to have to put down earlier. You're on your own."

The door is slid open, the wind rushes in, the engine noise drops. The countdown begins.

"Nice knowing you," the pilot shouts.

They both jump. The engines on the plane increase in power and it speeds away above them as they freefall. The ship seemingly accelerates towards them and although they've both pulled before, they know what night jumping can do to mess with your mind, especially when there's no light anywhere on the horizon to help you judge. In sixty seconds they will hit the water, there is little time to make a mistake. When waiting for anything, sixty seconds might seem a long time, but it's not when you are falling to earth at one hundred and twenty miles per hour. They both have friends who have died jumping. Checking their altitude meters, they deploy at two thousand five hundred feet, much lower than any domestic jumper would dare or be allowed to. There is no one-upmanship or playing cheat.

The parachutes rip open. Their bodies pull from 3 to 4g as the parachute instantly slows the descent to about 17 miles per hour, but drifts heavily with the wind. It's clear from their circle of the ship that both men feel landing on the deck with the drafts they expect is just a pipe dream. They, or the silk chute could cause damage to the ship or themselves.

As they turn around again they can see two life crafts already waiting on the ocean. What a day: a burst pipe, nearly shot in a bank, lunch meeting in the cruise village of Miami with wet feet, and tonight dinner with officers in the middle of the Pacific. Kieron hits the water first, goes under and bobs up, buoyant in the bright suit. He looks round to the lifeboat and sees two men with long oars splashing at the water in fear.

"We've been sent, we're expected!" Kieron shouts, "I'm not a pirate!"

"Get in quick! Sharks circulating."

Kieron looks around and sees he is surrounded by shark fins. The bright yellow suit seems even less like a good idea as he swims to the boat. The torch and whistle won't help on this occasion. He swims but he does not look around or back until he's being pulled on board. The crew are pushing the Great White Sharks away with the oars as Hunter swims in. A shark side rams the lifeboat, and they feel it lift.

"Let's go!" Shouts a crew member.

"Count my legs for me," Philips responds.

"Three, sir," a crew member reports.

12 MEET THE CAPTAIN

"Captain Neil Reynolds," Neil announces as he enters the cell down by security on deck 2 aft, and offers his hand.

"Hunter Witowski, Sir."

"Kieron Philips, Sir, here to help."

"I apologise that our incident room is in our prison, gentlemen, but space is a premium on a full ship stocked to survive an eleven-day crossing, and we want every little clue visible on a wall."

"Works for me," Hunter says.

"You've met our head of security, Senior Officer Ruby Jenkins," Neil checks, and then to create a chain of command he adds. "This is her incident room."

"It's my pleasure to reacquaint with an old colleague," Hunter says.

"Hunter trained me, Sir," Ruby says.

"Ruby, they sent me to finish the job. I can only apologise for your first instructor," Kieron adds.

"I hope you're not suggesting that I need more instruction?" She says making herself clear. "It's a case of three heads are better than one. The murders were only last night and so far I have very little. Most of the afternoon we've been catching up on sleep; we went right through last night."

Ruby draws their attention to the first area on the far left of the wall and walks them through all the details.

"Donna McGovern is the name on the top," she points to pictures of the large woman found on the deck. There are pictures of her in situ when found, pictures of the bruising around her mouth and the many very narrow stab wounds to her chest all in the heart area. "Weight. 22 stone. Age 57. Solo cruiser. Cabin A107. That is deck four, our reception level.

"This napkin was found in her mouth with a phrase written on. Autopsy findings so far are death by multiple but accurate thin round stab wounds to the heart. The doctor suggested a knitting needle. Death being almost instant. Her mouth appears to have been held while she was stabbed. The weapon used is thought to have been cleaned on the lower part of her dress. Blood wiping marks, also suggest long thin needle." Ruby indicates the area on the wide photograph. "Apart from her size, she was in good health. Her atrium photograph from earlier that evening sees her with two walking sticks, only one was found by her body."

Ruby looks at the two men who both appear OK to move on. She directs them to the second section.

"Peter Kershner, body found in the sea as you can see in these pictures, on the lifeboat and on the gurney. Weight 15 stones. Age 58. Solo cruiser. Cabin A103. That is near Donna but maybe a coincidence.

"Autopsy findings suggest death by drowning. Signs of bruising possibly from a fall or a struggle. Head injury, from a blow or hitting something during a fall. But the big note here is that he was found with another guest's cruise-card in his pocket, not his own. He checked in at the muster station roll call after the first death, after the mask was found in the ocean and about five hours before his body was found in the sea at sun up."

Ruby pauses as the two men take all this in. She makes to move to the next section but Hunter looks at the Captain.

"How many hours are you behind schedule?"

"Seven, but it shouldn't affect this."

"And the guys on the aircraft said bad weather was ahead."

"We're watching it," the Captain says, directing him back to Ruby and the boards.

"Eric Clifford is our section three," Ruby continues. "He could be the murderer and therefore on the run."

Neither of the two military men has followed her to the third section, they are both locked on the details of Peter Kershner. Hunter points to the note on his muster,

"Muster attendance was checked with the small infrared digital cruise card scanners?"

Ruby nods, a little put out.

"No facial recognition?" he asks.

"No, done the way it is always done. Plus, it was a masked ball night," Ruby adds.

"Guests still had masks on at the muster stations?" Kieron asks.

Ruby nods again. "Yes. We had one body but two guests missing, so the sea search continued."

"It wasn't a headcount; it was a cruise card count," Hunter suggests.

"You had two cruise cards missing and three people missing," Kieron adds.

"Certainly possible," Ruby admits.

"One person swipes two cruise cards; is that what you're thinking, Witowski?" Kieron asks.

"Could be. Seems three heads are better than one, Ruby Jenkins," Hunter says, giving her a wry smile as he's noticed she's a little edgy. The Captain nods with some relief, seeing the team come together after a crack was possible at this early stage.

"Let's do the third board," Ruby continues, retaking control.

Eric Clifford is the name at the top of the third section. Ruby talks them through it. He's marked missing. Below is his passenger information sheet and picture. The same information is there for his wife Betty Clifford. Then there is his detailed bar bill for the evening, revealing a drink every twenty to thirty minutes and all at the same bar. Kieron lifts the sheet and sees his bill going back throughout the cruise.

"A man of habits."

"An alcoholic?" Hunter suggests.

Ruby starts to read the notes and fill in the gaps again, "His wife says they were on board to celebrate their fortieth wedding anniversary. Due on the day we're in Bora Bora. Says 'they've never been apart in forty years', her words. But he was at the bar every night, drinking. She admitted he was a drunk and sometimes never made it back to the cabin at night."

"Then she asked for a large gin," Neil adds from behind.

Kieron turns to the Captain,

"Doesn't sound like they had never been apart."

"She has been in the casino at the machines most nights, so she says," Ruby adds. "From their cruise cards, it looks like she goes to bed about 2230 and leaves him in the bar until it closes. But, who knows. I haven't questioned her on that. She's still sleeping. The doctor gave her a mild sedative because she'd been up all night, like the rest of us."

Hunter turns to the fourth section on the wall, "Lawrence of Arabia?" he asks.

Both men start to digest the words that Ruby has had printed out and the picture of the evidence bag containing the napkin with similar inked words. Kieron looks between the sections, and at the napkin removed from Donna's mouth.

"Lawrence of Arabia was the first search result for that text and seems too close to not be relevant," Ruby suggests.

"Sure, but when did the killer write on the napkin? When did the killer put Clifford's cruise card in Kershner's pocket? Or did he?" Hunter asks.

"Is Kershner the killer and this is a deception that went wrong? Or was it an accidental switch of cruise cards, maybe by a waiter after drinks. Someone got my cruise card from a waiter on my last ship," Kieron shares.

Hunter looks at him accusingly. "You were just sleeping with so many women you didn't know who had your cruise card."

Ruby looks at him sternly. She does not approve.

"I'm just saying it's possible."

Ruby shakes of her disapproval and points to the bar bill. "Eric Clifford's drinking is so precise; he's a regular. I doubt it was a waiter error. Or, that he was sleeping around."

"I agree," Hunter growls. "It starts to give us a timeline. Clifford was killed before Kershner, or Kershner could not have the cruise card."

Neil is enjoying watching these three minds work together, taking it all in. "Unless Clifford is the killer," he adds.

"Sure, or the killer is one of the lifeboat crew who

slipped it in his pocket during the body recovery," Kieron tries.

Ruby writes those suggestions down the side of her board, very small. "Noted," she says not giving it too much weight.

"Consider Clifford was killed first. Before Kershner was tipped overboard. The killer gets out on deck. All before the mask in the sea which may or may not be relevant," Hunter muses.

"That killing is before the napkin was stuffed in Donna's mouth. The note can't have been written for her on the spot. It was too dark up there to write this accurately, right?" Kieron asks.

"Yes. Pitch black," Captain Reynolds adds.

"So, Clifford, who we've not found yet, triggered the killings. The napkin was written in anger against Clifford, or at the killer's own self-anger at murdering him."

"Hunter, you yourself said never to rely on assumptions being the truth," Ruby states.

"I did." Hunter nods, and moves to the fifth section which is a timeline of facts. He reads them.

"Lights out on sun deck, 2245 hours,"

Kieron looks at Eric Clifford's bar bill. "Last drink purchased at 2205 hours. But, you told us he always stays until the bar closes. Look Clifford vanishes early in our timeline for the first time in the cruise. Two things. That he's dead is an assumption, but an alive alcoholic needs to drink."

Kieron lifts the pages of the statement and points to the time spent in the bar every other night. He looks back to Hunter, who reads the timeline on the wall.

"Lights back on 2306 hours. Man overboard called at approximately 2307 hours. Floating mask seen by officers 2312 hours." Hunter circles the factual times in red and looks at Kieron.

"Where are you two going with this?" Ruby asks.

"It's possible all three were dead long before roll-call at Muster station, around one in the morning," Kieron states.

"But we only had two missing," Ruby stops.

"But you only check cruise cards at roll call, you don't match cards to faces," Kieron states.

"Correct," Hunter states. "Our killer could've checked in twice, once with his own cruise card, second with Kershner's card. Let's hope that's a mistake which starts to give him up."

"But, Clifford could be the killer who checked in with Kershner's card," she insists.

"Then he would've wanted to drink last night," Kieron plays. "Where has he found booze?"

"OK. Wanted dead or alive; Eric Clifford," Hunter says.

13 QUICK WASH, SAME CLOTHES

Washed but not changed, Hunter leaves his cabin door to swing closed behind him. He walks along the adjoining corridor to the suite on the other side of the ship and knocks on the door. Kieron opens it and lets him in, he's not quite as ready. Hunter walks in and looks around,

"I cruised for seven years, never had a cabin like this. This new job is working fine for me."

"Me too." Kieron smiles, sitting on the bed to pull his boots back on. Both men are washed but in the same clothes. "We need some clothes. Eight days' worth."

"We should expect to be treated like this from now on as well as a handsome paycheque" Hunter growls happily.

"Not sure about dropping into a sea full of Great Whites hunting for their supper, but apart from that, I think we work well as a team," Kieron concedes, standing.

"Sure do."

They fist bump and leave, walk into the 'CREW ONLY' restricted bridge area, and knock on the door to the Captain's quarters. Neil opens it, and beckons them into his suite which trumps theirs. Like the circling sharks, staff wait to serve them.

"Please sit, you earned this. I guess it's been a few years since you were dropped into action like this?" he asks.

"Its what we do, sir, and as the ships are in the sea, it's where it happens," Hunter shrugs.

The wine waiter offers him a choice of red or white. "Do you mind if I have a beer?" Hunter asks.

"Certainly, sir. Which one?"

"You have a pale beer?"

The waiter nods to him, then to another waiter who goes to the room phone, allowing him to move round to Kieron.

"White please."

The waiter makes himself scarce.

"Ruby is delayed, I asked her to come to dinner, but my guess is she's watching security footage to try and see who checked in Kershner's cruise card," Neil starts, "I doubt she'll be very long; we have so few internal cameras and they are by the art gallery and in the shops. Not the muster stations."

"She's a good one," Hunter smiles, then his face changes to panic.

"Problem?" Neil asks.

Kieron points at him, he realises what has forgotten.

"Do you mind if I phone my wife, sir, she's going to be worried?" Hunter asks.

The Captain indicates the phone. Hunter rises with some pace, but he encourages the others not to wait for his return.

"Dig in guys and I'm sure Ruby won't mind."

"If you don't mind, Captain, I haven't eaten since breakfast at Wild Mary's," Kieron says.

"Wild Mary's?" Neil asks.

"The diner by our office in Miami," Kieron adds.

"Not sure I know that one," the Captain admits.

"Come over when you're back in Miami, sir."

A waiter attends Hunter at the phone and he points to his selection from the menu. Kieron does the same and food is plated for them from the adjacent hot counter. Kieron and the Captain begin eating in no time.

"Head office has appointed someone to work with you on land to analyse evidence and information you send. They can also look at similar crimes on land I'm told." Neil explains.

"Great," Kieron says.

"Your pointman is Dwight Ritter. He was hoping you might know Holmes two?" the Captain asks.

"I saw Sherlock Holmes one and two, love Robert Downey Junior," Hunter chimes in from the phone.

"Is he British?" Kieron asks with some surprise.

"American I think, why?"

"Holmes 2 is a software program," Kieron

answers.

"What does it do?" Captain Neil asks.

"Collates and analyses masses of information from multiple sources."

"If he can run a check on everyone on this ship, working or guest; that would be a big help," Hunter adds.

"Exactly." Kieron answers.

"I'm glad you guys are in favour," Neil says.

"Big time," Hunter says.

A door opens and a bar waiter brings in a bucket of beers on ice. One is cracked open, poured and taken to Hunter, who toasts them both,

"Lovin' being back on a ship!"

"No offence but I'd rather you weren't here," Neil toasts with a smile.

"Fair enough," Hunter laughs, "I'm guessing Ruby's finished the cameras and putting together a to-do list, if not acting on some of it."

Kieron pulls out a pad and lays it beside his plate as they eat. "I wager our lists will be similar to Ruby's, but Miami will just want facts as we find them. We need to interview the waiters in Eric Clifford's favourite bar."

"He drank in the Crow's Nest. My guess is he sat at the same barstool every night. Real drinkers all sit at the bar, especially the solo ones, and his wife left him there for the casino. He did something to trigger our killer, which means contact. That could have been any time from embarkation until 2205 hours last night. Otherwise, he was there most of his cruise," Hunter says, still waiting for a connection to his wife Elaine.

"I favour that conflict being fairly recent. Maybe the night before," Kieron suggests.

Hunter nods, agreeing, finishing his beer and pouring a second. "Yep, real possibility. Clifford winds our guy up, triggers something enough to make him write that quote from Lawrence and carry it around. The Lawrence film needs to go on our timeline as a possible trigger. I bet he never wanted to go stargazing in his state of mind. Got caught up in a huge group on deck and went with them so as not to be noticed. Hide in plain sight, be one of them, be invisible."

"You think he's military?" Kieron asks.

"No idea but say he's lying on the sun deck, it's dark, he's annoyed, no one can see anything and he's laying next to Donna. He has just killed, still got the napkin, still got Clifford's cruise card, still got all the hatred and she just says something. The wrong thing. And she's dead." Hunter stops, and speaks into the phone, "Elaine! I'm on a job. Sorry honey, can you hang on just a second?" He looks back at the table.

"His brain's still in killer mode, we've been there, right Kieron? It's a place you go to when you have to, and a place which is damn hard to leave and get normal again. He ain't normal yet, Donna's dead. She's collateral damage. Then, under the cover of darkness, real darkness, with everyone looking up at the stars, he slips away down to deck nine. He bumps into Kershner who is another case of in the wrong place at the wrong time. Kershner sees him covered in blood? He can finger him, set him up as the double murderer. Bang Kershner's dead. The murderer takes Kershner's cruise card, plants Eric's card on him and tips him in the sea, and we have three murders, probably in minutes."

"Four murders," Ruby says from the doorway.

The Captain looks up, very concerned, Kieron and Hunter are far harder to read. The waiters all listen in because nothing like this ever happens on a cruise ship.

"We just found a fourth body," she explains.

"You're sure it's not Eric Clifford?" the Captain asks Ruby.

"No, sir, it's a member of the orchestra. Bogdan, the saxophone player."

"Elaine, sorry," Hunter whispers into the phone as the others move swiftly towards the door. "Sorry, sorry, I'm on a ship, we have a serial killer on board. Back in about ten days. Love you, darling. Put some champagne on ice to celebrate our first job. Gotta go."

14 THE BOX IN THE THEATRE

The Captain, Hunter and Kieron, follow Ruby Jenkins down the theatre corridor, past the old posters of classic productions, music song sheets and actor press photographs set in frames against the red flock wallpapered walls, just like any major theatre on land. She leads them past the rows of empty red velvet-covered seats that look onto the dark stage with vacant orchestra positions set back behind a single microphone, standing front and centre. She turns left into the narrow passage of awkward steps that lead to the entrances of the ornate theatre boxes. Their destination is obvious, a junior officer stands outside. He slides the red curtain open for them. Inside the lead medic, Manesh, stands above the body of Bogdan, who lays out flat in the chair, as if sleeping there.

"Jeez. Four deaths in two days; at least two are deliberate. That's a serial killer or someone who's completely lost it. Not sure which is more dangerous," Hunter states.

"This will panic the guests," the Captain worries.

"I think we should get this body to the morgue, finish dinner and get a good night's sleep. We need to be up first thing in the morning," Kieron suggests.

"I'll report back that we're discussing options and collecting evidence, and then re-join you," the Captain answers.

"It is a fine way to say hello to our point man, Mr Ritter. But we better send him photographs of Ruby's incident walls so he can get a start," Hunter adds.

Ruby looks at Hunter wondering who gave him permission to send her boards. The Captain nods, agreeing with Hunter,

"Where we sail next has got to be a head office decision. We're eleven hundred nautical miles out, thirty-three hundred to go. With a possible storm ahead, they could turn us around. It's three days if we turn back to Panama, which is not an ideal place to go with a problem like this. Six days all the way back to Miami. Or eight days to Tahiti at full speed to make up lost time."

"Sir, who are these pictures of my boards going to?" Ruby questions.

"Our head office, they are setting up a land-based team."

Ruby nods, caught up. "Fine. I'll copy them in on all my text reports as soon as you have a name and contact," Ruby asserts, showing that it is still her enquiry, that they are still her boards, and whilst Hunter was once her teacher and senior, this is her ship. Hunter nods, there was no malice in his suggestion.

"Well, we know where the killer is," Hunter states.

"Where?" Neil asks.

"Onboard."

"I'll be back at dinner as soon as I can," Neil says. He leaves, not amused by Hunter's statement of the obvious.

Ruby looks around the box, down at the empty bottle of vodka dropped on the floor, but the lack of any other clues. She's handed an evidence bag by the officer standing in the entrance, then a pair of gloves, which she uses to contain the bottle and seals the bag. She pulls a glove off and takes her phone out.

"Jason, can you join us in the theatre, level five. Same job as last night on deck ten." She hangs up and turns to Manesh. "Manesh, Jason needs to photograph him from every angle before you move him, then at every stage of the autopsy. Does it look like he was strangled?"

She places her hands around the neck briefly. Her fingers don't stretch even if she made contact and tried. She pulls them away. "Bigger hands than mine, he has a thick neck."

Manesh nods. "I think so, Miss Ruby."

Ruby leaves the box, followed by Hunter. Kieron lingers, looking over the edge of the box and down to the seats below, at the architecture. Like a climber or a thief, he is looking for places to grab and foot holes for an escape route.

"I would need a team chasing me with loaded weapons to consider that drop an escape route," Kieron muses, but apart from the dead body, Manesh and the officer outside are the only ones listening.

"You can exit up or down, down has a door to the stage, and from there goes out to the deck, but that route might be covered by a stage camera. I think the killer knows where the cameras are." Manesh shares.

"I think you're right, Manesh,"

Kieron steps out and looks up and down the passage. He strides to catch up with the others.

Back in the Captain's dining room, Hunter loads up a clean plate,

"Come on Ruby, eat. There's nothing we can do on an empty stomach or with tired minds. We need to plan tomorrow; day four of the crossing."

Hunter sits and starts to eat. Kieron enters and serves himself from the hot plate. The two men are used to death; occasionally it is emotional but this is not a colleague, not someone they knew. The remaining waiter passes Hunter a cold beer.

"Thanks, buddy. You know that saxophone player?"

"No, sir," the waiter replies.

Ruby starts to pick at the food, thinking out loud.

"The whole orchestra is Romanian. The musical director speaks good English; the others are OK but they do keep themselves to themselves. They all drink, big time."

The three sit at the table fuelling energy into their brains that are working overtime.

"Killing four people in two nights, with so many sea-days left is cause for us to panic, not just the guests," Ruby starts.

The Captain enters and jumps in where she left off, "As we have a working system in place between you and Dwight Ritter, we'll sail on to Tahiti, so we arrive in seven days. We're on our own for at least four. My guess is they will be flying people there and will have a vessel meet us before we get close. No pressure team, but I don't want another murder on this ship," Neil

Reynolds says coldly.

"Easy to say, but we don't have a clue who he is," Kieron states.

"Or she." Ruby corrects.

15 FOURTH DAY IN THE PACIFIC BEGINS

Kieron is the first on the sun deck at 0600 hours and the deckhands have not even begun to put the sunbeds out. The sun is already hot. He looks up and imagines the star show, then he lowers himself to the ground and lays down, looking up. He looks sideways and imagines the restricted view of anyone but those next to him.

"You're in the wrong place," he hears Ruby say and he twists his head back to see her standing behind him.

"It's not easy to look around when you're lying flat on the ground. Join me," he offers.

Ruby walks to the rail that overlooks the middle of the ship and the pool area. She lays down with her feet to the modern palisade that is part-way filled in with glass panels between the older wooden handrail and a white iron structure. It is all so much clearer in daylight than two nights ago. Kieron stays where he is and tries to move his head to see her.

"No way I can see you," he says rolling over and then crawling to where she lays, laying beside her.

"Now you can see why I don't wear my whites with a skirt very often. Once again I'm glad I have trousers on. And it's not even breakfast."

"This is weird," he says slowly.

"For you? I'm the one laying where Donna was murdered."

"Did you sleep well?" Kieron asks changing the subject.

"Very well."

"Me too. Like a log."

"I always sleep well on the Pacific, it's my favourite ocean."

"For sleeping?"

"And fishing," she jests.

Kieron spins onto her in an instant, covers her mouth with his hand, loops his leg over her body and he smothers her. She starts to resist, gasps for air but then figures it is not worth it, she cannot move. Then a thought hits her, she could be dead in a second and that makes her very uncomfortable.

"Housekeeping!" they hear in a deep voice.

"How does he get that low drawl?" Kieron whispers softly in her ear slowly releasing all his holds. She doesn't respond because she is pissed with him, he has way overstepped his boundaries. Kieron releases her allowing them to separate and look up at Hunter as she regains her posture.

"It's not what you think, we're just friends," Kieron says rising up from her.

"How was it for you, Ruby?" Hunter drawls.

"Quick," is the answer neither of them expected, but she works at sea with all kinds of banter and she can change the direction of any conversation when it suits her. However, she did not like being pinned down.

"Like most things, I guess it wouldn't be the same a second time," she adds.

The noise of slamming and dragging on the deck

below draws Kieron to look over the edge. Hunter joins him and they both look down at the deckhands arranging sun-beds around the pool in midships, to make the whole area on deck nine an open-air sun trap. Hunter looks back to Ruby still laying on the floor of deck ten,

"Are you getting up?"

In a burst, Ruby swings her leg in a wide arc aiming to kick at Kieron. But he has bounced up and gone. She hits Hunter. Kieron vaults the rail over to the other side and hangs from the wood. He lowers one hand to the top of the middle glass panel, now lop-sided he looks back through smiling.

"You need to be quicker," he says playfully.

Ruby rises to her knees to look back at him,

"Maybe I liked it," she says back through the glass.

His right-hand drops to the glass and he is hanging evenly. He then swings sideways and his left-fingers grip the deck flooring, then his right drops and grips the deck. All they can see are his hands gripping the deck to hang on and then Ruby's shoe slamming down on them. Then no hands, he has gone. She looks up at Hunter.

"I see you too have hit it off," he growls.

Ruby is up super fast to join Hunter looking over and down to the deck below. Kieron rolls out of the drop next to the pool bar. Had he been a few feet further round he would have hit the awning over the bar.

"Missing me already?" he shouts.

Deckhands on deck nine immediately run over to him.

"Are you all right sir?" the first asks, extending a hand to lift him.

"Yes, just taking a shortcut to breakfast," Kieron smiles waving them away with a slight limp, as his body recovers. As they leave him, he starts to look around the empty bar. He pushes the swing door next to the bar into the service area. It is unlocked.

"Sir, breakfast is this way," the returning deckhand offers, standing back and pointing to the back of the Lido deck.

Ruby and Hunter walk into the area and also start to scan. She catches the deckhand's badge.

"Thank you Panjang, excellent way to deal with the current concern," she smiles.

Panjang bows and retreats, but as he and the other deckhands continue to work they are watching the security detail with great apprehension and muttering between themselves. Hunter is watching them as he looks around.

"Rumours are spreading already. The crew must have heard that one of the guests is a killer, passengers will know soon," Hunter says.

"Empty and soulless," Kieron is fixed on the empty pool bar, which he can access easily whilst the drinks are locked away and no plastic glasses are out.

"Within hours it will be cocktails and fun," Ruby informs him.

"But at night?"

"It closes at seven after sundowners," Ruby says flatly.

"Exactly, it changes character. So what was Kershner doing here at nearly midnight?" Kieron asks in a low tone as he goes inside the service door again leaving the other two together.

"He's trying to copy your voice," Ruby says to Hunter.

Kieron comes out having heard her, "My voice has not woken up yet. It needs coffee, lots of dark coffee."

I don't keep my voice low by staying asleep all day, Philips," Hunter says, walking around the bar.

"Was he up here when the pool was lit and got caught here when the lights went out? And if so, why didn't the officers on watch see him?" Kieron muses.

"He was outside when the killer dropped down," Ruby says.

"I've gotta eat," Hunter says, heading towards the breakfast buffet and going inside first.

Kieron looks long and hard at Ruby, to the point where she begins to feel self-conscious. That moment of insecurity was what Kieron had been waiting for. He can read and twist human emotion.

"Nothing hurts as much as a betrayal. I thought we had something up there," he says flatly.

"If only you had a knitting needle."

"I didn't need one, it wasn't the murder weapon." Kieron boasts, and enters breakfast without revealing more.

16 THE KILLER'S ROUTE

They encourage Ruby to go in front of them at the buffet, which she refuses. She prefers to be considered equal. There is no queue this early. It is a vast area of well-lit colour. Ruby picks up a tray, takes a red napkin and a knife and fork then turns to them holding the red napkin.

"You two worry me."

They both stand silent, waiting for her to explain her statement.

"There is a difference between guys like you and ones like me."

"You're a guy?" Kieron asks, with well-delivered disappointment.

"I came up through the gym, martial arts, store security and night club doors. Even a stint doing stunts on movies, but you two, you guys have –."

"Can I stop you there?" Hunter interrupts her, "Could you pass me a tray? I'm going to get an omelette. I never get them at home."

"Not even at Mary's?" Kieron asks.

"Now there's a thought I can drool over," Hunter says.

Ruby stops him from leaving. "You two both think like killers."

Hunter shrugs and walks away, deliberately leaving her to look to Kieron for a response.

"He has a great voice. I can't ask him how he does it now you've grassed me up," Kieron asks.

"How he has a deep voice?" Ruby asks confused, but before she can answer he has left her. Both men have cold-shouldered her and she stands alone, no special treatment. Ruby rushes after Kieron,

"Did I go too far?"

"Yes. Full stop."

Kieron picks nothing up but stares at what's on offer. Every kind of food imaginable, fruit juices, fruit, pulses, nuts, pastries and various bread options, as well as every cheese, cold meat and fish you can think of. Then all the cooked items back at the first counter where they both walked out on Ruby. She appears next to him.

"Sorry if I offended," she says.

"You know that's not good for you," Kieron says,

looking at her fruit juice.

"Fruit juice?" Ruby questions.

"No. It's a huge myth."

"Fruit juice is bad?" she questions thinking he's mad.

"Worse than fizzy drinks. That apple juice has more sugar than cola," he says, pointing to her glass. "Sugar that your body doesn't want."

"How do you know what my body wants?"

Kieron ignores her friendly flirt, she is not getting out of going too far that easily.

"It wants to stay alive, we all have a survival instinct and it's that instinct that drives a soldier to kill. Full stop."

"Full stop?" she asks.

"The fibre has been removed from the juice, which your body does need."

"You said full stop," she adds.

"And the process of blending of the fruit turns natural sugars into free sugars; the bad kind. They have the same effect on your liver as alcohol. And we get back to the theme of death."

Ruby takes a moment, confused. However, she hasn't given up trying, "You care about me?" she delivers with disappointment.

"Juice is made from concentrates, stored for ages, depleted of vitamins and nutrients. Squeezed is not good," he says still very coldly.

"Then don't squeeze me."

"I won't," and he leaves her again.

Kieron joins Hunter in time to observe his omelette being turned out onto the plate.

"Are you hitting on her?" Hunter asks.

"Not that I'd realised," Kieron says.

"We need a 'romance in the workplace policy', I'll talk to HR here on the ship, get something drawn up for you to sign." He growls.

"Funny!"

"And what do you want my voice for? You've got one of your own. Girls in Miami are gonna love that accent." Hunter smiles and leaves.

Kieron turns to the omelette chef.

"All the vegetables and loads of onion. Do you have chillies?"

The chef nods.

"Go for it."

The chef starts the routine he will repeat for the next three hours. Kieron watches Ruby approach him again.

"How's this?" she asks, showing Kieron the fruit on her tray. "I dumped the juice."

On her tray are a banana and an orange.

"Not that you need to worry about your figure, but there's maybe five teaspoons of sugar in that banana alone. After the three spoons, your body has had enough and turns the rest of that banana into fat."

"So, don't eat bananas?"

"I didn't say that. Half a banana is OK. You should learn to share."

"Oh, sharing a banana. My mind is racing again, and I'm not sure whether you are trying to frighten me, help me, or chat me up."

Kieron sees no direct question and no need to answer her.

"Is silence an acquired interrogation technique or are you just waiting for your omelette?" she asks.

"Omelette."

"For a moment you frightened me upstairs."

"And then? The next moment?"

It is now Ruby's turn to make him wait.

"Have you ever killed a woman?"

Kieron stands stoic for what seems like ages, his eyes are locked drilling into hers but they offer nothing, they are empty.

"I was re-enacting our incident to try and save another life tonight. And here, I've been trying to save your life."

"From apple juice?"

"From all juices and most fruit. Eat berries; tropical fruits spend longer in the sunshine making sugar." He takes his omelette and leaves her again.

Kieron sits next to Hunter who has already polished off his omelette and is drinking coffee.

"Tea, coffee?" A waitress asks, holding a silver pot in each hand.

"Tea please," Kieron says, sounding even more British. She pours, and he adds the milk from a sachet on the table. "Thank you."

Hunter invites her to refill his coffee and he smiles and nods his gratitude.

"If you're going to smile at waitresses like that, I'm gonna need you to sign a waiver and romance contract," Kieron teases.

"Can I join you?" Ruby asks, appearing adjacent to them at their two-person only table.

"Why not?" Hunter growls.

"You chose a table for two," she notes.

"Just thought that you and lover boy would want to be alone. Sit down." Hunter indicates the adjacent table. "What colour are the napkins in the other dining rooms?" he asks Ruby.

"White."

Hunter holds up his red napkin.

"Killer ate in the buffet here on nine at the back of the ship then. Sat scribbling, getting angry. Went forward, killed Eric. Escape leads him to the back. Donna is next on ten on the sun deck. Killer drops down by the pool bar, Kershner was out there, don't know why, he goes for a swim," Hunter explains.

"Eric Clifford's body is a major missing clue to this," Ruby suggests.

"He should be between forward deck nine and mid ten, unless he got tossed overboard," Kieron agrees.

"There are cameras all around the deck," Ruby says.

"But for a few minutes, it was lights out," Hunter offers.

"I'm going up to Eric's bar. You two lovebirds can join me after," Hunter says and exits.

Kieron eats the last of his omelette; military people all eat fast. He leaves and Ruby has barely started her breakfast. She thinks about following them but stays.

"Room service uses red napkins too," she says to herself peeling her banana, "And trays are left outside rooms on all corridors." She bites half of the banana, folds the other half back in the peel and places it down on the tray, "I am a survivor."

17 EYE TO EYE

The Crow's Nest lounge is empty. It sits above the bridge and under the smaller forward sun deck, not the one used for stargazing. It is all windows, giving great views of the sea during the day and a magical black mirror-like reflection at night. Either side of the central bar is an entrance or exit with a short corridor to the elevator area. Portside there is a small chapel and a gentlemen's toilet.

"Guess the ladies is the other side?" Kieron asks as they walk in.

Hunter flips open his ship map. "Yeah, correct, and the library is starboard, where this chapel sits."

They walk into the lounge, both looking around at every detail. Hunter goes to the shiny dark-wood bar surrounded by bar stools, that overlooks the room. Kieron circles the windows, looking out to sea.

"No exit via the window system," he turns back to Hunter at the bar, "Wow. It doesn't need a dead body to feel any more like a morgue."

"The English have such a great way with words," Hunter mocks, spinning around on his stool. He spreads his daily programme out on the dark-wood, checks his watch which announces that the time is 0815 then looks down the day's listings.

"Ten-thirty; solo cruisers' get together. You should try that Kieron!" He swings around smiling at his own joke, then full circle back to the day's itinerary, "one o'clock is choir practice."

"That's here," Kieron says, having arrived at the central stage area of the raised inner section. He lifts the keyboard cover on the black grand piano and plays a few notes which encourages him to sit, not being able to resist, he plays. Hunter nods, genuinely impressed, but then focusses back on the daily event listings.

"At three we have craft, needlework and knitting. Now listen up people, is that where our murder weapon comes from? In the same room as Eric

Clifford, that event supplies the potential weapon that killed Donna?" Hunter swings round, pleased with himself, "After a small round of applause, I might take the rest of the day off!"

Kieron looks up from the piano keys and plays a little quieter so Hunter can hear him.

"Or," he says, "the killer used Donna's hatpin. Conveniently found on her own head, ready for the taking." Kieron sings a line. "This is my pin, for the taking."

Which finishes in a choking sound as he breaks one hand away to add a sarcastic mime. Seeing that he has not engaged his one-man audience he pulls an imaginary pin from his head and stabs his own heart over and over. Then he stops,

"Too soon? Look, a hatpin is a thing that British ladies of style sometimes use to keep their hat fixed on their hair."

Hunter just chuckles. "Yeah, that's not a British thing. We have hat pins in America. Partner. I bet Donna was in here for 'solo cruiser', I bet she was also in here for 'choir'. I bet she made that fancy hat pin, out of a goddam knitting needle at craft class and she wore it with pride. That would put Donna and Eric in the same room as the murder weapon."

"What time does that bar open?" Kieron asks.

"Why, you want a job? Going undercover as a cocktail pianist?"

"I could do that, but I hear the opening is for a saxophonist and as much as I like that instrument, I can't play it."

Kieron turns, segues into playing something romantic as Ruby enters with Lal who carries two files. She takes one from him and leaves him lingering at the door as she saunters towards Kieron and sits by the piano.

"Would you two like me to leave?" Hunter jokes.

"No, we have a problem," Ruby announces.

"Another dead body?" Kieron casually asks, still playing and smiling.

"The opposite, one of our existing dead bodies bought two drinks last night," she states.

Kieron stops playing. "And the company wants to know who to bill?"

"Eric?" Hunter asks.

"Not on his own cruise card, obviously," Kieron adds.

Ruby opens the folder and reads, "Kershner ordered two doubles. One at 22.43 in the gin bar and another at 23.15 in the Wagon and Horse downstairs."

"That was risky; what if his account had been closed as it should have been?" Hunter accuses.

"I'll get the three accounts closed," Ruby snaps.

"Is either on camera?" Kieron asks.

"No, my team searched before calling me. He might have got lucky because we have so few cameras, but I think he knew which table to risk being served at. Before you ask, the waiters don't remember him, but why should they? He's playing with us."

"How does he know we're on board?" Kieron asks, pulling the folder towards himself and leafing through it.

"Apart from slowing the ship to almost stationary, launching two lifeboats, you parachuting in from a passing plane and the rumours?" she asks.

"There is that. And he appears not to be stupid," Kieron says, without looking up.

She holds up the daily news sheet and then reads,

it.

"Captain Neil Reynolds would like to assure guests that they are safe. A disagreement between a couple of guests did result in an unfortunate incident. Two detectives were flown to join the ship and are now on board. They will deal with the issue, leaving the ship's staff to ensure guests can continue to enjoy their cruise."

"Nice phrasing, that was done in Miami," Hunter whistles.

"Why would you say that?" Kieron asks.

"If it was the Captain or anyone else English, there'd be a hell of a lot more words."

"So, Mr Linguistic expert, what do you make of the note from Lawrence of Arabia?" Kieron quizzes. "Let's try and put the note in this room."

"Dangerous to make assumptions, but I'd suggest an English love for the maze of words. I've got no idea what it means, so we will leave that with you, Kieron."

"But he used a short section. Notwithstanding the book is wordy, the section chosen was short. That makes him American on your calculations."

Ruby nods to her officer who takes the second file to Hunter.

"Thanks, Lal," Hunter says opening it. "Everything you had on the cell walls downstairs?"

"And more," she says. "My team's been busy."

Hunter turns the pages. Kieron is studying the verse from which the quote was taken, eventually reading it aloud in his best English accent.

"Sometimes one man carried various names. This may hide individuality and make the book a scatter of featureless puppets, rather than a group of living people: but once good is told of a man, and again evil, and some would not thank me for either blame or praise." He circles 'hide individuality' with a thick pen, "Hide individuality, is that hiding he's a drunk? Or being drunk is hiding him?"

Hunter has his file open at Clifford's bar bill, "Look at how much this guy drank? No wonder head office called us, they lost one of their best customers!"

"And I bet you guys are being paid a fortune for this," Ruby says with a touch of jealousy.

"Fortune," Hunter says, flatly engrossed in the file.

"Absolute fortune," Kieron agrees toneless.

"Jump in whenever, Ruby," Hunter says, which is not meant to be the insult that Ruby feels it is.

"Did Bogdan the sax player drink?" Kieron asks, "Don't answer that, he was a musician and from Eastern Europe."

"Yes, he drank like a fish, most of the musicians do. I worked that one out by the vodka bottle by his side. Who suggested I need you two?" Ruby throws in.

Both Hunter and Kieron look up at the same time with accusing looks.

"OK," Hunter starts.

"Sorry," Kieron follows, "so he was found with an 'empty' bottle of vodka?"

"Yes," she replies.

"Ruby, might we find out how much of that was in his bloodstream. It would tell us whether or not the bottle was shared?"

"Yes Kieron, we might," she agrees.

"Good call." Hunter agrees. "Bottle empty, no more booze, he's useless. Kill him."

"Sorry?" she asks.

"We need bar bills. Every dude who drank with Eric. Same bar, same time. Let Miami work canonical connections between the larger group of big drinkers."

"This is wild speculation," Ruby insists.

"That's why we feed Dwight everything, to let a computer run connections we can't see."

"I was just applying common sense," she offers, pulling out a picture of Eric and his wife taken at a black-tie evening. "To be fair, they don't look like healthy specimens, even dressed up,"

"Harsh," Hunter says.

"Is this a guy who could drop a deck, attack another man, the size of Kershner, swap cruise cards then throw him overboard all in the brief period the lights were out?" she asks.

"Hmmm… I have to agree. That was a serious superhuman vault to do quietly and a huge drop," Kieron adds, as he plays a run down the piano keys, "luckily it didn't hurt my fingers."

"If it wasn't him, then that theory requires a fourth killer and for Eric to be dead?" Hunter says.

The other two nod in agreement.

"I can live with that. So, Eric is a dead drunk. The killer's a smart drunk with a mental problem?"

"Then, Eric's either in the sea, or we need to turn this place upside down and look for his body. If he's on board, he's in here or close-by."

Hunter approaches Kieron at the piano and lifts the lid to inspect the strings inside,

"He ain't in here."

Ruby looks at him, "you're not really on board with this are you?"

"Let's get the doc to run a full tox-screen on all the bodies again. Let's see if there isn't a drug addiction that links them all together as well as booze. That could have them lingering in dark shadows, going behind doors, and owing money to a dealer who won't take the cruise card as currency."

18 THE CHAPEL

The Chapel is empty and has real flowers in its alcoves like a funeral parlour. Present there because of a renewal of vows service yesterday. Without people, it is a cold space. After opening every cupboard and door in the chapel, which they know could not hold a body, they walk around the room again, knowing they are fighting a losing battle to find a body in there.

"I felt sure the smart-arse would have buried him in here," Hunter says with sarcasm and disappointment. He is still thinking.

Ruby turns to Lal, "Can you check to see if the Cliffords ever renewed their vows, and ask the Captain when I might chat with Mrs Clifford?"

Lal makes notes on his phone.

"And can we find out if Donna was in the solo cruiser group, choir, or arts and crafts that all met in that lounge? And have the doctor test the hatpin for blood? Then re-bag it as it is essential evidence," Kieron asks.

Lal is tapping faster into his phone, but looks up at the possible importance of the hatpin. Ruby is surprised too,

"The hatpin a potential murder weapon?"

Kieron nods.

"I could have taken the pin from your head and killed you."

"Unlikely, I would have flipped you," she turns to Lal and continues, "Lal, check Kershner for his attendance at any groups in the Lounge, because he was in a solo cabin just along from her."

"I could have killed you," Kieron insists.

"You could have killed the slower and less agile Donna, I'll give you that."

Hunter marches out, ignoring their banter. Lal follows.

"Remind me to get HR to get a romance at work contract sorted," Hunter shouts back.

Lal starts to type that, then stops, wondering if it is a joke. He is finding it hard to tell the difference and looks at Hunter for a clue.

"You double-checked the service area?" Hunter asks him, pointing at the 'Crew Only' door before going into the Crow's Nest.

"Double-checked, sir. But it goes everywhere," Lal says, to defend their limited search. It is like he and Krishma are interns working to investigate the many ideas Ruby, Hunter and Kieron have. He does not have the resources for everything.

Hunter curves around the lounge bar which is still empty, exiting the other lounge door then entering the library. Lal stays glued to him and the others eventually follow.

Looking around the library, there is nowhere a body could be hidden. There are shelves and shelves of books, well organised and filled. The room is so efficiently designed it leaves just enough space for a guest to weave in and out searching for a book. Even the cupboards hidden behind the shelves are full of used paperbacks.

"Why are these in here and not on the shelves, Aishah?" Kieron asks, reading her name badge.

"It is a store of used paperbacks. When the book swap table is low, I use these to replace them. Sometimes I change them when the cruise route changes," she offers.

Ruby is now standing next to Kieron looking back into the library. Hunter faces the other way, transfixed on the ladies' toilet opposite the library entrance.

"Do you have any books on Psychopaths or serial killers?" Hunter asks, without looking back.

"Yes. We have a good crime section," Aishah answers.

"They need to go. What do you think, Ruby?" He asks.

"Yes, you're right, Hunter. Aishah, let's get all serial killer, psychology of a killer, and psychopath books off the shelf and locked in one of your cupboards," Ruby says.

Aishah does not understand why but agrees, and the two turn to look at what Hunter is looking at' the door to the ladies' toilet, and next to it the door to the disabled toilet, Hunter has his ship-map open.

"House-keeping checked all the toilets and cupboards, and engineering checked the plumbing access; one of my team was with each of them," Ruby says.

Lal nods, trying to remember if he was with each one as every duty took place. The investigation is racing forward at a pace.

"The other side, next to the men's toilet, the 'Crew Only' door. We keep avoiding it," Hunter muses.

"It is a crew door," Lal says.

"Does that mean you didn't search it? What if Eric was going to the toilet but got snatched into the crew rabbit warren?"

"Are you suggesting it's a crew member?" Kieron asks.

"You like assumptions Ruby," Hunter jokes.

"We shouldn't rely on them, or let them lead us," she says.

"We searched all the near areas inside," Lal insists, "beyond are stairs down and down."

"Our guy knows how to slip over a rail and vanish, he knows where the cameras are. He could know his way around below decks. He could have been a waiter last night, he could have been on the lifeboat. He might be a smart arse selling drugs," Hunter speculates.

"If it's a team selling drugs, he could have friends helping him cover up a mistake, assuming Donna or any of the 'Crow's Nest murders' were a mistake," Kieron suggests.

"I like the title," Hunter smiles, lips tight in frustration, "but why kill Bogdan? He ain't in the Crow's Nest."

Kieron notices that Aishah, whilst petrified at having heard every word discussed, is hovering.

"What is it, Aishah?"

"Bogdan was the entertainment in the lounge two nights ago. He was playing saxophone, solo," she reveals.

Hunter looks straight at Ruby, "we missed that."

"Look, we've been at full speed for two days. I missed that, we missed that, but we are still on our first pass," she admits.

"Killer ain't missing much," Hunter drawls.

"Anything else, Aishah?" Kieron asks.

She shakes her head nervously, in case she did something to get Ruby in trouble. Ruby waves a 'don't worry' and thanks her as the team move back into the lounge. They look once again at the raised stage where the piano sits. Kieron stands where the saxophone player would. He mimes playing the instrument.

"You're right, you would be a crappy sax player," Hunter says walking towards Kieron's position.

"The sax player can unashamedly watch everyone in the room. He sees everything," Kieron says.

"I thought you'd never stop playing!" Hunter throws away, as he leans back on the rail that surrounds the orchestra circle.

"So… he saw something," Kieron adds, and they are both left craning their necks to look everywhere they can from the restraint of the bandstand. They both focus on Aishah who has come forward from her door to the library. She is still watching them and looking worried.

"What is it, Aishah?" Hunter asks her firmly.

"He doesn't stand there, he walks around playing, all over the room. In fact, he climbs on tables, on to the backs of seats, he even balances on the rails while he plays. He was very funny," she replies.

Hunter walks to the side of the stage, far enough to allow him to see the other exit, the Crew door opposite the chapel.

"He comes here?" Hunter directs at Aishah.

"Yes, sometimes, often," she says nervously.

Hunter accelerates off towards the crew door.

19 RAW STEEL

Most 'crew only' areas are the same on any class of ship, white paint everywhere. White painted stairs, exposed and uncovered welded and riveted white metal walls and white pipes. No coverings, no carpets and no false ceilings where the sound is absorbed. Here, the sound bounces around and no one can move quietly. The ambient sound and background noise change as soon as Hunter opens the door and steps into the new area at the very top of the stairs. The three walk down just half a flight, and even their footsteps create a wave of sound. They all examine the area as if it is new, looking up and down at the cold steel and how narrow it is.

"Bogdan can't be on stage in there entertaining and in the middle of the sun deck killing Donna. Someone put his onstage times into our timeline for me," Hunter asks.

Lal is still standing on the top step where the door opens and again he is typing notes.

"Forty-five-minute slots. The last always starts at eleven-fifteen so it can finish at midnight," Ruby shares.

"Lights back on was twenty-three-zero-six, meaning the murders were all complete by then and our killer was travelling. So he could easily be back on stage by eleven-fifteen," Kieron adds.

Lal sighs and stretches his neck, he needs a break, but he re-focusses and types madly into his phone again.

"Let's not get excited people. Even if Bogdan is our killer, the killer didn't kill himself," Hunter says.

"No, and how strong would you need to be to drag someone inside here. Kill them up there at the top, then carry the body down?" Ruby asks, looking over. The second half of the drop from the turn on the stairs is about six feet. Kieron looks up.

"I'd tip them over the rail," Kieron says.

"No blood," Hunter offers, looking down.

"Crow's Nest is on deck nine. Deck ten is the sun deck, which has no connection to this," Ruby explains, "and that is deck eight, the back of your suite Philips, and just behind the bridge."

"Who but bridge officers and officers that were on duty at the stargazing would use this access?" Hunter asks, pointing out to deck eight.

"They wouldn't pull the body in the bridge area." Ruby exhales walking down the last steps.

"That's an assumption," Hunter growls behind her, and she leads them onto the deck eight service area.

"But I like it," Kieron adds.

"Officers would know house-keeping don't work after ten o'clock, so this area is abandoned," she admits, "and most crew know that."

"Anyone here at about 22.15, 22.30 hours would be alone… next to the laundry chute?" Hunter asks.

"Or recycling chute," Ruby says.

A female house-keeper rounds the corner dragging two sacks, she stops, shocked that there is a team including two officers in her area.

"Sorry," she apologises.

"No, come in, please. Continue." Kieron encourages, and Ruby nods to agree.

The small house-keeper can see Ruby, a senior officer, so she knows to continue as directed. She lifts the first sack, which is green. Kieron helps her and she is embarrassed.

"What does green mean?" He asks.

"Green mean towel. White mean linen," she answers and both sacks drop. She waits for permission to leave, then is gone as soon as they nod.

"Surely the laundry team would have found a dead body from two nights ago?" Kieron asks.

"Yes. They're on a twelve-hour turnaround. The sheet that comes off your bed today is on someone else's tomorrow. Your theory is falling apart here," Ruby says, but she already has her phone to her ear.

"Can you find out what the turnaround is for laundry and recycling dropped down the forward chutes over the last two days?" Ruby listens for an acknowledgement and then hangs up.

They look towards the forward service area of deck eight and back to the distance of the two half flights of stairs folding from deck nine above.

"Do these chutes drop all the way to the bottom of the ship?" Kieron asks.

"Deck two, that's not a huge drop. You wouldn't find chutes like this on any of the larger, newer ships, they would use the service lifts." Ruby explains.

"Maybe he dropped the body and then ran down to move it?" Kieron suggests.

"No. Six floors? And that area is staffed permanently," Ruby answers. "Laundry is in the middle, recycling is right at the front. The large bins get wheeled down i95 and sit in a queue behind a machine. They would be moved by the time he got down there. He wouldn't have a clue which bin to look in, plus the staff would question him carrying a dead body away even if he found it," she explains.

Her phone rings and is back against her ear, she listens just as she is observed, with interest.

"I need a detail on deck two checking all the stacked up laundry bins. You're looking for the body of Eric Clifford," she says, before ending her call. "One of our four washing machines is down, everything is going through three machines. There's a small queue of about half a dozen laundry bins stacked behind the broken machine."

Hunter smiles as he pushes the door on deck eight that says, 'Caution! You are now entering a passenger area'.

"Get far away, as quickly, as you can!"

"I bet he walked the full length of deck eight," Hunter suggests.

"We have no cameras on passenger corridors and few in the pool area," Ruby shares, as they all power along, glancing at watches.

They pass the busy pool area, the midship lift, then towards the rear of the ship they pass cabins again. They turn the corner at the last exit into the passenger stairs and elevator area.

"He'd have no chance getting on an elevator, they'd all be in use getting guests rushing from dining," Hunter starts.

"From restaurants on four," Ruby nods.

"Rushing past him like a herd up to star watching. His anger builds, people are fired-up, politely pushing on. He is adrenalin high, he wouldn't know if he was exhausted from walking the length of the ship. He mixes in. 'Become one of them, become invisible'," Hunter explains.

Kieron is nodding his head, they have a scenario, "Before he knows it, he is on deck nine, no idea why, he is talking to guests, no idea why. He wants to get out of there. He could leave them and go into the buffet, but that breaks cover because none of them are going to eat, they have just eaten. Plus, he is distressed, and that could get him noticed. He goes outside. The crowd lead him up onto deck ten and he lays down to calm himself. He has just killed someone and he is looking at the stars, no idea why."

"Coffee?" Hunter says. "We've done the next section."

"I did the next section," Kieron says.

Ignoring him, Hunter leads them into the buffet again. Now the ship has woken up and it is crowded.

"Both of you need to take an hour and go shopping. Please get out of yesterday's clothes," Ruby says.

"Are you implying -?" Kieron starts.

"Yes. You smell." Ruby says.

20 WHO RINGIN' ME?

Wild Mary is squeezed into her small storage cupboard, busy using a wrench to tighten a straight joiner on a section of new pipe she has inserted in the corner. She has crudely bashed a hole in the wall to reveal the burst, and can now see through into the maritime office next door. Her phone rings but turning and moving is not easy because she hasn't removed all the mops, poles, brooms and cleaning equipment in there with her.

"Who's ringing me? No one rings me," She rants, ignoring it.

Mary finishes nipping the nut tight. She turns, knocking the broom and mops out of the cupboard. She drops the wrench into her large toolbox and charges to the phone.

"This is why I don't do deliveries, people would be ringing me all the time."

She gets to the phone just as it stops. She looks at

it angrily. A phone now rings, but behind her in the unit next door. She walks back to the cupboard and leans in to look through the hole she made in the wall in order to repair the pipe. The phone is sat on the desk.

"They're not in!" she shouts at it.

The detectives' phone stops ringing. Mary is very pleased with herself. She turns and sees the large sixteen-pound long-handled hammer, she picks it up and attacks the wall in the back of her cupboard, knocking her way into the next unit. The phone rings again.

"Wait!" she screams, swinging the hammer until the wall has a large hole in it. She wedges herself through and into their unit, but has to wade through water and exhausted by the time she reaches the phone, which stops. She bends down, hands on her knees, breathing heavily. She looks around at the water.

"You boys expectin' a ship?"

She eventually stands up straight, hands on hips.

"Go on baby, now you can ring," she says with a smile.

The phone rings in her unit and she turns back, shaking her head, and levers herself back through the hole. Walking in, she messes her white tiles. Her phone stops ringing and she turns back again, angrily looking at the mess on the floor, the mess in the hole. The phone next door starts ringing and she explodes with power towards the hole, and with a hand each side she demolishes huge sections of hanging wall, then wades through the water to grab their handset. She would say hello, but for a moment she has no breath, so she listens.

"Is that Cruise Ship Crime Investigators?"

"They're out," she manages.

"Are they in the Pacific Ocean?"

"I'm in the ocean!"

"You're with them?"

"No, different ocean. But if you think they are there, why are you ringing here?" she says before slamming the phone down.

Mary looks to the hole in the wall.

"You owe me for plumbing and a new wall."

Mary picks the phone unit up and pulls at the lead to see where it is plugged in and how long it is. There is enough cable, so she walks it to the hole and leans through, placing it on a dining table in her premises near to the closet door.

She takes a bendy drain pole with a hook on the end from her own cupboard and wades to the back of their restroom, fishing for the floor drain. The phone rings again.

"They're out!" she shouts.

She yanks the drain cover up, then starts to wiggle the rod until the water begins to vortex away with a rude glugging sound. Mary gives a wide smile of self-satisfaction.

"Now you owe me for drain clearance."

Despite the phone still ringing, Mary moves at her own speed back through the hole and reaches for it.

"Sorry to keep you waiting, I've been real busy. Worked off my feet, don't know which way to turn."

"Can I quote you on that?"

"Sure you can."

"Can I get a quote from you regarding claims on social media that there is a serial killer on a world cruise ship currently in the Pacific."

"Sure you can," Mary smiles.

"What is going on out there?"

"Burt and Lee were taken out to the mid-ocean in a superfast jet, were dropped into the ocean using special forces parachutes and now they're on it. No worries."

"That's fantastic. What are their full names?"

"Oh. That's Reynolds and Majors."

"And your name."

"Wild Mary."

"And you work at Cruise Ship Crime Investigators?"

"That's next door, I'm at Wild Mary's breakfast bar next door. Everything goes through me. You want news, you come down and wait in line at the breakfast bar like all the other photographers and news gatherers. I got to go talk to the others. I'm coming, I'm coming," she says to no one. The phone hits the cradle with a heavy hand and rings instantly. Biting her lip she calmly answers but ready with a barrage.

"C.S.C.I," she says slowly working out every initial then giving a self-pleased nod.

"Who's that speaking?" A deep voice asks.

"That's real nice of you to ask, my name's Mary. Who you?"

"Dwight. Name's Dwight, Mary. I run your central office at the shipping office on Dodge Island."

"Hey, Dwight. Nice to speak with you. But, hear me out, central office. I was thinking the crimes were in the middle of the ocean. Miami ain't in the centre of the Pacific! Surely my boys are there so I'm the centre of detection?"

"Good point Mary, we're gonna get on fine."

"Well they ain't here," Mary says.

"I heard you on that, Mary. They're in the ocean. I

got the computer here, Mary. Every bit of information goes in, every. Eventually, I hope an answer comes out. So if you have anything I can put in…?"

"Yes, Dwight. At Wild Mary's Diner next door to the office, we do the best food, breakfast, lunch and supper. You be welcome working here and I might just teach you to jive!"

"I'm not sure you could, Mary. Not sure anyone could."

"You come down and meet Mary."

Mary puts the phone down and looks back at the draining water slowly revealing a very messy floor.

"Me need to get cleaned up! But you gonna pay for it."

21 SHOPPING

Shopping on a cruise ship is easy because it never feels like you are parting with money. The magic is the plastic cruise card. In the case of the Crime Investigators, they really aren't paying, because the charge is going elsewhere. They can't have been expected to pack a dinner suit, bow tie, changes of underwear and shoes in with their parachutes. They are buying everything from top to toe for a week at sea and the assistants can't believe their luck as they ring in the till sales, which aid their incentive points. The order has gone way over any basket size they have ever had. Some clothes and formal wear are already being walked up to their individual suites. The only other times people buy this big is on lost luggage claims, and with those the assistant is obliged to explain what the insurance is likely to pay for and what they are not, but this is as unusual as it is exciting. The two men genuinely have a James Bond-like status and the dinner jacket and white shirt is the easy start. It is the selection of casual wear which is causing a problem for both men. Kieron is being fussy, but Hunter is genuinely not finding anything close to that which he would appreciate being seen in. However, he admits defeat and he holds up a possible shirt.

"It's not like we have an option, right?" Hunter says.

"Which colour do you want?" Kieron asks.

"There's another problem."

"What?"

"Us, dressing the same."

"You get one colour and I get the other."

"That's a worse idea," Hunter says.

The female assistant is amused by their double act. "Choose what you need for a day or two and I'll search the stores for options. There's loads of stock below which might not get rotated for a while."

"You should be promoted," Hunter says to her.

"I should," she agrees cheekily. "I'll get all this sent to your suite."

"You have a key to my suite?" Hunter flirts.

"House-keeping does," she says, smiling.

Ruby comes in and pulls Kieron aside. Hunter senses it's a breakthrough, so leaves the assistant who realises she has been gazumped. Knowing they are being watched, they walk further from the shop. Assistants and guests can't help wanting to be first to have the slightest bit of information and embroider it into a rumour.

"It's like being a football manager, people trying to read your lips," Kieron suggests, with his hand up.

"What's up?" Hunter asks.

"Eric was where we expected. In the laundry. He's now in the medical centre," she shares.

"Guess they can't do much for him?" Hunter shrugs.

"We know one thing for sure," Kieron offers.

"Yes, he's not the killer," Ruby agrees.

"I'm gonna shower, eat lunch, then sit in the Crow's Nest and go over everything we know… which is not enough," Hunter says, leaving Ruby with Kieron.

Kieron stops to look at the lines and lines of guest pictures in the photo gallery. Ruby stops with him.

"Could be anyone right?" he asks.

"Yes," she agrees. "But we've really moved things along. Considering we're not set up to be a major crime unit, we've done well. I can at least report back that finding Clifford is in line with our developed scenario."

"I like that. But it's not enough is it?"

"No," she admits.

"You have a killer on board."

"Yes. And I have to stop it."

"Can you get a fingerprint off the hatpin? Excluding Donna's?"

"I've requested some better software for dealing with prints, our kits are being challenged, they are basic and so are the team, but they are enjoying the work. We don't do this."

"Have you done the officer's staircase, the laundry chute and then excluded all the officers, us and the cabin staff."

"I have two officers there but the workload is huge."

"Can you not step the manpower up?"

Ruby raises her eyebrows and gives him a look

with a pause that lets him know there is 'helpful' and there is 'interfering' in her department.

"I only have two synthetic white brushes and powder is running out."

"Baby powder?" he suggests.

"I'll ask, but this is an adult-only ship, so talcum powder might be limited," she shares.

"We've used flour before when we were stuck; you won't be limited there. Or icing sugar? Good job those synthetic brushes are washable. Do you reckon the kitchen might have a dusting brush you could use as a third?"

Ruby leaves a pause to ensure Kieron knows he has been talking too much, but she gives in. She reminds herself that the two men are only on the ship to help. Neither wants her job.

"I'll look into that. I need that staircase and laundry chute done so they can be made useable again. Nothing in a ship can stop for long."

"Should we have dinner later?" he asks.

"Maybe, where?" she says thinking. "I guess the Asian has the tables more spaced and there are alcoves, because we won't be able to refrain from talking about the case."

"Sounds good."

"I'll try and get up there and recce a table."

"Let me do that; you have non-stop work commanding your team. I don't have anything to do," Kieron says.

"Sure?" she says. "You don't want to re-read the folder?"

Kieron thinks, then shakes his head, "No. I want to think out of the box, and I'm ready for a night out."

"Shower and change clothes," she says, typing into

her phone as she turns away. "Oh. It's formal night!"

"I'm good then. I have a complete outfit that nearly fits me perfectly. But, I'm not sure I could run in it."

"I won't chase you then," she smiles.

22 C.S.C.I.

Hunter sits in shorts and his new shirt with a bottled beer right next to the handicraft class in the 'murderer's lounge'. He is reading a book on serial killers with the title hidden inside a larger thinner book on the island of Fiji. He is observing the workings of the lounge over the book, as light classical music plays on the address system.

He looks from an unlisted 'knit and natter' group to the bar which is not fully open, with no guest as yet sitting on a stool there. A beautiful female wine waitress is the lone patrol in the near-empty space. Kieron walks in wearing the same new shirt as Hunter but in the other colour, causing the American to shake his head gently in disgust.

"I could go and change." Kieron offers.

"Good idea."

"But, there's no one in here to worry about," Kieron says, sitting.

"Are you getting some kind of gratification from all this?" Hunter asks.

"Interesting you should ask that because it has given me an idea."

"Whatever it is, no."

"We should have a uniform, like matching shirts with logos."

"Great idea. Cruise Ship Crime Investigators. Chest pocket badge," Hunter says sarcastically.

"What was wrong with Philips and Witowski?"

The waitress approaches Philips, he indicates he'll have the same beer as Hunter. She looks to Hunter who signals a second. The waitress lifts Philips' card to ask if both go on that tab and Philips agrees. Not a word was spoken, but there is complete understanding as she takes Kieron's cruise card, swipes it in her handheld device and taps in the order, then turns to leave.

"I am not sure about the name." Kieron considers, sitting.

"Too late. I had to use a name when we got the gig. We've been contracted. It was the first thing that came in my head."

"Often the first thing in your head is as bad as the second and third." Kieron offers.

"Not this time, sheer brilliance."

"Brilliance? It's clunky and obvious."

"Cruise ship is the industry cache, always will be and works across all the brands. Putting crime next to it disturbs the universe, causes concern, makes people stop. Investigators means it's us that solves it. Four simple words."

"Not simple if you have to explain it like that every time."

"I would be forever explaining Witowski and Philips."

"They're our names! Philips and Witowski has class."

"According to our office manager Mary, she's getting non-stop calls from the press for the Cruise Ship Crime Investigators."

"She's fending them off by telling them we're out."

"No, she's had a better idea."

"Her as well?" Kieron asks in a very British accent.

"She's invited them to her diner and told them to bring cameras. She needs quotes because she's, in her words, 'running out of lines'."

"Oh. I guess our employers don't like that much?" Kieron asks.

"No idea. We're in the middle of the Pacific. Nothing we can do about it. And we report to Captain Neil Reynolds, it's his problem. That's Neil Reynolds, not Burt Reynolds whom she implied might be flying out to save the ship."

"Burt Reynolds, isn't he a little dead?"

"With Lee Majors," Hunter adds.

"That sounds pretty good, that we might be played by major Hollywood legends."

"Living ones would be nicer, eh?"

"Yeah, but I like the slightly older, romantic legends. We have a ton of really successful TV shows in the UK that have old detectives."

"Why?" Hunter asks flatly.

"I don't know."

"Back home, they cast the old stars in chief of police-type roles. Put them in an office. New actors play the cops."

"That seems more sensible."

"It's not sensible, it's right!" Hunter insists.

"Agreed. Then just run it by me. Why are us two, very retired and far from young or still of serving age officers, jumping onto ships in the middle of an ocean like a British TV show?" Kieron asks.

"Because ex-cops and ex-military serve as security on ships, we're experts. We're right on plot."

"Actually, we are still way, way younger than British TV cops."

"Settled then. C.S.C.I. a company of legends."

"By the way, I'm having dinner tonight with Ruby and three would be a crowd."

"Not interested. Let's get back to the killer," Hunter says.

A lady from the craft class is packing up her items on the nearest table to them, she looks over and smiles, "Nice shirts."

"Mum always dressed us the same. She passed some years back. We kinda do it as a tribute to her memory," Kieron says knowing that it will annoy Hunter.

'No need for that," Hunter says to him.

The waitress arrives and places their beers down. Kieron signs the slip and hands the pen back while looking at her name badge,

"Thank you, Jasmin."

"Manoj starts his shift in about an hour," Jasmin offers. "I have spoken to him on the telephone. He knows you wish to speak with him as soon as he arrives."

Both men nod and she leaves.

"Now Jasmin, I would like to have dinner with tonight," Hunter says.

"Not interested. Back to the killer. Good call on the interview," Kieron says, raising his glass to toast. Hunter raises his glass.

"Let's see if he looks fit enough to have swung over the rail and dropped a deck," Hunter grins.

"You don't like Bogdan for it?" Kieron asks.

"No. He's dead."

"To be honest, I'm not sure I like any of it."

"Me and you both, buddy, me and you both," Hunter worries.

"It's getting Eric down to the laundry chute. I think you or I would find that hard."

"You certainly would Kieron, you've started to put on some pudding. I'm still liking Eric walking down to buy drugs."

"Then why kill a customer? To be honest, none of it makes sense yet," Kieron says and they sit thinking.

23 FORMAL NIGHT

"Excuse me, sir… Sir," a voice mutters.

Kieron wakes to see a vision of loveliness, which takes him a second to digest.

"Sir?" She repeats.

Her beautiful hair drops enticingly towards him, her perfect face smiles. She grips a tray with her manicured nails. Her chest badge reminds him it is 'Jasmin', the waitress. If he ever has to be woken from sleep again, this is not a bad way for it to happen. The slender waitress stands above him. He must have fallen asleep in the chair. He looks over and Hunter is also fast asleep, he looks around and guests are dressed formally in black tie for the evening and his craft beer has gone.

"Sir, it is nearly six o'clock. There is a dress code." Jasmin instructs.

Kieron and Hunter who are both in shorts have been politely ordered to leave the lounge. Kieron stands and offers Hunter a hand to pulls himself up.

"Jet lag," Hunter growls, his voice even lower after sleeping.

"Funny guy."

They turn and walk towards the exit by the library, both spotting a lady in evening trousers and a smart top at the bar who appears to be scowling at them, quite miffed. Kieron stops, puzzled. Hunter pulls him out and past the library.

"It's our shorts." Hunter shrugs.

"Anger is the drive behind our serial killer," Kieron says.

"What so we should arrest her?"

"Someone should."

Hunter does an about-turn back towards the bar.

"Hang on, I was kidding!" Kieron says, bursting after him.

Back in the lounge Hunter leans over the bar and addresses all the stewards. "Manoj?" he asks remembering what he wanted to achieve in the lounge in the first place.

"No, I'm Prince, Manoj has not come in today, sleeping," Prince the other bar steward laugh.

"Please, leave," the woman interjects, scowling.

Hunter ignores her and continues to question the other bar steward. "You actually know he is sleeping, Prince?"

"He will be, sir," Prince says.

"Do I have to call security?" The woman says, having now pushed in between them and the bar. She invades Kieron's personal space.

"Not what I asked, buddy, d'you know he's actually sleeping?" Hunter repeats.

"No Sir, but if I ring him, I will wake him and we are not busy tonight," the Steward smiles.

"I asked you to leave," the woman says to Kieron venomously. She turns to the bar steward, "Steward, please call security for me."

"Please go back to your drink, madam" Kieron offers.

"I will not," she says poking his chest with her finger.

"You have just assaulted me, madam, and in front of witnesses."

She pokes him again, harder. "I will assault you again if you don't leave. Call security."

"Madam, I am security," Kieron exclaims.

"Get out," she says, now raging and prodding him.

"Madam, if you would accompany me down to the security office, you can quietly put any complaint in writing and we can ask you one or two questions about your conduct," Kieron says.

"My conduct! I will not! The head of security is a woman, get her here."

"Are you refusing to accompany me to the security office?"

"Blatantly!" she says, standing her ground.

"Madam, I am officially requesting that you come with us to the security office."

The woman stands stoic. Hunter now turns and gives a wry smile at the mess Kieron has got himself into, wondering where it is going.

"Please turn around and put your hands behind your back," Kieron demands.

"I refuse."

"If you are resisting arrest, I am obliged to use reasonable force to restrain you and escort you to security," he says, pulling at the belt in his shorts for his handcuffs. They are not there. Rookie mistake. "Stay there."

Kieron strides back to the chairs they slept in,

where Jasmin has found his cuffs and is holding them up.

"Looking for these?" she teases.

Kieron takes the cuffs and strides back towards the woman.

"Are you serious?" she demands, seeing the cuffs.

"Are you going to come with me to security, or are you resisting arrest."

"What am I being arrested for?"

"Assaulting a member of staff and then refusing to come to the security office, I have therefore formally arrested you."

"No."

"No one is above the law, some just think they are," Kieron says handcuffing her raised, objecting wrist dripping with gold bangles.

"I want a female officer," she demands.

"Noted, female requested." He handcuffs her to the gold rail that runs around the bar, "Cruise card please."

"No."

Kieron takes the house phone. He dials security.

"It's Philips. Send two female security officers to the Crow's Nest. I have arrested a woman who refuses to give her name or cruise card." He looks at his watch. "I make it 1810 hours. Please put her in a cell until I can get down to question her." He replaces his phone, "and it may not be straight away."

"You haven't heard the last of this. I will be contacting head office!" She fires at him.

"I am head office security," he says.

He turns to Hunter ready to leave, but Hunter has his ear to the phone.

"Manoj isn't answering, where would he be?"

Hunter demands of the steward.

The steward shakes his head in the way that westerners cannot. The closest signal we have is to disagree, but it only means the Steward is listening and has no idea.

"Are you seriously leaving me handcuffed to this rail?" the woman fires at them both.

"Yes, and you will be charged for any damage to it." Kieron offers.

"Manoj must be in room?" The steward offers.

"Number" Hunter demands.

"Three-seven-seven-one. Same number I dialled for you."

Both men march off towards the elevator.

"Let's go down and find Ruby," Kieron replies.

"You think you're still on for dinner?"

"I reckon I am."

"No way."

"Fifty dollars?"

"Make it a yard." Says Hunter.

Kieron thinks for a moment then shakes. "I'm even thinking she'll be wearing her whites with a skirt and heels."

Hunter shakes his head.

"I do have a proven track record with the ladies."

"No way man! You were so off last time, so off."

"Georgie and I will be friends for life. We own a property together."

"Good luck with that."

"Now do I report the woman you've just arrested to Dwight?"

"Who's Dwight?"

The lift opens, everyone inside is dressed for the evening and as they pass the looks of distaste at the two officers are obvious. They are left alone in the lift.

"There is enough arrogance in some cruisers to start a fight in many a mess room," Kieron says hovering by the buttons.

"You could arrest them all."

"No."

"Ruby's on two, press five and we can walk down," Hunter says, because the lift does not go down into crew areas.

24 THIS IS NOT A DRILL

Both men enter the security command centre looking like they've just come off the beach. Even though it is not yet six-thirty, Ruby for once is dressed in smart evening whites ready to go anywhere on the ship, as are her officers which causes Kieron to smile,

"Pay up."

"There's a way to go before we call this a date," Hunter explains.

Ruby and Lal are talking with a female in a long dark dress and her door is closed. The junior officers in the forward office are checking security footage frame by frame, still in their green daywear. Ruby sees the scruffy pair and waves them in.

"Ignore their dress, they're undercover," she starts. "Wendy is one of our entertainment hosts, the one who checked in Kershner's cruise card at the 0022 hours muster after Donna was killed, and this is the only security camera in that area. Amazingly it all happens on the edge of just off-camera, it's of very little use. Wendy's right on the edge of the frame. Our suspect only just clips in and out and all it shows is that he is slight."

"Could be female," Hunter offers.

"Could be," Ruby agrees.

"Same size and stature as the violent woman you arrested upstairs," Hunter suggests, turning to Kieron.

Ruby lets the eye contact play out between them, ignoring her ringing desk phone which Lal deals with away from them. Ignoring everything, she continues to brief them both.

"He or she walks in and out of frame quickly. Even if caught face on, we have no more than a mask which is one of the throwaway party ones from the ballroom. That and the dreadful video quality means we can't even confirm if it's the mask found in the sea. It gives us nothing."

"But the exercise is done," Hunter says.

"We should recommend there being a set mark to stand on when scanning cards on a muster drill, so that all the scanned guests pass by camera face on," Kieron suggests. "Like passport control."

"You're on fire today partner," Hunter says, weightily.

"Let's have it, what have you done?" Ruby asks.

"Luckily Kieron just arrested someone in the lounge, it could be her," Hunter reports.

"Why do I not feel hopeful?" Ruby adds as a commotion builds outside her office.

Ruby pushes past them. In the outer office, the woman from upstairs is very unhappy at being brought down here. She is struggling and giving Krishma and another female security officer quite a hard time. To the woman's amazement, Ruby ignores her and goes on to the second security detail, the one Lal has only just joined. Lal suddenly turns white.

"I was first!" the woman shouts.

"Lal, what is it?" Ruby asks.

"Another dead body, Miss Ruby."

"Manoj Bhatti, the steward from the Crow's Nest?" Hunter asks.

The words 'Crow's Nest' sink in and Wendy stands amazed, she has seen most things on a cruise ship, but this beats them all.

"That has nothing to do with me." The woman protests.

"Where was the body?" Ruby asks.

"Same chute, under the Crow's Nest. Laundry is waiting for permission to resume work." Lal states.

"You! Get these cuffs off me now!" The woman starts banging her cuffs against the wall.

Ruby turns around, "Where and why was she arrested?"

"I demand to see the Captain!"

"She assaulted a staff member in the Crow's Nest," Kieron says.

Ruby checks her watch.

"Eighteen-fifty hours. Lal, put her in a cell and make her comfortable. She mustn't see our incident room." Ruby turns towards the woman, but it is obvious it is not to engage with her, "It may be some time before we can facilitate her request to see the Captain. Log her request and the time."

"I have a name!" the woman insists.

"But you refused to tell us, and showed total disrespect for ship's staff, one of whom is now dead," Kieron says.

Ruby nods for her to be taken away,

"Get her name, check it against cruise card, pull up her file and her bar bill for the whole cruise," she orders to her officer.

"My bar bill?" she questions, as she is lead down a corridor she will never have seen on any ship.

Ruby turns her back on the mêlée as years of experience, not just on ships, has taught her to do. In front of her is a new problem, she has another dead body.

"We were waiting to interview him. The killer got to him first," Hunter growls, as the three set off with Wendy, the entertainment host still in tow.

"Only someone in the bar would have known that we were waiting for him, like that woman" Kieron adds.

"Wendy, did you check in any crew?" Hunter asks, changing the line of conversation.

"No, sir. All guests," she answers seriously.

"As the ballroom was already full, how did you do the muster station roll call?" Kieron questions.

"We got them to move around, we tried to make it fun," Wendy says.

"So it was a light-hearted affair, laughing, joking, in masks. It's possible a crew member could have been amongst them?" Kieron probes.

Wendy looks uneasy.

"You've done nothing wrong, Wendy. The person we're after is very cunning. There's a chance it could've been a crew member disguised and offering you a guest card." Hunter relates.

"I think I'd know all of the crew, no matter how they might try to disguise themselves," Wendy says.

"Thanks, Wendy, you can go. Don't worry, we'll get them," Ruby says, encouraging Wendy to leave, and when she does Ruby shares some other information.

"Preliminary findings on Eric Clifford show not

one bruise, not one mark, not even a blemish. Not even a bruise from the chute, no marks around his wrist to hold or lift him. Except on his neck, he was strangled. Easily."

"That doesn't follow our angry drunk scenario. It makes no sense!" Kieron says.

"If that lady you arrested is a flirt, maybe she enticed him down, then, strangled him and tipped him over? Hunter starts.

Kieron almost smiles.

"A female drunk complicates issues," Kieron suggests.

"If she's not involved, it's probably our last job," Hunter concludes.

25 ROLL WITH IT

Gently moving to a rock and roll beat, Wild Mary concentrates hard on painting a blue wave on the inside glass of her restaurant window. Her brush goes up and then down, then up under the hull of a ship that has been painted there.

"Mary, why don't you leave it to us?" A young male student, Croc, suggests. Croc is one of the many black students that spend most of their out-of-college hours in the diner. He is intricately painting detail to the top of the ship. He looks down at Mary and drops his head to the side to make his point, then hits her with a huge cheeky smile. He is ridiculously handsome and Mary can't resist him, but she finds it hard to leave the job. She looks down at a girl doing the sign who has finished the mainline, 'Cruise Ship Crime Investigators'. Underneath she is etching the outline of the smaller case line, 'Meeting and Waiting Area'.

Mary now drops her head to one side,

"You think that should read Meeting and Waiting Area in Wild Mary's?" Mary asks the girl who is painting the name.

Macey, another student, has more paint on her dungarees than on the window. Her hand is raised, meaning 'stop'. Although she can speak, she can sign, even if it is a street kind of signing. Her communication is often a mix of both, and well understood.

Mary puts the brush down, "My sea is finished," she says. "Looks damn good."

Both young painters nod in agreement.

"Looks good, Mary."

Mary turns away and walks back towards the larger area of the diner where couples are jiving. Outside, she notices the lights of a television scanner van with a satellite dish on the top. It circles the car park and stops outside the detectives' unit next door.

"Hey!" she shouts to her painters. "Finish up, we got visitors."

Mary gestures to hurry them away. She moves to the doorway and waits. She watches as the reporter jumps from the van to look in the detectives' window. It's painted black, with an immaculately written 'Cruise Ship Crime Investigators'. Underneath it says, 'Enquiries and waiting area next door in Wild Mary's.'

"Oh yes, come to mamma," Mary says softly.

The reporter turns and looks towards the diner, sees Mary's big welcoming grin, then waves for her cameraman to follow. He jumps from the van with his camera.

"It working," Mary says to herself, she holds her door open and invites them in. She turns inside and yells, "Put something lively on that jukebox and dance like Mary taught you."

As the media team arrive, the diner gets lively.

"Hey, welcome to Wild Mary's!" she enthuses.

"Is this the right place?" the reporter asks.

"Damn-sure it's the right place. It's been the right place since I opened it in 1999. I've seen you on TV," Mary says, encouraging them to come in. "It's 'bout time you see me on TV."

The reporter is hesitant, "Are the cruise ship detectives here? We've heard rumours they're in the Pacific." she asks.

"They ain't here and you talking to the office manager, Wild Mary, and maybe you should meet Stan…" Mary has them hypnotised.

"Who's Stan?"

"The man at the grill who's gonna take you order," Mary says, leaning out to see another truck parking. "Lucky you got here first, take a seat over here."

Mary waves them past the sign, 'no dancing on the tables', then towards the tables just far enough away from the newly painted window, where every clue that work was being done just seconds before has been removed. The reporter heads straight for the cleaning cupboard door, which is now matt black and wears the sign, 'Cruise Ship Crime Investigators."

The two students on nearby stools at the counter step up to stop them, but Mary is quicker and diverts them to a table for four in the middle aisle.

"I need a quote from them," the reporter says as the camera is pulled up.

"They ain't in there. When they call, Mary gonna give the phone to you first."

"Where are they?"

"They're not here," Mary says.

"Are they in the Pacific where a number of murders have been reported on the Cruise Doris Visits chat site?" The reporter asks.

"You better ask Doris. You talking to Wild Mary now. I hold the fort when they're not here."

"I need-."

Mary cuts her off, "When you order, I put the phone on your table and that make you first. But if that next team come in and order food first, they get the phone first," she says holding up the landline telephone with a long cable stretching back through the door to the investigator's office next door.

"Wild Mary, I need a quote. We are first on this story and I need a quote," the reporter annoyingly insists.

"OK, well you can write this, 'at Wild Mary's diner they run a faaaabulous programme of classic jive. It keeps the kids off the street and ensures they eating good food. And, it so happens to be next door to them sea detectives'."

"I need a quote about the murders or I will make something up. I need to go with the story tonight."

"Imma tell you this. Any quote you say tonight will be rubbish. But, it will fill me diner with reporters and cameras tomorrow when me have a proper story. So you'll be in a long queue and get no exclusive. I suggest you eat some food, pay your bill, you come back tomorrow for the best breakfast you've ever eaten. But if you talk about my diner and the good work we do, I'll make sure you get your scoop."

They do not order food, so Mary walks over and invites the next camera and reporter team in, with an even bigger smile. She points them to Stan at the grill who gives them his huge smile. The reporter goes straight over, orders and pays. Mary leads her cameraman over to a table closer to the closet door, sits him down and places the phone in front of him,

"You guard that with your life, baby."

The cameraman starts filming, first the phone then tilts up to his reporter who starts,

"I'm next door to the Cruise Ship Crime Investigator's office just west of Dodge Island but conveniently nearer to this great diner, 'Wild Mary's'. The crime busters are in the middle of the Pacific Ocean but Wild Mary herself and Stan, when he's not cooking up the best creole food, take their messages and today they have entrusted us with the phone. So as soon as the maritime detectives' ring, we will have a murderous cruise exclusive. This is Janey E for WBX25 NEWS."

She signs off, the camera goes down and their food is delivered by Mary. "Food comes with a guarantee that if they ring and it goes cold, it gets replaced."

The other reporter on the empty table is kicking herself, "crime busters! That is not proper news."

Mary walks back to her. "You know, you never even gave me your name."

Food finished, the WBX25 reporter is the other side of the diner, jiving on the dance floor with teenagers surrounding her. There is dancing on the tables as she cuts off for a second report to her camera,

"This might not be what I was expecting to do when sent to report on alleged cruise ship murders, but Wild Mary's, in true cruise ship style, is all about fun and good food and I can see why the Crime Investigators have their office next door. Still waiting for that call, Janey E on WBX25 NEWS."

The camera lowers to film shots of dancing feet. Then suddenly, the phone rings and the restaurant falls quiet with anticipation. The first reporter is the nearest and dives for the phone, but just as she gets to the table the phone is pulled away from under her arms. It slides off the table and bounces on the floor by Mary's feet. She holds the cable in her hand. Cameras pointed, the whole restaurant watch her pick it up and say,

"Cruise Ship Crime Investigators."

Mary listens then passes the phone to the first reporter to arrive, the one who didn't order food.

"It's for you, honey."

Shocked, the rather stiff reporter takes the phone. "Hello?" she says tentatively.

There appears an endless silence, but in reality, it is not long at all.

"Oh hi Ted, it's Gwen. Yeah, I'm waiting for them to ring."

Gwen puts the handset back on the phone cradle and hands it to Mary. "That was another reporter!"

"I guessed you know them," Mary smiles.

"I did."

Gwen is the subject of some directed laughter.

"You not feeling hungry yet?" Mary continues, as the phone in her hand rings again. Mary steps on a chair, then onto a table and standing high she answers it. The room falls silent.

"How that ship treating my boys?" she asks.

Janey E walks slowly up and stands close by but is not imposing.

"You got yourself a gaggle of reporters here, eating and dancing. I need you to say hi to Janey E." Without waiting for a reply, Mary hands the phone to Janey as she climbs up onto the table. Held in a two-shot standing high Janey smiles,

"I am connected to the middle of the Pacific Ocean!"

"Janey, you need to talk with Dwight," Hunter says.

"Dwight put us on to Mary," Janey says.

"Did he? That's a shame. Try the fried green tomatoes."

26 TEN TOMORROW

Captain Neil Reynolds enters the cell where Elizabeth Rowe has been held for two hours. She stands, annoyed and about to explode with abuse. He raises his hand and she is silenced, showing his total control. She listens as he reads from a sheet of paper.

"With multiple witnesses, you were verbally abusive and then assaulted a staff member. If you did not know they were a staff member both of those actions against another guest is a worse charge. With those actions alone I would be totally in line with company policy to have you removed from the ship at the next port and for you to find your own way home at your own cost. We have a zero-tolerance to any crime, violence, racism or exclusion. In the area where this assault took place, we have had at least one murder. The only evidence we have is a picture which whilst poor quality has a fleeting resemblance to you and we might like to ask you further questions. However, I am prepared to release you on your own recognisances,

1. Provided that you are aware that we are charged

with keeping all guests safe, so we have a duty to watch you.

2. That you agree to your fingerprints being taken and kept on file to aid enquiries

3. That you agree to be here at security at ten tomorrow morning, ship's time, for further questioning.

4. Should you be requested at any time by an officer, whether in uniform or plain clothes, after they declare themselves as security, you abide by the said request.

Do you agree?"

Elizabeth is obviously in shock. She can't formulate a response.

"I suggest you say little more without legal representation as anything you say will be recorded and can be used against you."

Elizabeth swallows, thinks and reluctantly nods.

"I might add, that we would rather rumours of the murders on this ship did not spread. If they did spread and you were to suggest to other guests you were in any way implicated or a suspect, it might somewhat isolate you and I suggest you enjoy the rest of your holiday without suspicion."

Neil Reynolds steps back and a junior security officer, watched by officer Krishma enters the cell with a fingerprint kit. The Captain leaves, looking at his watch. It is now eight-fifteen.

In the laundry, none of the machines are working and the team of workers linger, playing catch with a filled pillowcase. Machine four is still out of service and the whole area remains taped off even though the body has been removed. The Captain enters the area and

Ruby shows him where the body was found. Roy Stevens, head of house-keeping, is there with the head of laundry operations holding a flow chart which he has scribbled amendments on. Roy turns to the Captain,

"Neil, linen is normally changed every four days, we propose making that five days this cycle to get the laundry back on track."

Roy is head of the hotel and does not need the Captain's permission, but it is good practice to share knowledge when it involves the ship's guests. If there is any complaint, none of the staff likes to be surprised. Neil nods and looks at his watch again.

"Close this down and let's all have dinner. Let's try for nine o'clock."

Neil leaves with Ruby at his side.

"Are you sure it was Elizabeth?" he asks.

"Not at all, but we can't rule her out. She was causing a disturbance and however caused that needs to be jumped on."

"Nine o'clock, join me for dinner," he says and leaves.

Ruby thinks for a moment, she was expecting to go to dinner with Kieron, but maybe she still is. He will no doubt be there.

The Captain's rooms in the bridge area are impressive, no matter how many times you visit them. Dinner is a grand affair, however fast the staff cobble it together. Ruby and her two main lieutenants, Lal and Krishma are eating on one side of the table, Kieron and Hunter on the other, still in their short pants and summer shirts. Roy, the house manager joins them late.

"Good evening Roy, more relaxed?"

"Not really, Captain. I feel we need a headcount. A muster station roll call is the only way of doing that and bringing the monthly routine a few days early should not cause hysteria."

"Agreed, Roy."

"Sorry about the dress sir, we had our heads in the evidence folder," Hunter says.

The Captain nods.

"We need a statement, sir. Our office back home is under pressure," Hunter finishes. There's a pause as they wait for his response.

"Enjoy the wine, it is a very good one," the Captain suggests.

They all take a moment to eat and drink.

Neil puts his cutlery down. He obviously does have something to tell them.

"Head office called just before I came into dinner. The publicity machine is a strange beast. You have both been through this before for your countries."

"It'll never be quite like that, sir," Hunter growls.

"No, but head office is considering the diner next to your office as a way to leak stories out."

"I would want to be careful about what we say as a company," Hunter states.

"We can't be made to look bad because of bad reporting, it's our business sir," Kieron adds.

"It's not just that. Wild Mary would kill us if she felt she was being used, although knowing Mary I'm not sure she'd let that happen," Hunter objects.

"Sleep on it. Head Office is monitoring the overnight response to what she has already said, but on first reports, they might like the idea of Mary not really knowing what is going on but the news occasionally being led by her. It's actually their opinion that she might be enjoying the publicity. I have not seen her or what has already been said," Neil counters.

"Head office might have over-simplified a very complicated lady," Kieron delivers with a smile.

"I'll second that," Hunter toasts with his fine wine. He washes it around his mouth then considers his reply but the Captain is in first.

"I think HQ is hoping she might simplify things for them," the Captain toasts.

"One thing's for sure, her diner will be full of TV cameras for breakfast tomorrow, and she'll be happy about that" Hunter shares.

"HQ will have called me long before that."

"We're wagging the dog again," Hunter says slowly.

"Wagging the dog?" Neil asks.

"It's a movie sir, but let's just say, the tail's doing the talking," Hunter says.

"We're wasting time here, we should be solving a crime," Ruby says.

That brings the conversation to a halt and everyone digs into their food. Ruby looks across the table at Kieron,

"How are you enjoying our date?"

"I think it's going spiffingly well so far," he says to mock his position as a Brit.

The Captain, who's also British, rises, "Ladies and gentlemen, the bars and discos are still open around the ship, feel free to enjoy yourself, and we will meet here again at 0730hrs with Jason from photography, please. I want him on the team."

The Captain leaves. Kieron looks at Ruby,
"Disco?"
She shakes her head, "No."

27 DJ IS THE TICKET

Everyone leaves dinner shortly after the Captain, each going their own way. Whilst Kieron's light-hearted offer to Ruby of a continued evening in the disco was passed over, he isn't ready to go to bed. There is a lot haunting him; not Elizabeth who was arrested earlier, more that there is a killer still on the loose and it probably isn't her. The Crow's Nest haunts him and he feels he needs to sit at the bar at night observing its goings-on at the busiest time. He knows now that he can't do it in shorts and a flowery shirt. His formal dinner suit and shirt hang on the back of his door. It seems madness to put a dress suit on for an hour or two, but not so long ago that was his job, ceremonial duties for the army. He looks at his watch; it is just ten o'clock and many guests will still be at the last sitting of dinner, there is a ten-thirty show in the theatre and those guests would arrive in the Crow's Nest latest about 2330hrs. The suit is the ticket that will get him in anywhere, allowing him to walk the decks without causing attention. Dress the same and vanish, he thinks, as he takes the suit down. The first rules of undercover work come from simple compliance.

Re-dressed, he takes the 'Daily Event', the folded sheet of paper that tells of everything that is to happen today. There is little left to happen at this time of night. He notices a quartet in the Crow's Nest, and recognises the name of the performer in the theatre doing two shows, Paul Lopkey. He saw him on his last ship and he almost feels like he's an old friend. Half of him is tempted to go down and see his act but he got dressed for a reason. He leaves the paper behind, lets the door close behind him, as all ship doors do no matter the price of the cabin, and he strides to the carpeted guest stairwell. Ignoring the elevator, he jogs up one flight of the guest stairs. Seeing the bar and feeling the atmosphere, he feels himself relax; he is on holiday for a couple of hours.

In the bar, a quartet; piano, drum, guitar and flute are playing. He stops and watches for a second. Then he takes in the layout and ponders whether the saxophone player would ordinarily have been there instead of the flautist. These musicians must all be part of the orchestra and because a comedian is on the big stage, he doesn't require one.

A waiter offers to find him a chair, which is hardly necessary because the room is far from full, but Kieron wants a stool at the bar. He sits on the very stool that was Eric's favourite, he switches his phone to silent to respect the musicians who have deconstructed a song he knows, and are playing solo runs in turn. Kieron claps as the drummer finishes an interesting, though restrained solo. The pianist kicks in harder as the same waiter hovers by Kieron's side, they must be on some form of incentive or commission.

"I'll have a red wine, no, I'll have a beer, thank you."

Kieron swings around, looks at the pumps and taps one. He has been drinking very nice wine in the Captain's quarters at the rushed dinner, so he doesn't wish to disturb that taste with an inferior wine.

"Are you here every night?" Kieron asks the waiter.

"Yes, sir."

"Where's the saxophone player tonight? He was good."

"He has some time off now, sir." And the waiter

is away to the side of the bar to fetch the ticket for his beer.

Ruby is uneasy in her cabin, she too looks at her watch and it is far too early to sleep. Dinner was over in an hour and it is only ten-forty-five. She speed-dials seven and Kieron's name comes up, but it rings out. She decides not to leave a message but looks in the mirror at her formal white officer's uniform with stars on her epaulettes. She goes to her phone again and redials. Again, there is no answer. She texts, 'Sorry about disco, I thought I was tired. Are you still up for a drink'? She presses send.

Kieron is ordering his second beer, probably quicker than Eric would have done, and they thought he was an alcoholic. The Quartet finishes to light applause. He looks at his watch; it's ten-fifty as the pianist stands up and addresses the small crowd.
"Thank you, thank you. I didn't realise you were here!"
Kieron wonders if that was a sarcastic dig at the low number of guests, and the even fewer who applauded. Lopkey is a great act, so he will have them all in the theatre.
"I have a quick appointment with a Mr Jack Daniels, but I will be back at eleven… as it says in my contract! Then the quartet will re-join me at eleven fifteen and play until midnight."
"Can you play any Burt Bacharach?" A woman shouts from by the window.
"No!" The MD shouts back almost rudely, as he leaves the piano. "All his great songs have important horn parts and we have no horns with us tonight!"

"You don't need horns!"

"To do any of those songs justice, I certainly do. And I would not insult a good friend by trying."

"He's your friend?"

"I knew him when he was married to Carole Bayer Sager and I played with him."

"Wow," The woman replies now focussing more attention on him.

Kieron smiles considering the pointless conundrum as to whether it is she who has taken the bait, or the MD. The Musical Director walks in her direction but staying in the upper section, separated by a handrail.

"Do you know what Burt Bacharach's favourite song was?" he asks.

"Raindrops?"

"No," he says, now loving holding court. Jack Daniels will have to wait.

"Does this happen every night?" Kieron asks the bartender.

"No, it's normally my show. He's ruining it, but it is a small audience, he can have them," the bartender jokes, with a wink.

Kieron is beginning to imagine how much more goes on here than is in the 'Daily Event'.

"You know none of the artists he wanted to do Raindrops would do it. It was offered to Bob Dylan, he said no, Ray Stevens, and he said no. The ones that did record it were never his favourites." The MD continues.

"Do you think all this is true?" Kieron asks the bartender, who shakes his hands and face in a theatrical 'no'. He then takes a hand and extends it from his nose out, like Pinocchio. "If only his penis was that big," he says laughing.

Kieron can see the attraction of this bar. Quite simply the characters are fun.

"Alfie. He wrote it in three weeks and it was his favourite," the Musical Director reveals.

"You play it, I'll sing it," the woman challenges.

The MD is stopped in his tracks, but only for a moment. "There are bar stalls around the piano. If you're there with a double JD for me when I get back, I'll play it."

"Deal," she shouts back as he leaves, for what is now his very short break.

Kieron turns back to the bar, wondering where how that will go in just a few minutes. He is not a great musician but he can't listen to poor ones and the singer might just send him to bed. The MD got himself tied into a situation because he wanted to show off that he has known and played with the best. Kieron's mind wanders to his daughter, a brilliant performer herself, he owes her a phone call, not that she is waiting on him. She is now in New York planning a book tour with the publisher. Ruby appears next to him.

"I thought you were off to bed?" he asks enlivened.

"Well, I was already dressed to go out… I changed my mind. What about you?"

"I wanted to sit where Eric sat, drink his drink, be in his community."

"In that case, it's a good job I joined you."

"Why?"

"Because you can't see things through a woman's eyes," Ruby says.

"There is some truth in that."

"Some truth?"

The bartender is back, raising an eyebrow in agreement with Ruby. "Are you going to buy the lady a drink?" he asks.

"What do you want to drink, Ruby?" Kieron asks.

The bartender lets his head flop to the side, pouting. "I didn't mean her."

Ruby offers her card and makes her own order, "Large Merlot." She turns to Kieron, "Why don't you have any women in your company?"

"We do, Wild Mary."

"Who the hell is Wild Mary?"

"Good question, but shouldn't we be taking things in?"

The Musical Director comes back to his piano which means it is now eleven, that or he has seen his free drink. He is talking to himself, and maybe Jack Daniels. He takes far too long sorting out his music, it could be the woman on the piano stall, or the waitress, Jasmin, standing with his JD have embarrassed him.

"Can't find the music?" the woman asks.

"I don't need music for that."

The MD takes his drink, toasts her and her group by the window, downs it, and then nods to her. She starts singing on cue, brilliantly, and he follows her perfectly.

"She can actually sing!" Kieron says, applauding loudly.

"Never underestimate a guest," Ruby says clapping.

After the guest's amazing rendition, the MD stands and bows to her applauding and letting her take the plaudits,

"You can see why I could not play that alone on the piano."

"Now can we do Raindrops?" The woman ventures.

"No," says the MD firmly.

"He won't play Raindrops, he doesn't like it," the bartender chimes in.

"Do you listen to everyone's conversations?" Kieron asks.

"Of course!"

"Then I need to interview you."

"It will have to be in your cabin, I have bunk beds."

Kieron scoffs. He looks around the room. Eric had bought his last drink an hour before this. The room is quite dead apart from the quartet, they're almost playing to themselves. Ruby puts her glass down, the wine too easily finished.

"Would you like to come back to my suite for a coffee or a nightcap? They've given me a full bar." Kieron asks boldly.

Ruby shakes her head.

"We can use the crew stairs…"

"No," Ruby says, feeling no need to elaborate further. She stands and nods goodnight and leaves.

Kieron turns to the bartender who looks ready to start a new conversation but Kieron hits him with a firm look and stands. He has enjoyed the evening's break but he has work to do tomorrow. He walks away from the bar and turns down the short corridor, stalling by the fateful door marked 'Crew Only'. If he rushed to the elevator he might catch Ruby and try and convince her of that nightcap. No, he knows the steel steps lead to his suite, he should walk that safe route. He opens the door and steps in. He feels a hand on his neck pull him back, and his legs lift. He is in the air. Higher than he might be if he had stood on an improvised explosive device. Just for a few seconds, not even that, his life is a series of flashes with no reality to grab on to.

He hits the steel hard, crash. He feels pain. He fights to stay conscious, to look up at the assailant, but he blacks out.

28 WHAT'S IT ALL ABOUT?

Jason is in the Captain's dining room first, keen and ready for breakfast. The waiters are standing by to serve and watch him, but only because there is nothing else to look at. Feeling formal with his camera over his shoulder, he parks it on a surface away from the food, and edges towards the window. Looking out, he wonders what the protocol is, should he ask them? Even if they say to eat, does he want to be first? He checks his watch, 0720hrs. He is mega-early. Officers do tend to walk in on the precise minute, he thinks. He questions himself then turns to the waiters for a clue. They encourage him over. He goes for it, smiling as he takes a plate. The breakfast looks exquisite. How can breakfast look nicer here, an egg is an egg, right? It all comes from the same kitchen, he thinks, wanting to try several things.

"Looks better than upstairs," he says.

"It's the light, sir," a waiter shares with a smile. "Tea or coffee?"

"Coffee please."

The waiter pours a cup of coffee at a set place at the table, making a decision for him about where he is going to sit.

Jason sits, smiles and drinks. He nods at the waiter with a smile and says nothing because the taste of coffee is definitely not improved by the light.

Hunter enters. "Morning, Jason. I like a man who's prompt," he says merrily whilst he gathers food and sits quickly. "Good morning guys. Coffee please."

Jason looks at them realising he never said good morning to them, maybe never even said please, he worries.

"What am I on the team for?" Jason asks.

Hunter looks at his watch. "Meeting starts at 0730, we got four minutes yet."

Jason nods, takes Hunter's lead and tucks into his breakfast.

"You've never served have you?"

"No, how do you know?"

"You learn to eat. Someone puts food in front of you, you eat it."

Ruby enters with Lal and Krishma, three members of the same team but looking very different. Ruby is in her long black trousers and jacket with flat shoes again, Lal is in long white trousers and shirt, Krishma in a white skirt and shirt. They all go straight to the buffet to eat, only Ruby stops and looks at her watch. Jason copies by looking at his, 0728.

"Have you seen Philips this morning?" Ruby asks. She is the last to get her food before turning to sit with Hunter.

"We don't share rooms," Hunter offers.

"No."

"Did you?" he provokes.

"No," she snaps back.

"Back in the black and flats?"

"They hate it, prefer me in a skirt. I like to be a rebel and as I might have to chase someone, they can't argue."

Hunter lifts his cup of coffee and encourages an approving toast which she responds to. She likes these rare moments of respect.

The Captain enters and Hunter, Ruby and Jason all check their watches.

"Keeping tabs on me are you?" Captain Neil asks.

"No Sir, we're still a man down," Hunter reveals.

The Captain talks as he goes for food, "I have a suggestion. As much as this room is a pleasure and useful for guests, I think my only guests for the next few days will be you. What do you think about moving everything up here and making this the incident room? It will be easier for me to go between Dwight Ritter at head office and keeping an eye on things here, especially as there's a storm ahead."

"No problem with that," Hunter agrees, and looks to Ruby, who nods reluctantly at the idea of all of her evidence walls being moved.

Suddenly an officer opens the door behind them, and rushes in speaking urgently,

"Sir. Mr Philips has had an accident. He's outside at the bottom of the crew stairs, medics are with him. He is in a very bad way."

Hunter looks over to young Jason, who is both shocked and now very alert, copying the others in rising out of his seat.

"This is why you eat when you can, Jason. Let's go."

Hunter snaps a look to the Captain, who nods

back at him, allowing them to leave. Hunter is out of the room first, Jason grabs his camera, Ruby is straight after them. The Captain sits back down to eat with Lal and Krishma, wondering if they are about to leave him too.

"I think the right people are attending to Mr Philips!" he suggests.

Lal and Krishma eat tentatively as the Captain continues to pursue his plans for the new evidence room. He has obviously been sleeping on discussions had with Dwight Ritter,

"Can you two box everything up from the cell after we've eaten and start the move up here? We can use walls in the sitting room, they should be big enough to hold everything... unless more victims keep materialising. I want to keep a closer eye on this."

Ruby goes from carpet to steel flooring easily in her flat shoes. She turns into the area under the stairs and instantly chokes at what she sees. Manesh Hunjan, the senior medic has a drip in Kieron's body which lays mangled in a vast pool of blood. Kieron Philips looks dead.

A spine board is being run in by two medics.

Ruby pulls out her phone to start taking notes and add times to the orders she will give, but Hunter is in first.

"Manesh, give him morphine. Jason, don't wait to be asked. Photograph everything!" Hunter demands.

"He's unconscious, sir, he doesn't need morphine. It slows recovery," Manesh says, as the camera flash starts to go.

"When he wakes up, he's gonna scream. Big time. That'll be in a public area somewhere between here and the surgery on deck three. His body's done morphine before, he'll heal just fine."

Manesh looks to Ruby who nods. He gets a syringe ready, as another medic readies an oxygen supply. Hunter steps in, takes the morphine and plugs Kieron with the whole shot. He then helps out the fidgeting medic by taking the oxygen, placing the mask over Kieron's mouth and nose then running his hand down the clear plastic tube for kinks and ensuring his buddy has flow. He has turned into military-mode, working at the speed he would if under fire. His fingers feel Kieron's spine from the top of his neck down.

"OK team. Together, slide, on three!" Hunter commands, having completely taken over.

"I have this, sir," Manesh says.

"One, two, slide!" Hunter demands, ignoring Manesh.

The body is slid onto the board.

"I just have it faster. Lift, let's go. Central elevator, then down to three." Hunter says in a way that controls the scene without question.

Hunter runs ahead of them past all the cabins, through the pool area on eight and arrives at the central staircase. He hits the elevator button to go down. Ruby is there a split second later a little pissed that an outsider has undermined her staff. Guest breakfast in the buffet on this floor is now underway so the lifts are busy. One set of doors pings and re-opens. An elevator that was just about to go down but stopped in time, however, it is full. Hunter does not wait, he is in military command mode and only has one focus.

"Everyone out please, now!" Hunter demands in a way that makes everyone leave the life, except a mobility scooter that would need to reverse, and a man at the back who stops his wife from exiting.

"Out now, or you get thrown out! Medical emergency." He says, grabbing the scooter and lifting its back over so it can drive out easily. Hunter looks at the man standing defiantly as the scooter powers out.

"You're next." Hunter grabs the man's arm and forces him out.

Ruby, embarrassed by Hunter's behaviour adds, "Thank you for complying, sir. We would do the same for you."

The team enter the lift and Hunter presses three. Ruby takes a key and turns it in the lift control panel. All the lit buttons for the requested decks go out. She re-presses three. It is now an express. Ruby lifts her walkie-talkie,

"Someone check on the guests in mid-stairwell on eight." She looks at Hunter, but decides this is not the right time.

Lal rounds the corner and sees the guy in the mobility scooter wheeling into an open lift. He holds the door open to ensure he can ride in freely, noticing his name. Benny is painted on the front.

"Was that patient alright?" Benny asks.

"Let's hope so," Lal relays, and turns to address a man sitting on the stairs looking in a bad way.

"Can I help you, sir?"

"I need to go to the medical centre, I have been assaulted by a member of staff."

"OK sir, we can do that. We actually have a medical emergency on and we'll need blood donors." Lal says, "You can donate some whilst you get seen to, let's go!"

The man stands. "No, I'm good now."

The lift doors close leaving Lal inside with Benny.

"I can give blood. My name's Benny."

"That's great. Stay with me then, Benny."

The lift doors open on three and it is busy. Lal engages a nurse,

"Possible blood donor."

The nurse passes the order back, "Errr… OK, thank you, that's great. I'll take you from here."

Lal gives Benny a thumbs up and heads off through the warren of cubicles. He opens a door to see Kieron on drips and machines, his evening jacket is being cut away. Ruby, her hands covered in blood, takes the cut clothing and piles it on the desk.

"Lal, the clothes are all evidence, separate evidence bags please, no cross-contamination," she says.

The emergency is engaging all early shift staff.

"If we were anywhere near land he would be getting air-lifted," Doctor Simon Yates says.

Kieron's face shows very little life, as the doctor starts to cut his shirt open.

"That was a new shirt doc," Hunter complains in typical dark military humour, which is ignored.

Simon gives up on the scissors and rips the white evening shirt apart revealing a chest covered in blood. As a nurse starts to wipe his shoulder clean she reveals complex scars that make her stop.

"Old wounds," Hunter explains.

"He's been through a few wars," Simon declares.

"Just a few, Doc, just a few," Hunter says.

"I guessed you might need blood, seeing the mess at the bottom of the stairs, do you want me to put the call out?" Lal asks.

Simon re-attaches the heart machine onto Kieron's clean chest and a nurse takes a blood sample from his arm. Manesh Hunjan, the senior medic is now cutting away his black evening trousers.

"Ahh this is all probably a bit of a hangover, two grazed knees," Hunter says.

"He fell twenty-feet onto a steel floor," Lal reports.

"It'll be a lot more than grazed knees," Doctor Simon Yates says. "This is an interesting cruise, normally I spend most of my time prescribing erectile dysfunction medication, not dealing with dead bodies. Well, not this many."

"He ain't dead. He eats and shits stuff bigger than this the daily," Hunter protests, seeing for the first time the full extent of Kieron's old war wound scars. He points at a single bullet scar now wiped clean of blood, and while not new is still mending. "He got that saving my wife," Hunter boasts, showing huge respect for him. More than he has ever shared. "He'll live."

"I hope so," Simon says.

"I know so," Hunter demands.

"Lal, you could be right, I can't see the bleed yet, but we should put a call out for blood donors." The doctor suggests.

"I've got one outside," Lal says.

"One might not be enough, just thinking ahead."

"He's not dying, Doc. Get that in your head, he's way tougher than anything you've seen," Hunter stresses, as Ruby pulls him out. "Call me if you need blood," he shouts back.

"Me too," Ruby shouts.

Outside, Jason waits nervously with his camera. He has never had to take pictures like this; he does couples in evening dress in different areas of the ship, over and over again.

"Jason, get in there. Don't ask permission. Get pictures of everything. Then join us at the crime scene," Hunter commands on the move, but is slowed by the presence of a young officer.

"The Captain wants you back in his quarters ASAP," the young officer relays.

"Tell him we're travelling, officer, as fast as we can," Hunter says on the move. "Ruby, we need a detail guarding this medical centre, someone tried to kill him!"

Ruby turns back to Lal who is high fiving Benny, who has had the OK to give blood.

"Lal, stay here and guard this room with your life, call for two officers to assist you," she says, and is gone with Hunter.

"Give me a gun and I can stay guard!" Benny says, rocking with excitement on his mobility scooter.

"You might be a bit delirious after you've given blood, maybe you can take the second watch," Lal jokes. Benny nods, enjoying being involved in whatever is going on. A nurse approaches and addresses Benny,

"Have you ever given blood before?"

"I'm on guard at the moment," Benny says.

"I'll cover until you get back, Benny." Lal offers. "But don't be long!"

Benny turns and accelerates away behind the nurse, "Yes, I've given blood a few times. I stopped when they changed the biscuits," he says to her. "How long will this take because they need me?"

Hunter gets into the lift at level three with Ruby who uses her key and presses eight. It is empty because this is the only a deck with little to offer a guest other than the reception area, disembarkation and medical centre.

"Why's he in a penguin suit?" Hunter asks.

"Last night was formal night," she says, still processing that this all happened after their drink last night.

"He fell from the Crow's Nest, what was he doing up there?"

"He was with me," Ruby says, working hard to conceal her genuine upset. "I was questioning him as to why you have no women in your company," she says, now finding a little more grit.

The elevator door opens at eight and they burst out at a fast walking pace.

"He was already dressed and sitting in Eric's old chair at the bar when I arrived, it was a coincidence we met. Sixth sense I guess, we both went up to see the lounge working. We might have had the same thought but obviously, neither of us saw 'the something' we should have. We'd given up and were going to bed," she says.

"Separately?"

"Sadly yes, if I stayed with him he might be alive."

"He is alive."

"I might have seen the killer but I left before him, he must have taken the short cut down the crew stairs."

"He took a short cut, but it didn't involve stairs," Hunter says, turning into a crew area.

"You know what this means?" Ruby asks.

"Tell me," he says, holding the 'Crew Only' door open for her.

"He was targeted, you're next."

Hunter pauses for a second in thought.

"No. The killer's next," Hunter breathes, and he turns away into the service area, right at the end where Kieron was found.

29 THE STING

The cabin stewards' service area with the laundry chute, like many areas of the ship, is efficiently designed to cover multiple uses. These front crew stairs go all the way down to i95, and up to deck nine where there's a door to the Crow's Nest Lounge. For the stewards, here on deck eight, it is the work area they all use for the cabin cleaning along to the pool. Beyond midships, the stewards use a similar area at the other end, the aft. The area also has access to the bridge because it is the front of the ship. There is also the Captain's suite, plus the two top-class suites that Hunter and Kieron have, which are adjacent to the Captain and bridge area, or by closing doors can be part of the passenger area. On deck five, the promenade deck, is the public entrance to the theatre where Bogdan was found dead. Backstage drops with the rake of the theatre and comes out on crew deck four. The show cast and orchestra tend to use the backstage area, then use steps down to their cabins on deck three. On larger ships, the crew might have their own elevator but not on this ship, where there are few floors to descend to crew decks. Most of the senior staff would have cabins on deck four and others on deck three, like Manoj Bhatti, the dead bar steward from the Crow's Nest.

Hunter looks up to the platform on deck nine behind the Crow's Nest where the stairs end. Ruby runs up them, opens the door and looks down to where the body was. Seeing her action, Hunter walks through a move, imagining grabbing Kieron from behind to inflict the drop on him.

"They, he, she, it, was waiting behind the door." He shouts.

Ruby opens the door and stands behind it, then sees if it will still open. It does.

"A left-hand to his neck would pull across his body, the killer's right-hand grabs his belt lifting, then an upward leg sweep. Airborne instantly. That would catch him out, one move, executed in a flash. They would have to be super skilled not to lose balance and grab something. So let's check for prints!" Hunter shouts.

He tries out miming an off-balance move backwards having done the throw and grabbing for grip. Ruby can see where he means and starts down the stairs.

"A team is on the way," Ruby shouts.

"And check his phone. Did someone encourage him to leave the lounge and come down this way?" Hunter asks.

"I'll personally check his phone," Ruby says.

Hunter looks at her,

"Something you're not telling me?"

"If I find something you'll be the first to know," she defends. "If you're still alive."

Hunter turns round to address the scattered audience, but in a flash a dark image consumes him, he sees everyone as war-torn mercenaries. He feels himself raising an automatic weapon and picking each of them off in seconds. That period of his life was years ago, but the nightmare flashes, like the training, never goes away. Ever. Three cabin stewards are on this floor, watching and waiting. Four more in the stairwell below, just being nosey. Two security staff within the taped area measuring with infrared devices, and two more arriving with gloves and masks and small kits, obviously the print guys. Then there are two deckhands, standing near the wall where the blood spill is below the platform, waiting to clean up. Everything is cleaned fast on a ship, but quicker than that, in an instant, they could all be dead. Life is so vulnerable. Hunter shakes off his vision.

"Kieron Philips is superhuman to have survived that. Thankfully, he saw who did it," Hunter shouts. It gets their attention. "Superhuman. Doctor's got him sedated or I would have him going through every guest and crew picture. When he wakes up, he'll identify who did this."

"Is that the best we've got, spreading that he saw the killer?" Ruby asks.

"It's all we've got," Hunter says, watching the rumour spread - which is exactly what he wants. Ruby turns and stands face to face with him,

"You're using him as bait."

"He will have seen them."

"How do you know?" Ruby whispers angrily.

"How do you know he didn't?"

"How do you know he'll wake up?"

"He's spent his life on special missions, been shot, tortured and left for dead. He didn't survive all that to bail out on a fifteen-foot fall. You want the list of qualifications to join us? See his full but restricted curriculum vitae."

Ruby smarts at the remark. Hunter leaves her, walking off towards the Captain's set of rooms.

"We're on a cruise ship, not in the Mekong Delta or the Middle-East," she says to herself.

-

The Captain is looking at the boxes and boxes of material that were on the walls of the cell when used as the incident room and wondering if he has made the right decision inviting it all to invade his space. It is a lot more material than he expected. He addresses Hunter as soon as he enters.

"Witowski, I let the woman you arrested off our ten o'clock meeting; the day became complicated. I'm due to meet with Betty Clifford later, wife of the deceased Eric Clifford. Ruby is keen to ask her a few more questions. Dwight has a set of questions for her too." Neil slides a sheet of questions across the table to him.

"I've got one or two," Hunter adds.

"OK, go easy with her."

"Sir, she's just lost her husband. I'm not gonna leap in, sir."

"I mean go easy with Ruby. This is her ship."

Hunter picks up the sheet and starts to read the questions.

"Copy that, sir. But I'm just doing my job, looks like Dwight Ritter is too."

"I need to stay near the Bridge as we get closer to the changing weather."

Hunter looks at the second sheet of Betty's basic details with a handwritten note on top saying she has chosen to stay on board the cruise to the end.

"She's staying on board, sir?"

"They often do, Hunter. You know that. They're amongst friends here," the Captain explains.

"Sir, can we hold on this evidence going up on the walls in here," Hunter asks.

"You have a theory, Witowski?"

"I want everyone to think that as soon as Philips comes round he'll identify the killer. Ruby's got two men on the hospital door, maybe it needs to be a more considered bear trap."

"That medical centre is an essential busy part of the ship," the Captain offers tentatively.

"Dealing with erectile dysfunction?"

Ruby enters, but the Captain continues without distraction.

"Whatever reason people cruise, even if it's 'once in a blue moon nuptials', we offer a service. The centre needs to stay open and not one guest put in danger, not one guest held hostage."

"I am trying to keep everywhere safe, sir," Ruby says jumping into the conversation.

Hunter hands her Betty Clifford's sheet.

"I can handle this, sir," she offers.

"Thanks, Ruby, do you mind if Witowski here takes second-chair?" the Captain asks diplomatically

Ruby doesn't respond, but continues, "I am not sure about this trap we have downstairs, sir," she offers.

"No, I must admit, me neither."

"There's a killer onboard, prepared to kill guests." Hunter insists, "Is there a better plan than drawing them to Philips?"

"Wait until Kieron wakes up and ask who attacked him," she says.

Hunter turns to the Captain. "Philips never saw him, sir. Far as I can see, he was caught totally off guard from behind. The trap is an opportunity because no one knows that except us."

"Surely whoever attacked Philips will know if he was seen or not?" the Captain asks.

Ruby goes to the phone and makes a call, still listening to this play out.

"The killer left the instant he had thrown Kieron. If he even suspected Philips was alive, he would have gone down to finish him off. He assumed the fall killed him, that's the only reason Philips is alive." Hunter insists.

Ruby takes this in, then returns to her call,

"It's Ruby, I'm with the Captain. We need a status report on Kieron Philips."

Both men's attention has been stolen by Ruby and they stay silent until she thanks whoever spoke to her. She turns to them,

"So far, experts agree one stable break in the pelvic ring, limited bleeding but the bone is in place. He also has fractured ribs. Skull is cracked but stable and in place. They are double checking extremities now. His arm and leg bones, wrist and feet are next in a telemedicine system with Rostock University. The rest of him has all been stitched up. He'll be unconscious for some time but Simon is quite chuffed with his work."

"There is a lot to be added to my report," Neil says.

"Sound's like bed rest, which Philips won't do, or crutches which he won't want," Hunter adds.

"He'll be on anti-inflammatory and painkillers. He'll need eight to twelve week's rest," she adds.

"In the army, we substitute weeks for hours, he'll be up by the morning."

"You're not in the army and I'm in charge," Neil

reminds him.

"Yes, Captain. Can we ask for blood from guest passenger donors, for a medical procedure a guest needs? The killer might be curious, go down to donate if only to gather information. He won't want him to wake up."

"No."

"How about a temporary blood donor's area in the cells which leaves the medical centre running as normal and off the killer's radar?"

"That gives us two places to protect, sir because the killer might not believe us," Ruby interjects, pleased to be able to disagree with Hunter.

"There's a killer on the loose, sir. He can't let Philips live to ID him. He could give blood and poison it. The ship's past the halfway mark in the ocean and the clock is ticking."

"This is very risky, and a lot of this is pure speculation" The Captain suggests.

"You think they'll let us dock in Tahiti and let a killer walk free?" Hunter asks.

"We will berth there. We need supplies after ten days at sea. Everything has been ordered and planned," The Captain replies.

"If you dock and don't let guests off, especially with a killer on board, you might face a bigger mutiny than captain Lieutenant William Bligh did," Hunter stresses.

"I will allow you to make a list of guests who would be willing to give blood and a record of their blood types," The Captain agrees.

Hunter sits down and opens his evidence folder, the copies Ruby gave him yesterday of all the main material that would be on the wall if it were up. She has heard what he said and agrees that they are best at sea until this is under control, but they will need to dock for fuel and supplies.

"Looks like you don't need a whole wall," the Captain suggests, looking over Hunter's shoulder. "Maybe we could each have one of these folders?" He asks but he is now out of his depth.

"I'll get you one made up, sir," Ruby adds.

Hunter pulls out a pad and slides it towards Ruby, kicking a chair out, his way of inviting her to sit down. She hates these unsubtle orders.

"It is better on the wall sir," Hunter explains, turning to Ruby for support. "Ruby?"

"I'll get Dwight Ritter copies of all this too," Ruby says.

"Maybe we could go for mobile boards and start with them in Kieron's rooms? He might be an invaluable point man while he is laid up. We'll make him stare at them all day." Hunter tries.

"I don't envy him," the Captain adds.

"Actually he'll probably be relieved to be of use, plus it might keep him in bed." Ruby agrees.

The Captain nods. Hunter flips the pad open and draws a bird's eye view of the Crow's Nest,

"Who was still in the Crow's Nest when you left, Ruby? Maybe we can eliminate them."

Ruby draws her and Kieron's position and the bar. The Quartet, the woman who sang and her friends, and then dotted other unnamed guests around the room. Then in the corner, she adds slowly, four dancers, a singer and musician. Maybe Lopkey.

"You don't seem sure about these?" Hunter asks.

"It's the staff table. Not official but it's where the entertainment staff sit, the acts and some musicians.

Sometimes young officers. Every ship has one. On bigger ships, it's the back of the night club. I didn't pay it too much attention."

"Very odd," Hunter throws in.

"Why?" asks the Captain.

"All of these live below decks, directly below, probably by the theatre. Right?"

Hunter is unfolding a map of the ship.

"Yes," Ruby agrees.

"Yet they never saw Philips lying in blood, on the shortest route home?"

"The girls would have been in heels, so they wouldn't do metal stairs unless they had to. They would take the lift down to deck five then walk through the theatre to backstage deck four, that way there's only one set of stairs."

"Every member of the ship follows habitual routes," the Captain suggests.

"Who habitually uses these stairs?"

They both seem at a loss to suggest anyone. Hunter is not giving up,

"Seven members in the orchestra, four on stage in the Crow's Nest, one drinking at the staff table in the Crow's Nest and one murdered. Who is number seven?" Hunter asks.

"No, our orchestra is only six on a ship this size," Ruby replies and another idea is blasted out of the sea.

"You can see how it works having it on the wall, Sir." Hunter offers. "With a set number of suspects on board, we can eliminate some while looking for the killer. We are going to meet in the middle."

"By tomorrow we'll be in rough seas and high winds, my attention will be needed there, but interrupt me if anything breaks on this," the Captain says.

"Did we miss breakfast? I'm running on empty," Hunter asks looking around the Captain's empty dining room as he watches Neil go to the door.

"No, you ate breakfast. It's nearly lunchtime," the Captain adds as he disappears.

"Is the bar open upstairs?"

"Yes," Ruby replies.

30 HEY BAR TENDER

Hunter sits at the bar stool Ruby indicates; she sits next to him. The bartender wafts over with a huge smile that turns into a frown,

"Miss Ruby! Two men in less than twelve hours?" he says.

Hunter reaches over and bends his name badge to read it. The bartender grabs his hands,

"So strong," he says affectionately.

The badge is inscribed with the name 'Prince Dahoum'.

"Made up name, right?" Hunter asks.

The bartender frowns distastefully at him,

"I preferred the man you were with last night, Ruby."

"Prince." Hunter begins. "You were the last one to see Commander Philips alive. Were you the last man to see Eric Clifford alive?"

Prince shows genuine shock.

"Prince Dahoum, you were a friend of Manoj?" Hunter asks.

"I loved him like a brother."

Hunter is stoic, believes nothing. Prince Dahoum returns a disapproving look before moving to a guest along the bar who needs to be served.

Hunter turns to Ruby.

"What were you and Kieron talking about?"

"I was giving him a hard time about why are there no women in your company."

"There are."

"Yes, Wild Mary."

"You were talking to Kieron about women in our company? D'you think it's too early for a drink, I feel the need for a drink," Hunter says, looking around the empty lounge. "We need to put names to each of the marks on your map of last night. Staff, singers, everyone."

"I'll have Krishma get the bar bills and ask around, she says. "But removing ten or so people from twelve hundred doesn't get us far."

Hunter turns to Prince who has just finished serving the other guest.

"Get me an American Pale Ale."

"I am not sure we have any corn-based beer." Dahoum turns, looking at the beers, knowing perfectly well he doesn't have a corn beer.

"Corn beer? What?"

"Original American beer, sweetie. Native Americans were making corn beer before America became America, I know my beers, I just don't think I have one."

"Dahoum! I want an Indian Pale Ale, preferably an American one."

Prince Dahoum grabs a bottle from the fridge and shows it to him. Ruby holds her hand up kindly, she does not want a drink. Prince slides Hunter's cruise card across to Jasmin; bartenders never deal with the billing. He caps the bottle and half pours it into a glass.

"Many of the murders are centric to this place, right?" Hunter whispers to Ruby.

Jasmin approaches Hunter for a signature. She looks different, a whole different look and still just as devastating. He signs and smiles.

"Thank you, Jasmin. Were you on duty last night?"

"Yes sir, I served the man with Miss Ruby." Jasmin offers, before smiling and walking away.

"Was she on your map?" Hunter asks.

"No. You asked who was still here when we left. I couldn't place her then."

Hunter is nodding as Prince cheekily looks at Hunter's payment slip,

"I see your suite is just below, let me know if you ever want room service," he says with a suggestive smile, and he is gone again, dancing around his small space behind the bar.

"People love him, he's funny. It's all an act. He's harmless," Ruby says, not hiding her remark.

Dahoum comes back for the signed slip and his pen.

"They love the little dark one." Dahoum whispers.

Hunter downs the small beer and stands. "Let's go." But then he turns back, "Hey! Prince."

They meet head to head, leaning over the bar.

"I wasn't messing with you. Someone tried to kill my buddy Kieron last night on the stairs just behind this bar. Didn't work. Broke a few ribs, shook him up. He saw the killer."

"It wasn't me!"

"I know, you were here. He was left looking up from the floor before he passed out. When he comes round again, and he will, he'll ID the attacker for me."

"OMG."

"When I have the killer's identification I will find him, then torture him."

"Talents you've acquired over many cruises, I'm sure."

"What would you like to do with them before I kill them softly?"

"You are messing, right?"

"Only the 'kill him softly' bit, even as an homage to Roberta Cleopatra Flack, I couldn't kill that bastard without making him scream."

"Roberta Cleopatra?"

"Female singer, legend," Hunter says clearly to ensure it sinks in. But Prince Dahoum is not getting it.

"Lost honey, lost."

"Not that you could kill anyone with a song."

"Ah, the Fugees! Very funky number." Prince says then gyrating from side to side singing.

"No. The killer has danced for the last time, make sure everyone knows that."

31 YOU'RE STAYING?

Ruby and Hunter approach the Chart Room bar in the centre of the ship. She turns to Hunter just before they enter,

"Hunter, I can do this by myself, you need some time because this has got personal for you."

"Personal for me? You were on a first date with Kieron."

"Just offering to do this one alone."

"Sure, but no need," Hunter offers.

"I can collect evidence in my sleep, honestly."

"You said yourself, two heads are better than one."

Hunter walks off ahead one stride beyond her and sees Betty Clifford sitting alone in the corner. The Chart Room is very dark wood and brass, with models of older ships in cases. It is a very traditional lounge and it's quiet, though public enough for them not to be left alone with Betty.

"Hey, Betty. Can I get you anything?" Hunter asks.

"A large gin. Just to steady the nerves."

Hunter engages a waiter by flashing his cruise card, while Ruby sits with her.

"The Captain tells us you've decided to stay on and complete the cruise?" Ruby asks.

"Eric would have wanted me to."

Ruby types into her phone. "Do you mind if I quote you on that, you're not likely to change your mind?" Ruby asks, looking at her very seriously.

"No, I'm sure. Cruising was our life. I love it. He would want me to stay on," Betty says.

"Why would someone kill Eric?" Ruby asks.

Betty is puzzled by the question. She takes her drink from the waiter. Hunter signs for it and takes his bottled beer.

"That's what we want to find out, Betty," Hunter starts, sitting down, "Had he made any enemies since the cruise started?"

"Eric? Eric? No. Far too soft is Eric. No." Betty stumbles for words, but has her free hand clenched into a fist almost trying, but failing to push it up.

"He had a fight?" Hunter asks, and Ruby looks at him wondering where that came from.

Betty laughs and shakes her head, "Sometimes I wish he'd been stronger. Just had a bit more go in him."

"Did he watch Lawrence of Arabia when it screened earlier in the cruise?" Hunter asks.

"He did. I hate that film, but he loves it. He went. He's always different after he watches that. That gets him fired up."

"In what way?" Ruby asks.

"I don't know really. Maybe the war, he would never talk about it, but his grandfather died in that campaign."

"The middle-east?" Hunter asks.

Betty nods.

"I fought there, so did my partner. The treaty of Versailles signed after the Great War resolved nothing for that part of the world," Hunter shares.

Betty remains silent, her glass is drunk dry.

"Betty, would you like another drink or will that be too much before dinner?" he asks her.

"Very kind of you, another one won't be too much. Not in the circumstances."

"Don't want you missing an evening at the slots." Ruby jokes.

"I won't do that. Never miss that. But it's on Eric's bank card, I s'pose that's not right now." Betty says, shocking herself.

"Don't you worry about anything like that. I'll speak to the purser's office." Ruby offers. "What else do you need to do on his money?"

Betty is silent, Hunter wonders if that was a bit too soon to ask and eyes Ruby.

"Do I need to get any other standing orders sorted that are on his card or can they wait?" Ruby asks, more gently.

"As long as it works on the ship, and I can draw cash for the ports, I'll be OK," she says.

"How many cruises you been on, Betty?" Hunter asks.

Betty comes alive, it is as if a spotlight has been turned on her.

"Guess!"

A second gin and tonic arrives. Neither guess, but they wait for her to have her moment. Betty takes a sip of her drink. She is holding the answer like a poker player, an amateur who thinks they have a winning hand.

"Forty-three," she announces as if she would expect to win.

"That's a lot," Ruby says.

"We found our happiness travelling. We know most of the staff. Not you, you're new." Betty directs to Ruby.

"I'm relatively new to this ship, but I doubt you'd have cause to deal with my department on a normal cruise. I am in security and I only deal with cruisers when they break rules," Ruby smiles.

"You know the staff?" Hunter asks.

"Most of them," she says.

"And the ship?"

"Every rivet, Eric used to say."

"How did you make the time to cruise so much?" Hunter asks.

"And afford it. I know. That is always the question. Well, Eric was laid off at fifty-three. He had a final salary pension, the house was paid off. What else was there to do with the money? It saves me doing my own dishes."

"It certainly does," Ruby agrees.

"So I guess they do your washing as well as your dishes when you're on here. You use the laundry service?" Hunter asks.

"I do, it's fascinating," Betty says. "We always

wondered where it went and how everyone's bits get back to the right cabin."

"Eric liked to know how the ship worked?" Hunter asks, thinking that is a lead.

"Couldn't get enough of it, you should have heard him when he got started back at his club. He should have been paid commission for the number of people he converted to cruising… Oh, what will I do without him? I like these breaks. Will I still get his pension?"

"Not something to worry about now. The purser will see if she can find someone to help with that," Ruby offers.

Betty holds up her empty glass, however, neither Ruby or Hunter take the hint for a third drink so Betty has had enough.

"Do you mind if I go now? I'd like to get to my slots early tonight. I want to see the act on later. Eric saw the first show and raved about it."

"He went by himself to the first show?" Hunter asks.

"No. He said he went with someone he met who recommended it. No idea who."

"I bet they miss him in the Crow's Nest." Hunter ponders. "Which act is it?"

"Magician guy, tells jokes."

"Paul Lopkey?"

Ruby looks at Hunter, questioningly.

"No idea of his name."

"I saw him on another ship, I don't remember seeing his name for tonight. I thought tonight was a singer," Hunter says. He looks to Ruby for her to confirm, but she is not playing.

"Oh well, I'll see you around, thanks for the drinks," Betty says and leaves.

Hunter turns to Ruby who is looking at the list of questions.

"We didn't get the whole list done," she says.

"Which act is on tonight?"

"No idea," she says flatly. "But I hope it's not Paul or you will have caused an old lady to miss the show her late husband wanted her to see."

"Really?" he says sarcastically. "Did you gain anything from that?"

"That she knew nothing about her husband, the man from whom she has never been separated in forty years."

Hunter looks unimpressed. Ruby holds her hands out in a 'so what' gesture,

"Nothing there told us why he was killed," he says.

"I don't think she knows anything. You've made a friend, she'll be after you," Ruby says and stands. "I need to go and type this up. But you know that, you used to have this job," Ruby digs.

"I'm going to see Kieron and then go wash and change, but not by my habitual route."

"Frightened of being killed?" Ruby asks.

"The opposite. The killer's not been on my usual route so I am trying a new one."

At the medical centre, Hunter walks through the first door to see Lal on a chair and Benny the other side of the door seemingly keeping guard.

"You are?" Hunter asks Benny.

"Benny. I've been deputised."

"Really?" Hunter replies turning to Lal for an explanation.

"He's very helpful and keen," Lal says.

"Benny. You'd be more useful to me undercover.

You ever worked undercover?"

"Do I have to wear a wire?" Benny asks keenly.

"Usually yes, but we're on a ship, and I don't have that kit. If you need to record something, can you do it on your phone?"

"I sure can."

"Anything to report, get me through Lal in the security office. Go and have a wash, freshen yourself up, then carry on as normal. Mix with the guests and listen," Hunter instructs.

Benny accelerates off out towards the elevator.

"Thanks," says Lal.

It is Hunter's turn to use the 'so what' gesture,

"He's your man."

Hunter enters the recovery room where Kieron is still asleep. Dr Simon Yates follows him in.

"He's still sedated."

"Good. He could do with the rest. He sure needs it because I've got jobs for him when he wakes," Hunter says.

"He won't be able to work."

"From his bed?"

"Maybe."

"In a wheelchair?"

"Possibly."

"How about one of those electric scooters?"

"I'm not sure about that."

Hunter gives a huge grin,

"You ever watch Ironside?"

"Can't say I have."

"Don't worry. Any of your dead dudes leave a mobility scooter they're no longer using?"

"I might have an old one from a previous cruise,

maybe."

"Cool," Hunter says walking towards Kieron Philips laid out on the bed, asleep and looking peaceful,

"Look at you in clean white sheets. You know you've retired when you're a man-down in clean white sheets… You can stay sleeping 'til tomorrow bro', then I've got a list of jobs and an army vehicle for you." Hunter pats Kieron on the shoulder then turns. "Thanks, Doc. I'm gonna try and slow the flow of bodies down."

"Thanks, although I was going for a world cruise PB," Simon says.

"One more thing. Eric Clifford. He ever visit you for erection help?"

"Yes. Few times."

Hunter walks out and past Lal who is with an officer guard he didn't see on the way in.

"Lal. Doctor says there's an electric scooter of an old Jon Doe, see if you can get it requisitioned and have the engine workshop dress it up to look like a military vehicle for when Philips comes round."

"That's not normal practice, sir, taking dead people's property," Lal says.

"None of this is, Lal, none of this is," Hunter says and turns towards the lift shaft.

"Sir!"

"Yes, Lal"

"Aren't you worried about someone trying to kill you too?"

"No. They're not very good at it, are they?"

32 I'M ONLY DANCING

"Mary, what on earth is that noise? What are you doing?" Hunter checks his watch in a panic. He was taking a few moments to himself in his suite. It has just gone 5pm and Mary appears to have started the evening already. The day has shot by, and it hasn't been great.

Mary has her phone to her ear. She signals for the music to be turned down and the teenagers surrounding her begin to stop dancing.

"I'm dancing. I'm allowed to dance on my own table. I own the place!" she shouts.

Exhausted, Hunter is unbuttoning his shirt slowly, recounting how his day has slipped away. He switches to speakerphone,

"On a table, at your age?"

Hunter scrunches up his face immediately, he knows he's said the wrong thing but it slipped out. He is tired and angry with himself. He knows she's going to stick it to him for that.

Mary stands suddenly still. She is very angry.

"Yes. At. My. Age!"

Hunter pulls his shirt off scrunches it in one hand and throws it across the room. He catches his reflection in a mirror and his melancholy escalates. Where has the past gone? When did he start to look like an old dude? More importantly, what does his future look like?

"You owe me now. You hear me?" he hears Mary scream out of his phone.

"Yeah, I owe you."

"Gonna put my favourite reporter on, Janey E.

You gonna treat her well and give her something!"

"Mary?" he shouts but she is gone.

"Hi. It's Janey E," is all the new voice on the phone says.

"Janey. We spoke briefly once before. Look, one of the investigators was attacked last night. Thrown over a balcony. The has made one big mistake, he didn't kill him. So when Commander Kieron Philips wakes up he'll identify him. I will then personally handcuff this killer to the rear of the ship and we will tow him into Tahiti."

"There are rumours of more than one killing?"

Hunter pauses, then gives in. "I can confirm that and that there seems to be no motive. The killer's anger appears to be aimed at crew members."

"But, am I right in thinking that guests have been killed?"

"That doesn't seem to be his focus, but everybody is important. I can't say more until the company has informed relatives."

"Are we talking more than one guest?"

"Yes. Send me the email address of your picture desk."

"I want video not stills."

"Don't wait up. Nice talking to you." Hunter hangs up, tosses his phone, walks into his shower cubicle and turns on the water.

"Guess the Captain will be calling me again," he says to himself, because he knows he has gone too far. Way too far.

There is still a queue of guests waiting to give blood at the temporary medical centre down near the cells on deck 2, but now they are mainly dressed in smart evening clothes. This area is never seen by guests so in itself it is a reward and a talking point as they crane their necks to look down the main crew motorway known as i95. It is where everything and everyone moves below decks.

The Captain passes two guards and walks along the queue, shaking hands and exchanging stories but avoiding questions. He is a master at that as well as sailing his mini steel city. He gets to Ruby who is with two other guards. This would be a trap if the killer was daft enough to come in, and so far the one thing he has not shown is lack of intelligence. The Captain turns away to speak with her privately.

"You're not actually banking blood, are you, Ruby?"

"No, sir. They come in, get a quick scratch test onto a slide, and are sent away. We're collecting a record for an emergency blood bank we don't need. It's a trap, sir, Mr Witowski's idea."

"Can you see it working?"

"I don't see many of their ideas working."

"Close it down."

"Yes, sir. I didn't want to have to say this, but I wish head office had left this to me. They've discovered nothing so far, just formed opinions based on massive speculation and caused trouble. Now he's announcing his partner's attack to all guests, I have no idea what he is up to. I can't control him, sir."

"I feel your pain. Their Miami office released a press statement. Thanks to social media every guest will know an elaborated version of the story by the end of dinner."

"Can we not tell them to take a back seat?"

"For many reasons, Tahiti cannot come quickly

enough." The Captain turns to the queue and addresses them,

"I have to thank you personally for this wonderful show of support. I am told that we have enough information on every blood group. You have all been amazing. I hope we don't need to call on you again but we all appreciate such generosity on your holiday. Feel free to stay and add to our emergency database, but please get back to your dinner dates, your showtimes, or whatever you were doing on the ship before I lock the cells with you inside!"

There is laughter amongst his crowd.

"Enjoy your evening."

The Captain is gone. Ruby walks round to her office and Krishma dutifully follows a few paces behind and closes the door. Ruby turns to her.

"Get a closure notice at the top of the stairs or you will be here all night. When it's clear here, have two of this detail sent across to join the medical centre."

"This team are nearly out of hours, Miss Ruby."

"OK, rest them, work out a shift change with an overlap in the night when we can move Philips to his own suite and leave just one man on him there."

Lal walks in which puzzles Ruby, "You're supposed to be guarding the medical centre," she snaps.

"Mr Hunter asked me to requisition a mobility scooter and have it ready for Mr Kieron," Lal answers sheepishly, seeing she is under pressure.

"You work for me, not him."

"Sorry."

She is about to continue the dressing down but stops herself. "OK. Get it done. But ask both detectives to make their requests via me."

Hunter is still enjoying his hot shower, turning his face up to be pounded by the spray of water. A private moment to think, washing away the day and allowing fresh ideas in. Two days ago they boarded and he has hardly stopped, his partner has been attacked and the job is not panning out as he had hoped. It could all go wrong, including the yet-to-be-negotiated fee.

Then a thought hits him and his shower is over. He thrashes back the curtain, turns the water off as he steps out, grabs a towel and leaves the bathroom. Wrapping himself, he takes the internal ship security phone from his bed and dials Ruby. She fails to answer and he grows more and more impatient.

"Ruby, answer the god damn phone!"

Ruby is at Kieron's bedside in the medical centre, ignoring her phone which is on silent. He is still out cold, but there are no doctors and seemingly far less machinery attached to him now. He still has a plasma drip and a basic heart monitor. She holds onto his hand which is limp and non-responsive.

"Kieron. It's Ruby. Time to wake up. Time to show me that you're ok. Try to blink an eye or squeeze your hand. It's Ruby."

She gently squeezes his hand but there is no response.

"I'm sorry. Sorry, I didn't take you up on your offer but I did change my mind. I was calling you and texting you. You missed your chance, or I missed mine. Come on Kieron, it's time to wake up now."

Ruby turns and Hunter is standing there.

"How long have you been standing there?" she demands, embarrassed.

"A while. That's why you didn't want anyone else to check the phone?"

Ruby doesn't answer, Hunter has other problems.

"You're going to have to leave him, I've fucked up big time. Big time."

"The Captain told me, the press on the mainland are exposing a serial killer on board thanks to you?"

"The killer's going to strike tonight," he says.

"How do you know?"

"I just do."

"You can predict the future now? I don't appreciate you ordering my staff to do things."

"Do we have any unused security cameras? Any old, not working? To put up as dummies?"

"Were you listening to a word I was saying?"

"I was, but how am I supposed to react? I need bogus security cameras, not emotions. Do you have them?"

Ruby has to bite her lip before she answers. "I can ask, but it's unlikely. What are you thinking?"

"The killer is going to choose a guest."

"Why?"

"Because I told the press he was focussing on the crew. The one thing he seems to like is showing us and the world just how wrong we are. He'll try and prove me wrong, he'll go for a guest. We've got to try and stop him."

"How do we do that, wise guy?"

33 RULES AT MI5

"Jason, you're an essential part of this team," Hunter says.

Jason is dressed in a suit ready for the evening, even though it is a casual night. Hunter is wearing a white shirt but no jacket. They sit at a table away from others in the Crow's Nest.

"Yeah, but the problem, sir, is I just realised the team is getting killed," Jason replies, worriedly looking for reassurance.

He is a ship photographer. This whole thing seemed fun when he was photographing wounds and evidence, but now he sees the danger.

"How many in your team?"

"Five."

"They're all working tonight," Hunter firmly informs him.

"Five including me."

"They can't know why."

"I think everyone knows we have a killer on board, sir."

"No one knows what we know," Hunter growls deeply.

"Nothing. We know nothing. We haven't got a clue," Jason panics, "and look what happened to Mr Philips."

"Your staff must never know details, that's the first rule of working in intelligence," Hunter reveals.

"What's the second?"

"I can't tell you that."

"This is scary. Super scary," Jason worries.

"Yet another reason you tell them nothing. Do your cameras take video?" Hunter asks.

"Yes, but it rips their battery life."

"Can you work from local power?"

"Yes."

"I want you to shoot video, don't miss a thing.

Simple, not dangerous. Occasionally, manually fire the flash so it looks like you're taking stills."

"But you can see the little red record light."

"Not if it's covered up, right?"

"I get it."

"Put a photographer at each of the main entrances to the buffet."

"Are we looking for the murderer in the buffet?"

"Everyone has to eat. A loner, someone avoiding the camera, film them while they think you're not."

Jason puts his hand up like he is in class. Hunter pulls it down.

"Idiot."

"I have a good idea, it could be worth your while," Jason says, putting his hand out, signalling money.

"You're paid to have good ideas."

"Not enough for this idea. This is your department, security."

Hunter stands up and leans on the table, he is a huge unit to argue with. "Forget it. I'll talk to your team, you're fired."

"You can't fire me!"

"I'm from head office and I'm listing you as non-cooperative, a suspect, and putting you on office duties pending a career review when we dock."

"My idea is that we leave one camera on a tripod constantly shooting video, and we use a second stills camera to hold people up in front of it."

"Get it sorted! Then come and find me for your desk job. We all work for the same team on the same ship. Captain asked for you, you are now in intelligence."

"But my department has its own targets to meet."

"Let's hope the killer hasn't got a target on your

back. But then, why would he?"

Hunter leaves. Jason is left wondering what he has been tasked with.

Hunter has worked on a cruise ship before, not that long ago. Even though he was head of security, the overall crew were all tasked with giving guests the best holiday experience they could at all times. He's watching two maintenance men on a step ladder erecting a security camera to the ceiling in the narrow corridor which is the main thoroughfare to the theatre at the busiest time. Seeing the guest traffic build he knows he's going to have to dig deep to appease them. He notices Benny in his scooter watching from the elevator side and although he's not causing a disruption, his presence is not helping.

"No rush," Benny shouts, "The show won't start until you're all in, they know we have a little problem here."

Benny has produced Witowski's first genuine smile of the day and a grateful nod. But Hunter is desperate for a break in the case. He waves at a group of guests that have already passed him and shouts out,

"Thanks for asking, he's tough. He'll be up and about tomorrow with work to do."

No one had asked, they have no idea he is talking to them, it was a performance to excuse a comment, like a DJ saying 'this is a request' in order to play a record no one had asked for. Once again, Hunter is throwing into the ether that Kieron is going to be fine because he wants to worry the killer. But Hunter has not seen a likely killer yet and guests may be ignoring him. He is not in uniform or wearing a badge, so they may wonder who he is. Does he need to start wearing a badge? That is one for tomorrow because his audience has gone in and will have either ignored his remark, or be repeating it and embroidering the story with rumours, spreading news. He wants the latter, he wants the murderer to try and break into the medical centre and he is playing a dangerous game. The killer might not play into his hand, but he did buy two drinks with a dead man's cruise card just out of camera vision. Now, however, these cameras are going up to show the playground is getting smaller and smaller. By adding these cameras, even though they don't work, Hunter is hoping that the black spot into the theatre that allowed Bogdan to be killed, has been closed down. The photographers at the buffet and a few more cameras elsewhere should be doing the same.

Theatre guests will be out in forty-five minutes. The rush to and from events on a ship is as predictable as the timed events themselves. The cynical would say that the events have been planned so guests switch from one end of the ship to the other, meaning the programme has them forever passing the shops in the middle. Benny switches his scooter on with a beep and travels forward to follow the last guests in. He fist-bumps Hunter and as he drives past he throws a remark back,

"I got something for you."

"What?"

"I reported it to Lal as requested," Benny says back giving him a thumbs up before vanishing into the dark where the orchestra has started to play the overture.

Hunter wonders if he can leap out of that scooter and jump down a deck, or throw a man over a balcony. He seems too good to be true. Hunter may be reading too much into things but he also knows leaving any stone unturned is always the mistake that comes back to bite you.

34 RELAX, DON'T DO IT

In the hotel management offices behind reception, an area Hunter had yet to frequent, staff are not used to walk-ins. The puzzled group of junior officers watch him at a computer. To date, his requests had come via Ruby Jenkins or one of her staff. Whilst hotel staff have assisted him and shown him computer files as requested, this is different. He does work for head office, and though he out-ranks them, something feels wrong about watching him work on their computers, which is why they called their head of department, Roy Stevens, who has just arrived.

"My staff looking after you, Witowski?" he asks, swinging in and beckoning him into his office.

"Perfectly."

Roy holds his hand out to look at the sheets Hunter has printed.

"I wondered how long it would take you to arrive," Hunter says, closing the door behind them.

Roy flips through the sheets. Benny Raymond's customer profile and booking form. His social media profiles, groups he belongs to, and a newspaper article about the much younger Benny being stabbed while trying to save a shop assistant from a mugging in his local deli in Miami. His occupation is a data analyst, he's a big Dolphins fan, and supports many charities.

"Regular good guy," Roy says, handing the first few sheets of data back.

"In a shit world."

"You could have asked?"

"I'm asking, Roy. I need all the help I can get, we have a killer on board. I need to claw back any minutes and seconds I can because the shit is getting near the fan..." Hunter says.

Roy rocks his head from side to side, not sure how to answer. He places the rest of the sheets on the desk between them.

"Why am I looking at this hero and trying to figure out what might have flipped his switch?" Hunter asks, with some sadness.

"Does that say something about him or you?" Roy asks.

Hunter smiles, and the two men relax.

"If I had a bottle of something in a drawer I would pull it out now" Roy adds.

"That only happens in the movies," Hunter says.

These two have not had much to do with each other but there is an instant easy connection. Maybe because they're not under the pressure of studying crime boards.

"You could be a therapist," Hunter says, pointing at him.

"Not yours."

"Why?"

"There's too much shit in there, I wouldn't want that to hit the fan." Roy points at Hunter's head.

"Oh. That hurt."

Roy is steady with his reply. He means no harm.

"Did it? Not really. You know that. You're dealing with it."

"I am? You are a quack."

"I've seen enough of them."

"I won't ask."

"It's OK, I'm out now. It's nice to have someone to talk to, someone new, and I'm not hitting on you. I looked you up and saw you were married. Though that means little from my experience."

"I'll take that as a compliment. We've just moved from Madeira to Miami, not that we had much to move."

"I know, I read the news articles. I never knew security was so dangerous."

"We got a house in Coral Gables where the police patrol all the time and are never more than a block or so away, Elaine feels safe there. Now it's time for kids. Guess that's what happens when you marry someone younger."

"Do you play chess?"

"Used to."

"Love to play when you have time. My excitement starts and stops at running this hotel. And it's a pretty small hotel compared to my last ship. Had my last ship been on land it would have been one of the ten largest hotels in the world. But, as I don't need to tell you, guests at sea never eat out and expect to be entertained every minute of the day. I needed a rest."

"How's the small ship going for you?" Hunter grins.

"Having a serial killer on board?" Roy stops and thinks, then answers his own question, "- has not affected me much yet."

"That's what my buddy Kieron would have said until last night."

Hunter slides the papers back to him, "So, what do you reckon on this guy. Has he been ignored too long, has he flipped?"

"You know the answer to that one."

"I do, but someone has flipped. Someone has changed and we're not seeing the red flag."

"It's always the obvious, always the question you're avoiding," Roy suggests.

"What does the sign say on your door?"

"Friend, so come by any time."

"Is that a polite way of saying goodnight?"

"Not at all. We have a killer on our ship and no one has asked me or told me anything yet."

"So you feel ignored, maybe you could have flipped?" Hunter mocks.

"I work for a huge corporation, you get used to being ignored."

"I need all the help I can get, Roy. Especially from people who really know this ship."

"I know this ship, it's the same as your old ship, any ship."

"Roy, you're welcome upstairs anytime in the incident room, because I'm not seeing a signature to link these murders. Not anger, not thrill-seeking, not financial gain, not attention-seeking. And the murders are too diverse to be sex-driven."

Hunter stops. He ponders all he has said. Roy is enjoying his company. Then Hunter points at him.

"What?" Roy worries.

"Something you said."

Hunter stands up and shakes hands with him. Roy tilts his head, he wants to know what.

"Everywhere has its dark areas at night, where married men meet. Where is that on this ship? The pool area?" Hunter asks, revitalised.

"It could be," Roy answers, not convinced.

"The bar in the Crow's Nest?"

Roy gives the slightest of nods, Hunter is having a

breakthrough moment.

"I did say all ships are the same."

"It's people that are the same. Let's have dinner or a beer one night. And that is not a pass."

"Love to."

Hunter opens the door.

"Hey. A tip," Roy says, stopping him.

Hunter waits to hear what it is.

"Don't run around so fast you forget to appreciate your team."

Hunter nods back at him. "One other thing, Roy. I'd hate to find we have another murder hidden away somewhere. Like a cabin with a do not disturb up."

"We'll have a team chat."

35 BRING YOUR CAMERAS

Hunter enters the photography office, another space tucked away within the inner folds of the ship, where the team are locking away their cameras.

"Hey, paparazzi. Anyone fancy a drink?"

The team turn, puzzled because none of them has ever met Hunter and Jason has told them nothing. Sally, a female photographer, wears a black catsuit and looks ready to go out. Bill, dressed in a white shirt and black bow tie, waits for further explanation. The other two, Kusay and Michael are shy, they don't engage and continue putting the cameras away.

"First rule?" Jason says questioning Hunter's demand for secrecy.

"You said yourself they'd guess they were looking for a killer."

"What?" Kusay asks. Michael and Sally just nod at

each other. Both had guessed it was something like that.

"You didn't tell them?" Hunter says.

"No! You told me not to."

Well now they know but, hey, I'm buying," Hunter offers.

"Have you been drinking?" Jason asks, worried.

"Crow's Nest," Hunter states and leaves.

"Free drinks!" Bill says, slapping Kusay and Michael on the back.

"He wants something," Jason says suspiciously.

"But… free drinks," Sally argues.

Hunter re-appears around the door, "How good are your cameras in low or no light?"

"Some of them are brilliant," Sally says.

"Most are rubbish," Kusay adds, about to recite the full technical specifications of every camera they have.

"Bring a couple along," Hunter says, and he's gone.

"I told you, he wants something. He never does anything for nothing."

Hunter creeps into the back of the theatre, feeling the swell of the ocean has begun to change with each step he takes. He looks down to the stage where the singer is re-setting his position every now and then without skipping a note. It's easy to find Benny because there is an area for mobility scooters at entrance level. Hunter leans in and whispers in his ear,

"Crow's Nest after the show. I'm buying. Join us." Hunter leaves him.

Hunter enters the bar and finds a table at entrance

level. He orders a pint of lager and turns to see Jason leading his team in.

"So what is it?" Jason asks.

"Jason, for the first time since I arrived, I feel like I'm on holiday," Hunter tries to sell.

Jasmin is hovering by Hunter, who indicates that they can all order on his card.

"Gin and Tonic, please," Sally says.

"JD and coke," Jason says, and the others order beers.

"Large ones?" Jasmin asks.

"Go for it." Hunter says, as he sees Benny driving in, "What do you want, hero?"

"I'm not a hero, I haven't done anything yet," Benny says. "I'll have a Merlot please."

Jasmin taps the order into her device and heads towards the bar. The boys in the team watch her move as she goes. Sally slaps them all, one by one.

"You're a hero, I know it, you know it," Hunter says to Benny.

"Did Lal tell you?" Benny asks.

"I haven't seen him. Hey Sally, come here." Hunter puts his arm around her and positions the two of them between his team and the bar and encourages a picture.

"The job is to take our picture, but not. Aiming our way, but shoot past us and cover everyone at the bar, you don't need me or Sally in the frame."

"No such thing as a free drink," sighs Jason.

'You do', she mouths to the Bill. She then turns to Hunter,

"You couldn't take your shirt off? Make the picture more interesting?"

"No, Sally. I saw myself in the mirror earlier and

it's far from impressive."

"Have you seen the rest of my team?" She slips her fingers under his shirt between buttons.

"Now smile."

They both smile. Jason manoeuvres and enjoys the secrecy of photographing everyone who is at the bar. Bill, Kusay and Michael all do the same.

"Did you get us?" Sally asks.

Jasmin arrives with their drinks on a tray and stands to the side, where she thinks she's out of the picture. It is an art how bar staff manage whole trays of drinks as the weather starts to get rough. Tonight is a test, tomorrow their skills will really be needed. However, Jasmin is in the expanded camera frame, and as stunningly photogenic as she is, she is encouraged to serve and leave. Eventually, they have the whole bar photographed.

"Can we do that again in the wedding chapel? I want to freak my mum out," Sally says.

Hunter likes her, she's fun. He lifts his glass to Benny and encourages her to do the same though she has no idea why.

"To heroes."

"Heroes." They toast.

"Benny attacked a mugger. You are a true hero mate."

Hunter makes him feel special for a few moments. Benny, whilst embarrassed, enjoys being the centre of attention for good reasons rather than because he is in a chair. Sally moves to sit beside him.

"Take our picture for real," she says.

Benny encourages her to sit on the unit with him.

"Someone get that bouquet from next door," Hunter says, now much more light-hearted even though he is still gathering evidence, or preparing to.

Kusay is off, Sally stays next to Benny, cuddled up.

"I like this," Benny says.

"So, Benny, does your todger still work?" Sally asks.

"Sally!" Her team reprimand her in different ways for the embarrassment she is capable of unloading.

"Just asking. I'm interested," Sally says.

"No worries, good question. Wish more girls would ask. It does, just my legs don't work. I'm paralysed from the waist down," Benny says.

"This thing won't tip over?" Sally asks.

"No, you're perfectly safe."

She hugs him.

"It's capable of carrying a hell of a lot more weight than you and me."

The bouquet arrives and Sally goes to town on Benny, kisses and cuddles as the cameras flash. So much so, guests come over and congratulate them. Hunter is with Jason, cunningly shooting over the top of them at those at the bar who do not move, especially those by themselves.

"OK guys, we need one last set of photos outside, the pool bar area," Hunter explains.

"That's the cottaging area," Bill says, "I'm not dressed for it, my shirt will be a beacon."

"I'll do it, just need a balaclava," Sally says, getting off the mobile scooter.

"I'll be waiting for you," Benny is quick to say in jest.

"Anyone out there. Even voyeurs who are stand-offish. Stay safely hidden at a distance, use a long lens."

"I'll start above us. Sun deck looking back." Sally says, and she's off before anyone can volunteer to join her. The other photographers sit back and enjoy their drinks, wondering when they can get away.

"So, did Lal tell you my ideas?" Benny says to Hunter.

"No, I haven't seen him."

"The seven deadly sins," Benny says, grinning.

"Seven deadly sins?"

"You got it, pride, greed, lust, envy, gluttony, wrath and sloth," Benny enthuses. "It all adds up."

"Explain," Hunter asks, and everyone is looking at Benny as he drives his scooter closer to the table.

"Lust was Kershner, down in the cottages – you got that now. Gluttony was Donna, the large lady on Sun Deck."

"Harsh," Hunter says.

"Pride, I reckon was Bogdan. You could see his pride by the way he played the saxophone when he was allowed to do his solo show. Wrath is you two guys, they went for Kieron but watch out."

"How about Eric, where does he fit in?" Hunter asks.

"I've not got it all worked out yet, but maybe sloth, at the bar twenty-four-seven?"

"There's a lot of evidence you've not seen," Hunter suggests.

"To be fair, not much," Jason adds.

"There is, Jason. The first few days are evidence gathering, then it begins to tell a story," Hunter explains.

"Data always tells a story," Benny says, genuinely interested.

Jason is still unconvinced that either of them knows what they are doing. Hunter wants to convert him, he wants Jason to feel that what he is doing has meaning.

"Listen to the musicians, the songs change but the musicians use familiar runs and phrases. That's the artist's signature. Kieron explained that to me just after the Captain told us all crew have habitual routes around the ship. Serial killers have a signature."

"Is that what we have? A serial killer?" Bill asks.

"Yes, Benny is onto something, he's kinda latched on to a note left on the first night," Hunter says.

"What note?" Benny asks, with the photographers all listening carefully to the exchange.

"Guys, you are all in the team, you can't share this knowledge outside. Right?"

They all nod in agreement.

"The note was a quote from Laurence of Arabia."

"I saw that film," Kusay says.

"Boy, you must have been bored," Bill adds.

"I was."

"Not from the film, the book. The book relates to the Seven Pillars of Wisdom," Hunter adds.

"So I was on the right track!" Benny says, chuffed with himself.

"Not exactly. The book was written during the Arab Revolt against the Ottoman Turks of around nineteen sixteen. At the start of the book, there's a poem, the quote was from that," Hunter explains.

"What was it?" Benny asks.

"I can't remember."

"You can't build it up like that and not tell us," Bill chimes in.

"It was written in old complicated English, I would need to read it again, but it was nonsense."

"Obviously not. What are the seven pillars of Wisdom?" Benny asks.

"I think they're mountain peaks," Hunter explains.

An officer enters, interrupting. "The Captain would like to see you in his quarters, sir."

"I'll be right along," Hunter says.

"I was asked to escort you immediately, sir," the officer states.

"Has there been another body found?"

"I can't say, Sir."

Hunter is up and following the officer.

"Sally!" Jason gasps, and the team are off too, leaving Benny.

36 THE NIGHT IS OVER

"Sir," Hunter says, addressing the Captain in the Bridge which looks out at the dark swelling sea.

"I'm giving you a lot of rope on my ship, Witowski, but it can't result in deaths!" The Captain says very firmly.

"To be fair, sir, you were getting deaths before we arrived and at the rate of three a night," Hunter defends.

"This is someone you sent on a task, by herself, without the head of security's knowledge."

"Sally?"

The Captain hits Hunter hard with a confirming nod. He is shocked. Sally's death has is far more personal to him.

"How?"

"Initial thoughts are strangulation. Ruby Jenkins is there about to run the crime scene and I have authorised her and her two senior officers to be armed. I don't do that lightly, but we have at least one serious killer on board."

"Sir, that is not a good move. The guns were sent only in case there were terrorists onboard, and no doubt for Philips and me to deploy first."

"Officer Jenkins thinks there could be a dangerous drug ring on board and I don't want my officers ill-equipped to defend themselves. All of this started after we left Panama and Ruby has explained the contents of Kieron Philips's book, Cruise Ship Heist, which sounds unsavoury, to say the least."

"We were never armed, sir."

"That is not how she explained it."

"Not on the ship."

"I would appreciate it if you didn't challenge my orders. There is no need to get involved in Ruby's work tonight. I need time to talk with head office."

"Sir, I've spent many years on ships, most as head of security myself. I trained her."

"You trained her well and I will share all her findings with you and Dwight Ritter. I would rather you were not running around the ship sending my crew off on duties that none of us has any knowledge off."

"That's unfair sir, I was put on the ship to find a killer, not take a back seat, sir."

"You were put on my ship so the current crew did not have to get involved, and you have been doing the opposite, you have been using them."

"It's not about drugs sir, it's about sex," Hunter states.

"You're guessing, Hunter! I was not happy with the trap you set at my medical centre and I asked for it to be closed. I am not happy Sally is dead. Not one bit. Her death hits very hard."

"It hits us all, sir, but I think that's what the killer

wants. He's divisive."

"I don't think any of us know what this killer wants. Let Ruby run things for a day. Worry about Kieron and I will talk to head office."

"Roger that, sir, we've done two days of evidence gathering. It will be useful to analyse it, but when it starts to speak to me I will have to follow it again. That is what I'm here for."

"You were never trained as a detective were you, Hunter?"

"What do you mean, sir?"

"You were head of security, just like Ruby."

"No sir, I'm not just like Ruby. I spent many years with the CIA finding killers far worse than the one you have on this ship."

"But this is different."

"No two serial killers are the same. They kill people until someone stops them. And the more they get away with it, the more they show-off. Ruby's never dealt with a killer, sir."

"You're excused, Witowski. Stay away from the crime scene."

Hunter enters the Crow's Nest to see Benny by himself looking sad and worried.

"Let's walk," Hunter demands, almost rudely.

Benny follows him out to the stairwell where a lift is waiting. They both enter and Hunter presses five, the promenade deck.

"You know it's far too rough and windy to walk outside. The promenade deck is closed," Benny says softly.

"We can walk inside."

The lift arrives unstopped, little is happening

around the ship as it approaches midnight. On a world cruise, the guests have explored every part of the ship by this time and it has become home. Unless there is a reason to stay out, they will be in bed or watching television. That leaves Roy Stevens with a problem because the 'per head spend' on ship starts to drop but his targets don't. Hunter is lost in his thoughts.

"She's dead isn't she?" Benny eventually asks, as they get to the art gallery section.

There's not one person, staff or guest in sight. Hunter stops to look at a set of three paintings of a young woman. The colour palette is dark and misty. In all three the girl is walking away, just glancing back. Both think it could be Sally, looking back from another dimension, trying to tell them what only she knows. She was smart. Her murder is spiteful.

"She would have been almost alone on that deck. No one would have been out there apart from a few guys, looking for kicks. No one would have risked the weather."

"The smokers," Benny replies automatically, "they go outside in any weather."

"You smoke?"

"I have enough medical problems… She was a nice girl. It's hard to consider her life being cut so short," Benny says.

"Did someone follow her out?"

"No, look," Benny offers a sketch of the bar, "I mapped this out when the photography was being done, then ticked the ones still there when you all left. More guests had just arrived from the show, so they will be there until midnight for a nightcap. But no one left with Sally."

Benny studies the one painting of a young girl

Hunter seems mesmerised by. She is walking in the sun, but the palette is still dark. It is a fantastic image.

"These three different paintings all have the signature of the same painter, and I don't mean his name in the corner."

"To me, it looks like the artist is investigating her innocence," Benny adds.

"I'm not so hot on my art, but I mean there is a little of the artist in everything he does. The serial killer leaves the same inevitable signature," Hunter says, his finger drifting to the artist's name. "There is something about all the killings that should lead us to one person. The Captain is panicked, I understand why, but he's wrong."

"What has he done?" Benny asks.

"Armed his security team."

"With guns?"

Hunter nods, "Yet this killer has never used a weapon. Except for on Donna,"

"Why kill Donna with a weapon?" Benny asks.

Hunter turns to Benny. His face lights up, "That is a touch of brilliance."

"Won't save Sally though," Benny says, fixed on the picture.

"No, but if we can save more people, then that was a touch of brilliance worth having."

"So, what does it mean?" Benny asks.

"We're looking for a killer whose capable of strangling someone with their bare hands, but when he's in a crowd, under pressure, he'll grab whatever he can and kill with it fast."

"You think he panicked with Donna? He never wanted to kill her." Benny says.

"We always thought that."

"Then why kill her, Hunter? Why?"

"Because he could."

"But why not just stand up and walk out?" Benny asks.

"Because he's gone beyond caring. You're good at this, Benny. Very good. This is why we look at the boards and ponder on them," Hunter says, his mind racing.

"What?" Benny asks, looking at his face and seeing his brain work.

"Kieron got something wrong."

"He certainly did or he wouldn't be in a coma"

"I need him to wake up. Tomorrow you can study the boards with us, tomorrow's another day."

"I don't think I could sleep now. I'm not ready for the day to end."

"Bed is where you do your best thinking, Benny."

"I'll think about Sally. I don't want to be alone."

Hunter looks at him and can see he needs a friend.

"Can you sleep on a sofa?" Hunter asks.

"I can not-sleep anywhere."

"How about guarding Kieron? That kills two birds with one stone. Sorry, bad use of words. But he'll have been moved to his own room by now."

37 CLOSE PERSONAL PROTECTION

"Who are you?" Kieron shouts, which wakes Benny with a start. Kieron stands holding onto the door frame, dizzy on his first attempt on his feet, and the ship moving in the rough sea. His hand goes up and discovers that his head is bandaged, then he looks down and much of his body is strapped, under a new set of pyjamas. He groans in agony. Benny is thinking fast, caught on the couch in his room, still in the same clothes as the night before. Not that Kieron ever saw him then.

"Hi. My name's Benny. I'm your close personal protection detail," he says, sitting up.

"Just one of you?"

"Yeah. You shouldn't be out of bed."

"It feels like it, it hurts. Can you come back later?"

"I'm your guard."

"Really? No offence, but you were asleep."

"I was deputised."

"To sleep in my room?"

"Exactly! I need to call Hunter and tell him you've woken up."

"I'll do that."

"No, you go to bed, I'll call him."

"They got me a mobility scooter? They think I'm a bloody cripple?" Kieron struggles to say, as he uneasily crosses the room and focusses on the empty scooter.

"No. I'm the bloody cripple," Benny says, with no malice, using his huge upper body strength to connect with the scooter and swing his legs over.

"Sorry, man," Kieron is fast to add.

"No worries, been called worse, but they have got you a mobility scooter. It should arrive later."

"What?" Kieron says, going to the phone.

"Until then, you're confined to bed. You have a list of broken bones."

"Hunter, I'm awake," Kieron says into the phone, and then hangs up, not waiting for a reply.

"I can get you up to speed," Benny says enthusiastically.

"Yeah?" Kieron replies with a doubtful tone.

"You did something wrong."

"No shit!" Kieron says, struggling in pain.

"The killer is like an artist. Every painting an artist does is in part a self-portrait."

"And?"

"The killer is painting a story of themselves."

"And?"

"You got close to him but lived. How he tried to kill you should give us a clue."

"He threw me over a balcony?" Kieron starts to remember.

"You witnessed first-hand one of the things he has experienced in his life."

"What?" Kieron's eyes widen. He wants more answers.

"That's all I have, I think that's right," Benny says.

"You need to go to the rest of those frigging art lectures then," Kieron says, feeling a shot of pain and holding his head.

There is a knock at the door, Benny drives over to it, watched by Kieron. Hunter comes and stands in the door, holding it open,

"Morning, Benny. You want to go and freshen up?"

"Sure," Benny replies.

"You're relieved, I've got this detail," Hunter says, still holding the door open and standing clear.

"Back soon Kieron," Benny shouts, just before the door closes behind him.

"He is my close protection detail?" Kieron asks.

"Don't underestimate him. He was paralysed stopping a raid on a deli in Miami."

"What is going on?" Kieron asks, heading back

towards the bed.

"Good news; you lived. Not so good news; there's been another murder and we've been relieved of duty on ship. Ruby's back running the case. Worse news; she and her two buddies, Lal and Krishma have been armed."

"What?

"How long was I out? A week?"

"No, it's day six in the Pacific."

"What does that mean? How long have we been here?" Kieron asks, sitting on the bed, confused by the timeline.

"As of this morning, we've been on three and a half days."

"So I was out for a day?"

"And a half."

"And you lost the job? Did you fix our salary before we were demoted?" Kieron asks, wincing with pain.

"No."

"Next time agree on the fee and get paid in advance."

"If there is a next job."

Hunter lifts Kieron's legs so he can sit back on the very comfortable double bed in the special suite that only a few ever get to see on a cruise ship.

"Long as they don't take our suites away." He leans back on the pillows. Hunter sits. Kieron is in pain and exhausted from his first few moves, "What's the damage?"

"Broken pelvis, few ribs, lungs collapsed but they sorted that out."

"And the head bandage?" Kieron adds, feeling a thunder in his head as he lays down, sinking into the pillows.

"Saved you having whiplash."

"What did?"

"Your head hitting the floor. Stopped it whipping back and straining your neck. That could have been nasty. You know how many people in minor car injuries have whiplash and can't ever work again."

"Yeah, I was so lucky. I just feel dizzy and nauseous."

"Oh, I forgot, cracked skull."

"But what did I do wrong? Benny said I did something wrong."

"You didn't do something wrong, you got something wrong. Your reconstruction idea and our timeline."

"Go on."

"You rolled on top of Ruby."

"I should have rolled on top of Ruby the night we were out and I wouldn't have taken a hit," Kieron forces out.

"I think she phoned you with an offer but you didn't pick up," Hunter grins.

"I was busy bleeding."

"The killer never rolled on top of Donna, he couldn't have. Had he done that, people around them would have noticed. Sure, he could have contained her and strangled her easily, as you showed, but that wasn't an option."

"I get that. OK."

"Something happened. She turned towards him and said something or noticed something. Laying side by side of her he had no leverage to strangle her without stirring attention, so went for the exposed hat pin, and took it before he covered her mouth."

"So he never disturbed anyone on either side," Kieron says exhausted, but genuinely trying to follow.

"What did she see?" Hunter asks.

"That he wasn't looking at the stars," Kieron says, very sleepily now.

"So, what was he doing?"

"Reading the note, angry he hadn't left it with Eric as planned." Kieron just manages, and Hunter is unsure that he heard or understood what he said.

"So glad you woke up bro, go back to sleep and dream about rolling on top of Ruby."

"I'm starving." Kieron agrees, as he either falls asleep or passes out.

"I'll order in. You don't look like you want to get dressed and go out." Hunter says, straightening up his body.

Benny, Hunter and a wide-awake Kieron are digging into a silver service breakfast in the sitting room of Kieron's suit. Not only is there an incredible selection of food, but a private butler to serve and order anything that might be missing. A phone rings out in the background on speaker. Kieron is now dressed in shorts and a shirt, revealing more of his heavy bandaging. Benny too has changed his clothes. Hunter is reading sheets of paper then passing them to Kieron.

"Tox screen on all bodies is clear, so it's unlikely to be drugs. I fancy sex."

"I don't think I'm up to it," Kieron says, looking at the paperwork. "But, maybe after I've eaten."

"You guys are funny," Benny says.

"Yeah. Comes from spending all this time working together." Hunter growls with sarcasm.

"It shows. How long is it?" Benny asks.

"About ten."

"Ten years, wow."

"Ten weeks," Kieron interjects. "Ten very long weeks. Five weeks ago I took a bullet for him, now this."

"I'll send the tox results to Dwight, he's obviously not answering his phone." Benny offers.

The Butler opens the door for Lal.

"It is good to see you up, Kieron," Lal says.

Both men notice the gun in a closed pouch on Lal's belt.

"Can I bring the boards in?" Lal asks.

They nod and Lal goes out again with the Butler following.

"If I go through the boards in detail with Dwight and make a friend," Kieron suggests, "maybe I can rescue this gig."

Kieron re-fills his plate again. He has his appetite back.

38 GRATIFICATION

Psychological gratification is the usual motive of a serial killer. In most cases, it involves sexual themes, if not contact, that results in uncontrollable anger and eventual death. There are often elements of thrill-seeking, challenges and attention-seeking. In all of the killings, there will be similarities in the execution and a pattern to the locations. As these killings happened on a cruise ship, both the killer and his murders are confined to this steel motor vessel that has the population and facilities of an inescapable small village.

Serial killers are often hard to find because they look and act just like those around them, often being very close to the investigation. Hunter had read in his ship's library book about the over helpful school caretaker Ian Huntley in the British Soham murders. He had looked at Benny's enthusiasm sceptically but everything is an exploratory exercise, and that somehow triggered him to question Kieron rolling on top of Ruby. Now they have some knowledge it is time to exclude, as well as try to include. They need to build new boards. The first spreadsheet must be of known elements specific to each murder including the attempt on Kieron. The one thing that is constant is physical ability, strangulation favoured over any form of weapon.

"We don't have any canonical software on the ship, so we're using a good old fashioned spreadsheet model," Kieron says loudly at the mobile phone in the middle on the table.

"Doesn't matter how the data comes as long as I get it, it's actually better we talk it through," Dwight says on the conference call. "Love your timeline, I get the killer not rolling on top of Donna. It makes sense. She watches him read the note that haunts him about Eric, she gets it stuffed in her mouth. It makes her and very possibly Kershner both accidents."

"Physical fitness or gymnastic capability we have attributed in the first column next to the victims' names," Kieron explains.

"Great. I see some subgroups there. All good." Dwight says.

A dialogue has started, and this session is already proving that Kieron is a player again and Benny is a team member. Hunter may be a caged lion but he is totally engaged as they go through the board. Dwight is double-checking what he has picked up,

"Stop me if I get anything wrong. Donna McGovern was easily contained on the floor and kept silent while she was stabbed. It required quick thinking to take the hatpin and great ability to escape. The use of a weapon is unusual, the note everyone agrees was meant for Eric. Multiple scattered stab wounds are normally a pattern when emotions run high, when the victims are in an intermit relationship like husband and wife. But Donna was cruising alone and the stab wounds, whilst multiple, were all fairly accurately to the heart. The first one may well have been fatal. So whilst the use of a weapon is unusual, we're assuming it's because this murder was not meant."

Dwight takes a breath and continues,

"Peter Kershner was a large man, lifted overboard after being silenced efficiently with a blow, plus having his cruise card exchanged. That card exchange goes in column two as an impish act. However, even if the murder was off plot, once again physical ability is essential to have done this in the time restraints of lights-out."

Over the speaker, there is motor like sound and Dwight starts again,

"Eric Clifford was either encouraged downstairs or forcibly marched down, then tossed into the laundry chute. He is still considered to be the main murder and the reason all this started. The note is thought to have been for him. The note is from Lawrence of Arabia and his wife confirmed that he had both seen the film and loved it. I have your route and timeline, good work.

"Bogdan the sax player was strangled and is possibly the serial killer's planned second murder. Sally and Manoj were also strangled again reinforcing that the killer is capable and physically fit. Maybe the later deaths were to shut people up because they knew something."

Eyes in the room turn to Kieron because he is the only victim in the column whose horizontal row has nothing against it. He didn't die. The silence in the room is broken by the speakerphone.

"I guess you're all looking at the Brit?" Dwight says with a decent chuckle. It is nice that he has a sense of humour but he is always on point, a man of fact and data.

"Seriously team, in any murder investigation the body is the biggest part of the evidence. You have a live one here. Think. Examine him."

"I opened the door crew door, then I was in the air, there was no time to struggle, I didn't know I was being hit," Kieron says.

As uncomfortable as it is, Kieron is centre stage, he is trying to think about how he was attacked. He stands and with the restrictions of his pain, he re-enacts his step forward and again. Hunter who had rehearsed the move when he was at the crime scene stands next to him. Just as he had mimed when Ruby opened the crew door on the level above him, he puts his left hand across his body and on Kieron's neck.

"Yeah, that's it," Kieron says.

Hunter grabs the belt on his pants with his right hand and gently instigates a leg sweep at Kieron's shins.

"OK. Enough. It hurts."

Lal steps in to steady him and Benny watches in amazement as Hunter swiftly unclips and removes the gun from Lal's belt and re-seats it behind his own belt in the small of his back.

"Shit! That was the move, Hunter." Kieron admits having to sit.

"Quite some sneaky move," Benny says in automatic.

"Talk to me team, I don't have a picture link," Dwight says.

"So we know the killer has physical ability, but more than that he's got skills," Hunter says, moving behind Benny and performing a simple strangle. "Hand in face, cross arms, wrist turns into the neck."

Benny taps out fast. Nodding, he agrees it would work. Even being used as a dummy to be strangled, he is enjoying being part of the team.

"Let's ask Simon if the strangulations were wrist pressure, not fingers, but I think we know the answer," Hunter says.

Kieron is getting physically tired and has to sit, not that Dwight can see that. Hunter looks at the second column on the board.

"Dwight. Our second column, you could call character. There is a mischievous element: the note 'Scatter, you featureless puppets, scatter', the hatpin, the swapping of cruise cards, checking in at the muster station as an extra guest, the ordering of drinks on a dead man's card. This looks to me like attention-seeking."

"I like that. Again, it looks complex and the software can deal with that," Dwight says, absorbing everything.

"I wouldn't mind seeing that software when you're ready, Dwight," Benny says.

"Sure but it feels like day-one here and I'm drowning," comes the genuine voice from Miami via satellite and out of their speaker.

"Tell us about it, Buddy," Hunter says.

"One thing I do know is that I need more staff here."

"Something we can't do this end, the Captain's already not liking interference," Hunter shares.

"He's a suspect until eliminated. In fact, the great thing about this investigation is that we only have nineteen hundred suspects, that's twelve hundred guests and seven hundred crew and we know exactly where they all are," Dwight shares.

"The killer's hiding in plain sight," Kieron says.

"The best always do. Elimination will be key. When I get all your data in, I'll be able to start producing your spreadsheets for you," Dwight replies.

"Now you know why we're so glad to have you onboard, Dwight," Hunter says.

"Hurrah to that," Kieron says.

The Captain enters with Ruby and Jason. Kieron goes for the phone, "Let's get back on this later, Dwight?"

"Good call, time out."

Dwight is gone but it was perfect for the Captain to just catch them working as a team.

"Going well?" Captain Neil Reynolds asks.

Hunter hands him Lal's weapon.

Lal goes to his belt and realises his gun has gone.

39 CAPTAIN SAYS

"Sorry Lal, but Kieron and I have been doing this stuff a long time." Hunter turns from him to the Captain. "Just making a point, sir."

"The only point you are making Witowski is that

you're not a team player," Captain Neil Reynolds says, giving the gun back to Lal and making a point of his own.

"With respect, sir, the tox screens are back, all clear. This is not about drugs, we're not worried about a drug ring, the crew do not need to be armed."

"Noted Witowski, I shall mention your resistance in my log." The Captain turns to Kieron, "It is good to see you up and about, Philips."

The Captain walks to Benny and shakes his hand.

"Hi, I'm Captain Neil Reynolds."

"Benny Raymond."

"He's helping," Hunter says.

"Really?" The Captain looks disapprovingly at Witowski.

"You told me I couldn't use staff."

"I've been deputised," Benny tells the Captain.

"He's a data analyst, perfect addition to the team at sea." Hunter shares.

"I'm not sure as I approve of using guests while on their holiday."

"Captain, this is the holiday of a lifetime, the first time I have felt really useful since being put in this chair," Benny insists.

"Sailing the ship is your call sir, finding the killer is mine. I checked with head office and that is still the case. Now Benny here understands Ritter like none of this team does," Hunter states.

The Captain is uncomfortable being spoken to in this way, and his battle with Hunter feels like it has escalated. Ruby jumps in,

"I don't have a problem giving Dwight Ritter information, sir. This team need not get so big we don't know who is doing what; that was the problem last time," she says.

There is a moment of quiet as Hunter realises who his battle is really against, who has hung him out to dry. Kieron is a moment behind. Benny is not used to politics at this face to face level and Jason just keeps his head down as the tension in the room rises.

"Ritter will be inputting every member of the crew and every guest into his system now," Hunter says to Ruby.

"Head office has all guest and staff information they need," Ruby is quick to add. "Our job is to find the killer. Not annoy guests and crew."

"They need the headshot taken at embarkation and every picture Jason's team has ever taken, plus security footage of every working camera at the time of each murder," Hunter says. "I hope both your department and Jason's will oblige."

"That will take days," Ruby says angrily.

"Hey, who's got my phone?" Kieron asks, bored with the petty power struggle.

Ruby digs into her pocket and tosses him the phone which Kieron begins to check. He is looking for the messages from Ruby he missed the night he was attacked.

"The big problem we will have is bandwidth for uploading, but the facial recognition will do the pictures almost instantly and start to build timelines for almost every person on the ship," Benny says.

Ruby's phone beeps as she stands in the middle of Hunter and the Captain. She pulls it out, about to read it but Kieron speaks before she gets the chance.

"It's just me accepting your suggestions, Ruby," Kieron says in a business-like way.

"I don't think I'll be needing that now, and you

have enough on your plate while you're injured," Ruby says, defiantly.

Hunter smiles, he knows about the suggestive invitations to her room, "What's that, Ruby? Maybe Benny or I could jump in for you while Kieron's injured," he suggests.

The Captain senses the tension, "We need to work as a team and get on with this. Hunter, my guys are armed, your resistance is not teamwork."

"I'm on the team sir, and at the moment Kieron and I are the only two on this ship who are not suspects. The computer will start to eliminate people, not me, not Ruby, not head office. So, if you can let Dwight have the 'in and out log' for every officer on the bridge including yourself, sir. We might be able to eliminate you from our enquiries. Anything that any of your officers have that can help this investigation, however small, the computer can use."

"I have some research I have been doing on Lawrence of Arabia, something I didn't think anyone else would do, and only because I know the film," Neil starts afresh.

"Go for it," Kieron says, laying down, sinking into his pillow, finding it hard to keep his eyes open.

"All the bullet points or the punch line?" Captain Neil asks.

"Best we get all the points and let Mr Ritter's software connect what is pertinent," Benny suggests ready to take notes on his steering-column mounted touchpad.

"It's a very descriptive, stylish book, but it never mentions the seven pillars of wisdom."

"Neither does our killer," Hunter says, not as keen as Benny for intricate detail from the Captain's research.

"No, but the title of the book was originally for an earlier work. That intrigued me because all of you felt Donna was killed as an accident, meaning the note was meant for an earlier victim."

"OK," Benny says as typing.

"Team. I am feeling a little dizzy, do you mind if I just close my eyes for a moment?" Kieron asks, Ruby sits next to him and feels his brow for a fever.

"His book was going to be a work on the seven greatest cities of the Middle East," Captain Neil shares.

"Which are?" Ruby asks, keen to show she is interested in what he has to offer.

"Cairo, Izmir, which is a cruise port, but Lawrence referred to then as Smyrna. Beirut, Constantinople, Aleppo-."

"Syria, a place I'm never allowed to forget," Kieron drearily reflects showing he is not totally asleep.

"Plus Damascus and Medina. Lawrence destroyed that manuscript and started his diaries under the same title. But, none of these places are on our world cruise."

"Detectives often struggle down blind alleys," Hunter says, sure they are all just humouring the Captain now.

"Lawrence was, without doubt, a frustrated writer."

Hunter nods a little, then shakes himself from a bored semi-listening state. The remark has hit a nerve.

"Frustration? The pause before delayed gratification was in the book I read on serial killers. Killing, murder being a release," Hunter says. "Do you want to borrow it, sir?"

"No. Lawrence failed with the first attempt."

"Then the diaries became a marvel?" Ruby adds.

"No, Lawrence lost the diaries. He claims he fell asleep on a train and had them stolen in Reading. The published book appears to be a third attempt, the delayed gratification. It was also in a different style and quality to the eventually found lost diaries."

"Are you implying it was not his own work?" Kieron asks. "Like we have a copycat killer?"

"No." The Captain replies avoiding being drawn in. He continues with his story's journey.

"Reviews suggest that the film adaptation reveals much about the man that the book does not. More of his dark sexual desires otherwise only found in our poem at the front of the book. The note in evidence is from the poem."

"Very contrived; that will test the software, but sexuality might be our column three," Benny says, then looks up and sees Jason give him the zip-across-the-mouth mime. Benny knows he should not interrupt the Captain but the asleep Kieron joins in without opening his eyes,

"One of the key mistakes in any investigation is to consider the suspect to be without intelligence," Kieron states, and Ruby gently brushes his hair back and leans in,

"Just rest."

"Did Lawrence write the poem?" Hunter asks.

"Yes and no, he was quoting from a translation from Herodotus, an ancient Greek Historian." Captain Neil pauses for Benny to catch up, then turns to the evidence board. "Herodotus developed the method of systematic investigation, collecting materials and then critically arranging them as you are here."

"That is all too weird," Kieron mutters.

Ruby gently puts her hand over his mouth, but he

nibbles her finger. He is not as ill as he is making out.

"But good to have," Benny says.

"That wasn't the punch line," Neil says.

"Captain, I have an idea. Why don't I drive the ship and you run the investigation, you've got a flair for this?" Hunter says, in jest. A firm look from Neil suggests he is certainly not amused, nor finished, nor going to allow Hunter to sail the ship.

"I'm not sure such complexity is behind a killer knocking off cruisers unless he is just making his stage bigger and fancier," Kieron suggests, thinking the Captain's little show could now go on for as long as the film does.

"Do you not want me to carry on?" Neil asks, a little put out.

"OK Captain, I'm up with you," Benny says wanting more.

"Benny, I think you're right, the next column is sex," Neil says.

"Me too," Kieron says, enjoying Ruby's hands on him. She immediately takes them away and stands away from the bed.

"This poem, the clue in Donna's mouth is sexual. It starts 'I loved you, so I drew these tides of men into my hands, and wrote my will across the sky in stars'. Sex is then woven throughout with many references. 'Envy he outran me, and took you apart: Into his quietness. Love, the way-weary, groped to your body'," Neil continues.

"You British guys have some weird wordy sex. Couldn't he just put on a Barry White album and get on with it?" Hunter smiles.

"That is all sexual, right?" The Captain asks.

"Sure, but we hadn't settled on sex," Ruby says.

"I had," Kieron says. "No, actually, since when did we slip from alcohol to sex?"

"Since you were asleep," Hunter says.

"None of our victims have been sexually assaulted, but they all drank," Hunter explains.

"The poem dedication starts 'To SA.' Speculation is that S.A. is Selim Ahmed a boy from Syria of whom Lawrence was very fond of until the lad died, probably from typhus, aged 19. Lawrence received the news of his death some days before he entered Damascus."

"So you're saying we need to find a man who has recently lost a nineteen-year-old lover boy and is now attacking seventy-year-old guests," Hunter starts. "Hey, it's good to challenge."

"It's a good story," Ruby says.

The Captain smiles, "It's not finished yet."

Kieron closes his eyes again.

Hunter looks at his watch, "We'll be docking in a few days."

The Captain looks at him, disappointed.

"Joke, sir. This is the stuff that gets overlooked, we are with you," Hunter smiles.

"Selim Ahmed went to work as a water boy at the ancient archaeological site at Carchemish, on the modern Syria-Turkey border where Lawrence adopted him as his companion. Ahmed's fellow Arabs nicknamed him Dahoum, meaning, 'the little dark one'!"

"Captain," Hunter says, lifting the larger plan of the ship pinned to one of the boards to front and centre and pointing to the Crow's Nest, "you are officially one of the team."

40 THE WATER BOY

"Prince Dahoum and the Crow's Nest are without the doubt the centre of our investigation," Kieron says, circling the Crow's Nest in a bold pen.

"Column five should be Crow's Nest," Benny suggests.

"That wasn't the reason I actually came in," Captain Neil Reynolds says.

"Sure was, Captain," Hunter says.

"I felt my research underdeveloped, but I came in because we need to suggest a press release. The pressure is high in Miami," Neil says.

"You just wrote the best story, sir. One that keeps people happy but sends them off in all kinds of wrong directions," Kieron says, now sitting up and fully awake.

"Wrong?" Neil asks.

"Not necessarily wrong, but it's a story that takes them miles away, a great story to feed the press," Hunter says.

"I'm not sure about that, it rather drops a member of staff in the spotlight," Neil suggests.

"Trust us, we'll work on that. We wrote a whole book of misdirection to cover up a ton of mess on the last ship. Press will love it and it's not about the murders. It will give us more than a day as they go here, there and everywhere that is Lawrence. They'll be reading the book, watching the film, and finding experts…" Kieron says.

"We'll add some fluff to it," Hunter says.

"These stories just give you guys a bucket load of publicity," Ruby smiles wryly.

"We can quote it as your research, Captain?"

Hunter asks.

"No, no, no. You take that," Neil offers.

"We'll come up with another solution," Ruby offers.

"We could just say there've been six murders onboard ship and we don't have a clue who did them," Hunter suggests.

"I think head office will agree, taking the spotlight from the ship is a good route to take," Neil says, even though he can see Ruby disapproves.

"Are you sure, sir? They will be taking all the credit?"

"We need to embroider it a little, but leave it with us," Hunter says.

"No, let me help," Ruby offers sarcastically. "From the lifeboats, the ship's crew felt helpless as the heroes swam away from the circling white sharks."

"Desperate for their supper," Kieron interjects.

"Circling white sharks desperate for their supper," Ruby repeats in amazement, her anger growing.

"Hungry, add the word hungry," Benny suggests.

"Who are you?" Ruby asks, annoyed.

"A guest," Benny says firmly, feeling strong enough not to take any insults now the Captain has accepted him.

"Hungry lifeboats?" Ruby says.

"The two ex-special-forces in their bright yellow survival suits swam as fast as they could, exhausted from their high altitude parachute drop as every hungry shark in the area rushed in," Hunter says.

"...Nudging them! I can work that up, then distil the story around the note found in the first victim's mouth," Benny suggests.

"Really?" Ruby interrupts. "No!"

"Yes, sir. The point sir, is we're wagging the dog," Hunter says slowly.

"Wagging the dog?" Captain Neil asks. "I still haven't watched that film."

"When the tail does the talking, it manages to wag so hard the whole body moves. Fake news works; it doesn't have to be right or wrong, just sensational. So, 'they were flown out to join the ship, in the middle of the Pacific by the heroic US Coast Guard in a converted Airbus taken to the limit of its flight range'. That's a story that tells of heroes, but actually tells them nothing other than we're dealing with it. Stakes are high, but we're dealing with it," Hunter explains.

"We'll run it by you," Kieron says.

"Next we need to get Prince Dahoum down here and interview him," Hunter says.

"I agree, let Roy Stevens know." The Captain says, putting his arm around Ruby and walking her out.

"Prince Dahoum's not the killer," Jason says, now the Captain has left and he feels he has the ability to speak.

"No?" Hunter turns to put him in the spotlight.

"He was still behind the bar when you got news of Sally."

"And you said we knew nothing, had nothing, just shows how much we do have."

"It feels like nothing."

"It's not nothing."

"Ok, Ok, I get it, it's a whole elimination thing," Jason agrees.

Benny is studying the charts, he's data-centric, "In Sally's row on our chart, if we use the Crow's Nest photographs and each other, we eliminate Jason, me, Bill and Michael and all in their pictures, see my plan." Benny types.

"Jason, can you send every picture file you have, with its timestamp and add where it was taken? Benny can help," Hunter asks, "the answer is yes, by the way."

"Yes," Jason obeys.

Hunter holds the door open and Benny leads Jason out, leaving him with a very tired looking Kieron.

"I got a bed-job for you."

"I don't want a bed-job."

"Keep Ruby amused while we get on with our job."

"OK. I do want a bed-job. How long do you want me to keep her busy? A day or two?"

"We'll be lucky if you can manage a minute or two." Hunter smiles.

Kieron closes his eyes with tiredness.

The Captain leads Ruby into his adjacent quarters.

"It's how the press works. Let the investigators be the heroes, the press loves a heroic story."

"We deserve credit," Ruby adds.

"We do whatever keeps the ship out of the main story until it is over and then we can sell them the great features onboard," he pauses. "We're staff, Ruby. We get leave and all the comforts of working for a huge corporation. They've risked life even getting here and if it goes wrong they will take the blame. They will go down in flames."

41 LITTLE DARK ONE

The joys of a suite are manifold, not just the cabin size and additional rooms but a personal butler who can fetch drinks. However, Prince Dahoum previously offered a personal service and it is that service they need to exploit. The hotel manager, Roy Stevens, has conveniently worked the staff levels behind the bar in the Crow's Nest such that Prince can cheekily slip away. He is being trapped. Roy and Hunter are in the second bedroom, chatting until the butler answers the ring at the door. Dahoum stands behind it, looks at the butler and shows him the perfectly presented Paloma Hermosa.

"Testing me, weren't you, darling?" Prince Dahoum presents the beautiful drink with a flourish as he wafts in.

"I had no idea what it was," the butler replies flatly.

"That's why you do your job and I do mine."

"And I suppose the nibbles are in your tacky little pocket?"

Prince turns sharply on the butler. "Edible flowers! Tequila, elderflower liqueur, fresh fruit and egg whites. I did have to run to the main kitchen, but it's perfect."

"Well done!" Kieron shouts from the bedroom. "You didn't learn that onboard the ship."

Prince walks through with a smile and a swagger until he sees how bashed up and bandaged Kieron is. He stops dead.

"Should you be drinking?"

"That is exactly what I need to do," Kieron starts, and then switches tact, "was it you who threw me over the rail?"

"No!" Dahoum insists, placing the drink in

Kieron's hand slowly.

"Why am I getting flashbacks of your face?"

"Lots of men get that, dear."

"Why Prince, why in my confusion am I seeing you on the crew stairs balcony on deck nine, then at the laundry chute here on eight?"

"We've never been together by the laundry chute," Prince says firmly, "unless…?"

"Unless what, why? We were there," Kieron leads him.

Ignoring the butler, Prince sits on the bed and addresses Kieron softly, "were you in a mask?"

"The masked ball."

"Was that you?" Prince is now getting excited.

"And the night I was thrown over?"

"No. I was never there that night. Manoj had just been killed and I was alone, worked off my feet without any break. I had no time to play down there."

"I wasn't talking about playing, I was talking about throwing me over. I saw your face."

"If you nearly died, maybe mine was the face you conjured for a last moment of pleasure," Dahoum says with a little more cheek. He is confident of his alibi for every minute he was working that bar.

Kieron sips his drink and relaxes.

"If you are going to want more of those, I'll need to get some supplies."

"Where did you learn to make this, Dahoum?" Kieron asks more firmly.

"Mexico."

"You worked there?"

"No, I travelled, five-star!"

"As a companion to someone you met on a ship?"

Prince starts to look worried, but before his mind

can work, the connecting door opens and Hunter and Roy Stevens walk in.

"Sit down," Hunter demands.

"Not from this ship. It was years ago," Prince says in a panic.

Hunter draws a chair to the bed. Dahoum feels boxed in.

Ruby Jenkins is still feeling out of the loop, the security of which on this ship she is the head. Sitting in her office she calls Dwight Ritter in Miami, but he doesn't take her call because he's in a meeting.

"Would you mind calling him back?" The operator suggests from the office of the very shipping line Ruby works for.

"Just tell him Officer Jenkins, head of security called."

"Which ship?"

"He knows which ship." Ruby answers, even more agitated.

"I tell all my boys to watch the film, that's why it's always full. Mr Lawrence was a genius. Don't underestimate the number of married men who want to have fun."

"And you oblige?" Roy Stevens asks.

"We have to, the sexual fantasy is why they cruise."

Hunter is about to ask another question, but Roy places a hand on his shoulder to stop him.

"We, you said we. Who else is involved?" Roy asks.

"Mr Stevens, sir," Prince begs.

"Who?"

Hunter realises that Roy has picked up on something that could be vital to their investigation.

Dahoum may have an alibi, but if there are others then the circle of suspects increases.

"Who Dahoum? If none of you have anything to do with this investigation I promise no internal punishment," Roy snaps.

"None?" Prince asks in fear, looking between the three men. He also knows the Butler could answer this question as could many others, so it's better for him to take the immunity deal.

"Jasmin, just Jasmin," He reveals.

"Jasmin?" Kieron asks, knowing the beauty he is referring to.

"Yes, she's mixed nuts," he says.

"Mixed nuts?" Kieron continues in complete shock.

"Yes, baklâ bayot."

"Shemale?" Hunter asks bluntly.

Dahoum turns to him. "That's disrespectful."

"Disrespectful?" Hunter asks harshly. He is back to the no-nonsense approach.

"Shemale infers a sex worker, the correct term for Jazz is transsexual," Prince says.

"What the hell are you if you're not sex workers?" Hunter charges a little louder.

"No," Prince says. "No. We just offer a little therapy and fun in the bicycle sheds for customers who have left it way too late to come out."

"Bicycle sheds?" Roy asks.

"One of the guests nicknamed it that ages ago and it stuck. A little slap and tickle at the laundry chute and that's all they get," Prince says.

"And what do you get out of it?" Hunter asks.

"She's a man?" Kieron says, still in shock.

"Jazz? No. She's transsexual." Prince says. "Some

men are sexually attracted to transgender women and feminised men rather than admitting they're gay," Prince explains.

"But she has the body of a woman. She has no waist and great breasts," Kieron is totally confused.

"She has everything darling, everything. But neither of us are killers. Never."

"What do you get out of it?" Hunter repeats.

"We make sure they order their drinks through us. Our numbers beat any of the other waiters so we make a big company incentive, that's it."

"We need to tell Dwight, group four, sex. Has subgroups too," Hunter growls, thinking.

There is a knock and the butler opens it to a fake voiced fanfare. Something strange is happening outside but only Prince takes the few steps to look.

Hunter looks at him, "Stay put, we are far from finished with you."

Dahoum's excitement reveals nothing of what is to come, neither does the tube that appears through the door before they see Wendy, the entertainment host, wearing a world war two uniform, sitting astride a mobility scooter decorated as a military tank.

"Roy," Elvis says to greet the hotel manager he was not expecting to see.

"Not the best timing," Roy says to Elvis.

"We bring Mr Philips his tank."

"Gentlemen, this is Elvis our entertainment manager, and Wendy, one of the hosts. But I'm as puzzled as you appear to be," Roy explains.

"Some of this stuff clips off," Elvis says.

"Why-?" Roy starts, gesturing the tank-like scooter.

"That might be my fault," Hunter interjects, "I

asked for a mobility scooter to have a tank look, I wasn't expecting it to be turned into a tank. And I have no idea how the entertainment department got involved, though it is very nice to meet you, Elvis."

"We had some war set dressing that was ideal," Elvis explains.

"Or wasn't! I don't need a mobility scooter." Kieron states.

"If you want to go about the ship, you have to be on a scooter; doctor's orders," Hunter explains.

"Even if I had to use a scooter I would not take a tank around the shops, it's ridiculous!"

"I like it," Prince says.

Elvis turns to Kieron sitting on the bed, "Fine, I see we have gone over the top, but we need some help and I've heard that you are quite the dark one."

"Quite the dark one?" Kieron says.

Now everyone is confused.

42 A VIEW FROM THE BRIDGE

"I always think it looks scarier from here," Roy says, standing at the Bridge window looking forward at the raging sea throwing the ship up and down seemingly with no effort. A wave rises like a mythical god and strikes the glass hard, splashing right up over the deck eight's windows. Roy ducks back, which amuses the young officers.

"It's worse when you are underwater for a while," Neil says as Roy passes his Captain's workstation, where he is discussing fuel charts with his officers. Roy has decided to put as much distance between him and the window as he can. Not that a few feet would ever help him against any of these waves if a window was to implode.

"You're joking, right? Underwater?" Roy asks, as he joins Doctor Simon Yates and Hunter Witowski at the back of the Bridge waiting for the Captain to finish what are obviously essential duties. Neil turns, even he can't walk a straight line.

"Couldn't you have gone around this storm?" Roy dares to ask, but his question is ignored.

"Elvis is right, there is no way his mad unicyclist can go on stage tonight and the weather won't get any better until midday tomorrow, I think Kieron should do it" Neil shares.

"But we have nights when there's no show. Surely Elvis can close the theatre for a night?" Simon says. "As Kieron's doctor, I have to restate he really isn't a well man. Certainly not well enough to stand on stage and give a talk. Anyone else would be on bed rest for weeks if not months."

"They said that five weeks ago when he was shot. Look, if he does the show, he has to stay on the scooter, even though he is superhuman. But the real question is why do it? I'm only interested if it in some way helps further the investigation," Hunter says.

"If it causes more unrest about a murderer being on board, I'm with Simon. We are in enough trouble. If it helps the guests feel safer, then I'm with Roy. The guests are releasing statements on social media that the press then quote, we need to get control of this," Neil says.

"With regard to your point about the theatre being dark on occasions, Simon, that's true. But as we head further into the Pacific we always have more trouble with artists and weather than anywhere. We get more than our fair share of dark nights so if we can avoid one and make this a benefit to all, it would be nice," Roy explains.

"It's bigger than just that, Roy. Should the French authorities not allow us to dock in Tahiti or anywhere else in Polynesia, your entertainment problem will be secondary to fuel and food," the Captain suggests.

"They have to let us dock for essential supplies!" Roy says.

"There is no have to at all," Neil informs them.

"After them, it will be Australia saying no," Hunter adds.

"What is their concern about docking?" Roy asks.

"Apart from us having a serial killer on board?" the Captain starts, "Tahiti currently has representatives from Beijing, Shanghai and Shenzhen visiting the islands. It is a long-planned strive for a bigger slice of the booming outbound Chinese tourist market. Our head office has been told in no uncertain terms not to underestimate the importance of this. Apart from the events aimed at showcasing the region's attractions and culture, France has streamlined the visa application process and opened more visa centres in China. Chinese eyes are on the French Polynesian authorities to see how they deal with our ship trying to enter Polynesian waters and offload guests with a killer amongst them."

"Then they need to see we're on top of this," Roy states.

Hunter is quiet, listening.

"But Philips is too ill, he's not your answer," Simon re-states.

"My Entertainment Manager has heard Kieron has a very good talk he's done on a previous ship and can tow the company line," Roy argues.

"Roy, there's no question about that. He's brilliant with endless stories to tell. But he's not here to ease this political powder keg," Hunter adds.

"One show, thirty minutes only, sitting down on his tank. Helping reassure the guests we have everything under control would be a great help," Roy suggests.

"It could help quell the growing unrest on ship. The queues at reception and requests for guests to see me are out of control," Neil says. "None of which can be ignored if we hope to dock anywhere."

"To say the workload on my staff is high is an understatement," Roy adds. "Done properly this could do so much good and solve so many problems."

"By tonight, press then social media will have your story we talked through earlier, Captain. Isn't that enough?" Hunter says.

"Please don't refer to it as my story, and with the weather the way it is I doubt there will be internet for guests to post anything for a while."

"They'll get to hear tomorrow if not tonight. On stage, Kieron will be asked questions we can't even think of and he needs answers he doesn't have. So why is he doing it? Just to help reception staff?" Hunter asks, seemingly delivering a mixed message.

"Let him rest," Simon says, feeling the debate is over.

"And hope the murders are over?" Neil asks, cynically.

"Sure, and if the killer is considering he's finished, a stage act about him might just antagonise him to kill again," Hunter frowns, looking at each of them.

"I am no psychologist, but, serial killers rarely stop

out of the blue, normally their actions escalate. I'd say the killer will either be in the theatre watching or out killing again." Doctor Simon Yates says.

"Why is Ruby not here? It's me that gets it in the ear from her every time she's left out," Hunter growls.

"My error." The Captain says and he turns. "First officer, ask Ruby Jenkins to join me on the Bridge."

"Sir."

"If the murderer strikes while the show is on, we can at least rule out everyone who is in the theatre. That's if Ruby can figure out a way of knowing who is in the theatre," Hunter says, in a leading way. "Maybe the authorities might allow those eliminated to go ashore."

―

A torch scans an otherwise dark room in silence until a phone ring changes everything.

"Shhh!" Mary shouts to her phone. Both the blue light from it and reflected light from the raised torch light her face.

"Mary, we ain't gonna bring you on no more raids if you always making noise." Is a voice from the other side of the room.

"I don't want you doing no more raids, Croc." She says, then answers her phone, whispering, "Text me, I can't speak."

"Can we take these?"

Dressed in black, with a black hat covering much of his dark skin, a youth called Croc is looking at some old 45 vinyl records in paper sleeves.

"What? No!" Mary says.

He leafs through the singles, then dumps them back down, "I ain't never heard of any of these."

Her phone beeps again. "Shut up!"

An aimed and focussed light fires up and hits Mary. Caught like a rabbit in headlights, she looks up at Janey E, her favourite reporter. Next to her, the cameraman has lights on above his camera.

"Ok Mary, we've done the whole hiding bit," Janey E says. "You can begin your report to camera."

Mary faces the lens, slightly overacting.

"Hi! It's Wild Mary here, and we're in the dark because I don't want to get caught breaking in, it would be too hard to explain. Because I ain't breaking in, even though I did have to break in. You see my colour, 'five 0' ain't never gonna believe me. We looking for a USB stick and I don't even know what one of them is!"

The room lights go on.

"Perfect," Janey E says, having hit the switch. She looks around the room which is nothing but packed cardboard boxes, then takes herself to the most densely boxed area and sets up for her piece to camera. Just as she's about to start, Mary starts ranting loudly, so she has to wait.

"Why they taking so long to answer the phone, damn people, they just called m-" she stops herself, "Wild Marys."

"I know that's Wild Mary's, I just rang it. Is that you, Mary?"

"Yes, it's me!"

Janey E waves at the cameraman to turn around and the lights in the room swing onto Mary. She feels the spotlight again and smiles.

"Tell Izzy the boys just texted me a story. I'm sending it over for her to turn into a special Wild Mary press release."

"Is it rubbish?"

"Rubbish?! No, it's brilliant, BUT it doesn't mention my diner! Mix it in, then release to just a few special journalists, and you know our favourite Janey on WXB20 has to have it first, honey."

"WBX25," Janey corrects her.

"Yeah, damn right."

"No, you say it."

"WBX25."

"Mary, say the whole line again for me, right from I'm sending you a press release…"

"I'm sending you a Wild Mary press release. Let Izzy check it then release it to our few special journalists, but it has to go to Janey E on …"

Mary watches as Janey mouths the letters.

"WBX25 first."

"You just said that, Mary!" Says the voice on the other end of the phone.

"I know I said it once, but that was take-two!" Mary says, then she forwards the text.

"Mary, tell us what the text said, tell us straight into the camera," Janey encourages.

"You know, Wild Mary might be a little wild, but I don't like the trouble my boys are getting in."

"What trouble's that?" Janey encourages.

"Well, now you ain't never gonna believe this. They were flown out to the middle of the ocean by the US coast guard and dropped in the sea! Oh my! They were attacked by hungry sharks and saved by the lifeboat as they swam to safety."

"Are they alright?" Janey asks.

"Janey, they escaped the sharks, but Kieron fought with the killer on the ship and was thrown down a number of flights of stairs."

"How is he?"

"He's alive, baby. But he asked Wild Mary from Wild Mary's diner, to break into his apartment to help."

"It looks like he never had time to move in here," Janey adds.

"He always being whisked around the world to save people. He ain't never had time to move in! He needs a good woman you know, you available Janey? But first, we've got to find some secret computer programme and send it back to the ship."

"I got it!" Croc shouts.

The light spins to him holding a shallow but large cardboard box. On the side is written 'After Dinner & Stage Show'. Croc starts to rip it open.

"No stop!" Janey shouts.

Frozen, Mary and Croc look up puzzled. Janey and the cameraman move to Croc fast. The camera is pointed down at the box, filming the writing on the side then up to Croc's hands.

"OK go," Janey says.

Croc pulls open the box, there are two folded suit covers which he pulls out. Then the cleanest shoes you've ever seen.

"Man, you ever seen shoes shine like that?" Croc asks laying them down. He then takes out a long thin box and opens it. It's full of ribboned medals laid in a row.

"This guy must have done some crazy shit!" Croc says in amazement.

The camera pans up to Janey,

"The men who have been flown out to this ship are serious, they have dealt with international terrorists all over the world. We'll be back when we know more about why. Janey E, WBX25."

43 CN61

The photography office is even smaller with Benny on his mobility scooter and Jason crammed into it.

"That's all the photographs compressed into groups and uploading, Dwight. Good luck," Benny says into a mobile phone that joins him to the head office team in Miami.

"Within a few hours, I'll have additional staff with someone purely on photographs and timeline. I want progress on that job of excluding as many people as we can by morning, so anything you can do to section people on a timeline, do it," Dwight replies.

"Fantastic. Loving your work, loving your software," Benny says.

"Until you see a chart, trust no one that hasn't been excluded and that includes the Captain. I still haven't had the Bridge officers' log. Exclusion is going to be key, even for them."

"When Sally was killed, me and Jason, and the three other photographers were all in the Crow's Nest along with the guests you see in folder CN61," Benny explains.

"I will get that in ASAP. We can only trust those the computer excludes. No one else, and no one is excluded yet. Speak later, Benny."

The call ends with Benny on a high. He is really enjoying his holiday now he has a purpose.

"The face detection they'll have in Miami will be super cool and fast," Benny says to Jason.

"If we had something like that and were allowed

access to the security pictures guests had taken on embarkation, we could rotate their pictures for sale on their cabin TV."

"And they could click to purchase."

"We'd sell bundles."

"I think Dwight's in a chair," Benny says softly.

"What makes you say that?"

"Motor whirls in the background when he needs to move. You get to notice."

"We've all become detectives," Jason says, unhappy at the place he finds himself in, frightened of everyone.

"You want better technology for photo's, I want a job with Dwight when I get back to Miami. Or, you know, my legs back."

Jason looks at Benny as if he has been reprimanded for saying something wrong.

"Well, lots of things would be nice, like having Sally back, like not to have a killer on board…"

Jason stops feeling embarrassed. "How did it happen?"

"Sunny day, I was thinking of buying a soda when I saw a robbery going down. What do you do, how do you react?"

"I'd stay well away," Jason suggests.

"But would you? I called for back-up, staying outside, relaying everything that was going on, describing the robbers and the crime… until he took out a knife and held it at the throat of a child inside. The mum was screaming, I just walked in. I didn't run, didn't panic, just walked in. I even apologised for raining on their parade. I was just killing time, that's what I thought until the cavalry arrived. I dropped my phone and wallet as a distraction. The guy shouted leave it. I said I couldn't, it had all my wages in. He dropped the kid and went for my wallet. I guess I went for him and I got stabbed from behind. Then there were blue lights and gurneys, the rest is history."

"Was the kid OK?"

"Everyone but me."

"Did they get them?"

"Yeah."

"But you can't walk?"

"At least my todger works, not that it has been called into action since then. Apart from Sally with a test run." Benny smiles. "Trust no one apart from Hunter, Philips, me and your team!"

Benny drives backwards and lets himself out of Jason's little office.

"But even that's not official!" Jason calls out to no one now he is alone. He is even more worried about the deathly position he is in with fewer people he can confide in. He angrily stabs his pencil down into the desk and the point breaks.

Benny drives slowly through the empty photo gallery looking at a sea of printed faces, couples smiling thinking they know everything about each other. In twelve hundred guests there have to be many types, and whilst no two groups are the same, he knows as a data analyst that the larger the group, the more predictable its content and twelve hundred guests make a large group.

"Why has this not happened before?" he asks himself aloud.

"Why has what not happened before?" A voice responds. It's Bill, fighting the swell of the sea as he folds the boards into the wall and locks them. "Its gonna be rough." Bill leans against the wall and straightens his bow tie. "What's not happened before?"

"Numbers don't often lie," Benny says without thinking.

Jason joins them and helps Bill fold the last panel into the wall and locks it.

"What's he on about, Jason?" Bill asks.

Benny answers himself, "If someone leaves their house between seven and eight in the morning, we can't predict where they will go. But if one thousand people leave their houses we can know that 70% will go to the station, 20% will buy a coffee, 10% will be running late. That will be the same every day, without change. There will be a margin of error, but with twelve hundred guests like we have on this ship, the confidence level on predicting results will be high. On a ship this size, the computer will be predicting the routes walked when and where because the model is predictable."

"I get you," agrees Bill, "the model suggests there should be a killer on every ship if we have one on this ship?"

Benny shakes his head. "No, the margin of error is such that one in a thousand can never be expected."

"But if we had fifty killers on board, then we could expect killers on board on the next cruise," Bill says, using the maths as he had understood it.

"Yes, and we could expect the world has truly got out of control," Benny says thinking.

"You know what I was thinking last night?" Bill ponders.

"I've got a feeling you're gonna tell us, he always does Benny," Jason laughs.

"If trees gave off WiFi signals, everyone would be

planting trees," Bills says, looking at them for credit but they are both silent.

"They don't though, do they, neither do plastic bags," Benny says.

"That's my point," Bill adds. "If plastic bags could relay WiFi, they would never be banned."

"Benny, do you seriously think data will find our killer?" Jason asks.

"Maybe," Benny suggests. "Maybe he's the one who never walks those routes, who looks obvious to a machine but we can't see it."

"No mate, that's too easy. He walks these routes, looks like us and hides amongst us. And Sally knew him." Jason says.

"She knew him?"

"I think so. I think he caught her off guard, face to face off guard," Jason says.

"That makes it worse," Benny says, driving away. He is saddened and angry as he drives from photography into the art gallery, eventually stopping at the three paintings of the girl. One hauntingly reminds him of Sally, not that it looks anything like her. He finds himself looking at all the artwork that surrounds her. It is all screaming at him, 'look at me', that somewhere there is yet another signature, another recurring clue, but this is all so new. Dwight is a fresh set of eyes and ears who has been, like him, on the case about a day. Hunter and Kieron have been investigating this for three, but only the killer has four day's experience. What did Eric do to annoy him?

The ship continues to rock with the sea but Benny drives in a steady line to the end of deck five and arrives at the theatre and stops. On a screen outside is the picture of Kieron in his parade uniform and the full row of medals on his chest. Benny shakes his head in total disbelief.

"How do you fall down a flight of stairs, land on solid steel, walk away and end up on stage?"

44 DATA MONKEY

Benny drives into Kieron's suite to see Hunter approaching fast.

"Benny, Kieron needs some driving lessons."

"Press the button and steer, they're built for idiots," he says with no forgiving humour. Then he drives up to the other mobility scooter, still disguised as a tank and with a gun turret on the front.

"You're on stage tonight?" Benny asks Kieron without turning from the tank.

"How do you know?"

"Your picture is outside the theatre. Medals blazing."

"No going back now," Hunter says.

"But I don't have to do it on a scooter," Kieron argues.

"I'm not sure whether that was an insult or not, but there is nothing wrong with a mobility scooter, Kieron, some of us have to live with it."

"Sorry, I apologise. I'll use the scooter," he says.

"But as a tank?" Benny asks.

"It's show business Benny," Hunter adds.

"Benny, you know the funny part? Although I was in 'tanks', I never served in one. Tanks are actually part of the cavalry," Kieron says, sitting up.

"So I'll be watching Warhorse?"

"No, mate," Kieron says, not wishing to explain

further.

"I'm not your mate. It's convenient for you I've asked to help and I'm a data wrangler."

"Benny!" Hunter interrupts. "You did something no other guest did and that's step up. That makes you special. It makes you one of us. What's upset you?"

"Sally dying! Me dying!"

"You're not gonna die," Kieron says with a surprised smile.

"No?"

"Get that fist up soldier," Hunter demands.

Benny slowly raises his fist. Un-expectantly Hunter fist bumps him, Kieron is fast over the bed despite the struggle with injuries and he fist bumps his to Benny's.

"When you tell your story, tell of how you saved someone, you tell them so they know you're not just a survivor, you're a hero," Kieron states.

"The chair is what makes the stakes high. People want to hear what happened." Hunter adds.

"It gets hard for us too sometimes, to cope. I was trained to kill and inside I'm tortured, but there is a way I talk about it, because people want to hear uplifting stories," Kieron says.

"The nightmares get less, the flashbacks get less, but it means they hit so much harder when they jump back and hit me. So much harder," Hunter explains.

"He's definitely damaged," Kieron offers.

"But I wouldn't want to go to Kieron's dark places. And he won't be telling those stories on stage tonight, just how he is a hero. Inside is a mess that has caused a dozen therapists to go for therapy," Hunter explains.

"Harsh!" Kieron adds.

"But true. We are walking wounded," Hunter says,

now slowing down to the harsh reality. "But we're the lucky ones, we're alive, we're working, unlike so many we fought with, who found themselves forgotten and living on the streets."

"When you put it that way, how does anyone want to come in and listen to me talk?" Kieron asks.

"It will be packed," Hunter encourages.

"I'm not that big an attraction."

"Agreed, but there is nothing else on!"

They all laugh.

"Benny, your story would make an amazing presentation. Hey, maybe we should put it together for you and find you an agent," Kieron says.

"We are trying to solve a murder; why are you doing a show?" Benny asks.

"Ruby's idea," Kieron says.

"Well, she thinks it was her idea," Hunter adds, tossing Benny an infrared reader on a lanyard.

"We will reduce the entrances to the theatre to the four main ones and every guest will be checked in, if they go out, they get beeped again."

"That's confusing data," Benny says holding up the small infrared reader. Hunter takes it back from him,

"Best we can do with these."

"No, have two on each door. One beeps them in, the other beeps them out." Benny says.

Kieron and Hunter look at each other, shrug and nod.

"Benny, you're a genius!" Kieron says.

"I'm just a data monkey, but for this to be part of the elimination process we need one thing," Benny says.

Neither Philips or Witowski speak.

"We need a murder," Benny says.

"It's what we call collateral damage," Kieron says. "The killings are happening, they were happening before us and if we do nothing they will happen after us."

"If we do nothing, we have no way of finding the killer," Hunter adds, holding up the lanyard.

"But it might encourage the killer," Benny says.

"We can't know that," says Kieron.

"Ruby wants us ready if there is a murder," Hunter adds.

"Chicken and egg, and you made someone else think it was their idea," Benny stresses.

"We're at war Benny, there is always collateral damage," Hunter growls softly.

"It feels wrong to me."

"What is wrong is four nights back when Eric Clifford was killed. Then Donna and Kershner both being taken out because they got in the way of the escape, they were the killer's collateral damage. Three nights ago Bogdan was killed. Anger? Who knows. Two nights ago Manoj was killed for knowing too much and last night Sally was taken. Tonight someone will be killed. The killer has killed every night."

"And you hope it will be while you are on stage?" Benny asks.

"Yes," Kieron says.

"A forty-five-minute window?"

"Thirty-minutes. Kieron's doing thirty minutes," Hunter adds.

"What is the chance of that?" Benny asks.

"I can do forty-five minutes if he needs more time," Kieron mocks.

"It's not funny, you're talking about people dying

here," Benny insists.

"Maybe we are just a little more used to death. We mean no malice," Kieron explains.

"It was our career, polish it all you want, it was what we were trained to do," Hunter growls.

"Until we were put out of work by youngsters who fly drones," Kieron says, trying to change the subject.

"And I suppose they don't even need to be trained, they train themselves playing video games!" Benny adds.

"The voice of reason and understanding Benny, you're a good guy," Kieron says gleaming.

"From the voice of reason and understanding, the sample is too small. You need to check people in and out of the restaurant on both sittings too. If you are going to go for it, and really try to eliminate large numbers, do it properly," Benny demands.

"Where did you find him?" Kieron jokes.

"No idea, he's good though. Right?"

"Very good."

Benny enjoys their praise, but he has a job to do and that is to collate and send information back to Dwight Ritter in Miami, even though he has already sent enough to keep a small team up all night.

"Did either of you get any real data from Prince Dahoum?" Benny asks.

Kieron looks at his notes and studies them, "no."

"No?"

"Well maybe," Hunter starts to explain.

"Eric Clifford was gay, his wife obviously had no idea. He went down to the bike sheds," Kieron reads.

"Bike shed?" Benny enquires.

"Nickname for the laundry chute area," Hunter explains.

"With Jasmin during her early break," Kieron reads.

"Jasmin? You said Eric was gay!" Benny asks.

"She's transsexual," Kieron says.

"Has a working todger," Hunter adds using Benny's terminology.

"When she was sitting on my bed answering questions, I was certainly getting aroused. Anyway. Prince Dahoum went down a little later, during his break, with an unknown man in a mask," Kieron finishes.

"We suspect Eric was enticed down by another man to his death even later, that was shortly after 22.05hrs, but it wasn't with any of the staff. They all vouch for each other," Hunter explains.

Benny looks up at them in some disbelief, "This is serious, right?"

"Data," Kieron says flatly.

"Just data," Hunter growls.

"Column three," Kieron suggests.

"I know where it goes," Benny says confused.

45 THE SHOW

The show cast are not performing this evening so they have been requisitioned to the entrances of the restaurants and the theatre to check people in and out. Both the restaurants and theatre are easy to control because they have few access points. The emergency doors each have a security member standing by them and the whole operation has been organised by Ruby. Benny is collecting and wrangling data back to Dwight Ritter. His scooter has become a mobile technology hub.

Kieron is to be on stage, which means Hunter is on standby, and as it is early he can lurk at the back of the restaurant by the grand piano with the hotel manager, Roy, and the restaurant manager, Mr Aarav Kum. Aarav is a short but very elegant man, or at least he looks short against Hunter and Roy.

The ship only has one main restaurant, which could not hold all guests in one sitting, so the ornate chandelier and gold-trimmed room supports all the guests over two sittings. Some guests prefer the buffet, but the majority will eat here in the evening and dress accordingly. Men in an open neck shirt and jacket, ladies in a smart two-piece or cocktail dress, unless it is a formal night. There are few places on land that can match the stature of these dining rooms, few places would demand such a dress code. On the night of the masked ball, it would have looked like a movie set from an Agatha Christie film.

Amazingly few guests ask why or what is going on when required to have their cruise card scanned on the way in or out. Possibly because showing their cruise card is such a normal thing to do and possibly because they would all feel safer with the killer in the cells. The only problem that arises is if a couple has not brought both their cards, but as the cards are also their cabin door keys, and announcements were made earlier in the evening, that is very rare. The only one of the evening to cause raised voices sees Aarav excuses himself to deal with it.

"So, Eric Clifford was gay, and the only time he came out was on a cruise ship," Hunter says to Roy, now the two men are alone.

"Sixty-million people cruised last year so I guess

he might not be the only one," Roy says unsurprised.

"That leads us to believe the anger against him was his sexuality," Hunter shares.

"When you suspected it was alcohol-related, you fancied the killer as a sober drunk. Does that mean it is now someone refusing to explore their sexuality?" Roy asks.

"What a wonderful way of putting it, Roy."

"I've been through it, and before admitting it, it was tough."

"As our data wrangler would say, same column, different sub-section."

"And there are many sub-sections."

"With the officer's bridge log now submitted, they've all be eliminated from our enquiries," Hunter says with a smile, turning to Roy.

"I saw the questionnaire."

"And?"

"I genuinely have no alibi for any of those periods, I was in my cabin, alone."

"Alone?"

"As I am most evenings. I read a lot."

"Alone, no alibi?"

"Apart from my cat, alone"

"You have a cat?"

Roy nods, "A robotic tabby cat. Cat, book and a scotch."

"That means,"

"I'm still a suspect."

"That is how it works," Hunter nods.

"So, if I stay with you all evening and there's a murder, I'll be alright?" Roy tries.

Benny drives in beside them.

"All the data from the first sitting has been sent,"

he announces. "And Roy, many of the first sitting are already in the theatre. That show will be overcrowded."

Roy takes that information in and scans the full restaurant. These guests will be marching to the theatre in just over an hour. He pulls out his internal phone.

"It's Roy. How difficult would it be to put a live feed of the theatre show in the nightclub?"

He waits, as do Benny and Hunter.

"In an hour."

Roy puts the phone down and turns to the two men.

"That's happening."

Hunter pulls up his internal phone.

"Ruby. Roy has arranged for a live re-broadcast of the theatre to be played in the nightclub, can we cover it?" Hunter smiles, puts the phone down and turns to the other two.

"So who can I call?" Benny asks.

Captain Neil Reynolds walks backstage where he finds Kieron Philips at a table, editing one of his shows.

"I would like to introduce you, Philips, if you don't mind."

"Not at all, sir. Would you like to stay on stage for an informal chat about anything?"

"No, I don't think so. But, when guests ask if we have apprehended the killer it is best to be honest by saying no, then reassure them that a large number of guests have been eliminated from enquiries simply because we know where they were when the murders occurred, so that if you are asked to produce your cruise card more often it's so we can track movement and we thank them for assisting us."

"Certainly sir. Do I suggest that if we can dock in

Tahiti, it might be the case that only those eliminated from enquiries might be allowed to go ashore?"

"I think it might be a little early for that," the Captain says and pats him on the back. "Good luck. You have a full house and it's on in the night club, on the sea screen and on in the cabins."

Elvis, the entertainment manager, is introduced by a voice recording and the din on the other side of the curtain falls silent. He tells a few jokes that would not offend anyone and then introduces the Captain to huge applause. The Captain says very little other than apologising for the weather which we should pass through by lunchtime tomorrow, meaning the mad Paul Lopkey will be on stage tomorrow night. Then he introduces Commander Kieron Philips. The music Burning Bridges, which is the theme song to Hogan's Heroes starts. 'I am sure I could walk out faster', he mutters to himself. The Captain walks towards him shakes his hand, and is gone. Kieron organises the tank turret to face front, presses the button as directed, and a confetti cannon blasts out. There are screams and applause and he remembers this is show business so forgets everything the doctor told him and begins.

"So, those of you who read my first book, Cruise Ship Heist will know that I was shot just five weeks ago in Madeira. But, no rest for the wicked, they flew me out to the middle of the Pacific Ocean and dropped me from fourteen thousand feet to test the stitches."

The theatre fills with laughter.

"Did you all watch that? Did you see the sharks? So, we have a troublemaker on board which is why I am here. He and I had a little 'set to' at the top of the stairs and I got thrown over, so you won't mind if I sit down from time to time?"

Kieron has them, he knows that, but he sees Hunter and Roy turn fast at the rear of the theatre in the distance and leave, so he knows something has happened. The feared murder looks like it has taken place as predicted and Philips has to carry on for at least another twenty-eight more minutes to keep the crowds away from the crime scene.

'It's just an act', he thinks, as the audience laughs at another joke he has already forgotten.

46 COLD AND HEARTLESS

Breakfast on sea-day-seven is very relaxing for the guests; there is nowhere to go, just the ocean outside. Though still quite rough, it is a walk in the park compared with last night's testing storm. The long relaxing full-service breakfast taken in the main dining room, highlights what is now easily the longest spell at sea so far. Guests are somewhat soothed, amused and still chatting about last night's stage performance of Commander Kieron Philips.

Then their phones start to beep and all his good work distracting them is about to evaporate. News of yet another death last night, making five nights in a row on board starts to spread. It is digested in one of two ways; first are the confident, those who consider that it will never happen to them. Second, are the worriers and they have only just got started with their fear of death. Taking a superior position, the confident now also bask in the fact that the detectives will know that 'they' are not murderers as they registered in dining or at a venue so can be excluded. That active scanning programme adopted last night is already serving as a positive move as most chatter turns to focus back on the fact that the serial killer on board could be anyone, except them. Extrapolation develops the many options of what might happen next as social media escalates its interest, claiming that they will not be able to dock anywhere except back at their homeport in Miami because no one wants a serial killer. The various red top newspapers have their tag-line chosen names for the outcast ship ranging from 'Ghost Ship' to 'Hell at High-Water'. Again those guests eliminated are already claiming that they will be allowed to disembark when they dock because they have been cleared. Guests leap ahead of the international relations as experienced amateur seafarers confirm that the ship's course is still firmly aimed at Tahiti. However, there is still one piece of news they don't have.

Witowski and Philips are silent as they pick at their food. They took this job because it was a challenge, but they are realising that it's proving more challenging than they could've imagined and they are not yet succeeding. A close friend, however new, has now been taken. They are dealing with a monster. There are two more days at sea, and if Tahiti had long-range aircraft there is a chance they might drop extra military help on board sometime before dark tomorrow, day eight. But, Tahiti doesn't even have a full American embassy, let alone a US military detachment. It is one of seventeen foreign countries to have a consulate agency in Pape'ete but it is not a major office. The agency covering most countries' affairs for French Polynesia is best-staffed way down in Fiji. An office which, along with the US embassy in Paris, oversees the mid-Pacific Island. That means nothing is immediate and help from Hawaii is closer, but not close enough. Sadly, the French authorities are not playing ball so it is not clear how much help any office will get or what is going on. It is not that the two investigators feel that they have failed, but they have made no progress other than a possible timeline, a motive and the start of an elimination process which cannot claim to have a one hundred percent margin of error, as Benny would have reminded them, but he is dead.

The pressure is on. Despite storms, slowing to pick the two detectives up and it's many other problems, the ship is on-schedule to dock in Pape'ete early morning day ten. It's the land of romantic Ukulele music and pearl diving in clear blue seas.

However, French authorities have a completely different idea and are saying very firmly that docking is not a possibility under any circumstances unless the killer is caught and under lock and key. A French Polynesian State Department spokesperson has this morning released a statement saying,

"Every state has the sovereign right to regulate the entry, screening, and stay of foreign nationals in its territory, subject to its international obligations."

The officers around the Captain's dining table stare at the statement and begin to process the reality of the ship being a leper, and what they might have to deal with. The Captain is going to be busier than ever dealing with every department, from the laundry running out of soap to clean the sheets, to technical and mechanical problems of waste, fuel and food. If they are to have barges come out and supply them, there is going to be a pecking order of necessity. At this moment it is beyond comprehension how many people on land are working on the very many solutions, from fuel to food, for the nineteen hundred people on board the outcast ship.

Witowski and Philips are coming to terms with the very real loss of another team member. Benny was found with an electric cable from a cleaning appliance round his neck. He was hanging, still strapped into his scooter, halfway down the stairs. The weight of the machine meant he was hung in an instant. Kieron no longer wishes to use the scooter that was last night's stage prop.

"It might not have been a murder," Kieron says, breaking the silence. "I think he hit rock bottom and it was suicide."

"We should have done more for him," Hunter says softly.

"I don't agree. It was, once again strangulation. Our killer's signature move," Ruby says, and no one argues with her.

Kieron puts down his knife and fork, finishes his coffee and rises from the table,

"Excuse me."

Everyone in the room watches him leave. No one comments.

In his own apartment, the main sitting room is a fully functional central crime centre, the information boards are all around the room. Kieron goes straight to the house phone and presses one key, Dwight is now on speed dial.

"Good morning," Dwight answers.

"I'm not sure it is good, Dwight," Kieron replies.

"No, I heard. Benny was a good egg."

"What did he send you, what did he not send

you?"

"I had the first dinner sitting 'in and out', the second 'in' and most of the theatre 'in'. I say most because I expect there would be late entries. I don't have the second sitting dinner 'out'. I don't have night club 'in or out'."

"I've got my suspicions it was suicide but I don't get him leaving a job half done."

"Why suicide?" Dwight asks.

"He was in a chair and very unhappy."

"There are three of us in chairs here and we were looking forward to meeting him, the chair doesn't make it suicide," Dwight says.

Kieron stops to think for a moment, he had neither thought of them as being in chairs nor expected it.

"What's up Kieron? We don't all get as lucky as you each time we're hit."

"Sorry Dwight. That took me by surprise."

"What, that we are not just as you'd pictured us, normal walking-talking people?"

The door opens and Hunter walks in.

"Who came in?" Dwight asks.

"Hunter."

"That's OK, but I don't trust everyone."

"Morning Dwight," Hunter says clearly.

"He was uploading from his scooter, so he was hit while he was working," Kieron adds.

"You don't think it was suicide now?" Hunter asks.

"Dwight doesn't think so. Benny would have been going from the theatre to the night club at the back of the ship. So he got taken out at the mid staircase on the way."

"My guess, he was still uploading after his death because that takes time, especially in a storm. The theatre data was last and that was started at 22.05 hours. He would have started travelling after that," Dwight explains.

"That's the same time as Eric's last drink," Hunter reminds them.

"I can go one further, the data upload finished at 22.12 but the signal wasn't shut off until 22.14. He was dead before 22.12 or he would have closed transmission." The door opens again. "Who is that?" Dwight asks.

"Jason, photography," Kieron says.

"He's OK, he's excluded. Trust no one that has not been excluded by me! I need the rest of that data because we have an exact time of death here, hope the doctor agrees." Dwight closes transmission.

"Where's the scooter?" Kieron asks.

"Ruby had her team take it," Hunter explains.

"What is at the middle staircase, or anywhere there that would stop Benny going direct to the nightclub?" Kieron asks.

"The art gallery. He absolutely loved one of the pictures. It reminded him of Sally, but it looked nothing like her," Jason says.

"Can you see if you can find the rest of the infrared readers from last night?" Kieron asks Hunter.

"Stay in here, take it easy. We need a point man today," Hunter says.

"I'm going for a little stroll with Jason. Nothing else." Kieron says, turning to Jason.

"So you think Benny topped himself? He wasn't in a good place was he?" Jason says striding to keep up.

Kieron says nothing and slows down at the art gallery. Jason leads them to the wall but the three pictures are gone.

"It was here, but they rotate the stock, so it must have got changed last night," Jason says.

"Or he bought them?"

"No, not all three. He only liked one."

Kieron looks towards the central staircase which is not far away. He walks on, turns into it and looks at the stairs.

"Why come here?" Kieron says to himself but Jason is in tow.

"Well that is one of the art stores," Jason says, walking past and showing Kieron a section of flat wall sections that are actually doors, making an invisible storage section, "His picture could be in here."

Kieron stands in the space by the stairs, looking at the wall, then looks down along the wall to the electric sockets.

"He's here, on his scooter looking at the wall. Maybe checks his watch, but knows he needs to get on, turns the steering to about-turn, but to do that has to hard turn towards the stairs in the arc as he accelerates."

"Sure."

"The cable is snapped around his neck and pulled, it doesn't need to be tight; it's a distraction. His hands go up to the wire, the killer's hands go to his steering. A simple push. Instead of completing the turn it goes down the stairs and the wire does its job. He saw the killer, was shocked and caught off guard."

"Makes sense," Jason replies.

"You know Benny. If it was the last thing he would do he would reveal the killer," Kieron suggests. "He would type something in the pad."

Roy holds up a group of six Lanyards. "The last two from the restaurant, I stayed until everyone cleared. Then went to the night club and after the show, I collected all four from there. Two on each door. When I heard about Benny I kept them, because I knew it was his job and they would be evidence."

"So the only missing ones are the theatre, in and out," Hunter says.

"Elvis will have those, almost guaranteed. Let's go and ask him." Roy leads Hunter away.

"You still don't have an alibi do you?" Hunter asks.

"Other than working during last night's time frame, I don't."

The two men walk out from the hotel management offices behind reception, past the queues of disgruntled guests that have already formed, having heard the news that the ship appears unlikely to dock at Tahiti.

Elvis has his own office down the other end of the corridor from reception where each door is the office of a head of some department. Roy knocks on 'HoD ENTS', and goes in, followed by Hunter. Elvis turns and looks at them both.

"Your team were looking after the infrared readers at the theatre?" Roy asks.

Elvis looks at Hunter, "This has us all looking at each other suspiciously and I feel very uncomfortable," he says without the usual wide smile his job demands.

"Why?" Asks Hunter.

"Because I left them hanging here," Elvis says and he points to an empty hook. All three men look at it.

"What are you saying?" Hunter asks.

"They were stolen," Elvis admits. "Now, I know I can trust you," He says to Hunter. "You weren't on the ship when the murders started."

"I don't have them." Roy starts, "I had the ones from the night club, Hunter has them now."

Elvis pulls out a set of keys and unlocks a draw. He pulls out four lanyards and holds them high,

"As I said, I know I can trust you. The real ones I put in my desk, then four that were never used I hung on the hook. Don't ask me why, I just had a feeling."

"Good work. Can you schedule the movie Lawrence of Arabia to show again? Don't ask me why, just got a feeling," Hunter asks. "I'll get you a list of people you can trust."

"But I'm not on it," Roy adds.

"To be fair Roy, I doubt you're on anyone's list," Elvis adds, his smile returning. The banter and humour are still there, even if a little subdued and not without an undertone of serious worry.

Roy smiles and turns to Hunter, "Let me find you someone to deal with these," and he leaves.

Elvis nods slowly and turns to Hunter, "A rum business, they say."

"Who are they?"

"Those who do not cuddle a battery operated cat?"

"You've been to his cabin then?" Hunter asks.

"Once. Just once. Not my type."

"You're not into cats?"

"No. Allergies."

47 CODE READER

"Sir, I was asked to report," a female officer in white officer's skirt and shirt says, standing in Kieron's data centre. She carries a small bag like a cloth handbag. Her badge says 'Prisha Nah, Hotel Reception'.

"Roy is one efficient guy," Kieron says, impressed at how fast he has acted.

She nods her head but is obviously worried and confused as to why she's there.

"You will be pleased to know that you have a three-star security clearance," he tells her.

Prisha looks even more puzzled.

"Like a spy," Kieron adds, but she doesn't get his humour.

"I am not a spy, sir."

"No, you've been cleared as not being the murderer. Three times when there have been murders you have been on duty. You are eliminated as a suspect."

"I am not a murderer, sir."

"I just said the computer confirms that, but everyone else still is a suspect. Trust no one. Roy is not cleared."

Kieron points to the chart which she fails to understand and he does not have the energy to explain in full. However, Prisha can see she has three crosses and green ticks all along the line with her name in. She can see that Roy Stevens is not green.

"Mr Stevens is not a murderer. I can clear him."

"You can't. He has not officially been eliminated. Until then, you tell him nothing. What you do in this room stays in this room."

"Yes sir," she says, still puzzled.

"You any good with data and communications?" He asks, holding up the infrared readers on lanyards.

"I know how to read those, sir," she says.

"It's Kieron, Prisha," he says, reading her lapel badge again, his head still hurting. "We need the reader up here in this room, is that easy?"

"Yes, sir, Kieron," she nods, and holds up the bag. "Mr Stevens sent it."

Kieron walks across the room towards the house phone, "Dwight, you still there?"

"And waiting."

"Prisha meet Dwight, Dwight meet your new data wrangler."

Kieron hands her the lanyards and walks towards the door.

"Mr Philips, sir."

Kieron stops in the door; he looks exhausted.

"Your last data person was murdered?"

"Let's find that killer fast then," Kieron says. He leaves the room, unstable on the rocking ship, he gets to his bedroom and lays on his bed absolutely exhausted,

"Shit!" He says quietly to himself. He can hear Prisha talking to Dwight in the other room, asking if she will be OK, but there is no way he can keep his eyes open. One eye closes, then the other. He falls asleep, his breathing uneven. The inside of his head lit up by flashing lights like a firework display.

Kieron wakes with a vision of loveliness before him and he can't work out whether he is dreaming or it is real.

"Sir, Mr Kieron? What shall I do next?"

He fights to open his eyes.

"Sorry, Prisha. Familiarise yourself with those boards, just give me a minute," he begs.

Prisha watches him with concern but seeing him pass out again, her concerns about being alone in his bedroom vanish. She tentatively reaches to feel his forehead and instantly knows he is burning up with fever. She rushes to the phone and dials.

"Please tell Dr Simon that Mr Kieron is really not well. Not well at all. We are in his suite."

She slams the phone down and dashes into the bathroom. She grabs a face flannel, soaking it in water. Back at the bed, she loosens his collar as she mops his brow, neck and chest. Kieron lays lifeless. Suddenly she realises he has stopped breathing. She tips his head back, pulling a pillow under his shoulders, covers his mouth with hers and holds his nose to breathe life back into him, slowly and rhythmically.

"Sir, Mr Kieron?"

He hears her voice. His eyes open and he can see flashes of her standing in the doorway, flashes of her head above him. Was her mouth on his a dream? He feels awful, he knows he is coming and going but he has no control over his mind or body.

"Stay with me, Mr Kieron!"

"Always."

Doctor Simon Yates rushes in with Manesh, other medical staff and the nurse, Anokhi. Prisha backs out of the room to let them work. She stands distressed, lost and confused looking from him to the boards. She looks to the list of those murdered and sees Kieron Philips is listed with brackets around it. She shivers with fear.

Hunter enters data central which takes Prisha by

surprise. Seeing how upset she is, he puts his arms around her and she cries. She feels cold and is shivering.

"Sir, they took Mr Kieron to the medical centre."

Hunter fills with concern but cannot leave her yet. He also needs a rundown of everything that has happened; the murderer is still and large and he is under pressure to deliver results.

"He'll be fine, focus on this. What else happened?"

"I did the data with Mr Dwight and a lady called Elaine rang for her husband."

"And?"

"I told her that he had been taken to the medical centre, she was concerned."

"Elaine is my wife! I'll call her." Hunter is away.

"I am sorry," she shouts after him chasing him to the door.

"No worries, you weren't to know," Hunter shouts back, leaving with his mobile to his ear,

"Don't tell anyone anything. Not anyone, anything!"

Prisha is alone again and backs into a chair. She sits totally confused about her new status as a spy and now even more worried that she is once again left alone in this room. She turns to the phone and rings her head of department.

"Mr Stevens, Sir. I am so, so scared; I can't talk to anyone. I don't know what I am doing here."

"Where is Kieron?"

"He has been taken away by Doctor Simon, Mr Witowski has left, but maybe I can't tell you that."

"Stay there, just please stay there. They need you, think about how you can help. But don't talk to anyone, don't allow anyone in until Mr Witowski comes back. Close the doors and ignore anyone else who comes knocking."

Prisha checks that the cabin door is closed, goes back into the apartment and starts to study the boards again. She can see they are trying to work out who the murderer is and she tries to understand their process. The phone rings, interrupting a million thoughts running through her head. She stands looking at it, not knowing what to do before creeping forward tentatively.

"Hello?" she answers.

"Prisha, it's Dwight Ritter."

"Hello, Mr Ritter."

"I want you to tell Hunter that the first name that jumps out from the computer, for him to bring in for questioning, is the cabaret act, Paul Lopkey. He fits every category from knowing the ship, the entertainment office and having no alibi. Plus, his agility, ability and sexuality all match."

"Right. Is that it?" she asks confused and wondering if he can possibly be the murderer as she writes on a sticky note.

"Yes, that's it for now," Dwight concludes.

Prisha puts the phone down and makes notes more formally. 'Lopkey is our first match in all areas, please bring him in'. She goes back to the boards and places the sticky up. She is holding the note for Mr Witowski. She can see his line is red, no marks in any of the murder columns. She goes to Eric's murder trying to understand the context of the brief notes on Lopkey when there is a knock at the door. She stops and looks towards it, but does not move. The knocking persists but she has been told not to open the door. She hears a key card being used and starts to worry.

Ruby enters and Prisha relaxes knowing she is head of security. Ruby, however, is stunned at seeing her there.

"Prisha, what are you doing here?"

Prisha is struck dumb, all she can remember are the words 'talk to no one'. She looks to her left to try and read Ruby Jenkins' line to see whether it is red or green, but it is impossible. She is nowhere near familiar enough with the boards and Ruby is instantly more demanding.

"Prisha, should you be here?"

Prisha nods.

"Why are you in this room?"

"I have a three-star security clearance, and I have been told to work here?"

"Doing what?"

"Answering the phones at the moment, but I've not been doing that very well. I told Mr Hunter's wife that he had been taken to the hospital when it was Mr Philips."

"Kieron is back in the hospital?" Ruby asks, storming through to his bedroom. Seeing an empty bed she turns back to Prisha, "Is he OK?"

Prisha shakes her head as Ruby eyes dart towards the note. It's embarrassingly obvious, as is her poor acting. Ruby snatches it and reads.

"Lopkey?"

Ruby looks her straight in the face, but Prisha knows she can say nothing. Ruby rushes out and Prisha is left, once again sure that she must have done many things wrong. She tries to add up the things she told Ruby, knowing that she is not doing well at her new job.

Prisha has to figure this out. She moves back to the board, to the right-hand colomn, elimination'. The sheets of small print connect into a long column and are almost impossible to read at a glance. Even close-up, the names and information are hard to read. It holds the name of every crew member and every guest in the cross plot with columns downwards listing each murder with its date, time and name of the victim. Green, red, and orange, the colours make it easy to see who is eliminated and who is still a suspect. Orange is someone with only one cross, someone that has not yet been confirmed and made green, like Prisha was told she is. She can see that green lines have at least two verified eliminations. She finds her name which has three crosses, then she finds the Captain and can see it is still pending information and it's orange. She runs past her boss, Roy Stevens, who has only a question mark against Benny's death and is still red. Where has she missed Ruby Jenkins? Her finger scans up again, less rushed and more in control until she finds it. Ruby Jenkins has a line with one question mark, she's also still red. They have not been eliminated. Why does someone with a red line have a card to this room? Why can Ruby come in? Why did Prisha allow herself to be drawn in and talk to her? And why did she allow her to take the note about Lopkey?

48 GIRL ON ELIMINATION

Feeling guilty, Prisha is transfixed by the boards and the wealth of information when the printer starts up. She stands above it watching new sheets coming out, the lines of red and green. These have been sent from Miami and she is keen to see how they have responded to the information sent to them from the team in the ship's data centre. She lifts them from the printer tray and there's a familiar noise that breaks the silence. Her head snaps round in panic as the key card is being used again and the door opened. She looks towards the door and sees Captain Neil Reynolds.

"The storm is passing," he says to someone outside before seeing her. It is said as an expression of relief. He has had an eventful night, however, she knows there is no relief. This room presents its own problems. Her problem right now is that she knows the Captain's name on the old list was not green. She shuffles the new sheets to try and find the Captain's updated entry. But she has to stop as he walks into the room, making her back up and allow him to look at the boards. It is his ship.

"Sir, I am not sure I like my new role as a spy."

"Prisha, you are not a spy, you just work in intelligence now."

"I don't like it. I've already made mistakes."

"You are doing an invaluable job. Think about how to get more people in the green area."

She gives up trying to find him in the new loose sheets and moves to the board he is referring to. She takes the old sheets pinned in the middle of the board and moves them one by one to the far left.

"I cannot do that, sir," she says, wondering if he wants her to make his line green, remembering it was orange with a note written across it.

"Only the computer can make people green," she blurts out to excuse her from any request. She begins to pin the new sheets on the right and the difference is obvious, many more lines are green. She lines them up perfectly.

"These results are good. More green lines. You're

all doing a good job."

"I am trying, sir."

"The computer needs information, think of new ways of giving it more," he explains.

The Captain leaves Prisha pinning the last of the new sheets up on the right-hand side so the lines correspond. She writes the time and date on the top of the new column and steps back. The difference is positive. She fixes her eyes on the Captain's security level which is still orange and now reads, 'bridge log pending'. It's still not green. She second-guesses herself, thinking back to ensure she told him nothing. Prisha picks up her note pad and writes, 'why do people have key cards if they are not green?'

Determined to be a part of the team, she dashes out of the cabin with her note pad, then as the door closes behind her, she takes her cruise card and tries it in the door, but the lock shows the red light next to the card slot. She is not red, but her card is. As she walks away she pulls out her internal mobile phone and dials.

"Hi, it's Prisha here. Can you ask Mr Stevens to add room access to my cruise card for the starboard guest suite please?"

She deliberately hangs up after brief niceties, not allowing any questioning of her request as she marches through the pool area towards the middle stairwell. Whether she gets it or not she is acting a little more like a team member and a little less over-awed by her new task.

Prisha enters the medical centre down at level three, mid-staircase and goes directly to find Hunter in Kieron's room.

"Mr Hunter. I am not keen on being a spy. I am

not very good at it."

"What's happened?" he asks her.

"The Captain wants me to work harder at expanding the elimination list."

"We're all doing that, there'll be more ways, we'll think of them."

"Some things are concerning me. The Captain is not green yet but has access to the room."

"Good point, but hopefully that will change very soon now the bridge logs are in."

"Miss Jenkins is not green, but she has access."

"You have been busy!"

"I do not have access to the room but I am green."

"Oh."

"I wanted to ask Mr Stevens for help, but he's not green."

"Sadly, Roy does not have the clearance you have."

"Or don't have, the system is flawed."

"Already you are showing your worth, and you saved my best buddy's life. Relax."

"I can't relax, I made a mistake. Mr Ritter rang and then Miss Ruby from security came in and made me show her his message." Prisha refers him to her note pad where she has re-written it all down.

Hunter reads the message then turns to Simon, "Simon! Call me if there's any change."

He puts a friendly arm around Prisha as they leave.

"Is he going to die?" she asks.

"No he's like a cat with nine lives, you know that saying?"

She shakes her head 'no'.

"I mean a real cat, not a robotic cat, but let's not go there. Look I rang Elaine, my wife, and she knows I'm fine. I will speak with Ruby about Paul Lopkey.

Guests will be clocked into and out of dinner and the show again tonight. Prisha, we've let you down. You needed a lot more explained to you and we were expecting Kieron to be with you. But you have authority to get all the key cards stopped for that room except people who are green and the Captain. I mean everyone."

"I understand, but the Captain is not green."

"OK. Speak with Dwight Ritter first and double-check the bridge update. If he is still not clear, we will exclude him and I will talk to him about that. You are precise, I like that. It is essential."

"Thank you."

"Someone puts you on the spot, refer them to me, think of ways to pin people to where they were at the time of any murder. Every new person turning green is a help."

"There are strange listings, like all but two of the stage crew are green."

"Good, interview them, find out why."

"I don't have the power to ask them questions."

"Roy Stevens will set up any interview, he can do that. You can ask him for assistance, just don't trust him with information yet."

"I interview them?"

"Yes, but not in the data room."

Kieron does not look any better and once again his head has been bandaged.

"What happened, Simon?" Ruby asks.

She is shocked at how bad Kieron looks again, he's unconscious. Simon walks towards her.

"He is a lucky guy, I don't know how many lives he has been given to squander, but he is using them up.

There was swelling inside the skull, we had to relieve it. A serious operation on land, let alone at sea in a storm."

"Stop bigging yourself up, Simon, you're loving this. The storm's over and you've got the most stable area here, midships deck three!"

"Now you know why the medical centre is down here," Simon smiles and walks away. Prisha passes him on his way out and stands silently behind Ruby.

Ruby draws a chair in and holds Kieron's hand, "Hey, you. We're never going to get it together if you keep passing out like this. I'm very demanding you know."

Ruby senses someone behind her. She turns, but Prisha was not who she expected to see.

"I can come back, Miss Jenkins," Prisha says.

"What is it?"

Prisha draws a second chair in and sits next to her, "I have been tasked with accurately getting more names on the board to turn green. At the moment yours is not. I would like to change that first."

Ruby smiles, "Good, that's important."

"At each of the murder times, I am looking to place, without doubt, where you were. Then I can get your line green."

"That's simple and I'm glad you're on it."

"Me too. I just have to do the job very properly."

"Machines can't do everything and they don't know the ship like we do," Ruby shares, feeling a friendship building.

"Quite," Prisha explains. "I only need to pass you on two of the murders."

"I should think we can do them all. Donna was the first murder we can place and time. I was on duty, called to the scene and one of the first there," Ruby explains, then thinks ready to move onto the next.

"But, you did not have a specific position like a stair guard or a door guard during the minutes of the murder, so can you be more precise?"

Ruby was not expecting this. Prisha is exacting in her request for details.

"No, I was monitoring the guards working there from my office," Ruby explains.

"Who was with you in the office we can get to corroborate?" Prisha demands.

"No one, it was late evening. All my working officers went to assist in stargazing security. Others were called in after the emergency was declared," Ruby states.

"So I can't tick you off on that death. The man overboard and man down the chute we have no exact time of death for but even so, they would come under the same space of time and therefore the same problem. Let's find another one. The next night, when Bogdan was killed."

"I showed the two new investigators the incident room we had set up, at that time it was down in the cells by my office. Then I went with them to have dinner with the Captain to further discuss the problem."

"But there was a break between the incident room and the start of dinner. Also, you had not joined dinner when the murder was announced. I need something else if you have it."

"Well, I don't. I went back to my office to make sure I could give a perfect presentation at dinner," Ruby says, beginning to feel a little picked on.

"Manoj Bhatti. This is quite a wide timeline."

"Prisha. I am head of security, are you sure you need to do this with me in such detail?" Ruby asks.

"I was told to do this job, Miss Jenkins. I did not ask for it."

"Who by?"

"These orders come from Miami, and no one is exempt. The Captain is not yet clear."

"This is ridiculous. He was doing the commentary during the stargazing." Ruby states.

"That gave him a question mark, but you need two positives to go green," Prisha explains.

"Whose idea is this?"

"Miss Jenkins, you are making it difficult for me, I am already breaking rules by explaining detail with you."

"Head of security has no security clearance. Hunter Witowski has come up with this so he can take over."

"No ma'am, it has nothing to do with him. The US attaché and consulate general are working hard for us to be allowed to dock anywhere in French Polynesia."

"I am quite aware of all that."

"This is the procedure. If we can dock, then only those green on this list will be allowed off the ship," Prisha reveals.

"Pardon?" Ruby demands.

"Let me try to make this work, where were you when Kieron was pushed over the rail?"

"I was with him. I was in the Crow's Nest with him drinking."

"No miss Jenkins, you left first and he was alone when he left."

"He was coming to my room. I had texted him. Check my phone, check his phone."

"Miss Jenkins, that means you were alone with no alibi. I am trying to help you."

"No, you're not!"

"Where were you when Sally was killed? Again late night."

"In my room, getting ready for bed until I was called to the crime scene, to which I ran!"

"This is why there have been problems turning your line green. Under the terms that Miami is working to, there is no verification."

"Does that offer of coming to your room still stand?" Kieron says.

Both women turn, having forgotten that they are sitting by him in the hospital.

"Simon! He's awake." Ruby shouts. She then turns to Prisha, "So I'm his killer?"

"I am just trying to get the right data to clear you and have your access to the situation room allowed."

"What?"

"The incident room in Kieron's apartment is only accessible for people who clear green, that is why I need to help you first. Please help clear yourself."

"Clear myself?"

"It's OK. You can still come up there for sex," Kieron says.

Ruby is raging with anger. She looks from Kieron to Prisha.

"I don't think he's up to sex yet," Simon says, joining them.

49 INNOCENCE

Hunter and Prisha both grab lunch on the go into

the well-serviced data room, Hunter stands, remarking between mouthfuls while Prisha sits; she is far more formal and takes breaks from eating to talk. She has made herself a desk and work area.

"I met with the rest of the theatre crew and the two male singers who were not collecting guest data last night with the infrared readers. They were on a protest about working extra hours. They offered to verify each other's alibis but I would not accept that."

"Harsh!" grins Hunter.

"Am I too harsh?"

"No, I love it."

"When I explained it meant they are not eliminated, and as such would not be able to disembark in Tahiti, they agreed to work every evening."

"Are you getting this in there?" Hunter shouts to Kieron's bedroom.

"Yes. Laughing and loving it," Kieron shouts back faintly.

"Don't laugh too much, we don't want another brain bleed," Hunter shouts to Kieron, then turns back to Prisha, "What other departments have you convinced to work?"

"They all want to work all the time, but I have only turned one new person green," Prisha sounds disappointed, as if she has failed.

"Great job. Great job."

"It will improve when we get the timesheets in from all the other departments, from the engine room to the kitchen. I will then get that data to Mr Ritter."

Kieron appears in the doorway from his bedroom.

"Hey, soldier!" Hunter greets him.

"I can't resist the smell of food anymore," Kieron says, walking over to the self-service trolley. "How long was I out?"

"No time, you missed nothing."

"Did we get paid?"

"Haven't had those conversations yet, kinda feel we need to catch someone first," Hunter says.

"Do you think we should let Ruby up, give her door privileges again," Kieron asks.

"Maybe," Hunter says.

"But she is not green," Prisha insists.

"But she is head of security," Hunter reminds her, "and you know what he's after?"

"I have heard, but sex is not the reason to give anyone access to this information," Prisha says bluntly. "Perhaps we can get them a different room for that."

Hunter nearly chokes on his food.

"No, we're not having sex," Kieron says.

"But she wants to, clearly," Prisha adds.

"No, she didn't mean what she said," Kieron replies.

"It was her legal alibi, that she texted you and wished to have sex, she cannot lie in evidence," Prisha adds, then commences eating again.

Hunter likes her logic and is nodding.

"Actually I was thinking about us needing a woman join our company full time. Jenkins is a good fit," Kieron says.

"You know I am beginning to like working in intelligence, so you have options," Prisha adds, which shocks both men.

"Ruby has years of working in security," Hunter explains to her gently.

"And there will be times when we have to go undercover, as a husband and wife, as guests on holiday, and she has suggested…" Kieron says, deliberately leaving it unfinished.

"All cabins can be formatted to two separate beds," Prisha says.

"You're serious?" Hunter asks her.

"Yes, I like this work, and Miss Jenkins does not yet have the security clearance to get a room key back in here." Prisha finishes.

Prisha hands Hunter a printed Curriculum Vitae. She doesn't wait for him to reply and goes back to her lunch. Kieron and Hunter look at each other. They can now only talk about employment options away from either of the two women. However, they need to get Ruby back in the room where Prisha has asserted herself as head of the elimination board. Ruby is definitely going to have to prove herself.

Following a short but well-worded announcement by the Captain, eagerly listened to by all the guests, relief and hysteria still sit in two distinct camps. Whilst no guest can know who was actually eliminated under Dwight and Prisha's strict terms of adherence and therefore might be safe to go ashore in Tahiti, some know they weren't clicked in or out of a venue or a bar. They feel very strongly that they should not be punished for going to bed early. The need to prove one's innocence is about to divide the ship. Prisha is going to be incredibly busy interviewing guests who at the moment are red.

Ruby is deliberately avoiding calls, claiming she has an even bigger task to detail guest movement tonight to provide data for Prisha and Dwight. The whole ship is expected to want to be in a venue, selfishly hoping there will be another murder so that they can be proved to be innocent somewhere else.

Hunter moves to the Crow's Nest and settles down with a beer and a jotting pad to doodle on, chatting to Prince Dahoum or Jasmin as they work. He is sure something will click into place as the net tightens. He discovers that Bogdan was frustrated in the orchestra, felt he was a showman worthy of a specialty act in his own right and could be booked nightly going from ship to ship. He wanted to find an agent and was trying to improve his English. Apparently, he used to be in the circus and worked as a saxophone-playing clown. His antics during his show had been increasing, leaping from rail to table with guests lifting their drinks as his acrobatics increased. His audience in the Crow's Nest had been getting bigger and bigger, so no one said anything. It worked for everyone except the MD whose audience was getting smaller when he was alone on the piano. Jasmin thinks Eric might have said he would help find Bogdan an agent. He suggested he leave the ship and try for a big television talent show. Lastly, Hunter learnt that Bogdan was gay but had not come out.

Hunter doodled, writing notes and joining circles together as the computer did on a much grander scale. All this information fitted in with discoveries on Eric's and Kershner's sexuality. But as exciting as the story was, Hunter felt something was adrift with this thread. Perhaps the thread itself was the route but he was not convinced he knew the trigger or the cause. Hunter wanted to chat this through with his team, with Kieron and with Ruby, because she knew more than anyone about what happened on the ship. Prisha's experiences, on the other hand, revolved around the reception, this world was new and often shocking to her, but she was a stickler for the rules and calling Ruby would upset her. Running a company, even their small one was far from easy. He tossed the thin white beer mat at the table, then looked up at the handrail and out of the bar to the corridor, the entrance to the chapel, and the door to the staircase of doom. If the killings were sexual frustrations, triggered from the dark side of the film, then at least one of the other killings would surely have a note. Maybe Bogdan. And why not leave the note with Eric if the killer was so capable? Hunter writes on his jotter. The answer had to be that the killer was not a murderer. The thought makes his blood run cold because any man who has had to kill another man, has had to redress the difference. Hunter knows dark moments, he knows the rage and confusion that can build, he feels like he can get inside the killer's head. Eric was justified in his mind, Eric was disgust, Eric was planned. Eric was his first blood and he botched it up. As any soldier discovers somewhere along the line there is collateral damage. But the guests with military service records are 80 and 90 years old.

Hunter gets to his feet. He stands and looks from the rail where Bogdan played down at the 'Crew Door'. From here, Bogdan would have seen Eric and the killer go down and not come back. Then it hits him that the killer could not have not seen Bogdan, or Bogdan would have been killed that night. Bogdan was blackmailing the killer which is why there was a meet in the theatre box. Bogdan saw it as his ticket off the ship.

Hunter finishes his beer. Jasmin is there, "Another beer Mr Witowski?"

Hunter shakes his head and smiles, stands and

leaves. Jasmin is a dangerous woman who knows a world of secrets.

"Jasmin. You know this killer. You might not know it, but he knows you know. That is enough for him to make you the next victim."

Hunter turns and leaves, he deliberately leaves her stranded and worried.

"Mr Witowski!" She calls.

Hunter slowly turns, he knows this is going to lead somewhere.

50 TRUST, BUT VERIFY

Prisha is working like a machine with an office set up at the photo gallery's public counter, in the thoroughfare of the promenade deck 5. It is the perfect position because it affords a space for two people to work, and it is long and thin, allowing room for a queue. Jason is assisting her. She has worked out he not only has clearance but is a senior member of the team. And Jason has worked out that his being posted by the photo boards could be good for business. He can point out the pictures with a joke and a laugh. Every crew member on the ship is part of one big company, selling memories that the guests can take home. This cruise will undoubtedly have memories for all of them and the line is proving beneficial to photography sales, but their impatience is not helping Prisha. A new couple moves in front of her and the man holds his mobile phone up in her face.

"Look!" Is the blunt request.

Prisha reads silently. 'French authorities deny they have cut any deal to let any guests off the "ghost ship" at any island in French Polynesia.'

Prisha looks up at them.

"How can I help?"

"No one's getting off."

"I am part of the team investigating the murders, this is part of our enquiry. If you have some helpful information I would be pleased to send it back to Miami."

"You can send us back to Miami."

"That will eventually be an option, but American immigration would hold everyone there who has not been eliminated from the enquiry. The killer is on the ship, there were nineteen hundred suspects, and through our elimination, there is now a far smaller number."

"We want to be on that list." The woman insists.

"Then be in a time-stamped venue whenever possible. Most will be cruise card scanned again this evening."

Ruby jumps the queue and faces Prisha as the couple leave.

"A word please."

Prisha wonders what she has done wrong, but whatever it is, Ruby still does not have clearance so the conversation is found to be awkward. At the window away from the queue, though all the guests are watching them, Ruby lifts two sheets of paper up for Prisha to read.

"What's this?"

Prisha doesn't need to read it, she knows what it is. It is her application for the job at C.S.C.I. as their new female investigator. Prisha stays silent.

"I can't believe your nerve."

Prisha snatches them back. "I will talk to you when

you have been cleared."

Prisha strides away leaving Ruby, Jason, and his queue.

Prisha storms into the suite to find Hunter and Kieron at a table, both dressed for the evening, both with a beer. She approaches the table and shows them her CV and letter of application.

"What is this?"

They look at it but both seem a little surprised.

"It looks like your application for a job that doesn't actually exist yet," Kieron says.

"But a very novel way of presenting it," Hunter says, taking it.

"Please wait in the room outside and we will call you in for your interview in a moment," Kieron says light-heartedly.

"No!" She says loudly.

"That was almost funny, Kieron. You must be feeling a lot better." Hunter smirks.

"Very determined approach, this candidate," Kieron says.

"No! Miss Ruby Jenkins just gave this to me on deck five, in front of guests," she says.

Now the two men take more interest.

"How did Ruby get it?" Hunter asks.

"You tell me; it was here on my desk. She had no access to this room," Prisha says, quite put out.

"I can see how Ruby would be upset," Kieron says.

"I am upset. This is my property. Not for her to take," Prisha says stubbornly.

Hunter reaches out for another chair and drags it to the table. "Well, we've got it now. We'll look at it again after this job is over."

"How did she get in? It is a security breach." Prisha says, sitting down.

"Head of security is accused of a security breach?" Kieron says.

"Did you have her here for sex?" Prisha accuses.

Hunter, who was taking a moment to drink, chokes on his beer. "She obviously still has a key that can get in anywhere."

"And I'm not surprised she was seriously pissed when she saw this," Kieron says, "apart from this application, did you have a productive afternoon?"

Hunter gets up, walks to the fridge and de-caps another beer, handing it to her.

"I don't drink," Prisha says.

"I was just collecting your fingerprints."

She looks up at him, "And my DNA? Nice try, I'm excluded."

They both toast her and crash bottles. Kieron spins Paul Lopkey's information sheets to her.

"As we are the only three investigators here that can trust each other, let's chew over the afternoon's thoughts and discoveries," Kieron says.

"I made no progress. Not one guest went green, they all just wanted to vouch for each other. I didn't trust any of their verifications," Prisha explains.

"You know who came up with 'trust, but verify'?" Hunter asks.

Prisha shakes her head.

"It's an old Russian proverb, a motto used by the KGB, and then by Ronald Reagan in speeches made about nuclear disarmament."

"We trust the guests, they may all be truthful, but we verify it. Your instincts are perfect." Kieron adds.

"For a spy," Hunter concludes.
"I am a spy now," she says
They toast again.

51 ONE WHEEL

Kieron remembers Paul Lopkey's act from his first ship where he went to visit his daughter Auli'i, who was then a dancer. Nearly every throw-away ad-lib line Lopkey uses is exactly the same, almost every fall off his monocycle or unicycle is at the same time and in the same way. It makes no difference that this is a different ship and there are totally different members of the public on stage. This is a well-rehearsed, well-worked act and he performs with ease showing his incredible dexterity. He knows his show works and the audience loves it. The show finishes but there is not the usual rush for guests to be the first to leave, tonight is different. Guests linger and chat, wanting to be inside the known timed and registered circle. It also means that this evening there are people in the theatre who rarely attend shows and are surprised at how impressed they are.

Tonight, Kieron has watched the show with a third eye. He has seen an athlete who could flip easily over a rail and drop to the floor below, who has manipulated those he invited on stage to supplement his act with a push or a pull at the right point of the body at the right time. This is a man who could lift and throw someone, a man who might once have been his friend on another ship but could have caught him behind the neck and tossed him to his death a few days ago on this one. However, many performers are varied in their sexuality. Why would he have any frustration about being other than straight? Unless he is married. Kieron strains but fails to remember if the conversation went that far. He waits at the back of the theatre as he tries to recall more of the conversation he had with Lopkey on the last ship. Georgie introduced him and his daughter Auli'i to Paul Lopkey. Kieron wonders for a fleeting second how his daughter is, but the clock is ticking. He has to detail every characteristic he can about Lopkey because the computer says he is the number one murder suspect.

Memories rush back to him. Just as Kieron currently hurts because he plummeted onto steel a few days ago, he remembers he was in pain when they met. He had leapt onto another ship and hit the steel side, he was hurting that night. Kieron had been nicknamed Batman for the jump and Lopkey thought that was very funny. He asked a lot about the Commander's military background. He had a particular rhythm and punctuation as he spoke. He remembers his constant need to be funny. He remembers his eyes, his need to be liked and his insecurity that seemed to be hidden. A man who had no 'off-switch' to his laughter-Tourettes syndrome. He appeared a strange character, but it was the first meeting.

Kieron walks against the flow of the crowd leaving the theatre and stops when he reaches the empty stage. It could be a long uncomfortable evening interviewing Lopkey and he is digging deeper to remember more from that inaugural meeting. Kieron remembers asking if he could call him Paul. He remembers Paul quizzing him over and over again about what 'Investigator Philips' might be investigating next. Paul would have known that the real story on that ship was kept from him that night. He will now know there was a major drug baron's wife on board and gunmen. He will know we were armed then and several shoot-outs happened below decks. He may know even more if he read the book that was rushed to print just weeks ago, and the ghost-writer did dramatise things a little. Their meeting was only ten or so weeks ago so they should greet each other as old friends, even though Hunter may not have been a drinking buddy. Kieron smiles, a lot happier with himself that he is feeling good and remembering well. He climbs up the wooden side steps of the stage, aided by his walking stick knowing Lopkey, the comedian is likely to refer to him as Humpty Humpty rather than a superhero.

As Kieron gets to the top of the stairs, the stage lights come back on and Elvis the entertainment manager glides swiftly to the middle of the stage with a microphone. Kieron slips behind the stage curtain, out of sight and watches.

"Ladies and Gentlemen, I trust you enjoyed another great production and if you don't need to rush off to bed on a promise, can I ask you take a seat and we might just find something to entertain you."

Kieron knows he is thinking on his feet. Something has happened.

"I say this because you are logged in here, timed and registered and something might be occurring. Something, I know not what so don't ask me, maybe playing out elsewhere. Woosh!" he says turning his head. "Was that the flight of fake news on social media?"

Kieron moves backstage, down the steps to the men's dressing room. There is no Lopkey, as he might expect, just his clothes and costume changes and his tall unicycle. He walks through the dressing room and out into the forward ship's crew staircase on deck 4, where there are now some screams and shouts as people rush from below. Stage crew have watched something vanish down the stairs and are cautiously following with phones ready to film.

"Stop!" A shout is heard from way below.

Kieron discards his walking stick and runs down the stairs. He can see nothing on deck three, but there's noise from below. He jumps down two, three stairs at a time to deck two the main crew deck which has the motorway i95 straight down the middle.

"Stop or I shoot!" Kieron hears, sure that is Ruby's voice. I95 is always full of containers. Wheeled laundry trucks are at this front end and Kieron has to round them before he can see anything of what sounds like a standoff.

Food trucks way down towards the middle staircase are being moved from the middle towards the side. Equipment is being transported all along the deck but there is no sight of who is pushing it. Some workers are running towards him, to the front of the ship which must be away from the conflict zone.

Kieron advances fast, knowing those trucks are a barrier and he sees Lal and Krishma amongst them, one each side, crabbing slowly with their guns up like they are in a movie. Kieron sees the action is much further down and there is another set of trucks towards the aft scattered across i95. In the distance, Paul Lopkey accelerates out from behind one truck at speed on his monocycle, which is a single motorised wheel between his feet. He is so adept at riding it, that he looks like a cartoon character, leaning side to side, squatting and standing. He is obviously not shooting back at anyone but is escaping. Kieron is struggling but determined to catch up. He hears another shot which makes Lal and Krishma dive to the sides.

"Get up! That's a hand pistol. It wouldn't be accurate at this distance even if he wasn't riding a wheel with his back to us!" Kieron says, but he is feeling dizzy.

"Stop Lopkey, or I will shoot!" Ruby shouts.

Kieron sees her running from behind the same truck and then down the side of i95, her gun pointing all over the place as she runs. They are both way down the other end and more workers scatter towards them as Kieron tries to pick up speed, but he is failing.

"Ruby, don't shoot unless you have to!" He tries to shout, but he has no volume. He has no power. He hopes Ruby has the safety on her gun as it's getting waved about. He buckles. He forces himself to rise, digging deep to get in the game.

Running up behind him he hears the powerful sure footing of Hunter, so he favours one side to let him through.

"Ruby's running with a gun, chasing Lopkey on a monocycle," Kieron shouts to him.

"Step down soldier, that's an order," Hunter shouts to him.

Kieron does slow down now Hunter is in the game, his exhaustion and pain kicking in. Lal and Krishma catch him up with their guns out.

"Holster those guns now!" Kieron demands and they slowly follow his order. He does not want them shooting Hunter. "Right, now help me."

They take an arm each and help Kieron stay on the track. Gunshots are heard ahead and they try to duck, but Kieron stops them.

"Get up!"

Hunter ducks into cover to assess what is playing out. He is almost at the end of i95. The drama is around the service lifts to the main kitchen which is near the aft stairwell. Pushing forward too hard would force the target to get away into a public area. As much as his brain tells him the gunfire is Ruby's, Witowski has been in combat zones too many times to risk the target having a gun. The stalemate is tense and Ruby could also get spooked by him behind her and turn at any moment and shoot. This could be her first time in armed conflict. Hunter slips into the kitchen and looks for another route to the public stairs in order to circle round.

Kieron, Krishma and Lal cautiously push a large fridge aside to clear the way so they can see ahead and join the party at the end of i95. It turns slowly, revealing a kitchen porter swinging from a looped cable tight around his neck and hung over the large silver door. Kieron grabs him and lifts sweating with the effort,

"Release him!"

Lal opens the door and the cable lengthens, Krishma loops it away from his neck and he falls with Kieron. Kieron gasps for air, but the porter makes a gurgle sounds that sound eerily post mortem. Kieron rolls over to focus on the threat of what is now a confirmed killer upfront.

"It's a crime scene, don't spoil it," Kieron says, as he crawls forward leaving Lal and Krishma. He sees Ruby, her gun swings round to him, he shrugs at her, and she swings back.

"Got him! Guns down," Hunter shouts from an undisclosed position.

"Don't believe you. Show your face," Ruby shouts, still hidden.

"That's Witowski," Kieron shouts, moving towards Ruby's position, way out in the middle before collapsing with exhaustion.

"What are you doing?" she shouts.

"Stand down."

"No way, that could be suicide. I can't see Hunter."

Kieron pulls on her to get himself up, stands and hobbles past her, "Don't you dare shoot me in the back, or that job offer is off the table," he says, struggling up the stairs. He looks to the stairwell entrance where Hunter holds Lopkey in a manner that ensures he is not going anywhere.

"Paul, how you doing?" Kieron asks with a smile.

"Not so good, Batman," Paul answers.

Kieron turns round to Ruby, "Well done investigator. Cuff him."

Ruby attends to Lopkey as Hunter rolls him over and pulls his arms behind his back.

Kieron collapses and falls down the few steps to the half level.

Hunter grabs his phone and dials, "Medics. Level 2, aft staircase at i95, man down. Tell Doctor Simon it's Kieron again."

"How about me?" Lopkey asks, and Hunter looks down to see a pool of blood increasing fast from a bullet wound in his thigh. Hunter rips a strip off Lopkey's shirt. "Hey!"

He rolls it and rams it into Lopkey's leg. Lopkey

screams.

"Two men down. Confirm you have that," Hunter states into his internal phone.

Lal approaches them, "I think the porter is dead."

"Three men down and counting. Confirm you are travelling," Hunter corrects, leaving Lopkey with Ruby to go to Kieron. He gently turns him over into the recovery position and checks his pulse.

"He doesn't look well," Lopkey says.

"You better hope he lives," Hunter says in a low deep threat.

52 OLD PRESS CLIPPING

Day eight in the Pacific and all seems finally calm sailing straight towards the peaceful clear pastel blue waters of Polynesia. The bright yellow sunrise crashes in through the windows. Sprawled in the data room, making it look more like a fraternity house, the investigation team are still wearing last night's clothes, not having gone to bed. Hunter is wondering how his buddy is, as the Butler serves him coffee and clears away bottles. Lal and Krishma are both still asleep in chairs, not used to drinking. Empty wine bottles litter Prisha's desk, but she is in the bedroom asleep on Kieron's bed, fully clothed.

Ruby is anxiously waiting for a call from Doctor Yates to say that the killer in the medical centre has woken from his induced sleep. The entertainer might have been shot, but Hunter has told her more than once in the past few alcohol-fuelled hours that he has been shot a few times. He thinks a good shake and a shot of something would liven him up, but Lopkey is not a war prisoner about to be tortured. Even though the bullet hit an artery Hunter is calling it a scratch, and he has pulled a sickie to avoid questioning. Hunter, however, has a plan and Doctor Simon has been well briefed. Simon and Kieron will be on the case. Breakfast will soon be served in the Captain's dining room and the big man is ready to eat.

Ruby has added a new column for the murder of the kitchen porter and put in the time scale of his death from her brief but conclusive crime report. She has also ticked herself off for having proven whereabouts during his murder and turned her line green. She flops in her chair and is just drifting back into a deep sleep when it is time to wake. The green highlighter pen falls from her hand as her eyes close.

Prisha walks in just as the pen bounces. Although she has not been a detective long she knows what that means. She looks at the board and sees that Ruby has given herself security clearance. Prisha isn't sure that is right. She still thinks Ruby should not be in the room. It takes two ticks to go green and with only one, Ruby's line should be orange. However, it is not her call and she is up early and waiting for Dwight Ritter to wake up in Miami and send over the new elimination sheets. He has had Ruby's initial crime scene report from last night but that is unlikely to be in the first pass for today. Dwight will have had engine room and mechanics work logs put in and she expects more crew to be turned green. Then, there is another small matter that she is biding her time on because she is the new girl at investigations, even if she was invited to shadow Ruby last night and make her own notes on the crime scene. She goes into the bathroom, closes the door and locks it and the shower runs.

The printer starts and the phone rings. Jason is so tired and drunk he will sleep through anything even after being prodded by Ruby. Lal and Krishma both open their eyes but fail to wake fully. Ruby jumps to life and hits the speakerphone button. The sound of Miami fills the room.

"Miami's awake then," Ruby says sarcastically. "Good morning Mr Ritter."

"Who's that?" he asks.

Prisha comes out of the bathroom with towels wrapped around her, her long hair twisted up onto the top of her head. Hunter's eyes widen. She approaches the butler to take a coffee and ask if someone might bring her some clean clothes from her room.

"It's Ruby Jenkins. Head of security."

"Good morning Ruby Jenkins, head of security. Can I please speak with someone who has security clearance in this investigation?" Dwight asks.

Prisha tries to hide her satisfaction. Jason wakes and has to do a double-take, seeing her wrapped in a towel. She takes her coffee into the bathroom and starts drying her hair with the door open. Hunter silently chuckles. Ruby, annoyed, lifts the handset and the sound of Miami is gone. She offers it to Hunter who has not got the energy to get up.

"Hit the speaker again," he says.

Ruby hits the speaker button and the ambient room sound changes again.

"Morning Dwight, no Gloria Estefan playing this morning?" Hunter shouts. "You're back on speaker. Ruby is a special guest this morning."

"Hunter, when the computer gives you a person of interest we do not expect you to shoot them. We have a new person of interest this morning and we do not want them shot," Dwight says firmly.

Everyone's faces change and Hunter sits up, listening. That was not what they were expecting.

"But he killed a kitchen porter last night!" Ruby shouts.

"Is that your guest again, Hunter?" Dwight says.

"Yeah. She chased him and shot him," Hunter says.

"He's the killer!" Ruby adds.

"A court makes those decisions, above my pay grade, Miss Jenkins. I glanced over the report and saw no witness and no camera footage, so for now, Lopkey's just a person of interest being questioned," Dwight adds. "How many guests you got in there, Hunter?"

"Just the one."

"I am no longer a guest, thank you. I have clearance," Ruby says.

"I have just sent the new clearance list, sadly Officer Jenkins, last night's work has yet to be analysed in full. However, at best it is one tick against your name, and you need two to go green, two to be in that room. Or has someone overtaken my authority?" Dwight asks.

Prisha's finger makes a large tick in the steamed-up bathroom mirror. She remains in there, happy and now the only one who slept the night and is showered and refreshed.

"OK Dwight, we're going to breakfast next door. I'll leave you with the rest of the green team."

"Speak later. Who's left in the room please?" Dwight asks.

Jason sees he is vulnerable, he can't face work and

slides out fast with Hunter. Lal and Krishma leave with their boss. Prisha is left standing in her towel in the bathroom door, looking at the empty room.

"It's Prisha, I'm still here. Hi."

"Ah, Prisha, good morning. Please tell me that the crime report wasn't done by someone who's not security cleared for this case. I have to present all the facts to international cultural attaches, embassies, and the French police to beg for small things like docking rights. They ain't stupid." Dwight says.

Prisha opens Kieron's drawers searching for something to put on, they have very few clothes in them. She pulls out a pair of y-fronts and decides they will work, then pulls on a white tee-shirt. She answers him as she drops her towel.

"She has done every crime scene so far as the head of security, last night was not any different. Although Mr Hunter asked me to shadow her at every step and make my own report."

"Where is it? I can use that."

She hurriedly pulls her shirt on, "I have never done a crime report. I have pages of notes that need typing and I would like to..."

"Get it over to me fast." Dwight interrupts.

"Yes, sir. I will spend the day making it perfect and asking Mr Hunter if it is right." Prisha says realising the position she is in. She pulls on her white officer's jacket.

"Have you seen miss Jenkins report?"

"No. I just woke and showered."

"Good. Don't look at it, don't talk to her. Your report is all your own work. I don't care about the rest, you have green three-star clearance."

"Yes, sir."

"I'd like it by lunchtime."

"Yes, sir. Can you tell me who the new person of interest is?" Prisha asks.

There is a moments silence which seems to last forever and Prisha hears Dwight leafing through sheets of paper.

"Course I can tell you, you have clearance. The system is simple, right? Look in your printer and I'll walk you through it."

Prisha goes to the sheets in the printer. She lifts the familiar sheets of the new 'eliminated list' and places them on her desk to deal with as the butler enters, clearing away all the bottles. She looks at the new page then looks up in shock.

"You got it, Prisha?"

"Yes, Mr Ritter. But this is..."

"Yeah. Crazy right. Eric's goddam wife! Look on page two," Dwight asks.

Prisha looks at the second page. It is a team picture of a Miami college judo team from about forty years ago. The print colour, the hair, everything says America in the seventies. Not that Prisha was around in the seventies, or has ever lived in America, but she has watched old American TV shows, they get re-run all the time on ships.

"I can see Eric Clifford is in the team," she says recognising his sharp good looking features.

"Look at the girls, the young Betty Harris is the older Mrs Clifford, she was quite an athlete. Nearly made the Olympic team, but she fell pregnant."

"Oh."

53 TWIN BEDS

In the recovery room down in the medical centre, Kieron's eyelids start to flutter. He opens one eye but he is not seeing the vision of loveliness that he saw when he woke from his last deep sleep. Doctor Simon stands over him while manipulating his mobile phone into video camera record.

"Thought you'd never wake up," Simon jokes.

"Did I have another brain bleed?" Kieron forces out.

"Don't think so, but you should get a season ticket for here,"

Kieron smiles, he is awake. Simon passes him a glass of water to encourage the process.

"I think we should get that head of yours checked soon as we get into Pape'ete," Simon says.

"He certainly needs that doc, he's a complete crackpot," Paul Lopkey says from the bed next to him.

The doctor turns, still recording with his camera held out front in his left hand. His right-hand slips behind his back obviously palming Kieron a note, which wakes Kieron even faster. He is back in the game.

"So, you think I need to rest?" Kieron says behind him as he reads the note. 'Interview your mate Lopkey'.

"Last ship we were on he leapt off the dock, right into the side of the ship, like it wasn't steel!" Lopkey grins.

"Stop. That's a spoiler and I'm not up to that bit in the book," Simon replies. "But I'd like to have seen that."

"It's on the internet," Lopkey says. "Check on your phone."

Kieron pushes the doctor aside having read the note. He knows that 'your mate' means the interview needs to be subtle.

"Lopkey, what you in for?" Kieron shouts.

"I got bloody shot!"

"Shot?" Kieron says, and the doctor has backed off and is placing the phone on a shelf to work as a recorder all by itself.

"Done that, been there," Kieron says.

"You're trouble, tank-man. You never told me there were guns and shoot outs on the last ship."

"You never actually asked me."

"I won't ask again, if you are on a ship, I'm getting straight off." Lopkey laughs.

"I thought we were friends!" Kieron says.

"We can be pen pals, online friends, never face to face, get your butt shot friends!"

Kieron waves his hand over towards the next bed and they fist bump.

"So, how did you get shot?" Kieron asks.

"If you weren't in here out cold I would suggest you knew."

"I missed the first reel, catch me up."

"I was down on i95."

"Why? Theatre is on deck five, the motorway is on deck two?"

"Dude. After my show, I always go down and do a show for the workers. Ride up and down juggling."

Simon makes himself busy checking machines and read-outs, but he's listening. Prisha enters and Simon raises a hand to suggest she stays by the door and says nothing.

"I teach a little juggling, ride that monocycle which they love, and they teach me Bollywood dancing."

"You dance on the wheel?"

"Of course, man. You ever Bollywood danced?"

"No."

"It is the best."

"So your dancing was so bad, one of them shot you?"

"My dancing is improving. Their juggling is not, but I wouldn't shoot them for it!" Lopkey laughs.

Kieron laughs.

"Don't make me laugh, my head hurts. But, it's great to see you man, wish I felt better," Kieron says.

The two men are bonded like all workers on the ship circuit, truly 'ships in the night', passing each other.

"You ain't here just to give your talk, you're after the killer right?"

"I was. No idea what's happening."

"I heard, you hit the deck. I would have come in and seen your act."

"I had to get someone to shoot you just to get you in here," Kieron jokes.

"This was no invitation."

"Where did you get hit?"

"Leg. Major vein."

"I served under him." Kieron laughs.

"It was a major blood vessel," Simon adds.

"I was riding up i95, joking, acting out and someone shouted, 'Stop, shoot!' Seriously, we prank each other all the time down there. I thought it was one of the guys joking. Me, I carried on acting out – you know, 'not me', then bang! What the?"

"The killer was after you?"

"I guess he was," Lopkey says thoughtfully; the jokes are over.

Prisha walks forward and shows him a picture on her phone.

"Do you know this guy?" Prisha asks.

Paul takes his phone and looks at the picture of the dead kitchen porter.

"That's Kabir, he's a great mover. He's dead?"

54 DISARMED

"So when were you going to tell me?" The Captain fumes having stormed into the data room in the suite next to the bridge. Hunter turns slowly from the boards he is studying, not rising to the bait. Prisha looks up from her desk where she is still typing into a laptop.

"What, sir?" Hunter asks.

"That you've shot an innocent man and we have another death with no suspect?"

"No one from this investigation team shot anyone, and we do have a suspect who will be brought in as soon as I've gone over the reasoning sent from Miami."

The Captain stands with a fixed gaze on Hunter digesting his first remark, but before he can speak, Hunter continues.

"I suggest you talk to Ruby, your head of security, and maybe reconsider the order to have them all armed," Hunter says softly because he is talking to the Captain of the ship.

"Is there no way Lopkey did this?" the Captain asks.

"No, sir." Prisha answers. "Last night he was watched by too many crew. He was doing a performance up and down i95, sir, and they watched him right up to the stairs as Ruby Jenkins chased him. They thought that was part of the act. I have also double-checked all his offered alibis for three other murders and they are firm. All of that, plus a video of his interview has already gone back to Miami."

"This is a disaster. We will look fools when the French authorities hear we shot our only suspect who it transpires is totally innocent."

"Sir," Hunter interrupts. "This morning's story can be the same as last night, we have a suspect. They don't need to know the suspect has changed."

"Who is the new suspect?" The Captain asks.

"Clifford's wife, Betty."

"No, I don't see that," the Captain mutters, deep in thought.

"Me neither at first, which is why I'm here double-checking how Miami came to that conclusion. Stupid as it sounds, looks pretty good. Prisha's about thirty minutes off finishing the crime scene report from last night then we're gonna take a walk and find Betty."

"Very nearly done, sir," she says.

The Captain raises his arms. "What do I say?'

"Stay with the story, we have a suspect. No he or she, no name, no detail," Hunter explains.

The Captain nods but he is in despair, he knows the political problems mounting as they get close to the French territory.

"There is no way they are going to entertain us on any of their islands," the Captain says.

"They're gonna have to. We got a medical emergency. Kieron Philips has a brain bleed and needs a CT scan of his head according to doc. Why don't you talk to him, get a medical report and throw a little bit of maritime emergency law around?" Hunter suggests.

The Captain offers a wry smile in a moment of reflection. Both men have been at sea and dealt with international politics for a long time. Hunter is a perfect addition to the Captain's team and he is not sure how this would have worked out if he and Philip's had not been dropped in so fast.

"I will, but the French can be very insistent. I can't see us docking," Neil shares.

Hunter gives the smallest of shrugs.

"I'll reverse the order on carrying arms," the Captain offers.

"Thank you, sir. I'll let you know if something happens," Hunter adds as the Captain leaves.

"Phew," Prisha offers as a relief.

"No phew. No skin off our nose, we're fixing problems," Hunter tells her. "Now you gonna press the send button on that report?"

"Please sir, five more minutes."

"Five."

Hunter goes to the house phone and dials out with the handset to his face.

"Who's that? I thought I rang Dwight."

"I ain't never been a Dwight, ain't never had a Dwight," Mary says.

Mary is at the food counter behind which Stan is busy grilling large slices of green tomatoes, burgers and onion rings. She waves to Izzy, one of her young college devotees who hustles over with her note pad. Izzy listens at the phone and writes.

"I thought you was dead I hadn't heard from you in so long."

"You still have journalists there?"

"What, this early? They catch breakfast so late they don't have to buy lunch. They got less money than my students."

Mary covers the phone and speaks to Izzy.

"Don't you go writing that down, you wanna be a journalist you just stick to the facts, then add the grits."

Mary is back speaking with Hunter, "How's my other boy?"

"To be honest Mary, he ain't so good. He has had a brain bleed and they did emergency surgery in a gale force storm to do something to relieve pressure in his skull," Hunter says, stopping because he can feel someone taking notes, he can use them.

Mary looks down at Izzy's work and covers the phone again.

"You put that he was on death's door there, and add raging before gale force."

"That's –."

"That's the grits girl."

Mary goes back to the phone, she knows she is being played. "So, baby, what has to happen?"

Hunter smiles, he knows she knows the game. "He needs emergency medical treatment, he needs to get into that fantastic world-class hospital in Tahiti and get him a CT scan."

"What's that? Don't worry, we'll look that up later."

"So we are guessing one of those nice fast French authority customs boats, normally used to chase drug traffickers on behalf of the whole international community, will meet us sometime tomorrow and take Commander Kieron Philips off with our ship's doctor who has been treating him. They've got some top neurologist, trained in Paris."

"Have they shit?"

"I don't know. Look, both men leaving have been cleared of being the murderer so are safe to enter. We are going to need a new doctor to cover for Simon as we had another murder on board last night and a man was shot in the leg. We would also like a forensic pathologist with test equipment we don't have on board, or the bodies lifted off. We do have a suspect answering questions."

"OK."

"Thanks, Mary, you wanna go round and meet my wife?"

"Why I wanna meet your wife, she think we having an affair?

"No."

"I don't wanna take any pain if I ain't had the gain, you know what I mean? And as we working together, we should keep it biz, but thanks for the offer."

"Mary, I was asking you to check up on Elaine."

"I ain't-a social worker."

"No, guess you failed the interview on that one."

"I was a midwife for years, that paid for this diner. Many of these kids here, I slapped their butts and made them breathe their first breath."

"Yeah, well Elaine tells me she's pregnant, and I ain't home."

"You should have said, when she due?"

"About nine months."

"I got time then."

"Mary!"

"OK. I hear you. I gonna need a holiday after all this, and I ain't ever been on one of them big ships."

"You told me you didn't like ships," Hunter says.

"My people got a historic dislike of ships, but me

not talking your kind of ships. Mary's tired, and Stan wants someone else to be cooking for him."

"I hear you."

"Now let me go and try and get you that bullshit medical visit you want to the mainland."

"Thanks, Mary!"

"And Hunter! Don't be a stranger. I got a journalism student here called Izzy, and she need some more meat so she can add the gravy."

55 OUTSIDE IN

Hunter and Prisha walk together down the starboard side of the long outside promenade on deck five. It is not yet midday and her report with a map of i95, including people and trolleys has all been sent to Miami. The detail in her work makes them both proud, though Hunter only glanced at it. They now have to interview Betty, while all last night's infrared data slowly uploads to Miami. There is far more content than previous nights and it will time stamp and place more guests in various venues than they have before.

They have a rare moment to stretch their legs and take in the clear blue sky, flat sea and fresh air, now mixed with cigarette smoke as they walk from the front where their suite is to the rear where the security office is.

"Sorry Mr Hunter, we came out on the wrong side of the ship, but I wanted to see the sun," Prisha says.

"As unpleasant as the smell is, I don't think it will kill me for a few minutes."

On this ship, the smokers use the starboard side, the right side facing front, and they have the sun this morning. They won't get the sunset. Hunter has always had mixed feelings about the old shipping terms of port and starboard. The logic is that they diffuse confusion by being permanent. So no matter which way the ship faces, whether north or south, the east or west side of the ship may differ but port or starboard are constant. It is just that most people are confused by port or starboard. It could just be called the ship's left and right side but the other terms have lasted. 'Starboard' comes by combining two old English words: stéor, meaning 'steer' and bord, meaning 'the side of a boat'. The steering oars on old ships were always on the right, the stronger and preferred arm for the majority of sailors.

Just as the tradition of stronger arms being on the right, in the research of Betty Harris's very successful college judo career she also favoured the right. She threw with the right and strangled with the right, her favoured winning move. Now they have that information, doctor Simon Yates has been asked to re-examine the bodies considering whether the killer could be Betty or not. His small team will study another angle on the killer's signature moves and ask whether the killer favoured using their left or right arm.

Finding a guest on a ship should be easy because again they will have a pattern of favoured moves. Betty is known to rise late, buffet lunch, then spend most of the rest of the day on the slot machines. The gambling area is normally an area that any venue has covered by security cameras. Even on this ship with limited cameras, the card and roulette tables are covered. Miami based analysts have now sat and watched each and every hour of security footage looking for Betty to move, and she did.

Whereas the ship-based investigators had thought she sat there all day and all night, it certainly was not the case. Whilst her double gins were all bought from the waitress in the casino, she did occasionally leave. Maybe she is a smoker and she had to slip outside at regular intervals because unlike some ships that allow smoking in the casino, this ship has a different policy. It is amazing how little they know about Betty but they had always looked at her as a victim. Very rarely are serial killers' women, and it is even rarer for women to work alone. The female serial killers that both Philips and Witowski had read about in their brief breaks since being on board, seemed to be poisoners or often work in hospitals or care homes. Few used or had Betty's talents, although, approaching sixty she is not the athlete she was when at college. The skills a judo athlete has, the timing Betty would need are skills like riding a bike, they never leave you, even if they have to be revived. Betty had motive, rage, and she has no green line. Not once has she got a verified alibi.

Now the two are passing by Ruby's office, to see how she is doing, not to gloat. A fellow agent has shot someone by mistake and will be feeling shit. This is a peace mission, it is not to interrupt the work she still has to do which is no doubt building up because of the planning for a possible docking in Pape'ete.

Prisha and Hunter jog down the stairs from floors five to two at the back of the ship and turn into her office. She is not there. Krishma is at her desk yawning, and on seeing them just points towards the cells which are beyond this office. They walk through and see Ruby tearing into Betty Clifford. Prisha overtakes Hunter, unable to control her anger.

"Officer Jenkins, I must ask you to step outside

please."

56 DO IT PROPERLY

Ruby steps outside and Hunter steps into the investigation room and closes the door behind him.

"Officer Jenkins I am going to have to report this incident to Miami. Could I know what you have asked her and what you have told Mrs Clifford?" Prisha asks.

"I will type it up and let you have a transcript, but she's guilty. Just as I am for shooting the wrong guy who I'm now going see and apologise to. So you might have to wait for that report," Ruby finishes before bursting off.

Prisha turns and enters the cell. She sits down next to Hunter who is looking at the angry Betty Clifford. He says nothing as Prisha dutifully pulls out her note pad.

"I told the other officer everything," Betty states angrily.

"She works for the ship's security. We are a team of outside investigators working for head office in Miami, reporting to them, the American and French authorities. We are different." Prisha explains.

"So I've got to say it all again?"

"What?"

"Where I was at the time of each murder?" Betty asks.

"Betty, you are not under arrest, you can leave at any time. We can even do this upstairs in a bar," Hunter offers.

"You're buying."

"From memory, Betty, I bought the last two

rounds and as I get no expense account it's your round," Hunter says with a smile, lightening things up.

"Let's stay here then."

"My object is two-fold: one to green light as many guests and crew as I can to enable them to disembark in Tahiti," Hunter explains.

Prisha has written nothing down and is watching Hunter more than Betty. She is like a sponge to knowledge, learning from his pauses and phrasing, not just the questions.

"I don't mind staying onboard and sitting in the casino," Betty suggests.

"The casino closes when we dock, it re-opens as we leave the territorial waters of wherever we are," Prisha says.

"Let's try and get you off the ship," Hunter suggests.

"If I am not under arrest, how can I be kept on the ship?" Betty asks with a smirk.

"Good question. It will not be about us keeping you on the ship, so much as the French authorities only allowing people off who have been cleared."

"How do I get cleared?" She asks.

"Prisha here sends verified data back to Miami, the computer clears you, sends us and the French a list. The French authorities in Polynesia then decide if they wish to act on it, the same will happen for Australia afterwards if the killer has not been detained," Hunter explains.

"Some world cruise!" Betty says.

"Yes. And I am sorry for your loss, but tell me about Jasmin," Hunter slips in, without changing his inflexion in the slightest.

Betty is stopped in her tracks. Her jaw tightens in

her moment of silence. Prisha has lowered her pen, also quite shocked that Hunter threw the curveball in while the crowd were getting hot dogs.

Betty starts to shake her head.

"You weren't totally honest with us when you said you stayed in the casino all night every night," Hunter suggests.

"I didn't mean one hundred percent 24/7!"

"No, so you have been to the Crow's Nest?"

"I don't go in there, she's in there."

"Jasmin?"

Betty nods her head.

"It might have helped us if you had told us earlier that Eric was…" Hunter lingers on the unfinished question and allows her to fill the silence. Prisha notices that interrogation is about leaving empty spaces.

"She's not even a proper woman!"

"Now there's a phrase that could cause many a debate amongst all sexes," Hunter eases in gently.

"You know what I mean. I couldn't go in," she says.

"So where did you argue?" Hunter asks.

"Outside. Outside the men's toilet."

"Was it heated?"

"Damn right it was, and he went into the toilet and wouldn't come out."

Prisha starts to make notes that Betty can't read.

"The toilet next to the Crew Only door?" Hunter asks.

"I don't know," Betty offers.

"I thought you knew every rivet on this ship?" Hunter asks.

"Well I don't, he does. But he won't travel

unless she's working."

"He was a good looking guy, well groomed," Hunter says to lead her.

"Looking his best for Jasmin."

"OK. I'm gonna be straight with you, Betty. You're smart, tough and I would say you wore the pants in that relationship," Hunter offers.

"Damn right I did."

"So, you letting him book holidays to meet Jasmin doesn't make total sense to me."

"We've been together for a long time."

"Yeah. Great relationship, great understanding."

"And I miss him."

"I know. And I'm sorry. Forty great years."

"They were, forty years, never been apart," Betty reflects.

"He turned up drunk and you wished he'd stop drinking?" Hunter says.

"You remember?" Betty asks.

"Every word, Betty. He drank, so you drank as well?"

"Yeah. But it worked, and we both had fun," she says softly.

"But not together?" Hunter asks.

"If you mean like that, no."

"But you both had fun? Did you always come to the Caribbean?"

Betty looks up, resigned that Hunter is smart, that Hunter knows exactly how their relationship has developed. Betty nods to confirm exactly what she knows he is thinking.

"I didn't kill him," she says.

Hunter shrugs slightly and opens his hands a little in a way that means so much. He is saying he wants to agree and to help, but he needs more. Prisha is observing a master at work, her face is totally focused like she is watching the climax of a great movie and knows the end is moments away but she genuinely does not have a clue what is going to happen.

"You do know your way around the ship?" Hunter asks.

Betty nods.

"Through the crew doors?" he asks.

Betty nods.

"Bet you've seen i95?"

Betty nods again.

"Through the kitchen and their access areas?"

Betty nods.

Prisha switches her phone onto record because she feels he is about to get the confession, even though she knows it will probably not be acceptable in any court.

"You argued that night?"

"We did. The last time I saw him we argued."

"Did you go down through the crew doors?"

"We did and we had a very heated argument."

"In the service area?" he asks.

Prisha is amazed at how Hunter has got so much from her and she wants to jump ahead, to speed up. She wants to rush forward to how she ran to the other end of the ship, how she joined the stargazing, how everything happened but she forces herself to stay focussed and exact all the detail on paper. She has never written so fast but she knows she has to transcribe the conversation as she hears it live, then use the phone recording to verify it. Courts can be tricky, she has seen cases fall apart on TV because the detail was not exact.

"I left him there alive." Betty eventually says.

Prisha writes it down but does not believe a word of that comment and can feel her about to plead not guilty. Hunter remains silent.

"I didn't kill him. I wanted to, sometimes. Sometimes I hated what had happened to our relationship. But I didn't kill him."

"Why didn't you tell us this before?"

"Because I knew you'd think it was me, because when the others died I panicked," Betty admits. "And when he was found in the laundry, that was where I'd left him, at the chute."

Prisha wants Hunter to close the deal, she can't stop herself interrupting, "Why would you not kill him if he was having an affair?"

She has shocked herself, why did she ask that? Now she has to write it down. Was that stupid? She scribbles fast. Her eyes flash to Hunter, then back to Betty.

"Listen. You had a deal, you both enjoyed it. But he wasn't the one having sex was he?" Hunter asks.

WTF? Prisha thinks then scolds herself for even thinking the words.

Betty shakes her head just slightly to agree. "You know I would rather he came home but we hadn't had sex for years. He might have been gay, I don't know. I don't know."

"Barbados? Jamaica?" Hunter asks.

Prisha's hand is almost shaking with all this tension.

"Jamaica. It seemed like I was getting my own back, or maybe just something I needed, but that's how the relationship went. I'd never had sex like that. We cruised more and more." Betty says.

Prisha is desperate to hear what happened. Hurry

up Betty, spit it out, but she says nothing.

"So you became a sugar mama? But Betty, if you weren't early to bed on ship, and there is someone who can give you an alibi, let me suggest you ask him. I guarantee him immunity from company action. That means I'll be able to greenlight the pair of you. He will no longer be a suspect either."

Hunter stands, he has finished.

"I think you need a double gin," he smiles.

"Let me buy you a drink," she says standing.

He smiles and shakes his head.

"There's someone else you need to talk to."

57 SEARCH ONLINE

"You better get that report to Miami, I'll break the bad news to the Captain," Hunter suggests.

"Bad news?" Prisha asks as they stride down the inside corridor on deck five. Having left the cells at the aft of the ship, they need to get to the front and go back up to eight where their data room is.

"We don't have a suspect anymore."

"Not good," she agrees. "But I feel we're getting closer."

"Certainly getting closer to Tahiti."

"Why don't you come back and look at the boards and see if there is more from Dwight before you meet the Captain. He may have a new suspect."

"What I like about you, Prisha is your ability to keep a logical focus on the plot. But are you ready for the 'den of iniquity'."

"Den of Iniquity. That is a market place of thieves, from the Gospels."

"I was referring to Miami being a den of iniquity. Search online, for 'Sugar Mama' so you can explain in your report what was meant back in there. Conclude by saying we expect to clear her later today."

"Do I mention Ruby?"

"Just say she spoke with Betty first, that's enough. Jenkins is suffering. She shot an innocent man in the leg now she's shot herself in the foot. She knows there'll be an internal investigation."

Hunter slows down when he gets to the art gallery.

"What is it?" She asks.

"The picture Benny liked…"

"Which one?"

"It's not important."

They march off and hit the elevator up button at the front stairwell.

Hunter Witowski enters the bridge where the view through the front windows is of the flat blue sea hit by a low dipping sun which sends stars sparkling on the gentle ripples. It's a memorable sight that makes sailing such a treat, the earth seems so peaceful. The Captain turns from dolphin watching and greets him,

"I am not sure the world will survive social media."

"That's a bold statement. I'm thinking there's something deep and meaningful behind it."

"You asked me to claim a medical emergency. It was greeted with the briefest acknowledgement by Pape'ete port authorities with 'they would get back to me'."

Hunter smiles.

"Then the story appeared on social media early this morning, it spread to international press because our ship is famous, apparently it's now called the 'Ghost

Ship'. Print journalists picked up the story and stated international maritime mumbo jumbo. Then, apparently, the French authorities somewhat embarrassed, talked to our people in Miami offering to help and we are getting medical assistance."

"The world survived both the storm and social media," Hunter states.

"Has it? I understand what you meant now by the tail is wagging the dog?"

"Yeah. But that's the new world."

"Does Philips need medical treatment?"

"I'm not a doctor, but if you want my opinion, with a brain problem, a helicopter might not be the answer. But that's only my opinion."

"What does it get us if they take him?"

"Our doctor has to go with him."

"We lose a doctor and an investigator."

"We ask for a replacement doctor and some detectives to go over our work. Tahiti then has skin in the game. We have a man on their island, they have men on our ship."

"Tomorrow, a day out from Tahiti we normally get a local cultural act for the theatre that night."

"Push for everything and it will show how humane Tahiti is. The Chinese will love a huge show of strength."

"I feel another social media release brewing."

"Sir, there is something you might consider now we have lost our suspect. There are about seventy guests and about twenty-seven officers that are still red. I know it's late, but I suggest we get them all in one room tonight."

Neil turns to the deputy captain Vasile Nagy who is sailing the ship. "Vali, ask officer Roy Stevens to attend the bridge as soon as he can please."

The Captain turns back to Witowski, "One more thing, Hunter. We have to enter and dock as a military ship because we are carrying guns."

Hunter smiles. "Social media!"

Hunter leaves the bridge, now expecting to hear of a party tonight and a cultural show tomorrow. He knows cruise ships don't carry guns. Ships with any arms onboard are not normally allowed to dock at non-military ports. The way around this rule is to hire private security teams who board the ship when it has a problem or as it enters dangerous stretches of water like the Gulf of Aden. They then leave with their weapons once the danger has passed. Social media has revealed a shooting and it is obvious that the ship has arms on board.

Hunter enters the data room and sees Kieron at the boards catching up.

"You're supposed to be so ill, it's a medical emergency."

"Now you mention it, I don't feel a hundred percent."

"You can't be seen out tonight, we are demanding a fast boat meets us tomorrow and rushes you to an essential CT scan. I want you in Tahiti bugging the authorities like the local consulate can't."

"But I'm ill!"

"If they find nothing on the CT they'll release you."

"And if they find something?" Kieron asks.

"You'll be glad we got you to a hospital."

Prisha stands from her desk hoping their banter is over and she can interrupt. She walks over with a sheet of notes.

"I looked up Sugar Mama and found a woman on YouTube with an agency looking for younger men for older ladies."

"Well Betty is an older lady," Hunter says.

"I understand, I discovered a lot more about the Caribbean than all my years of sailing here have taught me," Prisha says with well-chosen language.

"There are lots of countries where younger men look to be saved from poverty by older women, normally single. Guess Betty is truly single now."

"I caught up. Betty rang up and said she was seeing two men on the ship's crew. Would our killer be a jealous lover?" Kieron adds.

Hunter thinks. It is not a route he had considered, but then this road was never mapped out before.

"Two men?" Prisha asks.

"Betty gave me two names," Kieron suggests. "They want immunity, then they will talk. Otherwise, they will deny everything,"

"Jealousy?" Hunter asks.

"Or money if she is a sugar mama, maybe a past young man she used to pay?" Prisha says obviously finding her new discovery a very strange affair.

"Can you two get to the bottom of this? Then rest, Kieron. Seriously, just rest while Prisha does the report."

"And Mary rang," Prisha says. Hunter nods, listening. "Izzy, her journalism student, has been preparing an article on the problems of seafaring. She has been researching. In 2017 there were 87 piracy incidents reported to the IMB Piracy Reporting Centre. A total of 63 crew members have been taken hostage."

"She sounds like a student," Hunter says.

"She wants to say that cruising is far safer and how in four days we have excluded nearly eighteen hundred of the nineteen hundred people on board from being the murderer."

"And tell her that tonight the other one hundred will be in one room," Hunter says.

"A den of iniquity," Prisha suggests.

"Just like a Hercule Poirot book," Kieron smiles.

"Who?" Prisha asks.

"A fictional Belgian detective, created by a writer called Agatha Christie," Kieron explains.

"Even though there is likely to be a murder in that room tonight, I would rather be in there than with Kieron interviewing the Sugar Crew," Prisha says.

"Prisha doesn't need a Sugar Daddy, she has us." Kieron smiles.

"Tell Mary she can run it provided they work in how helpful Tahiti is being by sending a doctor, detectives and a cabaret act for the theatre. They will also be taking away a seriously ill and dying guest," Hunter says.

"Who's that?" she asks.

"Him."

58 SIGMUND AND EDGAR

The West Wind specialty restaurant is closed tonight for a private party. Those who had booked it have been offered a free meal on any another night of their choice. It is a world cruise so they will have lots of time to make that up. The Captain was going to announce his 'invitation-only Red Party', but for so many reasons it has been kept quiet.

Every targeted guest has had a personal visit to invite them to the party. They are asked to wear something red because cruisers love themed parties and dressing up. All the invitations are taken personally by an officer and hand-delivered, not to be left outside in the post-rack. The officer has a red kerchief or scarf, and when they ran out of scarves a red fluffy boa from the entertainment stores. These officers are also all on the red list, meaning they have not been security cleared. Whilst they may have realised why they have been chosen, the guests are unlikely to have any idea. Parties are thrown all the time. Somewhere amongst this group is the killer, unless the murderer is from deep below decks, and neither Dwight or Hunter thinks that's the case. The two 'sugar crew' Prisha and Kieron will interview might be the exception but the team have to work on current information.

The officers delivering the invites know they are being timed and watched, because they have to report back to Roy Steven's hotel office, even though he has himself never managed to get off the red list. Each guest is then phoned to ensure that they feel special but more importantly to ensure they will be there and of course that they are still alive. It is not entrapment, none of the team expects any officer to kill or be killed in the cabin while delivering the red letter. That is why heads turn when one of the hotel staff making a call to check guests are coming, shouts out,

"I have a lady 7304 who thinks her husband is dead!"

Roy Stevens is fast to call the medical team. As soon as they acknowledge they are on their way he calls Hunter Witowski and then encourages his team to get back to work. This party has been arranged, invitations printed, a venue chosen, a menu prepared and staff arranged all in just a few hours.

Every cruise ship is required to have a supply of body bags and a morgue, but the morgue on this ship only has room for four bodies. They have had to be resourceful for some time. There is an old cruise joke that when they start giving ice-cream away free, they need the freezer space. Bodies of guests take preference in the mortuary because they have partners who may demand to see them. The ninth death is a huge problem for the medical team. The removal of bodies from the ship falls under local laws. Some ports require the bodies to be removed as soon as possible, using a door far away from the one being used by guests. Other ports allow the bodies to stay on board and travel back to the home port, but on a world cruise, there are a large number of ports and regulations to deal with. The ship has an overflow problem. Another problem is in the negotiation with the Tahiti shipping agent. Not only for the removal of a large number of bodies, which in turn go on to different countries which will issue the death certificates. However, as these are murders, a local post mortem may need to be done first by the French pathologists before the bodies can move back to the country to which it technically belongs. There will be a final post mortem there before the death certificate is issued.

Hunter waits outside cabin 7304, Prisha is inside with the distraught lady and the medical team have been given permission to move the body which is now in the last available body bag. Doctor Simon Yates leaves the cabin and Hunter walks with him down the corridor, following the stretcher team who take the first 'Crew Only' exit. Simon stops, now out of earshot of the guests waiting to console their friend.

"That looks like a heart attack. He had a medical history of heart attacks and strokes and had been in to see me earlier this week. I don't think it's one to add to your boards."

Hunter nods and walks back towards cabin 7304. He waits until he can catch Prisha's eye. His head rises for her to follow and he is gone. Prisha sits, arm around the lady, realising that as an officer she could sit with her for as long as it took, but she is on secondment to another unit. She smiles at the two women edging ever closer and stands to let them take over.

"Please call the hotel reception should you need anything," she says softly, then leaves.

Hunter is in the data room calling Dwight in speaker. The ringing fills the incident room. The door to Kieron's bedroom is closed, he is sleeping.

"Sorry, guys I am out, mobile. Who's calling?" Dwight says.

"It's Hunter. You taking a day?"

"No, I'm on your ship. Not your ship, but a mirror image that is docked here in Dodge. Very useful, and I have with me a psychologist who is an expert on serial killers, a consul from the French Embassy and a police lieutenant from Miami Dade who covers Port Miami."

"So good to have you as a lifeline to all those resources."

"I've also started to liaise with Interpol's i-checkit. What would you do without me?"

"Well, maybe we wouldn't have harassed two wrong suspects. But I'll forgive you."

"Ow! Back the truck up."

"I'll take another suspect off you any day."

"Everyone here is willing to stay on this ship when she sails so we can mirror whatever you feed us," Dwight says.

"You're sitting in HQ. Just ask."

"It's hell-of-a-busy there as you get near to Tahiti. We are all talking turkey but it ain't Thanksgiving yet. You will get into waters, your man will be taken off, but you may have to moor offshore and have a fuel barge come to you."

"That's stuff for Neil."

"Don't be surprised if you are surrounded by gunships and armed customs."

"Nothing surprises me," Hunter says.

"Don't worry, by the time you arrive we'll have a guided-missile frigate there."

"Sounds like over-kill. Are we causing an international crisis?" Hunter asks.

"No. Just increased theatre security in cooperation with the French Navy in the South Pacific. All to facilitate goodwill."

"So I will be able to get off and lay on the beach with a martini?" Hunter laughs.

"No!"

"OK, Dwight. I was ringing because we have all the red coded suspects in a party at the West Wind restaurant tonight, where they will also eat. So expect them to be in there between seven and ten."

"What do they do for toilet breaks?"

"Take a look at it, there are toilets in the stairwell which we will make part of the security area. Entrance will be at the top of the stairs."

"We're on our way."

"Can the psych think of something so we can spot our man?" Hunter asks.

"I'll put him on."

"Mr Hunter? It is Sigmund Henkel."

"Hi, doc, I assume you are the psychologist and not the police lieutenant."

"Correct, Edgar is with the police. I am sure we are somewhat breaking new ground here. In many respects, it is not technically a serial killer, though the FBI would no doubt still use that term. I say it's not, due to the lack of a cooling-off period between killings. It is a spree killer."

"Doc, how does this help me?"

"The spree killer does not have the return to normality between killings."

"There is little normality on a cruise ship, Sigmund."

"That I can see. The whole environment is like a pressure cooker, a catalyst. The confinement so unusual being caught is as much of a problem for them as it is for you to catch them."

"Sure."

"After the first, most of the other killings could be to protect themselves from capture, that again is not really indicative of a serial killer. The trigger may have been classic rage or sex, but the ensuing killings have more to do with either the desire not to be caught combined with, more complex, the growth in perceived power, that is power over you."

"What makes you say that?" Hunter asks.

"The ordering of drinks on the dead man's cruise card, checking in twice at the muster call. These are definite exhibitions of power to test you."

"Where you going with this doc?"

"We have just arrived in the restaurant you will use tonight. If you have the killer in a room, he will feel trapped. If there is truly no escape, it is likely he will make a power play. On land, I would worry about a gunman wanting to kill many people all at once, but you have no weapons so at least that is not an option. Do you understand my thoughts?"

"I do Sigmund. You are advising me to stay out of the room."

"Ha! Mr Witowski, if only that were possible. You were born to go into rooms like this and face trouble, I have read your file."

59 EXCEPTIONS TO THE RULE

Hunter rings his wife Elaine but his mind is not on the call and she knows it.

"You're thinking about the murderer."

"Sorry, Elaine. Just had a call with a psychologist in Miami."

"I didn't know you were seeing one, but that's good. It will help prepare you for fatherhood."

"Yeah, and his name's Sigmund," Hunter laughs, looking at a computer screen.

Hunter has rung her a few times and never been worried about the killer on the ship before, but something Sigmund said has made him address his own place in the room tonight. He is dressed in his dinner jacket and bow tie, ready to go, but his mind is racing. Sigmund was suggesting that the killer has no escape and Witowski knows that a killer who is trapped with nothing to lose, because all is already lost, is at his most dangerous and unpredictable. He knows if he continues to talk with Elaine she will sense he is worried.

"Can I call you in the morning, my head will be clear then? The psychologist has re-wired me."

They exchange kisses and 'miss you' and he hangs up, looking at Kieron's door. Kieron is his other partner, the one who can take the worry and walk into fire with him, whereas Elaine would rather he had retired to an easy cushy job.

Hunter walks towards Kieron's door but hesitates, his hand on the handle, thinking hard about everything he has seen in these few days, every kill that has been done and what Sigmund said.

"Who's at the door?" Kieron shouts.

Hunter walks in and gives him a big smile, "Nothing wrong with your instincts. How you feeling?"

"Head hurts, to be honest, I don't feel great but that might be because I'm thinking too hard."

"You do need some rest."

"After this, I'm gonna take a holiday. I've decided to call Georgie and visit our house in Bequia. Sleep, eat fresh fish, walk in the sand."

"Good idea," Hunter says. He knows that he has been hit hard and went back to work far too early. "Are you up to interviewing those two crew members?"

"Sure, but there's no rush, right?"

"Only brain rush, we have a psychologist with us in Miami."

"No shit. He'll want to write the book, don't tell him anything," Kieron says.

"Another book?"

"We can do this one together."

"Here's the thing. We know the killer is a professional or has some physical ability and training."

"Sure. They took me out very easily."

"Yeah, but that doesn't count," Hunter mocks, sitting at the end of Kieron's bed. "There are exceptions to standard serial killer criteria."

"They all make it up as they go along, they're observers, not doers. Look at the books written on military conflicts, why and how."

"But listen a minute. Harold Shipman was a successful professional doctor in the UK. Considered solid. He had won awards. He enjoyed power and wanted more. Nilsen was an ex-soldier. He became a civil servant and had no criminal record. No one suspected him. Then there was a reporter, I forget his name, but a proper crime reporter who even wrote a series of articles where he gave clues that he had murdered people. He dangled his power over the authorities. They all did."

"I get it, our man, he fits this group," Kieron says.

Our man wants power and knows he can't get off the ship. Ever. No one will get off until he is found." Hunter says definitely.

"Sure."

"My worry is we have shown our hand too soon, he might turn very nasty at the Red Party."

"Do you want me to come?" Kieron asks.

"I'll be there. I understand." Prisha says from the doorway.

"I was hoping you'd stay and look after me. Help with my interrogations."

"She's already watched the best at work, Philips. But Prisha, stay here and ensure he rests just a while longer. I have one last thing to do before any party,"

Hunter leaves.

"Rest!" Prisha leaves, turning into the data room, Hunter has gone.

Lal looks up as Hunter bursts into the security office,

"Lal, please open the safe."

"We are very busy, sir."

"I want to check the guns are still there."

"Of course sir, locked away. No one has touched them since Mr Lopkey was shot."

"Open it up!"

Lal goes to Ruby's desk and opens the drawer, pulls out the safe keys and then unlocks the grey safe which sits under the shelves behind the desks. The handle goes down and the door opens. Lal lifts out the kit bag and offers it to Witowski. Hunter opens it and counts out the guns. One, two and finally three. Then the holsters.

"There should be four."

"I know. I am in shock, sir."

"In shock when the keys to the safe are kept in Ruby's desk drawer and this office is often left unmanned?"

"Sir, I will ask Officer Jenkins."

"Lal, you will do nothing. Say nothing. Just lock the safe."

Hunter picks up the phone and rings the data room as he puts the guns and holsters back in the bag.

"Prisha, tell Kieron to get dressed for the party." He replaces the phone and looks at Lal. "Come with me."

He snatches the bag, then leaves.

60 DEN OF INIQUITY

Unusually, the entrance to the West Wind restaurant area has been set back at the stairs and the whole area cordoned off with a firm partition and an officer. Computer stands like the ones used to check guests and crew in or out when embarking or disembarking stand at the entrance, one each side This computer data is real-time, as anyone is checked in and out and it goes back to Miami via the satellite link.

Lal, Hunter, Kieron and Prisha enter together with wide smiles. All but Prisha, who has never had any gun training, are armed. Not that you would know. The men wear shoulder harnesses under their buttoned jackets, allowing the gun to slip alongside the chest almost under the arm. The first drink is free with the invitation. Normally on these occasions, some cruisers grab the free drink and then leave, but tonight, dinner follows so they should stay. Also, there can be no one on the ship who doesn't know that being in a registered area is good for their security clearance, should the ship dock anywhere before the murderer is found.

Hunter sidles up next to the Captain and waits for a moment when he can relay information. His hand goes up to his face as there are bound to be lip readers amongst the guests.

"Sir, I need to tell you that I am armed."

"Why?"

"Something was bugging me after I spoke to the psychologist in Miami. I went to the security office and one of the guns was missing, the possibility is, it's in here."

"Just you?"

"Three of us."

The Captain turns to Hunter and smiles but the smile is empty. He wants more.

"The killer is a professional, he wants power and possibly knows he will never make it off this ship. He is cornered and cornered prey is dangerous. This may be the setting for some form of final gratification."

"How did he get a gun?"

"The security office is often unattended and the safe keys are in the drawer."

The Captain takes a deep breath then turns away to continue mixing. It is his duty to meet and greet, but which of these people is a murderer hiding in plain sight.

Hunter re-joins Kieron and Prisha She is scanning the room, ever curious.

"They call us the ghost ship, but it is because there is a ghost on board we cannot see."

Kieron nods. "I'm going to last a lot longer if I sit down, in a corner where I can see everything. I think my aim is still good though."

"Lal, go with him. If his aim looks good, let him shoot, if he looks dodgy, you shoot," Hunter says.

The trays of drinks start to head back to the kitchen as hands bravely take a second glass even though they already have one. The trays arrive back empty.

"It's all about the free drink," Hunter growls.

"Alcohol is the start of so much evil," Prisha says.

"Can be fun."

"It can turn into a den of iniquity. And the room is full of the killer's ghosts. They can see him."

Hunter turns to Prisha who is very serious. "Have you been drinking?"

"No."

"Ghosts?" he asks. "You can see them?"

"Never ignore ghosts."

"No?"

"When travelling at night on an empty road, if you see a ghost on the road you must stop and offer a lift, then it will smile and let you pass. If not, it will appear on the back seat of your car and be in your rearview mirror for the rest of the journey."

"You think the ghosts are haunting the murderer?"

"They will always be in his head, always," she suggests.

"Good story. Can we torment them to explode?"

"I am just saying, someone in here has not been offered that kindness."

"Sigmund might say, they think they weren't offered kindness, they felt they were bullied at school, always the underdog, never respected by their parents., and now they're in here somewhere with a gun," Hunter says.

"Maybe, but maybe they're ready to talk. Maybe we need to a be a friend to them and not bully them," Prisha says.

"Who?"

"I don't know, maybe we need to appeal to them all. Ask each guest why they cruise? Are they enjoying it?"

"We'd need more staff to do that."

"We can ask the Captain, Roy and Ruby. And we have Lal."

She is quick to notice that Hunter is not listening because Kieron has caught his eye. Kieron offers a flick of the eye with a small head movement to send Hunter across the room. They are stalking a man who is awkwardly wandering without taking a seat. Hunter nods back to Kieron who is already up and approaching from the other side. Without being invited, Prisha slowly manoeuvres herself to a third line, the one that would meet him head-on. She has picked up the way they work, their body language and techniques very quickly and is confident enough to be first to meet with the man.

"Sir, would you like to come with me. We need your help with something special," she says.

Prisha links his arm and leads him towards the kitchen, flanked by Hunter and past Kieron. The man starts to feel worried when Hunter loops his other arm and he is in a polite frog march.

"What's going on?"

"Don't make a scene," Hunter says, making sure his grip is solid as they get closer. Lal and Kieron have circled behind them to obscure any guest's possible view.

Inside the kitchen, the man's face is planted into the wall and held by Hunter as Kieron searches every part of his body quickly and efficiently. Prisha again watches the unshakable approach the two use and the close contact no-nonsense way the man is dealt with. It is not the simple pat down the ship security staff do as you embark the ship having beeped the scanner.

"Hey, you can't do that," the man exclaims.

Neither Philips nor Witowski enter into any dialogue.

"Turn," Kieron instructs.

Hunter turns the man and plants his back firmly against the wall. Kieron runs the same body search again but from the front. The man decides to get louder,

"What about my..."

Hunter covers his mouth to silence him.

"Clean," Kieron declares.

"Sir, you looked like you couldn't find your seat. Why don't you sit next to Prisha?" Hunter asks.

"Come with me," She says.

The two men watch Prisha walk him out of the kitchen and up to the Captain, who shakes his hand easing any issue that might have arisen if he was not so confused.

Prisha talks to the Captain then walks her man to a seat and makes a fuss of him.

"She's good isn't she?" Kieron says.

Hunter nods his head and they scan the restaurant again as the Captain stands and taps a glass with a spoon,

"Don't worry, it's my spoon." He starts. "Tonight I would love to get to know you all better, that is why it is a smaller party. I want to know why you cruise. What this cruise means to you. What is it a release from? And, did you ever as a child imagine you would be here now? Think of those questions and chat about the answers with each other, the officers, and me whilst we eat. Now, please sit, dinner is ready to be served."

Hunter sees the Captain catch his eye and he nods, his speech was perfect. The chatter is high as people have wine poured at the beautifully laid tables. Prisha watches Hunter walk around the room and excuses herself as he passes her table,

"I'll be back in a moment."

"Good job. How did you relay all that to the Captain so fast?" Hunter asks.

Prisha smiles, she is becoming a worthy candidate. Hunter wants to circulate more,

"You may as well sit and eat. But keep your eyes

open."

"My eyes are always open but the killer is a ghost," she says.

"I've looked into the eyes of many killers, cornered, cold-blooded, enemy soldiers. There's something in the eyes. Something you learn to recognise," Hunter says slowly.

"They have already become ghosts. I've never seen one, but if I saw it I think I would know."

Prisha walks with him a bit, absorbing the master class. The Captain is on the other side of the room walking around the tables and saying good evening, Kieron is watching him like a hawk.

"I wish he'd sit down," Hunter says, looking in that direction.

"Why?" she asks.

"Just realised what Kieron's picked up on."

"What is that, sir?"

"The Captain's the prize kill."

Now Prisha looks like she has seen a ghost.

Neil Reynolds is a brilliant cruise ship captain, perfect at ensuring every guest feels he has seen them, said good evening them. He is walking from table to table, Jason shadows him, snapping pictures. Jason is doing his normal job, selling pictures, though his work is invaluable to the team. Hunter does not like that the Captain is so exposed but is relying on his partner Kieron who is up and always a table behind, watching each and every guest. It is a job he and Hunter have done many times but it is far from easy. This is now close protection.

The Captain walks between two tables and stops at Officer Ruby Jenkins, standing next to her for a moment.

"You're doing a good job, all of you. I can just make out your gun hidden under the jacket. I'm glad the other incident didn't stop you doing your job," Neil says.

Ruby looks at him and gives the smallest of acknowledging smiles; she has no idea what to say.

"Don't shoot anyone," the Captain jokes as he leaves her to take his place at the table.

Ruby puts her hand on the button of her jacket and loosens it.

Kieron's hand slips inside his open jacket.

Hunter steps forward.

Kieron walks straight past the Captain and stands tightly next to Ruby Jenkins. He might not be one hundred percent well, but he is two hundred percent focussed. Ruby caught him once before and nearly killed him. This time he is prepared and if she reaches for that gun she is going down hard.

Within seconds Hunter is at her other side and Lal is a table away with her as his only focus.

"What's all the attention guys?" Ruby asks.

"You're carrying," Kieron says.

"Damn right I am."

She walks away from them and starts to follow the Captain. Prisha crosses in front of her, which stops her. Prisha smiles, puts her hands on both shoulders and kisses both cheeks. "Let's not fight."

Hunter steps between them, "Why?"

"I got back to my office and all three guns had gone from the safe," Ruby says.

There is a moment's silence, an interrogation technique that fails to draw another word from her. They all stand and watch the first course being placed in front of the guests.

"Should we sit and eat?" Ruby asks.

"No," Hunter replies.

"Not with a weapon," Kieron adds.

"There's three stolen guns somewhere, I'm keeping this one," Ruby suggests.

"We've got the three guns, because the one you have was missing," Hunter adds.

Ruby turns to him and then to Kieron.

"This gun was in an evidence bag, locked in the drawer in my desk. It was the one I shot Lopkey with."

61 STILL WATER

There is a saying that 'calm comes before the storm', but today it feels reversed. Hunter leans on the rail on the promenade deck, looking out to sea, knowing the storm has been left behind. No one appears to have been murdered last night. It is very good news, but is unhelpful in the search to narrow down the murderer. However, had there been a murder outside the West Wind last night, with the only real suspects inside, that would have caused an even bigger problem.

There is hardly a ripple on the Pacific Ocean and not a ripple in his imagination as to how to find the killer. The ship may be a day away from Tahiti but he doesn't have a day. He opens the ship's magazine for day nine of the sea crossing which sports a picture of the Polynesian Cultural act in full traditional dress that will be in the theatre this evening. To get to the ship, their fast launch needs to leave the island at about midday. He closes the paper and thinks of all the preparation work being done for something that might not happen if international negotiations fail. The fact that the paper that went to print yesterday is just one example of the effort to let the boat to be allowed to dock alongside the ship. Doctor Yates having nine bodies and an emergency patient to travel with him is not without a lot of preparation and planning.

There are going to be about three hours of nerves in many departments as negotiations continue. Once that fast boat has left Tahiti, the largest French Polynesian island, the plan is half done. Until it docks alongside the ship as the sun sets and the personnel are exchanged, there is still a chance it could be recalled. Every effort has to be made to appease the authorities and the ultimate goal is to find the killer.

Sally and Benny will be leaving the ship for the last time in body bags. Hunter reflects on the many colleagues he has lost over the years, then decides to venture upstairs as Kieron should be awake by now. Prisha has taken to be his part-time nurse as well as a great trainee detective.

Hunter walks along the inside of the ship smiling at guests and saying good morning, then he stops by photography. He slips around the back to the small office.

"Morning, Jason."

"Hunter."

"Sales up?"

"They are! This is one cruise they all want to remember. Last night's 'red party' will be a hit too. Never have I seen so many officers being paraded to so few." Jason turns fully to Hunter.

"Winston Churchill," Hunter jokes at his misquoted remark.

"Who?"

Hunter shakes his head, it doesn't matter.

"Were you expecting a slaughter last night?" Jason asks.

"No," Hunter replies, a little uncertainty in his voice.

"Game of Thrones reference, red party." Jason excites.

"Never seen the show."

"There's a mass slaughter at the red wedding. So 'red party', I was cacking myself."

"Glad you're alive," Hunter says, and moves on to the art gallery.

Back in the data room, Prisha is on the phone with Dwight, discussing the geo-profiling of serial and spree killers. It is another example of the effect the psychologist is having on the team and Hunter is not sure it is helping that much. He listens silently for a moment, signalling to Prisha that his presence is not to be announced. He understands the point Sigmund is making, that serial killers are marauders and all their murders are near to home. But our murderer has no option, he is trapped on a ship by default. Hunter fails to understand why Sigmund has discounted him as a commuting murderer because the killer is on a large sea bus going somewhere. That surely makes him a commuter. Sigmund the brain box is missing something, but it is a waste of time arguing. Whatever deal they are cutting with the French psychologists and police is fine. They have tried everything else to nail the killer and now docking in Tahiti might just be what it takes to trigger something.

Holding Benny's artwork, purchased on his cruise

card (at the company's expense), he looks over the boards which he knows back to front, then discards them and walks into Kieron's room.

"I'll be up in a minute boss."

"You stay there, Kieron."

Hunter props the picture up on a unit at the side of Kieron's bed, directly in his eye line.

"What's that?"

"The picture that haunted Benny after Sally was killed. Might be nothing but I'm clutching at straws," Hunter says, holding up his thumb and first finger separated by a small gap.

"Me too. Something is smacking us in the face and you know what it is when you can't see it?" Kieron offers.

"Obvious," Hunter replies and they both nod.

"Let's talk about what you might achieve when you are on land."

"I should've been checked and discharged by midnight."

"First, it is about getting you well. Nothing is above that, not the killer, not being paid."

"I never knew you cared," Kieron teases.

"Elaine told me to say that."

"Immigration will no doubt check everyone off, if they allow anyone off at all. I'll be there. I'd like you to keep an eye on the re-fuel and re-stocking operation. The workmen coming and going."

"Then re-board the ship and travel to Bora Bora?" Kieron asks.

"I still think it'll be over before then, and we'll be flying home."

"Not me, I'm taking a holiday."

"Get some sleep, you might be up all night."

Hunter leaves the bedroom and re-enters the data room, announcing at the top of his voice,

"He's a professional, athletic ability, some training, and in that last one hundred, some of who were on mobility chairs. You must be able to get the number down to an interview list."

"Morning, Hunter," multiple voices chirp down the phone.

"Nice to hear the choir's up. Excuse me guys, work to do," Hunter says, walking through but not stopping. It hits him that his team have not interviewed the Sugar Crew. That is his next target. The door closes, then he re-opens it and re-enters.

"Prisha. Just in case Bogdan tried to blackmail the killer, check all his cabin phone records out after Eric's last drink."

Hunter leaves again,

"Yes, but..." is all he hears of Dwight's answer. The door closes behind him and he knows there will be something else he has forgotten.

Kieron stares at the picture until he falls asleep. He wakes less than fifteen minutes later staring at it. His eyes drift down to the signature.

"Hey," Prisha says as she enters, pleased to see he is awake. She flicks on the kettle and goes to sit on the bed.

"Prisha, what time is it?"

"You don't need to know. How do you feel?" She asks.

"Great," he says sitting up. "I'm now a professional power napper. Prisha, do people normally take their paintings with them off the ship."

"No. Most are sent to their houses by courier,

why?"

"Just trying to get into Benny's head. He was starting to go through the many ways the killer could get off the ship. He was thinking cargo, paintings, sculpture. Has anyone bought a really large sculpture that leaves in Tahiti?"

Hunter walks into the bridge and greets the Captain. "I was wondering if you had ten minutes?"

"Let's grab an early lunch. Vasile is covering my break and the launch has left Tahiti with a doctor, the cabaret act for tonight, and four local police officers. Things might be improving."

The Captain leaves the bridge and Hunter follows him through to his dining room.

"What's on your mind, Witowski?"

"I feel so close it's bugging me. Can you walk me through how investigators were called onto the ship so quickly when you only had two known murders?"

"Two murders aren't enough?"

"Sure, but the discussions, the thought process, the little things that were said that are the background to what is in the log."

"Much of it was all head office in Miami," Neil remembers.

"Let's concentrate on the ship, everything Miami was told from the ship, how they were led to that decision."

"Shall we call Roy and Ruby to join us?"

"Not yet, Neil, there's a gem of information that will unlock something. What happened first?"

"We were stargazing, lights out. All done properly, an officer at each stair. As the lights went back on there was a shout of man overboard."

"That fast?"

"Yes, it was almost instant," he says thinking back.

"Too quick?"

"No, as the lights go on, you-" the Captain stops. "Actually to spot a mask in the dark and then make the connection that it is a body when nobody has been seen… you might have a point."

"Do you know who actually gave that shout."

"No," Neil thinks hard then confirms. "No."

"Male or female?"

Neil shakes his head, "I think all the calls were female, it became a chorus. Maybe there were a few men eventually. The screams and initial calls were female."

"Can I ask Roy to put a call out for help. To interview all those who actually shouted man overboard?"

"Sure," the Captain agrees.

"What happened next?"

"All standard procedure. It's something we practice almost every week even though it's very rare. Our company alone had only four in over twelve million cruisers last year."

"So did you take it seriously?"

"Very. But then I was called to go back to deck ten as there was a murder."

"Who actually said it was a murder?"

"Vasile reported it to me, I was standing with officer Jenkins, planning the crowd control for guests watching the man overboard rescue."

"Who suggested the muster station headcount?"

"I did, then Officer Jenkins insisted."

"Where was she during the roll call?"

"You would need to ask her, I was making one of

my many reports; she was probably doing the same. She worked tirelessly all night. Later I went down to her office and demanded she get some sleep," the Captain remembers.

"When was that?"

"It was after roll call, way after, and after we had found the second body. I felt that was the time we should all get some sleep and start again in the morning."

"Shouldn't human resources be watching people's hours at times like this? I see mention of her appearing."

"Yes."

"And she is still on my red list."

"You will need to speak with her then."

"Yeah. Does she do reports to Miami? Who was reporting this to Miami?"

"The bridge. Vasile Nagy did basic reports under my instruction. I went up at various intervals and did full reports. They are timed and logged."

"When was the first time you actually spoke to a company officer in Miami?"

"That's in the log too. Two murders are more than the whole industry gets some years. I did make immediate mention of us not being equipped for such an investigation."

"Was that seed planted or hinted at by someone else?"

"I don't think so, it's obvious."

"Let's eat," Hunter says.

"You have something don't you?" the Captain asks as they start to relax with food.

"Nothing I like," Hunter says as he grabs a bottled beer.

"I need to talk to Madeline in Human resources, and the two crew you had exempted from retribution for having relations with guests. I tried earlier but couldn't find them."

"D'you want Roy and Ruby to join us now?"

"No. They are both still red, no alibi."

"What is it you're thinking?" The Captain asks. It is a direct question and Hunter should not really avoid it.

"It's that moment before a huge operation, when you rush around and check everything. I don't know yet. But I will."

62 THE SUGAR BABES

"Where have you been?" Prisha asks, as Hunter enters the data room.

"Solving a murder," Hunter replies.

Prisha draws him towards Kieron's bedroom. He lifts the board of the ship's population in red and green on the way and hopes his buddy is not any worse. It is a matter of hours now before he will be in a proper hospital.

"Please tell him to stay in bed," she demands.

"Stay in bed."

"I want to walk around," Kieron says. But, as he stands to prove a point he is definitively unsteady.

"Do me a favour, stay in bed, sleep, I might need you later."

"I don't know why I am so dizzy today."

"Because we agreed, a bedridden job and last night we had you up again on patrol at a party."

"What have you two been up to?" Kieron asks,

laying down again.

"Shall we get Dwight in on this?" Hunter asks, and Prisha bounces to the phone, ever alert. She pushes a direct dial number. No sooner does it ring than it is answered.

"Yo!" Dwight shouts.

"It's Father Christmas," Kieron replies. "Do you have presents for us?"

"Clear the chimney, it's raining men," Hunter says.

"Hallelujah!" Prisha says which shocks them all.

"So, Prisha, have you been visiting the Sugar Babes!" Hunter says.

Prisha's face instantly turns from fun to very serious and defensive.

"What do you mean? No!" She answers.

"Tell me," says Dwight, excitedly.

"I've always fancied a crew member or guest staff member for this," says Hunter.

"Me too, the knowledge of the ship and cameras is beyond even the regular cruiser," Kieron agrees. "And they would know how to get on and off undetected."

"No one gets on or off undetected," Dwight offers confidently.

"So, you've done the ship's tour," Hunter laughs.

"Dwight, you need to read our book, not only did people get on and off our last ship undetected but millions and millions of dollars," Kieron offers.

"Tell us about the elusive Madeline in human resources, Prisha, could she be our murderer?" Hunter asks.

"No!"

"Why so definitive, she is red, no alibi for any of the murders. I've never met her, never seen her, and she has never offered to help. Is she a ghost-like the killer?" Hunter asks.

"Madeline is wonderful, and she laughs all the time. She is a very large lady so there is no way she fits the action on our timeline. No way could she jump down from the sun deck," Prisha insists, defending her.

"But, an officer doesn't need to do the drop off the sun deck in the dark. If an officer decided to leave deck ten in pitch darkness, the stair guards wouldn't stop them. They stop guests, not other fellow senior officers they know. They would let them through without a thought," Hunter explains. "Kieron showing off his minor talents as a wannabe free-runner lead us all astray."

"That's a bit strong. If I was showing off I would have..."

"Trust me, that was his best move, Dwight," Hunter abruptly cuts him short.

"OK. I like where you are going with this," Dwight replies.

"We need to get hold of all the stair and door guards and interview them," Hunter says.

"I can do that," Prisha suggests.

"I might have something else for you. Help me out here. But what if," Hunter starts, "what if the killer's a woman?"

"Prisha, can you please bring me the note the killer left?" Kieron asks.

Prisha turns and leaves instantly.

"I don't want to sound sexist, but every time I asked myself who would write that note as their anger stewed up, I had problems thinking it would be a man."

"That is sexist," Prisha says to him firmly.

Hunter looks at Kieron and smiles and nods, he

knows that they have both been fighting problems within the investigation that have been ringing alarm bells.

"It could be a man," Hunter suggests.

"But, I could also never get why the killer never left the note with Eric. I don't totally buy into that being a mistake," Kieron says.

"Me neither," Hunter says.

"The note wasn't for him," Kieron smiles. "I have wanted to say that out loud for so long."

"The obvious," Hunter says.

"Guys, that's why we have these sessions," Dwight says over the speakerphone. "Loving your work, but who was it for? I know you're teasing me."

"It was for his wife, Betty," Kieron says.

"I agree," Hunter adds nodding.

Prisha hands Kieron the sheet from the board that they have all been looking at for days.

"Scatter, you featureless puppets, scatter." Kieron reads, "this is rage, this is jealousy."

"So why is it aimed at Betty? I don't understand." Prisha asks.

Kieron smiles and looks at Hunter. Hunter nods and smiles back. He wiggles his fingertips grinning with his teeth exposed as if he was being offered something he just could not grab.

"You can't see this, Dwight, but Fagin here is getting excited. He's gonna tell us in a minute." Kieron enthuses.

"Sadly not all of it, but I agree. It's a woman," Hunter starts.

"Wow! A female serial killer, wait till I tell Sigmund," Dwight laughs. "They are as rare as rocking horse shite."

"It's not a serial killer. She only wanted to kill one person," Hunter offers.

"Eric?" Dwight asks.

"Betty."

"I'm gonna keep quiet now," Dwight says.

"It's best."

"That's a curveball," Kieron says computing, "The killer watches Betty take Eric down to the bicycle sheds in anger and this is her chance."

"But she hesitated. She was seen by Bogdan then burst down too late," Hunter says.

"Betty has fled," Kieron says. "This feels so much better."

"Her outrage ends up being lost. Eric is still by the chute. She snatches his cruise card to stop him drinking, she wants him with his wife. She wants Betty out of the picture. She hits him once on the head in her temper and he is over. Had it been Betty she would have hit her repeatedly in anger. There is not another mark on Eric," Hunter explains.

"I'm loving this, that's why she still has the note," Dwight enthuses.

"And the cruise card," Prisha says thoughtfully.

"Cruise card and she still has the note," Dwight says.

"Shush Dwight! You're spoiling the movie," Prisha adds.

"Dwight!" Everyone in the data room shouts sarcastically to support Prisha's new found enthusiasm.

"She's not a serial killer. She fled upstairs and whilst escaping, killed Donna because she was outraged and angry. The multiple stabs to Donna were meant for Betty. Sigmund will like that bit. She stands up, she's an officer so no one will question her. She leaves by the stairs, sees Kershner who is stunned because he must have seen her kill Donna. So it could have been Madeline."

"Him looking up at the stars from the deck below means he would see them at the edge of the sun deck," Dwight adds.

"So you've been on a ship once?" Kieron asks.

"Kershner's stunned, he watches her come down and says something to her," Prisha adds then, thinking, "An officer could ask who Kershner is, why he is on deck, ask to look at his cruise card. The switch."

"Pop, Kershner has to go overboard, she has no option," Hunter explains.

"It's a great story, but we do not have a motive," Prisha says.

"Does it work for all the other murders? And why is she jealous of Betty? We need more. But hey, I enjoyed it," Dwight says as a bit of a downer.

"Who are these two?" Kieron asks.

"I didn't invite them," Hunter says.

"You did, you brought Prisha in and you asked Dwight to be phoned," Kieron blames Hunter sarcastically.

"I did, but they can go now," Hunter says.

"I'll be quiet, promise," Dwight says.

"Dwight, let's assume for the moment the others all saw something, we don't know what, but say they did and the killer had to cover her tracks…" Kieron muses. He then turns to Hunter. "I'm guessing you've got the key there in your pocket, partner? Let's open the magic box."

"Are you two always this jovial about murder?" Prisha asks.

"No idea, we only met three months ago. I was

called to save his wife," Kieron says.

"I got the key, I don't have the answer. And you are not helping like I'd had hoped. None of you," Hunter says, directing the last remark at Kieron.

"But you like Madeline for it?" Kieron encourages him.

"Apparently she's big, powerful," Hunter says still thinking.

"Forget who did it, please tell us what this key is!" Prisha pleads.

"The sugar babes!"

"OK. Someone fill me in," Dwight asks.

"Do you mean sugar mama? Betty was a sugar mama?" Prisha asks innocently.

"Prisha, you did your research on Sugar Mamas," Hunter states.

"A Sugar Mama is a woman looking for a younger man; in return for money. Betty had money; what did I get wrong?" Prisha explains.

"I met the guys," Hunter offers, not answering her question.

"Plural?" Kieron asks.

"There are two of them, great guys. Both huge fit guys and very proud of what they have to offer. Let me tell you I had quite the education."

"By that, I assume more than I found online?" Prisha asks.

"Let's just say this, basically it's the same. Women paying for sex, not companionship," he explains.

"Oh," Prisha says in some surprise.

"Sex," Dwight asks, "both of them?"

"At the same time?" Prisha asks in surprise.

"Err… I don't know about that last bit, but I think for Betty it was totally a sex thing. For many of the crew members, it appears that is the same, but I figure for one of the crew members it became more. Dangerous infatuation."

"Why did he not stay with her?" Prisha asks.

"Firstly, there were two of them. And secondly, they both have wives and families back home who they support with this income. Seems they almost support a whole village and they do not want to lose their job."

"So it was all about purchasing the exclusive rights. I can remember those terms used when we were signing the book," Kieron adds.

"It's not quite the same," Hunter contradicts.

"It is. Someone wanted exclusive rights. Betty was paying more," Kieron says.

"Money?" Prisha asks totally bemused.

"On a normal cruise, the passengers are gone within two weeks. Our crew member gets her man back. World cruises cause a problem," Hunter says.

"So we have a motive. Five female officers in red have no alibi," Dwight says slowly down the phone.

"10-4," Kieron replies to agree as he looks down the board and checks again. He looks up to Hunter. "I'm guessing they wouldn't name their crew customers?"

"Not first time out. I made friends, I have their trust, it might be easier to revisit if we have to further down the line."

"But we're so close," Dwight says.

"Women in the crew paying for sex?" Prisha sighs.

"Don't be sexist Prisha. This is an equal-rights world, no one's judging here," Kieron says.

"So we need to ask Madeline if she knows about any crew having 'relationships' with the two guys, but we think it might be her. She is the powerhouse in the ship, human resources, to whom all crew answer," Hunter says.

"Except you don't mean relationships," Prisha says.

"Don't care what you call it," Kieron says.

"But you're the one to do the asking," Hunter says looking at her.

"Me?"

"Could be dangerous," Dwight suggests. "But I think you're on target with this."

There is a pause as the two men look at Prisha, it almost feels like Dwight is looking at her too.

"I will do it, but I need their names. I know Madeline well. I'll be able to read her," Prisha says.

"Be very careful. If she's the killer, it's a side of her you don't know. I'm going to be outside her room listening," Hunter suggests.

"Should she have a safe word?" Kieron says.

"A safe word?" Prisha asks.

"That's something else," Hunter says. Just scream if you need me.

63 COME ALONGSIDE

It is hard to feel very much inside a cruise ship when the weather is fair and the sea has little swell. You can't even tell you're moving or let alone if it is fast or slow. Even in rougher weather, many cruisers feel nothing as all modern ships have stabilisers.

So when the ship slowed down at around 17.45 hours, only those having a last sundowner drink on deck knew the ship was in a manoeuvre and could watch the fast-approaching French launch. Almost everyone sitting at the bars went to the rails and watched as the small boat banked on the port side, swung around the ship and slowed down on the starboard side causing them to walk quickly across the deck with their drinks and look over at it. The launch looks smaller the closer it gets to the ship, but the sound of the Polynesian band singing, playing drums and other island-made instruments gets louder. They have modern over-clothes, but their faces are made-up with paint and their hair braided or tied back. Guests begin to feel like they are on holiday again as this is the first life anyone has seen for nine days, apart from the two investigators being dropped from the sky. The whole troupe are received by the ship first and are elevated to the sun deck as the French officers inspect paperwork.

On arrival, the local group arrive start to dance and play on the port side of the pool bar. Guests feel like they have arrived in the land of sun, hula-hula girls and Elvis songs. The only strange part of the act was it being flanked by an armed French policeman on each side. As with all great shows, the big flourish is to distract from the real work that no one wants to be seen.

One after the other, nine body bags are loaded onto the launch under cover of black cloths, checked by the last two policemen. Then Kieron and the Doctor step onto the boat, allowing the French doctor to step onto the ship. The policemen transfer, then the boat powers away into the falling darkness. The ship's mortuary is empty again and standing by ready.

Hunter stands on the promenade deck deep in thought as he watches his partner leave. They have spent the last hour talking over the many possible scenarios. Both are ready for anything but he is not prepared to see Prisha next to him, just as sad that Kieron has left.

"Maybe I will never see him again," she says.

"Guess I won't get that lucky. What did you get from her royal Madeline?"

"Nothing. She said all files are confidential and she cannot reveal any private information. I'm sure she's not the killer," Prisha says.

"I'm not. OK, just send Dwight a two-line report. Madeline refuses to confirm or deny any crew that may have had relationships with the two crewmen."

Prisha smiles and turns away. She strides ahead of Hunter before he has turned.

Two of the French police are in the data room to go over their investigation. Prisha and Dwight via the phone, are explaining everything in great detail but there is only one conclusion. The killer has not been caught. The red guests and crew cannot get off, and if they try, they will be arrested. It will be a tender port into the military floating dock that was installed by the French navy in 1975.

Hunter listens at the back of the room, he knows that many people are going to be really annoyed that they cannot get off. Roy Stevens and Ruby Jenkins being two of them. Hunter checks his watch. He is keen to know if his buddy is actually OK or if he's going to need to stay in hospital, but the boat will not reach the island for a few hours. He picks up an old green and red crew and cast list, the new one will be hardly any different as few, if any, have been cleared in the last day. With the rest of his team busy, he leaves before he can be asked a question.

Hunter finds his phone and dials home. First, he

speaks with Elaine and tells her he thinks it will all be over in a day or so. Then he rings Mary, updating Izzy with a press release. Mary updates him with his bill and the fact that she and Stan are looking forward to their cruise.

"We ain't never been on one of them ships. Have they got a grill?" Mary asks.

"Not like yours, Mary. I'll see what I can do."

Trying to pass the time he pops in to see the Polynesian show. He has watched many shows like this, from Fiji to Hawaii, so it is hard to concentrate. He walks out of the back of the theatre and looks towards the box where Bogdan was found dead. His phone records gave nothing. Hunter strides out, looking at the sheets of his list, heavy in thought that he is so close to working out who the killer is. He enters a crew door and runs down the stairs to the room of the sugar crew and knocks on the door.

"You're not entertaining?" he asks as the door opens a little.

One of the crewmen, equal to his stature but with a far more solid build, smiles and opens the door.

"Looks like we're gonna dock in Tahiti. You got the day off or working?"

"Both got the day off."

Hunter shows them the list where both of their names are red.

"Red. What's that mean?" they ask.

"Means you can't get off. Green would mean you could," Hunter explains.

"Can you change us up, man?"

"If you help me," Hunter says, laying out another sheet which is the eight murders and their suspected timings.

"Can you give Betty an alibi, for any of these times. If she cross-checks that she was here, I'll get you turned green."

One of the men goes to his drawer where there is a small notebook detailing names and times and the amount of money taken. He flicks through the pages and finds Betty at a corresponding time. Hunter raises his phone and photographs it.

"We good?" One asks.

"One more thing," Hunter says, pulling up the list and showing them the names of five red officers. "You know these women?"

They are silent, blank. It was not part of the deal.

"Come on guys I need more," Hunter persuades.

One of them runs his finger down the list and lands on a name, Officer Ruby Jenkins. Hunter's heart stops.

"I don't know this one, do you?"

His partner looks at her name.

"Not one of mine," the other one says.

"So the other four have all visited this room?" Hunter smiles. "How about dates and times from your book?"

They both shake their heads.

"You could give them alibis, and look at the list, technically to go green you need two clear ticks. I need one more from each of you."

"No man, only one of those is recent anyway and it's not right for us to tell tales on crew. We ain't the kind of guys who snitch, we're discreet."

Hunter stands, "One more to go green. I need your other recent customer."

"She won't help, she stopped coming when Betty got on board. She didn't know Betty was one of our regulars."

"Are there any other guests who could give you an alibi?" he asks pushing them.

The book is opened. Again and again, almost every night Betty is down with both of them. Hunter photographs each page.

"Guess we gone green now."

He holds a fist for Hunter to bump, but Hunter stands firm. "Call me with more names."

Hunter walks away sending Dwight the alibi for Betty and the two crew. Arriving at the mid staircase he climbs one flight and enters the medical centre.

The staff all know him and introduce him to the French doctor.

"Hey."

"Bonsoir. I cannot believe what you have here. It is like an 'hospital."

"What did you expect?"

"I know, but we are at sea."

"Did you eat?"

"Like a king."

"You want me to show you around the ship?"

"Is it safe?"

"You're with me."

Hunter walks off with the doctor on a tour of the ship. It is so easy for someone who works on a cruise ship to forget just how amazing the floating facility is. It comes back and hits you hard when you take someone new around who is amazed and impressed. His phone goes, it's Kieron.

"Hunter, I'm in the hospital. Waiting game now."

"Ring me as soon as you know anything, and by the way Mary's worried."

Hunter is going to clock-watch and spend the night thinking and worrying. Henré knows how he feels about his buddy, but as a doctor, he is rather mechanical about it,

"He is walking and talking. I am sure whatever he has they can fix it. They have time, he is in the right place now."

64 ONE TOO MANY

After maybe one drink too many that takes them up to midnight, Henré and Hunter see the bars closing, Hunter agrees to walk him back to the medical centre as he is sure he would get lost.

"This is a small ship, you know!"

"Small! Mon Dieu!"

Henré wants one last look around before he goes to bed. The medical centre is dark, just one desk light by one nurse on lates until the bars are clear, then she is clear. Henré starts to switch all the lights on again. He goes through it all, truly amazed, and then to the mortuary.

"Aussi un mortuaire," he says, sliding the first of the four drawers open.

"It's been pretty busy here this week," Hunter says, pulling at a drawer that will not open. The French doctor takes the drawer and pulls hard. There is a falling sound inside as the drawer opens. Hunter looks inside beyond the empty drawer and sees the body of Donna McGovern wedged down the back between drawers.

"Nurse!"

Within just a few sobering minutes the mortuary is full. Prisha, the two French policemen, the doctor, the duty nurse and Hunter who is still trying to ring Kieron,

"He's not answering."

"You're sure you counted nine body bags off the ship?" Prisha asks the police again, who are now annoyed they are being questioned and that they too cannot get anyone to answer the phone.

"Guys!" Hunter shouts to stop the chatter. "I'm going upstairs, there is nothing I can do here, though it might be worth searching to see if there are any other bodies left behind."

Hunter leaves, having dropped a deliberate bombshell to keep them off his back. He runs up the stairs to five and walks quickly along the deserted promenade corridor holding his phone to his ear.

"Dwight. You want the good news or the bad news?"

"There is never any bad news."

"We still have a dead body on board. The killer left the ship in a body bag."

"Are they armed?" Dwight asks.

Hunter does a complete about-turn and jogs to the back of the ship and down the crew stairs.

"Donna is in the mortuary. The police can't remember if any of the bags were heavy, but they think a couple were."

"You are down to four suspects, why not just wake them up?"

"I will, one job at a time," Hunter says kicking the locked door of the security office in. With alarms sounding he scrambles around in the desk drawer for the bunch of keys. The safe opens and he counts two

343

guns. He then spins around and opens every drawer in the desk. He finds the evidence bag the last gun should be in, it's empty.

"Two guns missing," Hunter reports. "I'm hanging up, try to get through to Kieron."

Lal appears at the door still buttoning his shirt.

"Lal, two guns are gone, re-lock the safe, call Krishma."

Hunter starts to dial on the house phone and impatiently waits.

"Roy, sorry, I need you up. Can we meet? Your office in five?"

The phone goes down and he dials Prisha, "Prisha, when you have a clear escape, tell the French police that the killer in the body bag is armed with two, I repeat two hand pistols. Then meet me in your old office, back of reception."

In reception, there are now five in their team, being watched by a curious skeleton night shift of one receptionist and the night security manager.

"We have four rooms to visit. Four female officers and I don't want to wait for them to wake-up, we need to know if they are in there. The empty room is the killer and that room will get searched from top to bottom. Split in two," Hunter orders.

Roy, Prisha and Lal rush off to officer Mary Wells' room. Hunter and Krishma rush to Madeline's. All these officers are on deck six in passenger areas so the public are going to start to wake. Hunters phone goes.

"Kieron, buddy. The killer left with you in a body bag. Donna's bag. She's armed with two hand pistols."

"OK. I'm on it." Kieron says snapping into action, finding his clothes and his shoes, a huge machine behind him.

"You're going nowhere," the local doctor shouts. "You're seriously ill."

"Doc, I will be straight back," Kieron says and leaves still dressing. His own doctor Simon Yates is studying CT scans in the next room when he hears the commotion and turns to see Kieron run out. He follows on shouting, "Kieron. You can't do this, you'll die!"

Failing to stop him, he turns back to the CT observation room and snatches his own phone and dials.

"Hunter, you've got to stop Kieron, he is seriously ill. He will die."

Hunter is standing in Madeline's room watching the large lady berate Krishma. He is numbed by what he has heard.

"OK stop! You've been no help. You're saying too much, and too loudly," Hunter says, pulling Krishma out.

Leaving Madeline, he follows Krishma along the corridor to the next room, but he is looking at his phone. He needs to stop Kieron, this is not worth dying over. The French police can take it from here. Krishma is knocking at the second room.

"Housekeeping, emergency!" She says, pushing the door open to find officer Shelly Summer.

"Headcount Shelly. Go back to sleep." Krishma says backing out.

Krishma rushes to the mid stairwell where the other team wait.

"Both present and correct," Roy reports.

"Then who's in the body bag?" Hunter asks.

65 THE DEAD GO THIS WAY

Kieron rushes down dark corridors in the basement of the opposite side of the hospital to where he was taken. He finds the mortuary is not as quiet or dark as it would be most other nights. Two staff are still quivering in the corner so he knows they have been shocked if not attacked.

"Where did she go?"

They both point to the obvious door that swings to a street access loading bay. Kieron starts to run and as he does he answers his phone,

"Bird has flown, I'm searching."

"Answer your damn phone!"

"My phones on silent, I'm chasing a criminal!"

"You're really ill, get back to the doctor now!"

"Not just yet."

"That's an order!"

"An order?" Kieron questions.

"Let the French Police deal with it."

"Seriously?" Kieron hangs up as he arrives in the street. He sees a taxi pulling away. He elbows the window of a small older style compact car and with his hand through the broken window, opens the door.

Hunter rushes down the crew stairs followed by Prisha, Roy, Lal and Krishma. At the bottom, he turns to Lal and Krishma, "Go and check Officer Jenkins room, she's your boss."

Leaving them stunned, he walks with haste along the narrow undecorated corridor to the sugar crew room he was in earlier. He bangs on the door but Roy uses his master card and they enter as a team.

The first of the two large men is up in Hunter's face, afraid of no one. Hunter floors him within a split second, spins him on the ground and has him screaming with pain as his wrist is locked against the joint,

"You lied to me. You know Officer Ruby Jenkins, don't you? I said don't you?"

"Yes, man."

"Yes man?

"Yes, we do."

"Did you help her escape?"

"No man. Never!"

"And?"

"And what man? She made us keep quiet, she was mad, she threatened us. She's a senior officer man, she has power!"

"Threatened you, why?"

"She fell in love, man. Worst kind."

"I would have thought that was good for business."

"No man. They don't think they have to pay when they're in love. It gets messed up."

"So you argued?"

"She'd had enough, she just wanted off the ship."

Hunter discards him, spinning back to the floor as he addresses the second man in the shared room.

"What are you, her puppets?" Hunter demands.

"No! We told her, stop calling us puppets."

"But you helped her?"

"No. I know her, but never helped her. Just called her to say you were in asking about her. I wanted to know what to say if you came back."

"What did she tell you?" Hunter asks, getting right

in his face.

"She said don't worry, she said not to say anything when you came back."

Hunter is out of the room, pulling at his phone and dialling. He gets an answerphone,

"Kieron, it's Ruby! She got the better of you once before."

"Then I owe her one."

Kieron throws his phone down in the passenger footwell and continues to follow the taxi in front. It pulls into a downtown motel so Kieron stops on the other side of the road. He watches as she goes into reception and while she is in there talking, he bends down and reaches back into the footwell for his phone. He grunts as he stretches with the effort. He exhales. His breath is uneven. Having grabbed the phone, he forces himself up. His nose is bleeding. He falls back into his chair and passes out. The phone rings, waking him again.

"Hunter, I'm in trouble. Confirm Ruby. Taxi. Walking upstairs. Motel…"

"Where is she? What motel? Kieron? Kieron?" Hunter shouts in panic. He throws the phone at a chair in the data room. "He's passed out, he's in trouble. We've got to find him!"

Hunter looks at his watch and bursts out of the data room ignoring the local police who are speaking to each other in French.

On the bridge the deputy Captain is on duty, the other officers stand out in their whites against the dark outside.

"Vasile. We got to get into Tahiti quicker, or get me there on a lifeboat." Hunter demands.

"I can't do that."
"Then wake Neil."

Kieron stands outside the car, blood running from his nose, holding himself up on the door. He tries to step but is unstable on his feet. He looks at the hotel. It's out of focus and the distance is near, then far, then spinning. He looks to his hand and tries to make his thumb press a key. He manages to hit redial but drops the phone which slides under the car. He falls to his hands and knees sliding down the side of the car which spins him the wrong way.

"Kieron!"

He can hear Hunter shouting from the phone.

"Man daaa..." Kieron's voice fails him.

"Man down? Kieron are you hit?" Hunter shouts.

"10-4. Man der."

Kieron starts to crawl across the empty dark road like a lost hedgehog. The city hasn't woken up yet so Kieron might survive if he can get to the other side.

On the bridge, the Captain has listened alongside Hunter.

"I'll see what I can do, but you need to use the local police," Neil says to him.

Hunter leaves the bridge and runs back to the data room. "He's down somewhere," he announces as he enters.

"What did he say, exactly, word for word?" Dwight asks over the phone.

"He said something like Manda, so I asked him if he meant man down. I said Kieron are you hit? He said 10-4 and then mander," Hunter says, annoyed.

"Hunter, listen to me now. He said 10-4 and then

said what exactly?" Dwight asks.

"10-4. Man daa. It was definitely daa."

"So, he agreed man down, even in a mess he wouldn't then try and repeat 'man down'," Dwight suggests.

"I hear you, Dwight. I asked him for the name of the hotel. Man daa could be a motel," Hunter says, looking to the French policemen who appear blank and at the same time dialling on his phone again.

"Doc, you lost a patient. He has passed out, outside a hotel with the name Man da something, get in a taxi," Hunter whispers, then turns to the room again. "I need to get off this ship."

"And go where?" Prisha asks. "Hotel Manda, Mandarin, Mardina, Manderlay, Mandow, or even Man down?"

"Guys it's your island, what Hotels do you have like Manda?"

"We are here to send information back to our police. Especially now your killer is on our island. We are not instructed to help you deal with anything." The first French policeman says.

Prisha holds Hunter's hand firmly down on the desk and whispers to him,

"Calm. I can do the research."

Hunter turns to her and whispers in her ear,

"My friend is dying somewhere out there."

"He's my friend too."

66 TAXI FOR ONE

Simon is driving around Tahiti in the back seat of a taxi. The driver is worried that the meter is getting to a large number.

"Don't worry, I can pay."

But he can't. Simon has no money on him and certainly no local currency. He only has his phone. The day is just waking up in Pape'ete as they stop outside the Le Mandarin, opposite the town hall which is in mid-downtown. Then he sees Kieron, slumped over in the road.

"What's the name of this road?"

"Rue Colette."

Simon rings the doctor at the hospital.

"What do you mean he's gone home? I have found the patient. He is passed out in the middle of Rue Collette."

Simon listens for a while then leans over to the driver.

"That is my patient. I need to get him to the hospital."

"You have money?"

"Yes!"

"Let me see."

"I work for the biggest shipping company in the world, you will get paid. That man is important."

"What ship?" The driver demands.

"It docks tomorrow," Simon offers.

"Tomorrow. But it is today, no ship."

"I am from the ship!"

"Ghost man, ghost ship, with killer? You kill him? Get out!"

Simon gets out and the taxi drives away. He runs to the grass verge in the middle of the road where Kieron is propped up against a palm tree sleeping like an old drunk, but less healthy. He takes his pulse as he starts to dial Hunter.

"Hunter, I've found him. We are in Rue Collette. Town Hall on one side, Hotel Le Mandarin the other. I need help. He's not in a good way."

Kieron stirs, "Simon, walk me across. Out of sight."

"Walk him out of sight, Simon. Ruby will kill you both if she sees you. Hopefully, she's still asleep. We just dropped anchor, I'll be on a tender across to the island before you know it."

Hunter is in the security office where he has taken charge of the last two handguns and is taking all the spare American dollars from the safe, which will not be enough if things go wrong. He has no idea how he will get the guns on land. He tucks them both in the rear of his trousers. Staying on deck two, he walks along until he finds which door the tender is using. It is open and the first lifeboat can be seen circling ready to come alongside to receive the first people to cross, which is a crowd of locals who were all in the cultural show last night. This morning you would not recognise them, dressed as civilians with their stage costumes in cases. The ship is on schedule, the tenth day of crossing and this group of people will get back for their day jobs and even have time for breakfast. They start to board and Hunter gets on with them.

The tender swings out and around the ship and Pape'ete is clear, the capital of the largest island of Tahiti. Docked in the cruise port is another small ship that Hunter instantly recognises, the Regent Seven Seas Navigator.

He looks around the tender and settles on the girl who sits opposite him who may have just pulled the short straw. She has a large bag with a headdress carefully placed on top of it which is obviously expensive. She has obviously not packed it as she doesn't want it crushed. She will be his target, he has done this before. He is on a mission. Hunter's eyes flick back to the fast-approaching dockside, he knows Pape'ete, he has been here many times before. He can see that this craft is heading for the cruise port right next to the other cruise ship. It is where they should have docked but their ship was told they couldn't. Little do the French know that there are no weapons on board now. The killer left with two guns and Hunter has the other two.

He looks across to the military pontoon and can see that there is another lifeboat from his ship unloading the standard twelve-foot square easy up. He recognises it even folded, as he's had to lift it ashore, erect it and take it down on many occasions. He can see police with blue flashing lights and other officials gathering there to meet with the ship's immigration officer. It reminds him of the rescue he had to arrange for Kieron on their last cruise in Panama as he canoed back from an excursion. He wonders if the French customs officers will board to inspect the ship as happens at every cruise port, which basically means going to the buffet to get their free breakfast, or whether they will stay away from the killer? No, he thinks, the attraction of free food will be too great, but they pulled the short straw too, the Regent Seven Seas is a much nicer ship.

Hunter can't believe his luck, he might get ashore with the cabaret act and get lost amongst the Seven Seas guests. His enclosed lifeboat ensures that no one on the cruise dock will have seen who is onboard, if anyone is bothering to look, which he doubts. It docks easily and the first of the cultural dancers get out to almost no reception. No other tender is going to use this dock today so they are slowed up by just two policemen who jovially check the performer's passports. The first few off are obviously the elders who carry nothing. Then large bags are handed off and the police with clipped down sidearms help lift the bags away from the boat in this very informal re-immigration. This act must come and go every day there is a ship in, and another version of this same act will have got off the other ship where passengers are now disembarking. Hunter stands at the back of the queue having observed those in front showing their passports, he knows he can only produce a cruise card. His friend is somewhere dying, Ruby is no doubt still at large and he has seconds to formulate a solution.

What he does not want to do is shoot or be shot. The police are innocent guys doing a job and will have families at home. A gunfight is never a solution. He looks at the girl next to him again as she lifts her bag and drops it a few feet further on. It is heavy. He smiles at her, then with a nod asks her permission to lift her headdress from the top of her bag and inspect it. She agrees and he scrambles to find his phone. With nothing but more enthusiastic gestures, he asks if he can take a selfie of the two of them, her in her headdress. She obliges and then offers him the headdress. This was his ploy all along, he wants it on his head as he leaves the boat. They move along a little further, this time Hunter moving her bag. He arranges the side beads to hang down around his face and then they come together for selfie mark two. He is ready to snatch her, pull a gun and use her as a shield as he escapes. He knows he only has to cross a road which is right along the dockside. No more than about thirty feet and he will be in the welcoming mayhem of the cruise guests and the police will not shoot.

Kieron sits on a chair in the hotel reception holding an old magazine as cover but looking up at the clock above the almost sleeping night shift guy. It reads 0742 hours as Simon arrives back with a bag. He takes out a bottle of water and then rips open a Dioralyte sachet, then a second. He pours them into the bottle and shakes the water to ensure they have dissolved. These will hydrate Kieron faster and more effectively than water alone, though not as well as a drip into his arm. Then Simon produces three locally branded pain relievers that should also reduce swelling.

"We need to call an ambulance," he says in a firm whisper.

"No way! Not while Ruby is in there," Kieron says drinking from the bottle. "We wait till Hunter comes."

Simon pulls his phone out and rings Hunter again.

Hunter stills wears the headdress and is carrying the girl's large bag, which looks smaller on his shoulder. His phone goes. He pulls it out but says nothing. He is looking down the queue at the two out of sync policeman checking passports.

He edges away to the other side where an entertainer has just passed the policeman and is pocketing his passport in the rear pocket of his jeans. Hunter takes it unseen and unfelt, turns to the guy behind him, who he had pushed in front of by changing lanes and apologises.

"Pardon," he whispers with an acceptable accent, then leans into the girl who had the headdress to get her to speak into his phone. "Bonjour," he encourages her.

"Bonjour mon ami!" she shouts into his phone as Hunter flips open the passport he has stolen and she shows hers to the policeman. He offers the phone up to the policeman.

"Bonjour!", he encourages the policeman to say.

"Bonjour!" the policeman shouts and Hunter is through. He walks across the road at a determined pace with the girl, still carrying her bag. He knows that there is often a delayed reaction that could still catch him. He sees she has a car waiting, so with eyes surreptitiously on the two policemen he loads her bag in the trunk. He places the headdress carefully in there and the stolen passport on the top and closes the trunk, clocking one of the policemen now watching him. He kisses both cheeks of his new friend and slips backwards through a crowd of cruise guests into a mini tourist park that sits between the dock road and the entrance to Pape'ete city. No one is going to shoot him in here. He notices the policeman is crossing the road towards him very fast. Drumbeats bang out in a violent chorus from a small group of Polynesian natives sitting in the middle of the craft stalls playing for a solo dancer. Hunter picks up the pace and slips out of the tourist park as fast as he entered it. The town is in front of him, just across the busy city street but he is now exposed waiting for traffic lights to allow him to cross. Looking back, he can see two police advancing through the tourist park looking left and right. A man on a Segway swings past then turns and hovers. He is selling Segway tours of the city. Without a thought, Hunter shoves the unsuspecting rider off the machine, mounts it and rides it fast down the road and into the traffic.

He races up a side street with stalls and vendors, past an old yellow building and up to the market building he knows well. He discards the Segway for the owner who is shouting at anyone who will listen, racing after him. A block behind, the police are running his way.

Hunter slips into the busy market building where the decorations suggest they are still celebrating a long finished Chinese New Year. He rounds to the other side and exits by the taxi rank, sliding in the first taxi he sees,

"Hotel Le Mandarin, Rue Collette. US dollars OK?"

"Dollars are fine man."

"We are going to pick up a friend and take him to the hospital."

"Which one, we have many," the driver asks.

"He will tell you."

Kieron is looking a little better when three police officers walk in and wake the receptionist. They speak too fast for either Simon or him to understand, but what they do understand is that Ruby is walking straight towards them, giving the lawmen a wide birth. Kieron is about to shout out when her left arm darts out, grabbing his chin and holding it up it so he can't speak. Her right-hand holds a gun under a shawl which remains pointed at them.

"I was watching out for these guys, but never expected to see you two. How nice. Say anything and you say goodnight, then they do. Let's all stand up quietly and walk out through the back."

They follow her instructions. She walks behind them poking them with her gun.

"You'll be quite a star. Female serial killer." Kieron

says.

"I'm no serial killer. I was angry at Betty. Her stupid husband got in the way. The others just got too close, knew too much. All I wanted to do was get away. And they send you idiots!"

The taxi stops.

"I could have walked this," Hunter says looking back at the few blocks he has been driven.

"You could, but…"

Hunter tosses him twenty dollars. Wait here, I'll get my friend."

Hunter rushes in and sees three policemen, but no one else in reception.

"Were there two men sitting here?"

The receptionist obviously speaks no English, the policeman steps forward and translates. The receptionist looks behind Hunter which causes him to turn, but there's no one there. Hunter knows they would have stayed unless Ruby ran. He looks at the policemen who have split. Two start to run upstairs and the other one stays put. Hunter looks outside at their car and assesses she would have gone out of the back if she has gone. Kieron would be after her. He walks purposely round to the back looking for a door. There is an emergency exit wide open which he takes, looking left and right. He turns into the access alley and spots Ruby, no more than twenty yards away with a gun pointing down at Kieron. Simon is arguing for her not to shoot him. He is right in the way of Hunter's shot.

"Jenkins!" he shouts, knowing he has to fire the instant she turns, before she can use either man as a shield. The trigger is pulled. He can almost see the bullet leave the gun. He knows she has moved and he will have missed. She backs away, confused. She has never been under fire before. Her gun points down, she shoots Simon who takes a hit and falls. An instant rain of bullets from Witowski sends her off. The first policeman runs out behind Hunter his gun held high.

"Release your weapon," he shouts, his gun firmly pointed at Hunter.

"I can't do that. The killer is there! She has shot two men," Hunter shouts back, holding up his cruise card in his hand like it's a CIA badge. It is an action that alone has some meaning when everyone is in panic, one Hunter has used before. The policeman looks beyond him, sees both Kieron and Simon on the floor and he charges senselessly forward to the corner Ruby went around. Hunter shakes his head, thinking he wouldn't last two minutes in the Basra Province. He hears more gunshots, telling him she is still near enough to engage the police. The other two police run out.

Hunter helps Kieron and the doctor get to their feet, "You'll be fine, doc. She just winged you."

"It hurts."

"You get used to it," Kieron says.

"I hope they have that covered," Hunter says, struggling to get the two men back in the emergency door. "But somehow, I doubt it."

"We're fine, go," Kieron says.

Hunter drags them through reception and out to the waiting cab, "Which hospital?"

The driver runs to help Hunter as Simon replies, "Main hospital!"

The driver then notices that they are both bleeding, "No. They bleed on my seats," he shouts.

Hunter pulls out all a handful of US dollars ranging from fifty to twenty dollar notes and pushes them into the driver's pocket.

"OK, OK. Ta'aone?"

Simon nods yes. They both slide in and Hunter slams the door. The driver runs round to his seat.

"You deliver them. Him for neurology. You come straight back here, right here, and wait for me and you get the rest," Hunter says, leaning in the passenger window and showing the driver another handful of dollars.

The car screeches away and Hunter turns to look at the street layout for the first time. The access road ran behind the hotel but must come out in the street to his left. As he starts to move, he sees Ruby running fast in the traffic across the junction and leaping onto the back of a jeep. Hunter turns and runs up to the junction. The three uniformed police run after him, he turns and shouts back,

"Get your car! Ta voiture!"

One of the policemen turns and runs back, the other two follow, but the jeep stops three buildings in front of them and they are advancing on a standoff between Ruby and the very annoyed driver whom she has now pulled a gun on. One of the Policemen stops, stands and shoots forward, with no chance of a hit. He shoots again and Ruby jumps down.

She runs in and out of traffic for cover and into a gas station where cars are refuelling. Hunter runs to the sidewalk and along the buildings. She is trying to take a car but with no luck when Hunter catches up and takes a position. Ruby realises she cannot shoot anyone, but if she's cornered she will. An explosion waiting to happen. No one should shoot.

The French police run in and take positions but Hunter is praying they don't fire or they will all be toasted in a giant fireball. All the vehicles in the gas station face, away from him and there's a queue of cars beside him waiting to go in. Even though some are trying to back out against the traffic, if she steals a car she can only exit one way: the other side of the gas station.

Seeing the police have Ruby's attention, and that he has not been noticed, Hunter drops down behind a car and crabs the long way around the station. He drops back to the exit, staying out of sight, anticipating her next move.

The taxi driver skids up outside the hospital shouting for help. He opens the taxi door and drags Simon out who bumps on the floor.

"Aidez-moi! Aidez-moi!"

Medical assistants run out and shout back inside for help as the taxi driver pulls Kieron from the back seat. He turns to a senior attendant next to him,

"Il a été abattu, il est pour la neurologie. Neurologie!" he says then runs around to his driver's door.

"What?"

"I go to get more," He shouts.

"We no pay commission!"

One of the police is getting dangerously close to Ruby. She panics and starts shooting at him. She backs away and hits a man with her gun, snatches his keys and takes his car. She shoots towards the police again and drops into the driver's seat as the two police run after her. They shoot at her driving out, but by default, they are shooting towards Hunter. He walks forward into the road, shooting at Ruby through the windscreen. She is hit but she drives straight at him. He jumps up and is on the bonnet grabbing for the screen wipers to stop him swinging off. She accelerates away and the police car picks up the two other officers and races after her, siren going. She swings the car from side to side but Hunter pulls himself up at an angle and aims his gun through the windscreen. Ruby pulls her gun and aims back at him. Hunter shoots first, once, twice, three times and she crashes into an oncoming car. Hunter rolls off her car, onto the front bonnet of the car she hit, he rolls up over the windscreen and off the back.

The police quickly surround the car. They open the doors each side of her and see she is a mess of blood. They turn to Hunter who is just getting to his feet, dizzy and unbalanced.

67 BEST HOSPITAL FOOD IN THE WORLD

Captain Neil Reynolds walks into a private sideward, past the French police guarding the area. Just three of the beds are being used. Simon Yates is in the first one, Hunter Witowski in the second, then a French doctor stands over Kieron Philip's who is on several drips, with a machine either side of his bed and his head is bandaged again.

"Guys, I would love to stay and see all your court cases play out but I have a ship to sail," Neil announces with a large smile.

"Did you find out why she did it?" Kieron asks.

"I understand they wanted to talk to her, but she was riddled with bullets," the Captain says with an almost straight face.

"She didn't say anything then?" Hunter asks again.

"Apparently the police want to interview you to ascertain whether it was necessary for you to shoot her," Neil says, looking at Hunter.

"I was just trying to wipe her windscreen, she started to shoot at me!" He replies.

"Inconsiderate," Kieron says.

"I think so," Hunter adds.

"I am shocked that this man is even awake," the doctor says, looking down at Kieron then moving towards the Captain. The uniform and all it's trimmings always attract attention.

"I hope you were able to sort out his brain, doctor. I'm Neil Reynolds," he says introducing himself.

"It is nice to meet you, Captain, I'm doctor Mancini. Most men would be dead with the bleeds he had. I have repaired the damage but as for his brain, that is for therapy and I wish the therapist much luck."

"He trained in Paris, Captain," Kieron says.

"Why did you come here, doc?" Hunter asks.

"Apart from the sunshine, the beautiful paradise beaches and the best hospital food in the world, I have no idea," Mancini smiles, then turns back to the Captain. "The quiet one at the end you can have back."

Doctor Mancini points to Simon. These two can't leave today.

"No worries, I don't need them back. You can keep them," the Captain announces.

"That's nice isn't it?" Hunter responds.

"I can't believe it. I undergo brain surgery for him," Kieron says flabbergasted.

"I get shot, thrown over a car!"

"To be fair, you didn't know you were shot."

"I knew I was shot," Simon says.

"No one's asking you doc, he's not leaving you in this... this heat."

"Too hot," Hunter says.

"It's sandy," Kieron starts.

"Too sandy."

"Can we get him dressed so I can leave? Ten days of these two has driven me mad," the Captain asks.

"Sure. Doctor Yates, you should get dressed," Doctor Mancini says.

"Don't suppose Ruby's alive?" Hunter asks.

The Medical staff and Captain all shake their heads without saying anything.

"Typical," Kieron starts. "He's not the kind to take prisoners."

"I was hanging on her car trying to stay alive!"

"You should still have read her her-rights."

"I was going to when she stopped!"

"Well, she won't be talking much now. But her cabin did, seems like while you worked hard to find the killer, she was working harder to try and ensure she wasn't caught," the Captain says.

"I suppose you'll be leaving us then. Got a ship to catch?" Hunter says.

"Do you have any idea what day it is, Hunter? The ship left yesterday. Vasile is in charge, company executives are on board and she is now docked safely in Bora Bora." Neil reveals.

"Oh, sorry Captain, we didn't mean to make you miss your ship. Hope you don't get sacked," Kieron says.

"I slept for over twelve hours?" Hunter asks.

"You were awake the whole of the previous night, and did have a bullet removed," Neil explains.

"It's a long swim to Bora Bora, is Simon up to it?" Kieron asks.

"We have a plane booked to take us on," Neil explains. "Simon, as soon as you are dressed, I can escape this abuse."

The Captain is smiling, he walks forward and shakes Hunter's hand. "Thanks." He turns and shakes hands with Kieron. "Thanks, Philips. And I loved your act, come back and do the whole thing. But leave Hunter in Miami."

"I would've loved to have said goodbye to Prisha," Kieron says.

"Me too."

The Captain nods his head to the side and there at the door is Prisha, dressed in her white uniform and her huge smile. She rushes in, opens her arms and hugs Hunter.

"That's great, isn't it? He gets a little nick, I have major brain surgery, out all night, and she goes to him," Kieron says.

She stands up, twists to Kieron and hugs him. Simon is dressed and joins the Captain.

"You know, I don't think Officer Ruby Jenkins is taking that job offer, do you, Hunter?" Kieron asks.

"She hasn't said anything in the last few hours, so I'd say we are entitled to retract any offer we may have made," Hunter says.

Prisha stands up in mock shock, "You offered it to her before me?"

She swings a full open-handed slap at Kieron's head. The doctor goes to stop her, Hunter tries to move to stop her. But she's kidding, she stops just before his head. She smiles at him,

"I have been awake all night reading a criminal behavioural science book I found in the hospital library. I wondered why Ruby was making verbal sexual advances to Kieron when he was in a coma. It was because she knew I was listening, it was for all of us. She was covering her tracks."

"Why did she kill Benny?" Kieron asks.

"It was about power. She had got to the top of her career tree here on the ship and when you were not offering her a job, she was challenging your ability."

"And it started in a jealous rage about love," Dwight offers.

"But she was trying to piece together clues; the book, Lawrence of Arabia," Neil says.

"No, Sir. She was looking to confuse us all more and more," Prisha says. "I am not sure I am ready for Miami if it is like this, Mr Kieron. I have two children back in India where it is safe, and you guys get too near to death."

"We could probably throw in medical," Dwight says.

"You'd need that," Kieron says.

"No, thank you." She kisses them both. "I have a plane to catch. But stay in touch and let me know if something comes up when your lives are less dangerous."

To be continued, very dramatically, in

Cruise Ship Laundry Wars...

CRUISE SHIP SERIAL KILLER

CAST GLOSSARY

SHIP

Kieron Philips (old scar that starts just below the sleeve of his shirt on his right arm, and reveals itself just in the neck line, the mess between is hidden –mentioned in first sex with Georgie book1sc32)

Hunter Witowski , 6ft 3. Mid to late forties. (wife Elaine ten years younger) (two healed bullet wounds in the left shoulder, deep voice)

Neil Reynolds (Ship's Captain)
Roy Stevens (HoD Hotel Manager)
Prisha (Hotel Staff - data wrangler)
Elvis (ents manager)
Wendy (ents host)

Vasile Nagy (Deputy Captain)

Ruby Jenkins (HOD Security)
Lal (security)
Krishma (security)
Madeline (HR)

Jason (Hod Photography)   team of 4 below him
Sally – Photographer
Bill, – Photographer
Kusay – Photographer
Michael – Photographer

Simon Yates (Doctor)
Manesh Hunjan (Senior Medic)
Anokhi (Nurse)

Panjang (deck hand – sun beds)
Aishah (Librarian)
Benny Raymond (Guest from Miami, in a chair, eager to help)
Woman Guest (arrogant arrested)

Manoj Bhatti (Crow's Nest Bar staff)

Prince Dahoum (Crow's Nest Bar staff)
Jasmin (waitress)

MIAMI
Dwight Ritter - on land ex FBI
Sigmund Henkel – Psychologist
Edgar Hawthorne - Police Lieutenant

DINER
Wild Mary (African American Breakfast bar owner)
Stan – cook and husband?
+
Various college kids and dancers inc
Izzy – college girl wanna be Journalist
Macey - painter
Croc – painter and goes on raid of apartment
+
Various reporters including
Jenny E – WBX25
Gwen
Ted

BANK
Isiah Success (Bank Guard)
Ron Stone (Bank Employee)

FRENCH CREW
Henré – Doctor
Receptionist at hotel, various police, Segway man.

THE DEAD
1 Donna McGovern
2 Peter Kershner
3 Eric Clifford   (Guest) - (wife is Betty Clifford (Harris))
4 Bogdan (Sax player)
5 Manoj Bhatti (Crow's Nest Bar Steward) Rm 3771
-   Attempt on Kieron
6 Sally Photographer
7 Benny (Guest in mobility scooter)
8 Kabir – Kitchen Porter
9 Guest in 7304 – natural causes.

ABOUT THE AUTHOR

Stuart St Paul started as a writer and broadcaster working mainly on radio. He moved into television in 1980 and following the career dollar line specialized in action, having been an athlete. He ended his career as a movie director of his own projects and directing sections of other people's movies as either second unit or pick-up director. The tails of his career, the highs, the lows and the near misses make a great after-dinner treat. He now concentrates of formulating CSCI as a book series and possible television series.

He lives near Watford not far from his son Luke and his family, and a trip into London to his daughter Laura and her partner.

Stuart is represented by Champions UK

He is active on the cruise resource centre Doris Visits.

www.DorisVisits.com

www.Youtube.com/c/dorisvisits

As we write, **Laura Aikman** is due as the new guest character in the Christmas special of Gavin and Stacey. She voices Space Chickens, Shane the Chef and is a character in many video games. A career better researched than we try to cover here. She went to Habs Girls and lives in London with Matt and Eric the French Bulldog.

A FEW WORDS FROM STUART

As a director, I love working with talented creative actors. With the others on a film set they create a team that need not ask what to do, but occasionally check we are on the same page. That is often a phone call or a chat over coffee before the film set. Rehearsals are to engage with the set and allow the crew to set lights and sound without shadows or other problems for the camera team who are looking for that special moment.

Film making is teamwork and with that in mind, I want to explain that Laura Aikman, my daughter bring a lot to the project that I would not see. She removes much that might embarrass me later, and it all works. I like the team that worked on this book. Laura with her creative input, Jean my wife for deciphering my dyslexic code before the others are challenged, and David, new in, who did a great proof of an early draft making the cook very happy.

You may often hear directors say they hate their films. It is because they have to see them so many times at so many stages. It is because they know they could do better with time and money. I now love Laundry Wars, but it frightens me that, firstly I have gone too far, and secondly that it will be hard to be beaten.

Come say hi if you see me on a ship.

2019

This is the first book in the series, it covers a very threatening cruise out of South America. It features Kieron's first love and how he meets Hunter

….. but you don't need to know any of that.

March 2020

This will not be the cover!

There is a problem in the laundry, the centre of all the ship's gossip. CSCI don't do general guest matters so why have they been called.

The mystery turns into the most threatening and darkest book in the series.

Other books are planned for this series.

Printed in Great
Britain
by Amazon